RED IKE

Borgo Press Books by S. Fowler Wright

Arresting Delia: An Inspector Cleveland Classic Crime Novel
The Attic Murder: An Inspector Combridge & Mr. Jellipot Classic Crime Novel
The Bell Street Murders: An Inspector Combridge & Mr. Jellipot Classic Crime Novel
Beyond the Rim: A Lost Race Fantasy
Black Widow: A Classic Crime Novel
The British Colonies: No Surrender to Nazi Germany!
The Capone Caper: Mr. Jellipot vs. the King of Crime: A Classic Crime Novel
Crime & Co.: An Inspector Cleveland Classic Crime Novel
Dawn: A Novel of Global Warming
Dead by Saturday: An Inspector Cleveland Classic Crime Novel
Dream; or, The Simian Maid: A Fantasy of Prehistory (Marguerite Cranleigh #1)
Elfwin: An Historical Novel of Anglo-Saxon Times
The End of the Mildew Gang: An Inspector Cauldron Classic Crime Novel (Mildew Gang
    #3)
Four Callers in Razor Street: An Inspector Combridge & Mr. Jellipot Classic Crime Novel
Four Days' War: The Alternate World War II, Book Two
The Hanging of Constance Hillier: An Inspector Cleveland Classic Crime Novel
The Hidden Tribe: A Lost Race Fantasy
The Jordans Murder: An Inspector Combridge & Mr. Jellipot Classic Crime Novel
The King Against Anne Bickerton: A Classic Crime Novel
Megiddo's Ridge: The Alternate World War II, Book Three
The Mildew Gang: An Inspector Cauldron Classic Crime Novel (Mildew Gang #1)
Murder in Bethnal Square: An Inspector Combridge & Mr. Jellipot Classic Crime Novel
The Police and the Public: Some Thoughts on the British System of Justice
Post-Mortem Evidence: An Inspector Combridge & Mr. Jellipot Classic Crime Novel
Prelude in Prague: The Alternate World War II, Book One
Red Ike: A Novel of Cumberland (with J. M. Denwood)
The Return of the Mildew Gang: An Inspector Cauldron Classic Crime Novel (Mildew
    Gang #2)
The Rissole Mystery: An Inspector Combridge & Mr. Jellipot Classic Crime Novel
The Screaming Lake: A Lost Race Fantasy
The Secret of the Screen: An Inspector Combridge & Mr. Jellipot Classic Crime Novel
The Song of Songs and Other Poems
Spiders' War: A Novel of the Far Future (Marguerite Cranleigh #3)
Three Witnesses: A Classic Crime Novel
Too Much for Mr. Jellipot: An Inspector Combridge & Mr. Jellipot Classic Crime Novel
The Vengeance of Gwa: A Fantasy of Prehistory (Marguerite Cranleigh #2)
Was Murder Done? A Classic Crime Novel
Who Murdered Reynard? A Classic Crime Novel
The Wills of Jane Kanwhistle: An Inspector Combridge & Mr. Jellipot Classic Crime Novel
With Cause Enough?: An Inspector Combridge & Mr. Jellipot Classic Crime Novel

RED IKE

A NOVEL OF CUMBERLAND

by

J. M. DENWOOD &
S. FOWLER WRIGHT

THE BORGO PRESS

An Imprint of Wildside Press LLC

MMIX

FOREWORD

As Mr. Walpole's preface was written before I had received the ms. of this book for the assistance which I had undertaken, and as his absence in the West Indies, closely following my own return from America, has allowed no opportunity for subsequent consultation, I think a word of explanation is due both to him and to myself—and, from a different angle, to Mr. Denwood—as to the extent and limit of my own contribution to its present form.

The manuscript, as Mr. Walpole saw it, suffered from a radical defect of construction which a practised novelist would have avoided. It was in the form of a narrative by William Moffatt, commencing at the time when he returned from America, and the earlier events were told by Red Ike to him in the course of a long conversation which completed the first book.

The first person is often used by the inexperienced author, who is least aware of the difficulties he will encounter or skilful to overcome them. It is the least satisfactory of narrative forms (excepting that of a series of letters) and the most difficult to handle (excepting the diary). It should never be used unless it is intended to confine the tale to such facts as are naturally within the narrator's knowledge, or such emotions as he can have experienced or observed.

The use of two first persons, and the inclusion of much which could not have come within the knowledge or observation of those who told it, forced me to the reluctant conclusion that the book could not be adapted for publication without the major operation of changing it to the third person throughout, and placing the incidents in chronological order.

With greater hesitation, I have occasionally modified the exuberance of the more violent episodes or conversations, not unaware that a good melodrama may be preferred to an indifferent comedy.

But in such redaction as I have indicated I have added little of value. It is not an instance of two authors pooling their inventions, nor of one writing a tale of which the other has provided the plot.

My part has been no more than that of arrangement and modification, and the re-writing of some earlier portions where the plan of reconstruction which I adopted rendered it unavoidable.

The finest prose passages in the book (as also the lyrics, except for two slight modifications) are Mr. Denwood's unaided and unaltered work.

—S. Fowler Wright

PREFACE

I will not delay readers of this remarkable book for more than a moment. That it is a remarkable book, no one who reads it will, I think, deny.

Mr. Denwood is *not* a professional novelist; that is, in fact, the very last thing that he is. He tells here a story and he paints some vivid and memorable characters, but it is neither the characters nor the story that gives this book its character. *Red Ike* is memorable because of its feeling of place.

Now Cumberland has not, as yet, been very generously dealt with by English novelists. There are the stories of Professor Collingwood, the *Helbeck of Bannisdale* of Mrs. Ward (and that is *Westmorland*), that old but rather child-like favourite *Hope the Hermit*, the *Sorrowstones* of Mr. Calvert, *The Secret Valley* of Nicholas Size—it is difficult at the moment to recall more than these.

I am, I think, quite safe in saying that none of them, not even Mr. Calvert's *Sorrowstones*, a fine work, catches the breath and life of the Fells as does this novel of Mr. Denwood's.

It is because he is not a novelist so much as a poet that he has here so extraordinary a spirit. All his life long he has breathed the air of these hills and dales as though he were part of them. He has never self-consciously thought: "Now I will make a story of this." The hills themselves have simply driven him to do so. It is so often a tragical thing that the people who know the country best, its sights, sounds, colours and skylines, are least able to write about what they know. That is why a book like Mr. Denwood's is so rare a thing.

I do not know whether it is rash to compare him with George Borrow. Perhaps it is—and yet the comparison must be made. Borrow is a very great writer. I do not say *Red Ike* is another *Lavengro*—but I do say that it comes nearer to the true spirit of *Lavengro* than any other English novel of recent years.

This book will perhaps be chiefly loved by those who care for Cumberland. Perhaps because I care for that country so dearly I am a little prejudiced in *Red Ike's* favour. But I do not think so. One criticizes most severely those whom one loves the best, and the spirit of *Red Ike* is really independent of prejudice.

For many years to come lovers of Cumberland will treasure this book.

—Hugh Walpole.

BOOK ONE

CHAPTER I

DESTINY or freewill? It is the old insoluble question. If Will Moffatt and Red Ike had not lain out under the stars by the Brutchstone (A wonderful phallic stone on the top of Naddle Fell about three miles southwest of Keswick.) that warm June night in 1883? Or if Joe Gream and Peg Shore had wandered another way? Or, say, if it had happened to rain? Perhaps destiny would still have led them by other no less sombre paths to the end that they could not guess. But we have enough to do to watch the growth that followed from that unlikely chance, without guessing what crop might have come from seeds that were never sown.

Red Ike watched them embrace. They did more than that. When he saw what they would be at, he rose suddenly and rushed away. They might have heard, had they been less self-occupied than they were, thinking themselves to be out of sight or knowledge of men on the lonely height of the moor.

As to Will Moffatt, he lay and watched. He was curious—and amused. He was not over-concerned that his friend went off as he did. Red Ike had his sudden moods. And he partly guessed how he felt. Will Moffatt looked at Peg with rather different eyes. She could bring as many men as she would to the Brutchstone in the moonlight hours, and let them do with her as they pleased, and his sleep would be none the less. But to Ike she was a pure dream that he doubted his worth to win. It was in that hope that he worked and saved. She knew that well enough. He could have bought her at a less price, but she had the shrewdness to see that it was one that he would be slow to pay. Meanwhile, it was not only that Joe had the better purse He was more of her kind.

We must observe that they were both young at this time, Will and Ike. Will was twenty-two, and Ike was younger than that, though he had come to a strength that it would be prudent to fear, if his anger stirred, as it would at times in a quick way. They looked at life as the young do, through the half-light of the dawn, which may be golden or grey, but it is alike to them, for their eyes and thoughts are for that which the mist hides.

Will lay as he was and let his friend go. Had he known that it would be seven years before they would meet again, he might have done differently, but how could he guess that? And by the next day he had trouble enough of his own at Sandyflatts, so that even Red Ike had little place in his mind.

He let Joe and Peg go, and lay still under the stars for a time. He was in no hurry to go home. There is time to sleep in the day. But the night's poaching that they had planned must go, now that Ike had rushed off in that sudden way. He was not troubled at that. He would have thought (had he thought of it at all) that there were other nights that would do as well. But he could go home when he would. There was no one living at Sandyflatts except his mother and he.

So, meaning to go home, but being in no haste, he lay still, and, the night being warm and the heather soft, he went to sleep in the end, and waked to see the summer sun at a good height, and then he went home at a quick pace, though he had no thought of what he should find, for, if you often poach at night, it is well to be home before you may be watched from a mile away.

CHAPTER II

THE morning was well advanced when Will Moffatt came to the door of his own home. Even as it then was, Sandyflatts was forbidding enough. A grey-built solitary house set in the desolation of the moors that stretched round it in miles of barren undulation, interspersed with masses of heather, gorse, and bracken. Its wild tract was lined with countless runnels in whose peat moss banks, tunnelled by the fierce spates of many winters, the small, yellow-bellied trout fled for safety when the shadow of a heron or wild duck crossed the water's surface. There the curlew comes in early March, and the whole moor is continuously athrill with its tremulous, wailing cry until the frosts of the falling year. There the nightjar sits on its favourite old grey stone, which is the very colour of itself, and sings its strange song to rising moon or lonely star.

And there the eastern hill is faced by a Druids' Circle of stones, some of which mark the course of the year as a sundial marks the hours of the day.

On this hill in olden days were seen the mirages of marching armies. But in later times these have been replaced by scenes of festivity. There shadowy pleasure-fairs are held, with showmen's booths and the gathered crowds before the platforms. There the modern electric switchback, hoopla stalls, and all the sordid paraphernalia and flotsam and jetsam of a virile civilization perform, as if in mockery, the mimic antics of present-day humanity. The country folks scattered over this sparsely-populated district view with awe the wild revels thus held in the daylight hours, and have named it "The Hill of Devils."

Will Moffatt had no such thoughts as these as he came whistling cheerfully to a door which had been opened already, and entered a kitchen at the table of which sat a woman dead, her head upon her folded arms.

When a bullet crashes through bone and flesh there is often little pain at the first. The stunned nerves fail to respond. A man looks foolishly at his shattered limb, uncertain of what he thinks or feels. The pain will come soon enough, but it is yet to begin.

Will Moffatt said "Mother" in a cheerful and then again in a puzzled way. Then he touched her and knew.

Half an hour after that, he had lifted her onto the kitchen sofa as best he might, and set out to get help from those of whom he thought as his friends, and (except Red Ike) the only friends that he had. He set out over the moor to where John Lynd farmed at The Bents—three hundred acres of "as good land as ever lay out of doors," as they would say in those parts.

No one knew how long the Lynds had farmed on that land. Extra land had come to them from time to time under the several Commons Enclosures Acts, and John Lynd was a prosperous man enough, though not one who had saved. He owned a good blood-horse, and no better cross-country rider followed the hounds than he.

He was something more than a common man of his kind, having been an only son, and better educated than was usual in his class at that time, and beyond that he was of a restless ambition which was not easily stilled. He had tried to make a place for himself in the public life of the county, but he was lacking in the gift of oratory, and had been embittered by the failure of his efforts in that direction.

He had a wife, and a daughter, Jean, of about the age of Will Moffatt, who had been free enough of the house during his boyhood years, where he would go to borrow books, or to ask guidance of the older man at some point of difficulty on the hard path of self-education, some point of grammar, history, or philosophy, for he did not attempt to penetrate the mysteries of modern science till a later time.

Up to that time Will Moffatt had taken the world for granted, as youth will. He had not even concerned himself to wonder why his mother's home was bounded by the walled-in eighth of an acre behind it, though he knew in a vague way that his ancestors had owned all the expanse beyond.

He sought eagerly for the knowledge that came within reach of his hands, absorbing the books he read as he absorbed, unconsciously as a flower, the beauty and glory of the Nature around him, revelling in the storms, or lying with his head on a stone until he felt as much a part of ever-changing, everlasting scene as were the inanimate fells and moors themselves.

Now Jean saw Will approach. She waited for him, leaning on the fold-gate. She called him a light good-morning, and then her tone changed quickly as she saw his face. "What's wrong, Will?"

It seems strange to tell, but Will did not know how to begin. He stood there telling nothing but by the silent misery of his face. When she asked him again, in a sharper fear, he said, "Can I see your mother?"

"Mother's not very well. She's not down yet. Tell me, Will." Her hands reached his as he told.

If he loved her at that time it was that which he scarcely knew, and her own thoughts lay quiet in her own mind, and, to the man who watched them from the bedroom window above, the way they stood may have seemed to mean more than it did, he not knowing of what they spoke, but it happened that Will lifted his eyes, and met a black anger in those of John Lynd, at which he was puzzled enough, and would have been more so at another time, for Jean's father had always been kindly enough in a rough way, and, not thinking how the scene might look to the older man, he could have guessed no reason at all.

"I'll tell Mother," Jean said. "You'd better come in and sit down.

He was sitting on the kitchen settle a moment later when John Lynd came in. He said brusquely, "What are you doing here?"

Will met that tone more easily than he had done the questioning sympathy in a girl's eyes. He said briefly, "Mother's dead."

"Well, what do you want us to do?"

Will said that he did not know, but they were the first people he had thought of in his distress.

"Then you'd better go back. Mrs. Lynd will find someone to do what's necessary, and drive over later."

John Lynd turned with these words, and left the kitchen. Will stood silent a moment, and turned away also from that unexpected brutality. He went back with his grief across the open moor, pondering in vain the meaning of this conduct from a man who had always shown a careless friendliness, and a disposition to praise and help his studies even up to two days before. At another time, under other circumstances, he might have puzzled over it to the point of elucidation. As it was, when his mother was buried three days later, he hardly noticed that the Lynds were the only family within miles of the Church garth who were not present at the funeral.

It was the next Sunday morning that realization came, when he went to the churchyard, and saw Jean standing by his mother's grave.

When Will Moffatt hesitated, he was always less likely to do the wrong thing than to do nothing at all. So he had lain on at the Brutchstone when Red Ike went; so he had been silent to Jean's question, doubting how his grief should be told. Now he drew back and watched. He had not seen Jean for a week, and now she prayed at his mother's grave. He knew how he loved her then, and he saw at the same instant that it was that which had roused the black anger in her father's eyes, and the brutal words that had sent him home. He could not guess what it meant. He did not know that John Lynd was his mother's brother. It was many years before he learnt the wrong he had done her. But the storm broke the next day.

They met on the open moor. There was no one within possible sight. John Lynd meant to have it out once for all. He came to the point in a curt way, and when Will admitted his love for Jean, he burst out with an oath that he wasn't going to see his daughter wedded to a penniless, bastard brat.

Will Moffatt's anger leapt into sudden flame, as that of those who are of a slow nature may sometimes do, at this refusal, and at the vile and unexpected imputation which it contained. He shouted, "You lying cur!" His hand reached for a stone.

John Lynd stood his ground, a cynical smile on his lips. He tapped the barrel of the gun which lay across his arm. "Do you want a charge of shot in the legs?"

Will looked back with eyes that were as wrath and resolute as those of the older man, but the stone dropped. There is little use in arguing with a loaded shotgun in the hands of a man who has a reputation for violence of temper.

John Lynd observed the action with the same cynical smile. He went on. "Now listen to me, Will Moffatt, and it's the last warning you'll get. You'll be gone from here by tomorrow night, and if you show your face again on any land of mine, or where my word goes, you'll be harried to the devil, if you don't get a charge of shot, as a polecat should. There's not a house on the moor that can shelter you against my will. You can make up your mind to that."

"I can live at Sandyflatts, Mr. Lynd, as long as I like, without asking you."

"Oh, yes? Whose do you think it is?"

"It's mine, now my mother's dead."

"It's no more yours than it was ever hers. I can turn you out when I will. You'd better clear while you can. Now go."

Will Moffatt looked at the sneering, contemptuous eyes, and he knew that he had heard the truth. He controlled the impulse of passionate reply. He saw the hands that were restless upon the weapon that his opponent held. It was not his hour. He turned and went without further words.

He lingered for a few days in the depressing atmosphere of his solitary death-haunted home, feeling that the hands of all men were against him. What chance had he with slender means, in such a place, with such an enmity? He decided to quit the moorland forever to forget his miseries and make his own career in another world. The next week he sailed from Liverpool to New York, telling no one of where he went.

CHAPTER III

RED IKE fled through the night. He cast himself down on the heather of Lonscape fell with his mind in a tumult of revulsion and anger, shame and grief.

He had worshipped Peg Shore, and she had encouraged his advances. He had known well enough that Joe Gream was in love with her also, and that he had far more to offer. But he had had her word. He had trusted her with the unquestioning simplicity of his own nature.

Now he told himself that he had always known she was wanton: that he could have had her, if he would, on the same terms. He cried *Fool!* to the fells, and the fells echoed in mockery. Hearing that mocking cry, he knew the falsity of his own thought. He cried *Liar!*

and the fells answered again. He writhed, clutching the earth with his hands in an extreme of passion that must find some physical outlet. He leapt to his feet again and rushed deeper into the night, and the wilderness of the fells.

He lay down again, exhausted by the pace at which he had thought to flee from his own self, and faced his grief again. The pure love which he had thought his own had dominated his life until that night. It was for Peg that he had hoarded and schemed, for Peg that he had haggled over the price of the game that he and Will had poached on a hundred nights. Now he lay like a wild and wounded thing, resolving that he had done with love, and with all the restraints and reticences that had ruled his life. Then in the pause of exhausted passion at which men may turn to suicide or self-control, he stood up, stretching his arms to the void. He made a gesture of casting-off, crying aloud, "This for a woman! Have there not been many men—how many men!—in worse case than mine? Men who have not learned the truth till they have been tied for life to a wanton's will. I am a free man still!"

He laughed aloud, and was startled by the echoed sound, which had a hollow and discordant jar, so that his own voice seemed strange. He thought, "At least I can be a man and let the woman go, or take her for what she is, pure or impure." He walked home with a quiet and steady step, and was soon in bed and asleep.

He rose after a few hours' sleep, and was first down in a room in which a siskin sang. It was Peg's gift, and with a quiet smile he took down the cage. "Go," he thought, "with the peace of God. You will be loyal to the mate you choose. There is no creature of the wilds that is so base as mankind."

It was a month before he saw Peg Shore again, and then he came upon her at the stepping-stones on the moor. The beck was in flood, and she stood in doubt on the edge. She saw a man who was taller and better-made than any other she knew. He had the vigour of early youth, and the clean health of the open life that the poacher lives. He was a good sight to her, though he had the dreamer's eyes, which are not easy to read, and she knew he worshipped her for that which she could never be. In the shallow shrewdness of her mind, she thought little of his prospects or purse, but the man himself was of a desirable kind.

He stopped as he came up to her side, and she raised confident smiling eyes. "Won't you help me over, Ike?"

He looked at her silently, as one who studies a strange thing.

"What's the matter with Red Ike?" she asked in her teasing way. "Has a bogle frightened him that he hasn't come my way for a month past?"

He answered that. "We saw two bogles, Will Moffatt and I. They were at the Brutchstone a month tonight."

Not a muscle of her mouth moved, nor did her eyes fall before his as she answered, "Sneaks and eavesdroppers always see and hear more than is good for them."

"In this case it was better to be without sight, and beyond hearing."

"Why?" she asked, lifting her eyebrows in a puzzled way.

He looked hard in her eyes and answered with a slow deliberation. "Because I did not wish to hear the gurgle of mating."

She did not drop her eyes, which showed a sudden realization of what he knew, and a fierce anger that followed, but she flushed purple as she answered in a torrent of abuse before which he stood unmoved till her words failed.

"Well, Peg," he said, when she paused at last, "who's at fault, you or me?"

"Coward!"

"Not at all. I was glad to know your relations with Joe before I was too late. See—this was for you." He held out a ring which he had bought some weeks earlier, dreaming that it would not be long before it would have been on her hand.

"You bought that for me?"

"Yes. That's the fool I was."

"Then I wish it had been on my hand when I went with Joe Gream that night, now I know what a sneak you are. But I'll be even with you before I've done, so you'd better beware."

"Yes?" he answered. "And you'd better beware of Joe Gream. Few men want a soiled woman, not even the man that soils her. If Joe Gream can get Jean Lynd, she'll be the woman for him, though I reckon she's got her eyes on a better man."

"How do you know of that?" she asked in a sharp, changed tone.

"Because I'm a sneak and an eavesdropper."

"I think you're a devil," she said bitterly.

"Well, look for yourself. The Lynds' house is open to you. You're Jean's friend, and Joe Gream is there half his nights. It's nothing to me. Look here."

He took the ring between finger and thumb, and shot it towards the boiling cauldron of the falls a dozen yards below.

CHAPTER IV

RED IKE walked away feeling that he had had the best of that encounter, as, perhaps, he had; but it had brought Peg back to his mind in a way that he found it hard to shake off. He learnt, as many others had done before, that it is easier to ignore a woman than to forget her. He had been drinking more than he should during the past month, which was a new thing to him, and after a time, during which he did nothing but let the money that he had been hoarding up for Peg slip away as it would, he joined a gang of gypsies that had camped at Mirkholme, and roamed with them into Scotland, and spent about six months in the Rob Roy country.

They welcomed Ike, because he had the name of being the most skilful poacher on the Borders. The gypsies knew how to poach, as they knew how to thieve, but there were things in the making and using of nets that they had not learnt; and now, as they went idly and merrily through the countryside, they levied generous toll on the lordly preserves that skirted the public ways. Sometimes partridges by the score would fall victims to the sweep-net, or they would stove a full clutching of pheasants with a long pole and a box of fuming sulphur from the thick black firewood plantations, and would soon be boiling them in a bule pan over a turf fire, or spitting and frizzling them in a savoury circle beneath the midnight sky.

Nor was venison an unknown joint. Long before a beast could be missed, its skin and entrails would be buried miles behind, and the carcase eaten. The gallant salmon was their easy prey in many of the narrow, boiling streams of Scotland. When Ike had taught them how to use the double-armed net, with pole and bladder, hardly a day passed that they did not dine on fresh fish.

The gypsies looked at him as a valuable addition for these services, but he came to sicken of an existence that was wilder and more lawless than anything of which he had dreamed before, and from which the common decencies of life were too often absent. His departure was hastened at the last by a singular incident.

The women were of the ordinary type of the nomad tribes, dirty, gaudy, loud-tongued, and brazen, but there was one exception. Jael Boswell, in spite of her surroundings, was of a natural reticence which contrasted with the free and shameless familiarities of her companions sufficiently to suggest that she was, in part at least, of an alien race. Red Ike was drawn to her by this difference, and paid her some attention, which she accepted with an apparent willingness. Yet he held her always at arm's length, his experience of Peg Shore not being easily forgotten.

She came to him once when he was reading a tattered volume of Shakespeare's plays that his pocket held. She drew the book from his hand.

"Which play do you think the greatest, Red Ike?"

He looked surprised as he answered, "*Macbeth.*"

"Why?"

"Because its sombre power fascinates me."

The shadow of a smile passed over her face as she said: "You mean, I suppose, that it appeals to the instinct of wonder inherent in you, and yet you pretend to hold in scorn the gypsy's lore," and continuing, "Where, Red Ike, would you draw the boundary between a gaping crowd held entranced by the witchery of Shakespeare, and the fool who is having his fortune told? Both are swayed by their love of the marvellous. I grant that the sophist might draw a distinction, but it would be purely one of degree. What do you say to that?"

"Jael," he answered, "your question is not so subtle to me as is the mystery of how you have come to know anything of such a matter, or of the ease with which you express yourself. Have you had some schooling?

"I am the only woman of my tribe who has had any education. From my eighth until my thirteenth year I was sent to a private seminary, for what reason and by whom I know not. I made rather rapid progress and since then I have followed up my advantage as far as might be amid the bustle of our roving life. Old plays and present-day verse have long been a source of delight to me, though I have not entirely neglected other kinds of reading. Tomorrow, if you wish, I will show you my books."

The strident voice of old Abegail cursing Jael for some neglect, or owing perhaps to the hag's mistrust of her companion, put an end to the conversation. That night Red Ike went out poaching on the banks of Loch Lomond with Ben Faa, a young gypsy with whom he was on terms of a rather surly companionship. They returned to camp about an hour before sunrise, hid their catch within the double floor of the van, and then went to snatch a few hours' rest before the tribe would be on the move again.

No sooner was Red Ike stretched on his pallet of bracken than he felt a hand placed upon his breast, and a pair of warm lips pressed to his cheek. Turning on his side, he felt the head of his companion, and his hand wandered down the body to the hips, and he knew by the length of the hair and the curves of the waist that it was a woman who lay beside him.

But who? was the question. If the wife of one of the gypsies, and they were caught together, blood might flow, but if a single woman no harm would transpire, but he would be looked upon henceforth as the woman's mate. To speak would be to betray her to others within earshot. How came she to be lying beside him? Was she mistaking him for another in the darkness? What should he do to get rid of her? He attempted to rise, but she clasped him round the waist, and held him down.

Then he felt her face—her long eyelashes, her mouth, her nose.

Yes, he could not be mistaken, she was Jael Boswell.

He placed his mouth to her ear, and whispered: "Jael, not now. Leave me tonight, and I'll find means to confer with you tomorrow. We'll lag behind on the march, and I'll explain myself." But her only answer was to cling closer to him, and solicit by silent gestures his body's contact with hers.

"No, by God!" he said, fiercely, and tearing her arms apart, he threw her from him, and rushed from the tent. He was miles away from the camp when the daylight came.

Cursing all creation, at the close of the day he threw himself down on the Gleniffer Braes, and gazed into the blue void above. Was there ever such a mad-brained idiot as he? Flying first from his native place because of a faithless whore whom he loved, and now from the solicitations of a woman whose love was perhaps purity itself, judged by the morality of her class. He who had sworn a few months back to take his pleasures wherever they might be found, was leaving love behind him, and unconsciously returning to his native country, and to Peg Shore!

"Returning to Peg Shore!" he cried. "If we meet again, I'll slit her throat, or may the next thunder levin strike me."

Nevertheless, he continued his journey southward, and arrived at Carlisle weary in body and reckless in soul. He had not been there many days before an episode of sudden violence landed him at last in prison.

He stept into freedom to behold Jael Boswell holding out her hand. If any act could have moved a man's heart towards a woman, this was one. But some perverse devilry in his nature withheld him even then from greeting her as she deserved, and he coldly shook her hand, showing neither surprise nor welcome.

She gave him a look that showed at once her disappointment and that she would give no further trouble; but when he moved along the street she walked beside, and pressed money upon him. He glanced at the coins, accepted two half-crowns, and returned the rest.

"Come and have a meal," she said.

He would not assent to that, but promised to look out for her at the oncoming hiring fair to be held in November. "I shall be at The Roaring Militia Man," he said, and they shook hands, and parted.

He arrived home in darkness, to a house that was tenantless. He went on to Sandyflatts, where he expected to find Will Moffatt. It also was tenantless and desolate. Next morning beheld him at daybreak standing beside a new-made grave in St.-John's-in-The-Vale church garth. He had no need to ask whose it was. It was side by side with his father's, and he turned and left the spot with the bitterness of a black past and a dark future weighing upon his soul.

He returned to Sandyflatts and examined windows, doors, and chimney. He clambered over the garth-wall and found the milkhouse window blocked up, and wondered and puzzled to solve the meaning of this desolation. Then he remembered the secret passage from the old well-pit in the garth, which as he thought was known only to Will and himself, and lifting the flagstone that covered it, he dropped from sight. Then a further riddle awaited him. Everything smelled musty as a grave, and he knew that the place had not been inhabited for months. He struck a light, and examined every nook. There was nothing to be learned. What had become of Will Moffatt? Was he dead and buried? Should he enquire? No. He would remain here until nightfall, and then find out what could be learned in his own way.

Having settled his mind on this point, he stretched tired limbs on the wood screen, and slept through the day. He was not one to pay the supernatural the tributes either of belief or fear, but it seemed to him as he woke that Will Moffatt's mother stood at his side, and that her hand was on his brow with a cool and pleasant touch.

Her words came clearly to his waking ears, *"Wait here for Will,"* but when he raised himself and looked round, there was nothing to hear or see.

CHAPTER V

HOW was he to act for the best? Whilst pondering on this he heard the sound of footsteps upon the highway, and the indistinct talk between a man and a woman as they approached the house. They stepped to the door, inserted a key into the lock, shot the bolt, and lifted the latch. He did not move, because he did not care who they were.

"Damn!" said the man, "the door's been barred inside."

"It can't be that. I tell you the house is empty," the woman answered.

"Let's make sure," said the man, "there's no saying what freak Will Moffatt might take into his head."

He came to the window, and tore down the hoardings someone had nailed before it. There was a smashing of glass and a bull's-eye lantern shone into the room. Red Ike seized the arm and wrenched the lantern away, turning it full upon the pair outside. It showed the frightened angry face of Joe Gream, with Peg's startled eyes over his shoulder. Dropping the lantern, Red Ike gripped the arm with both hands. The frightened man struggled furiously, but Ike did not loose till the arm snapped like a match-stick over the window sill.

Cursing and screaming in mingled pain and fear, they fled into the darkness. Red Ike picked up the lantern, blew out the light, which still burned, slid the bars of the door, and stepped out into the night.

Luckily, the new-made skeleton key, which had no doubt been forged to fit the lock of Sandyflatts, was still in the keyhole. He turned it silently, and then ran on across the pathless moorland, his thought being to reach Joe Gream's forge before the return of the frightened pair. As he approached, he saw that a light was streaming through the unblinded window, so climbing onto the shoeing shed, from which he could see into the kitchen, he lay flat to wait and watch events. Joe's mother was busy preparing supper. A simmering pan of oatmeal porridge hung over the fire, and a large bowl of buttermilk and two platters were on the table. Evidently Joe and Peg were not wedded. The thought gave him a grim, unworthy satisfaction; yet, as he watched the old woman busy with her household duties, a feeling akin to sorrow crept over him, that his act of violence was about to cause her trouble. Then a pair of strong arms gripped his feet, and pulled him from the roof of the shoeing shed. The next moment he was struggling under a powerful adversary. He felt the pressure of a fierce grip on his throat, and a knee pressing him down. He strove in vain to break the grasp of those merciless hands, until he jerked his own knee between the thighs of his adversary. In an instant the grip on his throat relaxed. The man rolled over, groaning in agony. Red Ike knew the voice for that of John Lynd, and it was a simple thought that it would have gone ill with him had his face been seen. He rose and dashed into the darkness.

Yet his purpose held, though he knew that he must use every precaution if he were to find out what he sought and remain unrecognized. If Joe had not gone home with his wounded arm, it was at Peg's cottage that he would be. Very cautiously Ike approached The Knoll, and was about to step up to the window, and peer into the house, when a half-bred mastiff bloodhound sprang upon him. He felt its paws on his breast, and its hot breath enter his mouth, but, with the presence of mind of a practised poacher and wrestler, he cast the brute over his leg and away, and then drawing his clasp-knife he awaited the next attack. As it sprang again for his throat, he gripped it by the forepaw and turned it onto its back, by a trick that the gypsies knew, holding it powerless, till his knife was across its throat. The warm blood spirtled over his hand, as the dog rolled over without a cry, for he had severed its windpipe, feeling, in the heat of the struggle, as little compunction as though he had pressed his boot on an adder's head.

It had become increasingly apparent that things were out of joint, and that something had happened of which he was ignorant, quite apart from his own quarrel with Joe Gream. He could not guess the mystery in which he had become so rapidly enveloped. But he was determined to solve it, even at the risk of prison or death itself. As he watched, the light which had been in The Knoll window went out. He turned to seek shelter on the moor among the whins, and to debate with himself on his next move, when he stumbled and fell over the dead dog. An oath burst from his lips, and before he could regain his feet he was once more in the grip of John Lynd. He felt himself in a powerful grasp, and guessed it was he by his method of tackling. He guessed that he would try to make sure this time, and went limp in his hands. He sought by a ruse of non-resistance to delude his opponent to think that he was going to take things quietly. And then, bending his body until he was well underneath him, he quickly gripped him by the right shoulder, and buttocked him clean over his head. He struck the ground with a thud, and lay shaken and winded. With a jeering laugh, Red Ike bounded onto the moorland, and the darkness again became his friend.

High up on the breast of the Hill of Devils he lay till the next morning came, and he could watch the comings and goings of the scattered community below him. The Naddle fells and the northeastern shoulder of Helvellyn range were one mass of purple and gold. The more distant ranges were dark purple and blue, beautiful to behold to a stranger. To him, born and bred amongst them, they were the walls of God's temple, and he gazed with deep transport upon them. The Bents' chimney was the first to smoke, after it The Knoll, then the cottage adjoining the forge. The forge itself would be fireless for many a day.

He longed for a pair of good field-glasses to bring within ken the moving mites of humanity below him. But the distance baffled his sight, and so he turned onto his back, and watched the passing clouds, and the revolutions of the hunting buzzard hawks as they scanned the fell sides for quarry, circling slowly till every yard of ground would have been surveyed, and they would wheel away to the inspection of an adjoining area.

He had not slept through the night, and now the warmth of the morning air soothed his body, and he fell into a dream-free slumber.

It was high noon when he woke, and, turning on his side, beheld, in the far distance, upon the Mosedale road, a gypsy's van, and knew by its colour and build to whom it belonged. He half rose from his point of vantage, and then sank as quickly. It would not do for him to be seen.

If he moved in that direction, it must be by night. Hour after hour he watched the gypsies drawing leisurely nearer Mirkholme, their old and favoured haunt. That part of the moorland belonged to John Lynd, and he had often wondered why he allowed the gypsies unmolested to remain there for indefinite lengths of time. The motives of men are sometimes hidden and strange, and the ties of blood are often the prompting of deeds which would be otherwise inexplicable.

He lay thus while the sun circled three parts of the heavens, and as it sank to nadir behind the highest fells, the longing to be up and away to the moorlands below was insistent within him. He watched with increasing impatience the slowly dying embers on the fringe of the world gilding the hilltops with reflected glory; and as these gradually lost their glow, the ravines on the shoulders of the fells became full of shadow, sombre and restful, as eternity shall be when man with his fierce passions, vain imaginings, high hopes, and base desires has passed through folly to the eternal night.

When the darkness fell, Red Ike made his way back to Sandyflatts, and found it silent and deserted. He replaced the boards which Joe Gream had torn down from before the window. He locked and barred the door from the inside, and then left the house by the passage through the old well. He was determined, at whatever cost, to solve the meaning of Joe and Peg's visit to Sandyflatts; of John Lynd's attack on himself, of Peg's ferocious dog, and finally why the solitary gypsy's van had returned to Mirkholme at the fall of the year, and who were its occupants.

He crossed the moorland cautiously, giving a wide berth to all foot trods, houses, and outlying buildings.

The Bents, when he approached, was in darkness. Wondering at this, he was about to cut across an angle of the moor leading to Mirkholme, when he heard voices in the distance, and hurriedly climbed into one of the black yew-trees that half encircled The Bents.

"I tell you, it was Will Moffatt," said John Lynd.

"Are you sure?" questioned the other. It was the voice of Ben Faa, the gypsy.

"Quite. I know by the way in which he buttocked me over his head, after he cut the dog's throat at The Knoll. No other man in these parts could have thrown me so cleverly and cleanly. Besides, I taught him that trick myself. He used my method exactly."

They then passed on and entered The Bents.

Wondering what devilment those two might be planning together, Red Ike dropped from the branches of the yew-tree, and next minute he was tearing across the moorland to Mirkholme. There, himself unseen in the darkness, he saw Jael Boswell standing before the van door in the leaping fire light.

Looking over the half-screened doorway, and watching her intently, was old Abegail, not a bad type of gypsy, but a gypsy still, and no matter in whose veins the blood of the tribe runs he had learnt to trust them not at all, or as little as possible. Retiring further into the darkness of the whin-clad moorland, he uttered three times the wild, weird cry of the brown owl. The old witch looked in the direction of the sound. Jael stood still, apparently unmoved, but he knew otherwise. He saw her lift the lid from the bule-pan hanging over the fire, and examine the contents.

Satisfied that all was right, she ascended the steps, and entered the van. A few minutes passed, and he heard the old woman cursing her for a pariah, and driving her forth onto the moorland again. By the light of the fire, Jael turned and raising her clenched fists towards the old hag, she poured the most fearful maledictions upon the whole gypsy race, and then fled towards him in the darkness.

"Jael, what is the uproar about?"

"Hush," she said, "the devil himself's abroad tonight."

He laughed, and answered, "No doubt he is. His name is legion, and his machinations are manifest and always abounding."

"Come," she answered, "I have something to tell you."

"Where shall we go, Jael?"

"To Sandyflatts."

"But the house is tenantless."

"You were there last night, Red Ike."

The urgency and straightforwardness of her speech impelled him to follow. Yet as he did so he was debating inwardly how best to hoodwink her, for he knew that he could only enter by the passage from the old well, as he had not only locked the door, but barred it on the inside.

But Jael dispelled his dilemma with the words: "Over the wall with you. I'll follow. I know the way." And before he could answer she led the way, and he followed in her wake.

In the darkness of the empty house, he lit the bull's-eye lantern he had wrenched from Joe Gream, and then hung a quilt before the window, making sure that no gleam of light could be seen from outside. This done, he turned to Jael, and stood transfixed in wonder at the apparition before him. Her eyes were as brilliant as twin dog-stars on a winter night. The glow of her pure skin from her bare shoulders to the forehead was like the tint of a June rose shining through a thin gauze of olive. Her hair, glossy and black as pitch, rolled in delicious waves down to and about her waist. She was moulded like to Milo's Venus, flawless, and thrice as entrancing, being a living woman, alluring, enticing, and with arms outspread towards him. He leapt to her embrace, and time was not; past and future had no meaning. The present alone was reality.

Midnight passed.

The early hours of another day were at hand by the calling of the moorfowl, and by the indefinable feeling or realization so distinctly understood by all lonely inhabitants of the out-of-the-way places of the world. Not even Wordsworth has fully expressed it, rich as were his gifts of intuition and suggestion.

Jael was sleeping peacefully on the stone flags by his side, the incarnation of natural womanhood. What cared she for the laws of country or church? Being a gypsy, unshackled by custom or convention, she did not understand the meaning of ostracism, and might have cared little had she done so.

To her, the gratification of her instincts was of paramount moment. Earth was her heaven. Red Ike her god, and sensuous delight the realization of the worth of living. A Keats might have flown, from the cold atmosphere of a Fanny Brawne, to that of the rich, warm, and fragrant, if lawless one created by Jael.

Red Ike touched her bare pulsing breast, and in her deep satisfying slumber she spoke his name in such a dreamy, rapturous, abandon of passion that he folded her in his arms and kissed her lips.

Yet, even then, he felt that he did not love her, as men adore the ideal woman of their adolescent dreams; in fact, he could have parted from her, or seen her happy in another's embrace, without feeling the emotion that had been stirred within him by Peg Shore's infidelity. And yet he knew that she was true and pure, as Peg could never be. He felt with a confident certainty that he was the first dominant sexual power in her life, and knowing this he might have lived with her during the rest of his days had she wished and willed it. But she did not. She had no thought of settling down to a formal routine of life, or breeding through long years of semi-poverty, a brood of future half-civilized children to be the semi-slaves of those who harried the tribe to which she belonged. Her instinct was for a freedom of love that left her with absolute independence of thought and action. Hence she had no desire beyond the present hour, no fear, and no care; she was resourceful in emergency, but without plan; impulsive, loving and daring, a splendid type of animal womanhood. Lacking the low scheming cunning of the house dweller, she was in many ways the exact opposite of Peg Shore. Tomorrow was an unknown quantity, to be reckoned with when it arrived.

So, roused from her sleep, she sat up. A low musical laugh, like the first note of a throstle on an April morning, broke through the darkling room.

"I was dreaming of you, Red Ike."

"And I am here."

Leaping to her feet she ejaculated: "Light the lantern."

"Why, Jael?"

"I can hear the rumble of carts."

"Well, what of that, Jael? The highway lies outside."

"Hist, there is someone at the door."

The lock was shot, and the sneck lifted.

"I told you so," said Jael.

"Blast it!" came a voice from outside, "the door is barred again."

Jael held her finger to her lips: "That's Joe Gream."

The thunder of a huge stone banged against the door shook through the house, but the impact made no impression on the stout iron-barred oak woodwork.

"There's someone else outside, as well as Joe Gream, Jael. I broke his arm yesternight."

A glance from Jael told him she knew.

"He thinks 'twas Will Moffatt."

Red Ike lifted his cudgel as the rumbling cart stopped by the door. Then a hurried consultation followed, and they caught the low, cynical laugh of John Lynd.

"Back the cart against the boarded-up window," he cried.

Ike motioned to Jael to step inside the milkhouse, and blew out the lantern. As she did so, the shuffle of a horse and a grinding cart prepared them for the event. Ike stood in readiness. With a crash the window was hurled out of its bearings into fragments on the kitchen floor. Still he did not move.

The morning was yet dark and overcast. The dawn would be delayed. A wind was rising and rain was falling. It seemed as though the elements were about to league themselves with the scoundrels outside Sandyflatts. The cart was drawn back from the window onto the highway. Still Ike waited. His time to strike was not yet. They moved cautiously, remembering his assault on Joe Gream the night before.

The flaring light of an old bag saturated with paraffin oil was held through the window, and shone full upon Jael standing in the milkhouse doorway. A howl of jealous rage and amazement broke from Ben Faa, and he leapt upon the window sill. Red Ike's cudgel swung, and knocked him back to the feet of his confederates.

"By God!" exclaimed John Lynd, "I'd burn him out now if he were the devil from hell."

And cursing Will Moffatt as he did so, he backed a cart up to the stoved-in window. By the glare of the burning bag outside, they saw that it was loaded with straw, and that John Lynd held a revolver in his hand.

Joe Gream was at the horse's head. John Lynd set fire to the cart-load of straw, and Ben Faa forked it into the house.

The wind had risen, and rolling peals of thunder broke over the moorland. Great flashes of lightning tore through a deluge of rain, and from time to time would show for an instant the three men at their devilish work.

The two inmates of the house, blinded and choked by the smoke of the burning straw, were driven back to the milkhouse, where they watched, for a time, the furniture blaze up, and heard the downpour of the rain that beat on roof and walls as though to frustrate the attack of the deadlier element.

Thinking it impossible that the house should be saved, they were about to retire into the secret passage to the old well, when there was a rending crash, and part of the roof fell in an inward ruin, as though struck by lightning, or demolished by the fury of the raging storm.

CHAPTER VI

WONDERING how he came to be lying in darkness with a broken head at the well pit bottom, Red Ike sat up and began to collect his thoughts. Resting his head upon his hand, as his brain cleared, he tried to find a solution of the strange happenings of the past few days. But in vain. Truly there was mystery upon mystery, and the reason for burning Sandyflatts the crowning mystery of all. It was evident that John Lynd and Joe Gream thought that he, Red Ike, was Will Moffatt. But he knew nothing of any enmity among them. They had always appeared to be friends.

What had come to pass? He gave up the problem.

Then suddenly, and last of all, he thought of Jael. He called her name, and received no answer but the echo of his own voice from the farther end of the secret passage.

Had she perished in the burning house? Anxious and in doubt, he raised himself and made his way to the milkhouse. A sheet of clotted blood caught his sight, but no Jael. He rushed into the kitchen and drew back appalled before the destruction that met his view. The once neat and clean home of Nance Moffatt had become a charred and rain-drenched ruin. He searched around until convinced that Jael, harmed or unharmed, was not there.

Then he fell to wondering how he had got to the bottom of the old well pit. He concluded that he must have been hurt by the falling roof, and that Jael must have dragged and left him there. A chance view through a broken mirror on the charred wall showed that his head was bandaged. Doubtless, he thought, the clotted blood on the milkhouse floor was his. Seeing that there was nothing more that he could hope to discover there, he retired into the secret passage, and lay down again at the bottom of the old well-pit.

It was then little beyond noon. He resolved to take no risks of being recognized by daylight, and so composed himself to sleep, and did not waken till night was far advanced.

He emerged from his resting place into the serene beauty of a starlight sky. A brown owl hooted from the old bullace tree that hung against and over the garth wall. Stretching his limbs, and feeling well and fit despite the experiences of the last two days, he was soon out of the open moorland. When he came to the cattle-pool, fed by the meeting of the three runnels that form the main beck, he stripped and washed. The bandage Jael had wrapped round his head he rolled up carefully, and placed beneath a stone amongst the great clump of broom on the edge of the pool. There was a deep cut across the back of his skull, and feeling it, he found the wound had been carefully trimmed of hair, and salved. He knew that this must be Jael's work, and the thought determined him to go to Mirkholme and demand to see her. Caution whispered "Beware," but he told himself impatiently that he was afraid of no man, and striding determinedly along he reached the camping ground and found it deserted. Cursing his luck, and knowing the uselessness of appealing to anyone but Jael to clear up the points that perplexed him, he resolved to circumvent the design (if such it were) of John Lynd and Ben Faa, of hurrying Jael from his reach. So he crossed from Mirkholme at an angle, and made straight for Lonscale gap, and then held eastward, after skirting the shoulder of Saddleback. Within an hour before dawn, he hoped to be at Sour Nook, and felt sure that he should find the gypsies there in camp in a favourite wooded howe above the banks of the clear-winding Caldew. So he did, and without pause, as being one of themselves, and of a certain welcome, he walked up and stood before the camp fire. A huge brindled lurcher which he had trained to retrieve its kills, and to do other things as valuable and useful, bounded towards him with joyous contortions of its lithe body. Too well it knew that to bark was to earn for itself a fierce thrashing.

Watchful and silent, he gazed into the blebbing, boiling pan over the fire, guessing that the eyes of Ben Faa, Abegail, and Jael were upon him. Assuming an abstracted, indolent attitude, he waited to see who would be first to speak. After a few moments of suspense, Ben stepped from the van, and accosted him in an offhand manner, yet with furtive glances over his body, and roused him to an additional alertness.

He could feel the tension between them, and braced himself up for the coming contest, which he knew was inevitable. If by sheer intelligence he could overreach him, well and good, if not, then he would fight him with a good will, though not for Jael, for he did not feel, even then, that the event of the night before, which he had not sought, had united them in an enduring bond. However, as if to remove his suspicions, Ben cast himself upon the ground, and held out a plug of tobacco towards him.

He declined it, saying he did not smoke.

"I had forgotten that," Ben answered, and rolling over onto his back he gazed covertly up at him.

At that moment, old Abegail appeared at the van door.

"Jael, here's Red Ike," she cried.

With the air of an amorous princess of the Arabian Nights Entertainment, Jael stepped from the van, and lightly hailed him. A loosely-fitting robe of amber-coloured merve silk, girdled with a curiously fashioned belt, and fastened with an ivory clasp inlaid with gold and mother-of-pearl, added a sensuous grace to her perfect figure. Thrown over her shoulders was a transparent gauze scarf, through which the luscious delight of her dark-glowing healthy skin drew the eye with subtle power, an alluring witchery, arresting attention and capable of overwhelming the balance of a susceptible or artistic nature. Over Red Ike the glamour of her presence fell, but without enthralment. Admiration he would give to beauty in all its forms, whether human or animal, mountain, and lake, and cloud, or bird and flower, but there was an element in his nature that resisted even the domination of beauty. He would be free in his own soul, though the hands of all were against him. He had fallen once to the spell of love, and it had roused him only to anger and self-contempt and a bitter pain. Nor could the memory of what had been during last night—not even that—entirely obliterate from his mind the earlier episode when she had made the first advance and he had fled from her in the night.

He took the hand that she stretched out to greet him, as she came forward, and said, "Where has Red Ike been since last we met, and why did he leave us?"

The form of the question prompted him to an equal caution. He said, "A presentiment of my mother's death impelled me to return home. She lies buried in the church garth over yonder."

Old Abegail, watching in the rear, gave a mocking laugh. "Has the gift of the seer fallen to Red Ike from the gypsy caravans?"

"Stranger things may have happened than that," he replied carelessly.

A curious smile was lurking about Jael's mouth, as she questioned him, as if at random, "Have you heard that during last night's storm, Sandyflatts was struck with lightning and burned to the ground?"

"No," he answered coolly. "I hadn't heard that. I hope no one was injured."

"We don't know that. Abegail read it in tile crystal. We were on our way to Mirkholme today, but have received an urgent summons to Scotland. We shall be returning at once."

"Wait till tomorrow, and I'll go with you."

At this unfortunate remark, Ben had turned onto his elbow, and in a defiant tone swore there was no room in the van for another traveller. He saw that jealousy alone prompted his surly attitude towards him. Did he really believe, he wondered, that Will Moffatt was with Jael during the burning of Sandyflatts, and that he knew nothing of the affair? Had John Lynd's delusion that, in his encounters with him, he was Will Moffatt, had the effect of dispelling the doubt which he had heard Ben suggest to him when he stood hidden in the black yew tree at The Bents? There was the dissimulation of Jael in his favour, and he resolved to profit by it. He did not believe they meant returning to Scotland. But unless he made a pretence of wishing to go with them, he would have no chance of having any private talk with Jael.

So every objection that Ben made he waved aside, until at the last the gypsy broke out into open and threatening enmity.

But the opposition only stirred Red Ike to a colder determination that he would have his way. The evident jealousy of the gypsy only roused him to an open challenge for her whom he had thought but a moment since he could resign without difficulty.

With folded arms he looked down on Ben Faa, and taunted him with his lack of good fellowship. Then he turned to Jael, and praised her beauty and dress, thanked her for the affable welcome she had given him, spoke of the delight that he always had in her company, and finally offered her marriage. Would she care to become a house dweller? If so, his hand and heart were hers. A shadow flitted over her features and passed again, and then her face became as inscrutable as the Sphinx that forever and changeless gazes across the desert sands, and forgotten generations of buried cities, temples, and gods. She looked at him without reply, and in her eyes was the age-old mystery, the enigma of the daughters of Lilith which is never answered, though it has been asked since the world's dawn.

And while they stood thus, old Abegail thrust herself between them. "Will Jael wed the like of you?" Her voice rose in a shrill derision. "You marrowless scum of a rotten race, born, and cradled, and fed, and doomed to die in the shadow of a superstition at which the gypsies laugh! You, whom law and custom harass through life, like bloodhounds at the heels of a fugitive! You wed our Jael, and crush her free proud spirit into the narrow bounds of a parish no bigger than my hand! Jael, our Jael! The glory of the gypsy race! There's not a camp in the three continents but boasts her beauty, and will own her power. Their hope today, their queen tomorrow, when the film of death glazes the eyes of Abegail Faa."

Red Ike stepped back in astonishment as this tirade was poured upon him. He was about to answer the sibyl when Jael stepped between them and spoke with an aspect of authority, and a natural dignity. "The answer belongs to me. I want no husband but the one of my choice, and my choice today"—she looked straight into the eyes of Red Ike as she said this—"may change tomorrow. I am a free spirit. I will be free as the eagle that broods on the black crags above the highland strath where I was born."

As the old witch realized the tenor of this reply, she drew aside and began to chant a low mystic rune, and to dance, weirdly gesticulating the while, around a curiously carved stick, which she had planted upright in the ground. Ben Faa, who had so far watched the scene without interposing, now lay crouched up like a dog in fear and trembling until the rite was over.

Red Ike said nothing. He looked at the witch's antics with a laugh that was half amusement and half contempt, and then turned and walked a short distance away, and sat down with his back against one of those great upstanding stones erected by early races, which are found dotted, chiefly near the banks of rivers, in the seaward-sloping dales of Cumberland.

The oncoming dawn was now breaking with a faint tinge of orange; anon quivering shafts of light, shot from that wonderful archer, the sun, burnished the orient. Then the great globe itself rose resplendent from the depths of space, and began its circular march again. Red Ike looked at the symbol of human destiny. Of birth and death; of resurrection maybe, and new-born glory; a never-ending process between, at the farthest, every three score years and ten. But to what end? Who can guess?

He thought it to be a strange book that none may read. Nor (he thought) can the sibyl Abegail more than another. No, not by a single step. 'Tis a dark and gloomy vista, and he who hopes and he who doubts may well be fooled at last.

Then a low sweet laugh-sounded on his ears, and rising to his feet he saw Jael, a mocking gleam of merriment in her eyes.

"A penny for your thoughts, Red Ike."

"They'd be dear at that."

"Then they are very worthless."

"I should like to talk with you, Jael."

"So you may, but fate wills that we shall part for the present."

"Nonsense, Jael. In this case I shall take fate into my own hands, and mould it to my will."

"There are too many lumps of clay to begin with at once, and all together," she rejoined. "Deal with each lump separately. Watch and wait. When I can help you I shall."

"Then do you know why Will Moffatt left Sandyflatts, Jael?"

"Yes."

"Why?"

"Ask Jean Lynd. She'll tell you."

"Where shall I find her, or Will Moffatt?"

"I don't know that."

"Are they together?"

"No."

"Do the three scoundrels who burned down Sandyflatts know that I was there with you last night? Do they think Will Moffatt was with you?"

"They're puzzled."

"Do they think anyone was there with you?"

"They saw no one but me."

"What happened in the milkhouse?"

"Something struck you when the lightning came, or else you stumbled and fell."

"Good. Shall I go with you to Scotland?"

"You can please yourself; you'll have to fight for it if you do."

"Then I shall fight in any case, and please myself whether I go or not afterwards. Why did you speak so strangely, Jael? And why did Abegail dance and chant round the carved stick? And swear by the eyes of the Pyramids and the North Star?"

"To impress a fool, Red Ike."

"Was she conniving with you, or was she in earnest?"

"In deadly earnest. She believes her incantations have an efficacy most powerful, especially when she chants them round the carved stick during the dark hour of night that always precedes the dawn."

"What was she soliciting the fates to do for her?"

"To take you off by death. Did she dare, she would remove you by poison or the knife. She wishes me to mate with Ben Faa, so that he may become the consort of the gypsies' queen after her day."

"She is not so old, Jael. She may outlive you yet."

"No, no. She is in the grip of an incurable malady. The wonder is that she's alive today. But she has an indomitable will that does not suffer her to think of defeat or death. She has ruled our scattered tribes with unequalled power since her ascension to the gypsy throne almost forty years ago. She was then a young woman about my age, but thrice as beautiful."

"That is not possible, Jael."

"Next year is her jubilee. She is resolved to live till after that event, which will be celebrated in France within the stone circle of that once mighty structure, the still-imposing and majestic ruin of Carnac. For each standing stone of that wonderful amphitheatre there will be a representative from a gypsy tribe, and I shall be chosen Abegail's successor. And, oh that that cringing dog, whom you saw curled up in abject fear less than an hour ago, were a man like Red Ike! The gypsy consort whom I shall choose…"—and here she laughed bitterly—"…must be no weak-kneed craven, afraid of the wreck of an old woman, dancing and chanting around a carved stick, and mocked by her own shadow cast by the firelight of a gypsy's camp in the dark hour before dawn."

During this conversation, Red Ike had never taken his eyes from Jael, but though a sign of emotion, well under control beneath a careless laugh, showed itself now and again, she was an inscrutable enigma still. True, her words implied contempt for Ben Faa and but little respect for the gypsy rites, yet the darkest side of her nature still lay outside the pale of his comprehension. The fact was that he was but glimpsing the undeveloped character of a personality, strong, stern, and unbending. One of those strange types of humanity whose ultimate realization of themselves depends so much upon circumstance, to which they will adapt themselves so readily that it will appear to be their creation, and not, as the fact is, the creator of that which they become.

Red Ike arose from his seat against the upstanding stone just as a gleam of morning sunlight touched Jael with its glory. And lo! She became transfigured; and he, astounded, gazed upon her. She was no longer the gypsy Jael, but another, the veritable counterpart of Jean Lynd, exact in every outline. A sweet, modest, refined woman of the sheltered class. Was he bewitched? There she stood in the flesh before him. A cloud crossed the sun's disc, the glory fell, and he exclaimed, "Jael?"

"Well," she said, "have you seen the devil? You're as white as a ghost."

And the old inscrutable mask of the Sphinx settled upon her face again.

He answered nothing, turning from her presence into the depth of the wooded howe. He broke through the thick undergrowth of bramble and wild raspberry canes, and green, five-fingered ground ivy, till he was far enough away from the gypsies' camp to be secure from observation. Glancing round to make sure he had not been followed, he threw himself down amongst luxuriant bracken, on the edge of a bold crag above the swift-flowing, white-foaming, roaring Caldew.

He knew that he had seen that day, with a flash of intuition, that which might have remained for ever an unexpected thing. Jean Lynd was Jael. Jael was Jean Lynd. They were not one single entity, he knew, but the striking resemblance between them was no mere freak of nature, but the sure result of a close relationship of blood, near enough to be guessed at correctly.

This then was the clue to John Lynd's forbearance with the gypsies on his land at Mirkholme. He resolved that he would not abandon the search till he had uncovered the heart of the mystery.

CHAPTER VII

THE sun was past its noon when Red Ike rose refreshed from sleep amongst the cool lush bracken. He descended the face of the crag, and stripping himself by a deep pool he revelled in the ice-cold water.

A snowy-breasted cusel sat on a moss-covered boulder on the far side of the beck, and sang cheerily as he swam past. A lone dweller in the solitude, had it not learned to distrust the near approach of man, or was it aware by instinct of those who did not mean it harm? He left it still singing there after he had dressed, and ascended the face of the crag, and set out again for the gypsies' camp.

Jael and old Abegail were not to be seen, neither were the horses. Ben was lying asleep, or feigning it. He was couched in a well-defined circular hollow in the centre of the wooded howe. Many such hollows are to be seen in secluded places all over England. They are the game cockpits constructed by our forefathers, and are ten to fifteen yards in circumference. After the passing of the Act against cock-fighting, their use gradually passed from the knowledge of all but the oldest inhabitants of the countryside. Yet around these arenas in the grey light of dawn occasionally gather lovers of this old English sport, even to this day.

He walked up to the van, and seeing that it was unoccupied, sat dawn upon the steps of the doorway. The great brindled lurcher came and stretched itself at his feet. Ben raised himself onto his elbow, and called the dog to him. It blinked up at Red Ike, and wagged its tail, but did not move. With a curse, Ben leapt to his feet and called again to the dog. Still it did not move. Striding forward, he grasped the poor brute by the neck, and began to thrash it unmercifully. Red Ike rose and strode up to him. The sight roused him to one of the sudden angers which his strength made perilous for those upon whom they fell. His fist caught the gypsy behind the ear, with all his might in the blow. Ben Faa rolled over, and lay still. The dog fled, and crouched its quaking body in the bottom of the old game cockpit.

Red Ike saw that his chance had come. He entered and searched the van. In an open black ebony case which was fixed to the van's side, he saw the carved stick. A small table of the same wood, the top of which was curiously inlaid with ivory, gold, and pearls, stood by the bed. He had no time to spare to examine the table-top, but he noticed it was slightly tilted. Raising it further, he uncovered a cunningly-devised space in the top of the table-bole in which was a small, black ebony box. Lifting the lid, he glanced at the contents. There were some letters which he thrust hurriedly into his pocket, leaving the empty envelopes. There was also a gold chain, with a pendant attached. He sprang this, and saw inside two miniatures, John Lynd and Jael. Satisfied with the proof it gave, he dropped the bauble back into its box, closed the lid, and left the table-top tilted as he had found it. Then, with the carved stick in his hand, and the key for its locked case in his pocket, he passed from the camp, leaving Ben Faa lying where he had fallen, and the brindled lurcher crouched at the bottom of the old game cockpit.

For the moment, he thought only to retreat to some quiet spot where he could examine the letters without fear of interruption, and consider his future plans.

He had no fear of pursuit. He thought that days might pass before either the letters or the stick would he missed. Probably the gypsies would leave the district at once, and not discover their loss until the old sibyl had again some reason to overawe Ben, or some other members of the tribe with her gymnastics and contortions and chanted rune. But he knew that when the loss was discovered the whole gypsy tribe would be roused to restore it to her.

He did not think that they would scruple to murder him, if, by so doing, they could regain its possession. He decided that he would consult his own safety, as well as secure its retention, if he should deposit it in a hiding-place which they could not find. He would make straight for Carrick fell, and lie low in the bracken on its mighty breast until nightfall. Avoiding the open country roads, and taking advantage of all available cover, within an hour he was safely ensconced in a position of vantage, whence he could overlook the moorlands that spread below, one wide expanse almost level to the distant Cumbrian capital, that city of contentious border warfare, of legend and song, of Wallace and the Bruce, of Edward Longshanks, of the gallant De Harcla, of Kinmont Will and the bold Buccleugh, and hosts of others of fearless lawless kind, who had played their parts like puppets on the stage of life, to pass at last, one by one, within the shadow of eternity, but to remain reflected through the magic pages of romance, the delight and wonder of the generations that were to follow.

From such thoughts as these, which filled his mind in the long solitary brooding hours, when he would lie out on the huge fells under sun or stars, he was roused to the memory of the peril in which he lay by the sight of the great brindled lurcher, with its nose to the ground, running upon his trail. Eagerly scanning its course, he saw no one in its wake. The brute, responding to the only constant kindness it knew, was coming to share his life. A glad thrill of comradeship swept through him with this realization, and a few minutes later it lay at his feet, welcomed with a caress, and the words of praise that it understood so well.

The carved stick was lying beside him. He took it up and examined it carefully. Like the table and the box in the gypsies' van, it was black ebony and richly carved with quaint devices of rare invention. The workmanship revealed the skill of a master-hand. A serpent, beautiful and life-like, wound its sinuous form around it from end to end. With mouth agape, the reptile held between its jaws an ivory ball movable on a gold wire pin fixed through the centre. On the ball was carved the universe, the Old and New Worlds, oceans and islands in the minutest detail, the sun, moon, and planets, and the twelve signs of the Zodiac. On the stick itself, in addition to the serpent, were carved the nude figures of a man and a woman standing on either side of a Sphinx. There were also birds and fishes, and a wealth of foliage and flowers. The marvel of all was that each object was enamelled in colours with exquisite perfection. A wonderful piece of workmanship, worthy to hold its own with any example of the rarest craftsmanship of Benvenuto Cellini.

The stick was old, undoubtedly, but not earlier than the fifteenth century, as was shown by the representation of the New World.

He was about to lay it aside when, whim-led, he pressed the serpent's jaws. The ball opened in halves, and in dark purple lettering, the colour of human blood, were written these words:

THE GYPSY'S LUCK

Whoever owns The Gypsy's Luck
Need fear no evil fate.
Face thou life's chance with grit and pluck,
And heart and soul elate;
Hold fast to me with all thy might,
And I shall serve thy will,

And bring thee luck through all despite;
Mine owner triumphs still.

"This stick then," he said to himself, "is a fetish, prized and perhaps held in reverence and awe by a race that is supposed to hold no religious belief, and to scoff secretly at all human and divine law. The Christian looks up to a cross and the mangled Christ, the Mahometan to the crescent, the gypsy to a stick. And all are swayed by one powerful feeling—call it what you will, it is rooted in wonder; it was so at the beginning, and will be till time is not."

Stretched at his ease on the wilds of Carrick fell side, he waited patiently for the coming of night. He had resolved to take refuge for at least a week in an underground drift of an old slate quarry on the steep side of Helvellyn. Once there unseen, he had little doubt that he would be safe from all intrusion, save that of the brown owl, or occasionally the sweetmart, or fell fox.

Thinking himself to have been unseen and unfollowed, he reached his destination by midnight, and after examining every corner of his retreat, he prepared himself a bed on a rough-hewn ledge, with a wisp of dried bracken pilfered from a stack as he came along. Whilst doing this, he noticed a bore in the rock-face about four inches in circumference, and finding it dry he hid the carved stick therein, and sealed it up with a stone and some clay paste.

This done, he sat down on his bed of bracken, when suddenly he remembered the letters he had taken from the black ebony box, which he had forgotten in examining the curiosity of the gypsies' stick.

Now, by the yellow light of a flickering candle, he went over them, till there was only one that was left unread. From them he learned that Jael's mother was daughter to the old sibyl Abegail. That John Lynd, in his early youth, had joined the Faa tribe, and travelled with them over the British Isles, and then through France, Spain, Italy, and Egypt. Also that he had been at Carnac when Abegail was enthroned and crowned Queen of all the gypsies the world over. There was no open confession in any of them that he was Jael's father, but of that he had no doubt. The letters were all in the handwriting of John Lynd. He was about to read the last one when the lurcher lying at his feet stood up and bristled its back, and turned its erected ears to the entrance of the drift. Laying the unread letter beside the others on the bracken, he went towards the entrance of the drift, to see what might be disturbing the dog. The next instant the report of a revolver rang out. A bullet whizzed past his ear, and struck the candle where he had left it behind him. The light went out. He dropt quickly to the ground, and waited in the darkness.

"He's done for," said a voice he did not at once recognize. "I heard him fall."

"Don't be too sure, he's a cunning fox. And he's one to fight like a devil. Strike a light, and I'll shoot again if necessary."

"John Lynd and Ben Faa, by God!" thought the crouching man, "and I'm trapped here like a rat."

"Devil take them," cried Ben, "I've lost the matches."

"Then crawl in, and fetch the letters; you saw where he laid them, on the ledge to the left."

There was a grumbling protest from Ben. It was evident that he did not like the idea. John Lynd's voice was raised in an overbearing anger. "You'll fetch them out, or, by the blood of Red Ike, there'll be another bullet for you."

"Mr. Lynd!"

"Blast you! If I don't hear you move in a second…it's your last chance."

Red Ike's arm held the lurcher down while Ben felt his way along the drift for the ledge. Once he stepped onto him, and shrank back from what he thought to be the body of a dead man. Red Ike heard the papers crinkle as Ben Faa picked them up, and crawled back out of the drift.

"I've got them, Mr…."

"Hand them here. Is the Red Devil dead?"

"Dead as the Brutchstone," said Ben.

"Damn you and the Brutchstone. And damn him for a meddling fool. I can smell the reek of his blood from here. Come along now."

The steps and voices withdrew.

Red Ike's first thought as the men passed from the drift, was that the gypsies could not be aware that he had the carved stick, unless John Lynd's impetuous desire to recover the letters had driven, for the moment, the thought of it from Ben Faa's mind. Were there other gypsies, he wondered, placed on guard to prevent any possible chance of escape from the drift? He could not know, but he felt certain they would return. To clear out quickly was the best thing to do. But at the entrance he paused.

From the opening of the drift an old sledway falls with a sharp incline to the dale below, and here, without warning, detached boulders will often break from their hold on the crag-face that frowns above, and roll with frightful speed, rumbling like thunder on their course, and carrying death to man or beast that stands in their path. Red Ike had seen such falls smash trees a century old like matchwood, and fly at last into a thousand splinters on striking the debris of their shattered fellows, heaped in fantastic and motionless disorder. There they lie like buried generations of bygone mortals— waiting, waiting, waiting for they know not what.

Now, as Red Ike stood at the entrance, he heard the warning, sliddering, crackling noise of the crags in motion above him. He drew back into the drift and listened. A terrific roar like thunder broke the midnight silence. Thousands of tons of crag fell sheer from the heights above, and crashed headlong down the brant incline of the old sledway, and he knew that only by a miracle could John Lynd and Ben Faa have escaped death on their way to the dale below. But it was still his need to find another and safer shelter, and he again made his way to the entrance, which had become darker now, so that he must feel his way by the wall.

He found that it was now almost entirely blocked by a huge boulder several tons in weight. With great difficulty he squeezed himself through an aperture, beyond which he could see the stars, and, followed by the lurcher, he stood once more under the wide sky. But what a scene met his gaze! Tons on tons of rock blocked the one-time sledway. Falling on hands and knees, he crept along until he found himself once more among the bracken and whins.

Elated at his escape, he stood up and swept his glance from peak to peak of the dark looming heights around him.

The Pole star was on his right, and so, turning leftward, he climbed to the summit of the fell, and lying down beside a cairn of stones, slept with the lurcher curled up beside him, until the black-cocks crowed to the advancing dawn.

His nerves braced with sleep and the high mountain air, he felt fit and ready to do battle in a just cause with any living man. The lurcher stood looking up into his face with the questioning gaze that the poacher knows so well, and that is rarely noticeable in any but a highly-trained, intelligent crossbred's eyes.

Stooping, he caressed it and said, "Good lad, how-way fetch."

With arched back and wagging tail and nose to the ground, it completed three-quarters of a circle, struck the "drag" of something that had passed in the dark, and bounded into the thick bracken. Shortly, a shrill scream told its own tale, and the lurcher, with the air of a conqueror, came racing back, and laid a splendid hare at his feet.

One good meal a day is enough for a dog, no matter how hard it be worked, and, strange though it seem, the garbage of a new-killed rabbit or hare is preferred to the fleshy portions. Had it been otherwise, it is likely that Red Ike would have made a smaller meal. As it was, he took the two hams for himself, and the lurcher had the feast of a lifetime.

The sweet morning air, rich with the blended scents of heather and late-flowering whins, and a thousand blooms that come to perfection in early autumn on the Lakeland fells wandered on a light southwest wind. Far and near the voices of the inhabitants of deep solitudes fell on the ear. The bark of a raven gloating at the sight of a stricken sheep, the sharp cries of a pair of kestrels, the lowing of cattle, the neighing of fell-bred ponies, the bleat of wild goats, and then the loud blast of a hunter's horn rousing the sluggards in the valleys below to rise and join the hunt.

Tally Ho! Tally Ho! Tally Ho! Hurrah for Blencathra! The most splendid pack that ever threaded a mountain pass. Fleet as lightning, and with sinews of steel, they are out to track the plundering fox, and run him to earth. Yonder they go, Tally Ho! Tally Ho! Five-and-twenty couple. White, black-and-white, and liver-and-white, with tails erect and stiff, running in full cry. Up the steeps of Latrigg, through leagues of bracken and ling. Away! Away! They are turning for the deep dens in Skiddaw forest, where the peat-moss, spongy and springy, defies the feet of man to make quick headway, but over which the light feet of the greyhound fox, that knows every inch of the pathless waste, passes swift and sure. Red Ike heard their chiming cries, faint and far and mellow with distance, and knew that very shortly the whole pack would burst into view over the heights of Blencathra, or the Hill of Devils. Yonder they came, tireless and relentless, not a straggler amongst them. A glorious sight that makes the pulse dance, and the eye flash with the lust of the chase, that terrible instinct that lies latent within us all, and, though unguessed at, is yet close to the roots of life itself.

He now watched the fox, glimpsed again and again as he made straight for the ancient borrans amongst the crags that fell last night. Poor Reynard, flee thou to another shelter. Here there is none. What the fates will must be. From a thousand feet above he saw the fox running to the dale below him, and, standing upright on his hind legs, gaze in wonder at the masses of rock lying before him. He could see him sniffing the air. Clearly he was nonplussed and unable to decide his next move. The pack behind, ever drawing nearer and nearer, and in front almost impassable piles of sharp-edged, newly-splintered rocks, with no known track amongst them. The old sled-way was blotted out of existence. The borrans his fore-elders had known and inhabited from time immemorial were no more. Buried under tons of debris, those erstwhile populous catacombs would never again be the noisome mansions of the four-footed denizens of the wild. That day was past and gone. Realizing the hopeless and helpless position he was in, he turned and faced his pursuers. He could die snarling and fighting. A not inglorious end, when the odds are fifty to one. Dropping into position, he waited the oncoming rush of the foremost hound, a gallant bitch bred from the renowned John Peel strain. The "drag" being hot, she ran up to him before realizing the nearness of her prey. Red Ike saw both their backs bristling, then the fox dart forward like a red bolt and bury his claws in the hound's eyeballs, but ere he again recoil, the ravenous pack had seized and torn him into a thousand shreds.

By this time the foremost hunters were on the scene, and soon a small group gathered in animated discussion. The hounds were called together and coupled, a sure sign that the hunt was being abandoned for the day.

Closely and eagerly, he watched their next movements. Had someone been caught and maimed or killed by the fall of rock? Yes, they were slinging a dark object across a horse. He would have given much to know, but would not change his position to see whither they bore it. John Lynd might yet be alive. When they turned towards Mirkholme, the gypsies' camping ground, he knew at least that some of the tribe were again at their old haunt.

Having leisure to think, Red Ike began to ask himself whether he had done right or wrong to steal the carved stick. It was worthless to him, who had no love for curios. As long as he kept it from the gypsies, he judged his life would be safe. He did not consider that it might have a money value. That they would use whatever extreme measures, short of his death (which would not help them), to discover its whereabouts, he did not doubt. But if he kept his own counsel, not even an expert quarryman, let alone the gypsies, in spite of their boasted occult knowledge and divination, would be able to unearth it from its tomb. Of that he was certain. He doubted even if anyone but himself could find the drift. For the entrance was almost blocked, and the whole surface of the crags had been changed.

But thinking to see for himself how far the fall had extended, he was in the act of descending to the drift when he beheld two figures advancing rapidly towards the dale from Mirkholme. Withdrawing himself into the bracken again, he lay down with the lurcher beside him. He pointed out the distant figures to it, and knew that it recognized one of them by the quick tension of its body, and he guessed rightly that Ben Faa was alive and well. On a nearer approach he recognized John Lynd also. He too had escaped. Who then had been killed by the fall of rock? Probably a gypsy sentry, if such had been with them.

Now, anyone lying a thousand feet above a dale, if the wind is favourable, can hear distinctly a conversation taking place below him.

Red Ike lay there, feeling, curiously enough, no resentment towards either of the men as they approached, but rather a curious satisfaction in knowing that he had outwitted them so far, and was master of the situation. He had the carved stick, and he knew the contents of all the letters but one; though that one, as he could not guess, contained the most vital information of them all.

He watched them coming through the narrow opening of the dale mouth, and then ascend the very boulder from which the fox, standing upon his hind legs, had surveyed the new-piled fragments of rocks that blocked the way to the borrans and the drift.

What would they do next?

He was not kept long in doubt. John Lynd led the way. He could hear him cursing the gypsy, body and soul, as they scrambled along, until both stood directly below him.

"Right here was the location of the accursed hole," said John Lynd, "and I'll be damned if there's a vestige of it to be seen. I'm sure of the spot. That rowan-tree that now overhangs the face of the cliff grew twenty paces further back before the fall. There is no doubt that Red Ike and the carved stick are buried for ever, and a noble cairn they've got. May the fires of hell consume them both!"

When the gypsy spoke his voice had a strange ring. "Neither hell-fire nor any element can harm the carved stick. It is immune from decay or destruction. It was grown on the shore of the Dead Sea when the world was young, and under the charm of a mighty wizard, whose direct descendants are Abegail and Jael. Were it hidden in the very centre of the earth itself, it would finally be restored into the keeping of the gypsy queen."

"Then why the devil bother about coming to recover it?" The slow wit of the gypsy found no ready answer, and without further parley the two departed whence they came.

CHAPTER VIII

RED IKE crept back to Sandyflatts in the night, and made it his abode for several weeks, never stirring out by daylight, and living on the toll of game that the lurcher and he took, ranging several miles over the moors. By this time his beard was a foot long, so that it, and his unkempt shaggy hair, both as red as a fox, gave him a wild and unrecognizable appearance. He would have been hard for any to know, except by the tone of his voice.

It was November now, and the long nights were in his favour, enabling him to travel miles out and in before dawn. The freedom from restraint, combined with constant bodily exercise on fell and moorland, made his already robust constitution as hard as adamant. He became fleet-footed, reckless of danger, and of such abounding spirits that he laughed to scorn the idea of anyone grappling with and holding him in the dark, or of running him down, be the race ever so far.

To dispose of his poached merchandise, he waylaid travelling butchers when returning from their country rounds, and never haggled over the price when selling it to them, or bargaining for future orders. He only stipulated the times and places of meeting, and that they must come alone and ask no questions, nor pry into his mode of life, nor inquire who or what he was. They were well content to keep a still tongue, making the bargains they did.

Whilst he was thus waiting one night at the crossroads, it being near the Martinmas hiring fairs, the jostling of show-men's vans crossing the moorland on their way to Carlisle kindled a fierce desire within him to mingle with the crowds that foregather there. A longing possessed him to see the wild horseplay of the dancing lofts and drinking dens, and to listen to the merry songs and tales, only to be heard at such times and in such places, from the mouths of scallywags and loose women, often no better than ministers of lust and disease who flit from fair to fair until they fall out of existence in some loathsome lazar-house, or die by their own hands in the throes of insanity.

He had withdrawn into the shelter of a thick clump of whin bushes as the vans were passing, when a white lurcher bitch trotted up and rubbed itself against him, and before he could lay hold of his own dog both had disappeared into the darkness.

At the crossroads he waited the dog's return until the dawn was about to break, and then hurried home to Sandyflatts. But the dog was not there.

Surmising that it had followed the showmen to Carlisle, and was now probably a prisoner chained to one of the vans, he resolved to go to Carlisle Fair in search of it, and by the next night he had taken up his quarters in Dan Lockering's lodging-house, hiring his bed for two nights. This was the most disreputable lodging in the city, but probably the only one that would have admitted him in his unkempt condition. Thinking he was a hanger-on of the shows, no one took the least notice of him, so, after his supper of ale and bread and cheese, he stripped himself stark-naked, as enforced by the regulations of the house, counted what money he had brought with him, and handed it and his clothes to the landlord for safe keeping. Then he slipped into bed, beside an unknown roadster as nude as himself. But not to sleep. Fresh arrivals kept thundering on the door continually, and the stifling, fetid atmosphere of the place at last became unbearable. Jumping out of bed, to the wonder and annoyance of his bedfellow, he roared for the landlord, and cursing his lice, fleas, and all creation, demanded his clothes, dressed himself and sat in the kitchen until morning—the morning of the day that was to prove one of the most eventful in his life.

All that day he dodged from van to van in the hope of finding his lurcher, but without success. Chagrined and disappointed, at the edge of the evening he went into The Roaring Militia Man Inn and called for a drink. A goodly company was in the room, and a general smile broke out amongst them at his appearance and unexpected order. The landlord, looking him over, asked him to step round to the bar at the back of the house, where he would be served. This he refused to do, and sat doggedly and stolidly still. Seeing he was, or might be, a rough customer to meddle with, the landlord laughed, and jokingly said, "All right, Man Friday." Red Ike took no notice of this, nor of the many uncalled for and unsavoury remarks passed about him, making allowance for the merry jests of the fair day. However, when jest became license, and a young fellow tilted his hat to the side of his head, and called him the King of the Yahoos, he pushed him aside with an impatient gesture, and when he came at him again and lifted up his chin to look into his face, he rose to his feet, and with a double fist and all his force caught him under the jaw, knocking him into a heap at the far side of the room.

"Christ! I thought he was an old man," ejaculated the startled landlord.

"I only want to be left alone. Can't I have a quiet drink without being insulted here? You," pointing to his late tormentor, "are the type of riffraff whom the landlord should order round to the back bar to drink." He then drained his glass, and was about to depart when the landlord laid a hand on his shoulder, and said, "Sandy, do you want a job?"

Red Ike guessed the job that would be offered after the scene that had just occurred. He asked only: "The price?"

"A pound."

"Right." And he was forthwith engaged to be the chucker-out at The Roaring Militia Man for the rest of the drinking hours that night. Not a position of high importance in law-abiding England, but nevertheless one with possibilities of trouble on a night like that.

A cold heavy sleet came on as the night advanced, and the dense crowds on the fair grounds began to disperse, the lesser and more staid portion to the peace and warmth of their homes, the larger and wilder and more insatiable, to the dancing lofts and drinking dens.

During the day he had not seen a gypsy, although he had scanned closely and keenly the hucksters of both sexes vending their trashy wares to a credulous people, whom no amount of trickery practised upon them takes a step farther on the road to wisdom. Autolycus was here as of old, a merry rogue and wise in his day and generation, making use of the talents he had to his own benefit, and letting the foolish world jog along as it liked.

Soon The Roaring Militia Man became packed to the doors, and hard drinking and uproarious shouting and singing was the order of the hour.

Red Ike sat behind the bar on the edge of a beer barrel, drinking glass after glass, content that no disturbance was taking place to call for his interference, when Jael's voice, sweet and clear as a bird's, came to him from the adjoining room. Her singing, to the accompaniment of a guitar, hushed everyone to silence.

She had come to the fair then, he thought, in spite of the belief of John Lynd and Ben Faa that he had perished under the fall of rock. He remembered his promise when released from prison that he would meet her here, and for the first time in their acquaintance he felt for her a feeling new and strange to him. Yet had he not loved Peg Shore? And the memory of that dark incident in his life, the scene at the Brutchstone, still rankled in his breast. No, he would not trust Jael. She might be no better than Peg, and he thrust the delight of her from mind and heart, swallowing glass after glass of noxious hell-fire, that it might turn his thoughts from a temptation to which he was resolved that he would not yield.

Meanwhile Jael, unconscious of his nearness, sang song after song, now a merry ditty, now some tender Border lay whose liquid burden, distilled and purified through the medium of her rich nature, was pouring out unconsciously upon a fair-day rabble, for a few pence, the suppressed vehemence of a passionate, hopeless love. For whom?

For Red Ike, and what was he? Nothing, but yet a saint to what he was shortly to become in the mouths of men.

And now he fell to wondering. Was Ben Faa with her? He would see that for himself. Yes, he was there collecting into a hat the money at the end of each song. Red Ike clenched his fists, and felt a sudden desire to throttle him. Yet he knew that he had no right to interfere between him and Jael. If she wished to attend the fair, for whatever purpose, it was no concern of his. He had heard her declare herself a free woman, with the absolute right to bestow herself whenever and on whomsoever she thought fit. Yet the devil of jealousy tore at his heart, and his drink-addled brain was past the stage where calm reason is possible. Gloomily he returned to his seat on the beer barrel, and called for his glass to be filled again.

The hours took wings and flew under the spell of song and drink, until but one remained before the roisterers at The Roaring Militia Man would be turned out of doors.

Even yet, the night might have passed in peace, had not a free fight broken out, some trivial drunken quarrel, in the room where Jael was singing and playing. Doing no more than the duty for which he had been engaged, Red Ike pushed his way into the room, crying "Hold!" and flourishing his cudgel above his head.

But at the sound of his voice, Ben Faa started back, yelling "Red Ike! Red Ike!"

"Or his ghost," he shouted in answer.

Jael forced her way through the press, the guitar still in her hand. She laid a hand upon his bare neck, and the blood leapt lusting through his veins at her touch.

"Nay," she said, "he's quick."

"Yes," he cried, "and by the carved stick and the devils in hell, a match for the whole bloody gypsy tribe."

At that word, a sign passed amongst five or six of them that had gathered there, and like mad dogs they leapt upon him, and like dogs he threw them backward to right and left, striking them down with the cudgel, one by one, till the space around him was clear. Then he saw Ben Faa skulking behind Jael, while he shouted the others on. He stepped forward to settle him too, but spreading wide her arms so that he could not strike without harming her, and looking him straight in the eyes, she said quickly: "Enough, Red Ike, I'm afraid there's blood on your hands already."

Then, turning to Ben, and pointing to the door, her voice hoarse with emotion, she said: "Go—Go."

Like a beaten cur he sidled past into the darkness and sleet outside.

Bending over the limp prostrate bodies on the floor, Jael examined each, and then stepping up to Red Ike she whispered, " Fool, you've killed the Weasel. Clear off, while you can." But it was too late for that. Before he could gather his wits to realize the enormity of his act, or the desperate position in which he stood, Ben Faa was back, and half a dozen stave-armed constables blocked the way to freedom and the open moors. Seeing no chance of escape, he held out his wrists for the gyves in a sullen silence, and was marched off to the doom that overshadowed him.

CHAPTER IX

RED IKE stood his trial for murder at Carlisle at the New Year Assizes. The principal witness against him was Ben Faa, and if hard swearing could have hanged him, our tale would have ended there. But Jael offered herself as a witness on his behalf, and showed that he had not even been in the room when the fight began. She said that he had no interest in the quarrel in which it originated, and had not known the dead gypsy, even within an hour of his death.

The judge eyed her keenly and watchfully as she gave this testimony. "Wait a moment," he said, when her cross-examination was concluded, and she would have left the box. "There are a few questions that I should like to ask you. The dead man was no friend of yours?"

"He was not a friend nor an enemy," she answered. "I did not know him at all."

"But he was one of your tribe?"

"He was a French gypsy who had just come to England." She went on to explain that he was one of several who had come to make arrangements with the English tribes to send members to attend a great festival to be held in Carnac the following year.

"What is the purpose of this festival?"

"To crown a gypsy queen."

The judge made no comment on this. It was not easy to tell what he thought. But Red Ike noticed that John Lynd, who had been in court since the trial commenced, seemed to wince at the words, and a pallor spread over his face, which puzzled him, so that he forgot for a moment the peril in which he stood.

But the judge's questions went on. "How long have you known the prisoner?"

"Several months."

"Under what conditions and where?"

"He was with our tribe in Scotland for some months."

There was a moment's silence as the judge considered this answer. He knew that there was falsehood either in her evidence or that of Ben Faa. There was a man's life on the issue of which of them should be believed. That was for the jury to say, but it was his part to guide them to the right end. He was a merciful judge, but there had been too much of lawless and sometimes murderous violence at that fair during recent years. An example was needed, and if Ben Faa had told the truth.... He watched the witness intently as he said, in his quiet way, "He was with your tribe in Scotland for some months—will you swear that, beyond that, there has been no personal intimacy between you and the prisoner, either at that time, or since?"

There was a hushed silence in the court, waiting for her reply, as Jael looked at the judge, meeting him with a gaze that was as inscrutable as his own.

"My lord," she said, "I came here only to tell the truth. I did not know that I should be asked such a question as that. The prisoner is a house-dweller. He is of your own kind. I am a nomad, and there is a gulf between us that neither could ever cross. He is nothing to me."

As she said this, she thought of the great traditions of her own race. Of their tents in the frozen North, where they had been the first men, camping around the icy Pole, of their wanderings through the then tropical Siberian forests where the mammoth ranged, of China, of Egypt, of how they wandered today in every part of the world, having no tenure, no dominion, no ties but the common bond of the gypsy blood, which to contaminate is the unpardonable sin.

"My lord," she added, "you may know that we gypsies go with our own kind."

The judge weighed her answer in a very shrewd mind. He saw that which she did not say, and if he had made a guess, he might have been near the truth. But he saw also that she was one who would not easily lie, even with some cause. He said, "Then you can swear that the evidence you have given the Court is not biased by any personal feeling?"

She answered boldly to that, "I swear it by the bones of my ancestors under the Polar ice, by the eyes of the Pyramids that point to those graves for ever, and by the Sacred Stick, which is the symbol of all we are."

The judge said "That is all." Afterwards he summed up fairly enough. It might be murder or manslaughter. It was for the jury to say. If they were in doubt.... They took the hint. They agreed on a verdict of manslaughter almost as soon as they left the box.

But the judge did not take a light view of the crime. An unarmed man had been killed. The prisoner had been in trouble before. Jael might call him a house-dweller, but the description did not fit overwell. The jury had very properly given him the benefit of the doubt. It became his part to give him a sentence of seven years, with hard labour.

BOOK TWO

CHAPTER X

IN the early Autumn of 1890, after an absence of seven years, William Moffatt came back to Sandyflatts.

The previous afternoon he had tramped from Carlisle to Sebergan, and slept during the night at a wayside inn on the outskirts of that village. After breakfast he had called the host, and after paying what seemed to him a wonderfully cheap reckoning, he set out, having timed himself to reach his destination by sunrise. The night had been clear and frosty. With a light raincoat thrown over his shoulder, and a stout stick in his hand, he stepped out into the darkness of the winter's morn.

Full of health, having come to mature manhood, and feeling sure of himself in every way, he strode briskly along. His way lay over one of the wildest mountain passes in the Lake District, but he had travelled it so often in past years, and at every season, that he could have crossed it blindfolded and in as straight a course as a heath-going sheep.

When he reached the summit of the pass he was halfway on his journey. A new moon like a sickle was visible oh the skyline, and Orion, girt with his shining belt of stars, was standing on the farthest rim of the distant Solway Sea into which he was about to plunge, to be resurrected again by the revolution of the circling universe.

Gazing over the wide expanse of space from his lofty stand, he beheld the infinite majesty of the starry creation outspread before him on all sides like a scroll, and bowing his head to the unknown power that brought it into being, he instinctively and dumbly worshipped in the presence of that great Panthos whose spirit he felt, with Aristotle, to be the very essence of thought which shall endure forever.

As the mood passed, he resumed his journey and began to descend the fell at whose foot lies the moor on the far centre of which stands Sandyflatts.

Around him he could feel the presence of the wanderers of the night returning to the shelter of borran and cave, surfeited with the flesh and blood of their hapless victims. He heard the bark of a fox within a few yards; the hoarse croak of a startled heron sailing past on the wind; the yelp of weasel or stoat; and the wild whoop of the owl calling its mate back from the chase to its home in the old disused close-head quarry.

Suddenly he felt a sharp wind rise and begin to bite his ears, and turning his face towards the crest of the Hill of Devils he saw the first faint streak of morning light flushing the dawn. He was now within a quarter of a mile of Sandyflatts, and hurrying forward he stood opposite the bourtree that blocks the doorway, just as the sun surmounted the fells, and shot a shaft of prismatic haze over the outermost southern stone of the Druids' Circle, and enveloped him in its glory on the flagstone of the doorstep of his old home.

With a sense of satisfaction, he stood and surveyed the scene before him. The distant fells almost to their very tops looked black and forbidding, except where the brown bracken was tinged with winter sunlight. Wherever juniper or heather grew rankly, those particular parts of the fells seemed devoid of vegetation. It is the dead brown bracken alone that gives such a wonderful charm to Lakeland fells in wintertime.

In the distance, here and there, the smoke from lonely farms began to taint the morning air with the unmistakable scent of burned peat; and the halloo of shepherds, and the barking of dogs, told him that soon these inseparable companions of solitudes would begin to breast the toilsome mountain tracks in search of straggled members of their hardy flocks. Just as there are oases in the deserts, so are there patches of sweet herbage in the innermost recesses of the fells, and thither, despite the most careful watch of their shepherds, the oldest sheep will often wander. The danger is that, unless they be kept during winter months within an easy journey from the farms, they may be overtaken with sudden snowstorms and perish in the deepening drifts.

Coming within sight of his childhood's home, after so long an absence, it may seem strange that he should have stood thus, within sight, and yet delayed to approach it. But it had puzzled him more than once on the journey back to say why he should return at all.

Driven, as he had been, as a leper from the neighbourhood, he came back to gaze upon the scenes of his childhood, having, with one possible exception, no friends in the district, no acquaintances with whom he could expect to be on terms of more than formal speech. Even the woman he had loved had become little more than a shadowy figment of the brain, a lost ideal that sometimes taunted him with an unrealizable desire, and at others had been a lure to turn his face on the homeward path.

And then one night below him, on the darkening Narragansett waters, where the stately passenger ships plying between New York and Boston were lighted from stem to stern, a vessel had glided past with the band in the first-class saloon playing *The Waeful Heart*. Oh, what is the thing called tune? In a moment's space it seemed to him that he had lived through an eternity of anguish and despair, and as deep calls to deep, he arose and faced the pathway of the river to the Atlantic Ocean, calling aloud, *"My love, I come."*

And on that impulse, no richer than when he had gone out seven years before, he had come back to his childhood's home.

CHAPTER XI

BEFORE leaving Sandyflatts, Will Moffatt had boarded up all the windows, locked and double-barred the doors, and cemented a blue rammel flagstone over the chimney-top to keep the owls and jackdaws from nesting in it, or descending into the rooms below during his uncertain absence. He had then squeezed himself through the milkhouse window and bricked that up, and turned his back on Sandyflatts, The Bents, the wild fells and moors, his mother's grave, and the woman he loved. His return, like his departure, was unnoticed and unknown to any. Now he approached a house which seemed little changed when seen from a distance in the winter dawn.

There was still the old bourtree blocking the door, still the overhanging ivy, still the lintel of blue rammel stone with the rude carving J. & E.D. 1669 to propound the mystery of who built it, which there were no title deeds left to show. So he noticed first the ivy over the walls and windows, and not that the house was roofless and windowless, until, parting with his stick the ivy that dropped across the door lintel, a startled robin flew into the kitchen, and perched upon the rannel boke of the fireplace. Then he clambered after the robin, and gazed upon the desolation around him. The charred remains of his old home told their own tale. Yet he was not greatly affected by the sight. He knew that, unless his prospects and circumstances altered considerably for the better, Sandyflatts could no more be a resting place after his day's labour, nor a sanctuary he could enter, and shut himself in from the hostility or coldness of the world. But who had set fire to all his possessions, and why had the thing been done?

He now began to search the ruins, and noticed that the small milkhouse at the back was intact, and pushing open the low door, he struck a light and entered the room. The sconces where his forbears had set up their milk to cream, and where his mother and he had cured their yearly supply of bacon, was, with the aid of rude unbarked posts and layers of fir wood, improvised into a comfortable bedstead, and littered with a heap of bracken. In a corner was a stool, originally meant for clipping sheep on. These things were all the place contained, and he could see that it was, or had been very recently, used as a sleeping-room. Having seen all he could, he was about to leave the place when he heard someone step through the branches of the bour tree in the outer doorway; and slipping hastily aside into a corner, he awaited developments. Within a minute he could feel beside him in the palpable darkness the body of a man, and knew by the smell of him and by instinct that he was in the presence of a healthy and vigorous personality. He seemed to have brought with him the very life and breath of the moorlands and the sense of the wild nature upon them.

Without a word he threw something heavy, and what Will Moffatt judged to be a bag of game, from his shoulders to the floor, and stepping with unerring precision towards the window that Will had bricked up years before, he struck a match, and lighted a candle. "Red Ike."

In a moment he had snatched up a stout cudgel, and swung round to face the intruder.

Will Moffatt held out his hand, but he looked doubtfully at him, keeping his cudgel poised and ready to strike. "What fetches a stranger here?" said he.

"I have come to see my old home, Ike, and surely you are the last man in the world to deny me the privilege."

"This place belongs to Will Moffatt, and until he comes to claim it, I shall allow no man to set an uninvited foot in its walls."

"But Ike, I am Will."

"You are? Then step outside, and let me see you in daylight and I shall make sure."

They went out together, and Ike said doubtfully, "You're like him. Can you tell me what we saw pass between Peg Shore and Joe Gream at the Brutchstone?"

Will Moffatt described the occurrence.

"Aye, you're Will Moffatt sure enough. There are but four folk alive who know that."

"Then we are friends, Ike?"

"For life, Will Moffatt."

"How does it happen that I find you living at Sandyflatts in this manner, Ike?"

"Why did you leave Sandyflatts, Will?"

"Through misfortune and the loss of a woman, Ike."

"Your reasons for leaving the countryside are mine for burying myself in it. Come back into my den." And turning he led the way. Motioning to the shearing-stool, he sat upon the bed-edge, and began: "You wonder at finding me here at Sandyflatts, and now that you've turned up again, I can leave it when I choose. No. Don't interrupt. Wait until I explain myself. It's a long tale to tell."

With the memory of old-time friendship quickening in the hearts of both, they sat there while Red Ike told the events which had followed Will's disappearance, and of the disaster which had wrecked his life.

Red Ike had been released from prison but a week ago.

"I came back," he said, "at once, and made myself a bed of bracken on the sconce of the old milkhouse, and settled down to await your return."

"You felt sure I would come back?"

"Yes. I was sure of that. Had not the spirit of your mother begged me to wait? My one fear was that you might return, and I should not be here."

"What do you mean to do now?"

"Drift to the devil, I suppose. I've nothing to live for now."

Before Will could answer there was the sound of a dog whimpering round the door. The next moment it burst its way in.

Red Ike leapt to his feet, with his head thrown back. He said, "It's the lurcher, by God!"

The dog stood still as a stone, save for the act of respiration, studying Red Ike and showing its wonder that it was not welcomed by the questioning of its brown eyes, the attitude in which it held its body, and even more definitely by the curve of its long-stiffened tail.

"Ike, have you nothing to say to that? You have one true mate in the world even yet."

He held out his open hand towards the lurcher, which raised itself on its hind legs, walked forward, and put its right paw into his, sealing once more the compact between them which lasted till its death.

Ike called it Prodigal, and the two were seldom parted in the days that followed. Will Moffatt had no place in its life. When he called its name, it lay still and blinked, but the moment Ike stepped to the door it rose and strode promptly to heel, ready for any emergency at any time, day or night, and in any weather. The old allegiance was firmer than ever despite their six years of separation, though it might never forget that it was Ben Faa's dog.

This may have been well for Red Ike, as was the return of the friend of his earlier years, and one of a less impetuous and more equable disposition than his. As it was, Will Moffatt came to fear for a time that the long incarceration under the iron discipline of our penal laws had warped his nature, that he had become no more than half a stranger and half a friend. Until late in the evening, thinking thereby to dispel the shadow of restraint which they both felt, he sprung this question upon him: "Did you feel the loss of freedom very badly when in prison, Ike?"

Watching him narrowly, he saw that he had touched his nature to its very depth. Rising from his seat, he several times strode back and forward in the small milkhouse, then stopped and faced him. "Why do you ask that, Will?"

"Because I want us to be on the old footing. We were always the frankest of friends in the days gone by. Square and above board in all things. The friend I had was clean-spoken and clean-thinking, beyond the ordinary order of men. Besides, he was my friend, and you can't have friendship you cannot trust."

"But," and his voice fell, "I killed a man."

Then by a mighty effort of self-control, under which he could see his face twitch, he grew calm and proceeded.

"Yes, I felt keenly the loss of personal freedom. During the first year, when winds were loud, and the moon riding high, I gazed often through the iron-barred window of my cell, and longed to be abroad on the wild moorland with Prodigal. I yearned for the scent of the wild mint crushed beneath my feet by the river-pool, in whose far depths lay the shadowed stars that broke into a thousand shimmering rays when a startled moorhen shook the water's surface. And oh, how my heart ached for the song of the willow-warbler, low, sweet, and plaintive, by the dark edge of swamp or tarn. And when I heard, during the migratory periods, in early spring or late autumn, the trumpeting of the wild swans, the clonking of geese, the call of curlews and duck, on their outward or inward journeys, the desire of my old life became almost unbearable. Had I then had the means, I might have put an end to my miserable existence.

"Wretch that I was, with long years yet before me of helpless and hopeless bondage! However, my good conduct in prison earned me, by degrees, some special consideration. I was allowed books, and my choice in these attracted the attention of the prison chaplain, McPherson, himself a man greatly interested in the fauna of Lakeland, and an authority on that subject. Many an hour he spent with me discussing matters which, until then, I had not thought of much importance."

"That would be an unexpected kindness from him."

"Yes, I began to look forward to his visits that brought a gleam of moonlight into the darkness of my night. However, at the end of my first year in Carlisle Jail, I was removed to Dartmoor, and set to work in the quarries. Here, as before, I applied myself diligently to work, and became rapidly an expert craftsman. There is now no branch of that trade of which I am not a master hand. I can drill a bore in the rock-face, and fire the shot, hammer the blasted blocks into shape, and finally dress them ready for transit from the quarries.

"The work was hard, but the thirst for reading was always with me in those days, and, finding way and means to get books which lightened my life, I spent all my spare moments in study. The Bible I read diligently and carefully. Then the Greek philosophers, playwrights, and poets. From them I wandered through the provinces of the best minds of the Roman Empire, sifted the good from the bad, and found them largely an echo of the Greeks. The European Renaissance then fascinated me, and after that I exercised my mind in the study of English grammar and composition alone, comforting myself with the thought that when my term of imprisonment expired, I might still devote my life to the achievement of some imaginative work of art."

CHAPTER XII

THE morning after they met in the ruins of Sandyflatts. the two friends climbed together to the top of Helvellyn to gaze once more upon a scene which they had known from childhood, but which was now almost equally unfamiliar to them, the one returning from prison, and the other from a more voluntary exile.

Different in many ways as they were, there was in the minds of both a half-contemptuous, half-resentful consciousness of the social ostracism to which they had fallen. They would have said, with more than partial truth, that their portion was the result of hostile circumstance rather than of any action of theirs. Yet no man is the passive victim of destiny. Each must have his own share of responsibility for the fate that meets him.

Had he been approached from another angle, Red Ike would not have been slow, even after the hard and regular discipline of the prison life, to laugh derision at the narrow timidities and conventions of the social order around him. He thought of the dwellers in town and village as of people under a constant restraint, losing at last all sense of individuality, self-satisfied and cautious, following a routine of eternal drabness, uncolourful and unrelieved.

There may be greater safety and softer comfort for those who move at the crowd's pace and who follow in the common way. The way of transgressors is always hard. That is no more than the operation of a physical law of a very obvious kind. Yet there are compensations in all things. Health was his, and leisure to think and feel, and the delights and freedom of the open moors.

Now, lying on the fell-top, thinking of nothing in particular, and absorbing the invigorating atmosphere with every pore of his body, Will Moffatt's eyes fell on a curl of bluish-white smoke that rose from a chimney of The Bents. He said aloud, but as one who exclaims to himself rather than addressing his companion, "I wonder where Jean is now!"

Red Ike looked sharply at him, but did not speak, and having betrayed his thoughts he relapsed into a moody silence.

On the morning breeze the mellow sound of a single bell wandered among the crags and fells like a lost spirit of melody subdued and forlorn. Over moor and dell, far below along grassy tracks, folks were going to worship in the grey, barn-like Chapel-of-Ease, in whose garth lies the dust of bygone generations. From The Bents two figures emerged. Even at that distance Will knew them. They were Jean's father and mother. A new pang thrust its sharp arrow through his heart. Was Jean wedded and lost? Unable to endure the thought, he questioned Red Ike, who knew no more than himself. "But," he added, "that's a thing that's soon learnt."

Will answered nothing to that. He turned the conversation aside. "The gypsies are in camp at Mirkholme; they are lighting their fires."

"I thought as much," Red Ike replied, "and when they miss Prodigal they'll go to Sandyflatts to look for him, and perhaps not for the dog alone."

"For what else then?"

"To learn where the carved stick is. They'll know I'm out by now."

"Then you have the bauble yet?"

"I don't know. Probably, it is in the bore in the drift where I placed it nigh seven years ago."

"Shall we go and see?"

"Yes," he answered, and together they descended Helvellyn, crossed an angle of the moorland, and soon arrived at the dale of the fall of rock. The change in the valley was so great that Will could not locate the position of the drift, but Red Ike, without fault, walked up to it, and examined the boulders that almost blocked the entrance, overgrown with whins and bracken.

Having satisfied himself, he turned to his companion, and said, "Not even an owl or a fox has entered the drift since the night I hid the carved stick in it."

Knowing his knowledge of wildlife was too great to be questioned, Will only said, "Then we'd better leave things as they are."

"Yes, we'll leave it there, but we'll first see if it has taken no harm."

They went together into the drift, and struck a light. Ike removed a stone from the bore, and drew the treasure forth. It was quite unharmed, and after Will had examined it, with delight at the exquisite workmanship, they replaced it in the bore, and sealed it up again.

Then they sat before the entrance of the drift, and waited until the shadows of evening fell in sombre silence ere they returned to Sandyflatts. It was a windless night, and save for the hoot of an owl, or the bark of a fox, all was peaceful. The lurcher curled upon its bracken bed, and went quietly to sleep.

"Ike," Will Moffatt asked, after they had sat for some time in a common silence, "You spoke of devoting yourself to some work of art. What is the line you've mapped out?"

"When in prison," he said, "various projects passed through my mind. I felt myself capable of many things, but my chief source of solitary pleasure was the writing of verse. I saw that to become a major poet was to reach the sublimest height of human achievement, but I saw also that the greatest masters in song had almost without exception died miserably poor, had been compelled to beg for patronage, and to hang onto the coat-tails of the wealthy, and to debase their talents to please the fashionable taste of the age.

"Nevertheless, I thought, and still think, that I possess sufficient fortitude to remain poor, and to work out with patience, and in obscurity, the task I have allotted myself. I shall not sing to please any one class; though, naturally, my leanings are with the needy and op-pressed.

"To be a poet of the people; to rouse them to higher deeds; to clear the mist from their sight, so that they see kings, statesmen, priests and demagogues, in their true guise; to bring heaven close to earth; to fill the world with music, light, and song, and happiness, and peace; this is the mission I have proposed to myself. Even to fail in this will be to suffer defeat in a glorious cause."

The enthusiasm of the poacher-convict, as he burst out in this way, striding restlessly as he did so within the confines of the nar-row room, waked some wonder in his companion's slower and more practical, if not more prosaic mind, but it waked also a generous admiration and a kindred sympathy.

"You can count on me, Ike," he said, "to help, if that's what you're aiming at—to help in any way that I can—and that your spirit of independence will let me do."

The conversation completed the resumption of the old spirit of confidence that they had known in the earlier days. It was with a closer understanding than they had felt on the previous night that they now prepared their beds of bracken, and were about to lie down when Prodigal rose, and holding its head on one side, gazed intently at the flagstone that covered the secret passage to the old well. Red Ike put his finger to his lips, laid hold of a cudgel, and signalled to Will to raise the flagstone. But before he could do this, it slowly moved, was cast back altogether, and then the head and bust of a beautiful woman rose through the opening. Will Moffatt saw at a glance that she was of gypsy blood, and guessed she was Jael.

"Come," she said. "There's not a minute to lose. Blow out the light. The secret passage will hold us all. Bring the dog with you."

As she spoke, there came a rush of clattering feet outside. Will Moffatt extinguished the candle. He allowed Red Ike and Prodigal time to descend, and then replaced the flagstone. He had been driven once from his home, but that was seven years ago. He was a differ-ent man now. He thought he would stay where he was.

A thundering blow sounded on the milkhouse door. He lit the candle and shouted: "Who's there?"

A voice he knew to be John Lynd's roared: "Down with the door."

Without waiting for their assault, he flung it open, and stood with a revolver pointed through it. "Who comes thus to the ruins of my house at this hour of the night? The first man that crosses my threshold, I'll put a bullet into him."

There was a pause, and the rabble fell back.

"I ask again; what is the meaning of this uproar? Am I a fugitive from the law that John Lynd should bring a crowd of ruffians to tear me from the scant shelter of my old home? If so, show me on what authority you come, or go and leave me in peace."

Not a man amongst them moved, so keeping the revolver pointed through the door, he continued: "If you stand there till Doomsday, I'll keep you all covered."

A swarthy gypsy of powerful build, whom he rightly took to be Ben Faa, spoke: "It's not you we want. It's Red Ike."

"He is not here."

A derisive laugh broke out amongst them.

"Yes, he is," cried Ben Faa, "and there's a lurcher with him that's ours."

"If you think that, I'll allow any one man amongst you, providing you first bind his arms behind his back, to examine the room."

To this proposal, after some consultation, they agreed.

"But remember," he added, "at the least sign of treachery I shall shoot in self-defence, and the law will uphold me in the act."

Ten minutes later, he had the satisfaction of seeing them depart.

For several days Will Moffatt stayed in the solitary house expecting that Red Ike would return. But he did not do so, and at last, fearing that some foul play had befallen him, he began to upbraid himself for inaction. Putting the revolver in his hip pocket, which he had learnt the habit of carrying while abroad, he set out to reconnoitre the gypsies' camp.

Through a pair of powerful field-glasses he kept it under observation for several hours, but had to return to Sandyflatts without gaining any satisfaction. He then resolved to visit John Lynd, and demand an explanation of his conduct both past and present. He therefore made his way to The Bents, but instead of the farmhouse which he had expected to see, he found that a new house, or rather mansion, stood on its site. Red Ike and he had noticed from the top of Helvellyn that there was some change around it, but he was not prepared for the one he saw. About ten acres of the surrounding moorland had been fenced in and planted. A macadamized drive led up to the house. The outbuildings were spacious. An atmosphere of prosperity was everywhere evident. Not allowing himself to be daunted by these signs of affluence, he rang the front door bell, with a half-nervous wonder as to whether Jean would appear, and was almost relieved when a servant answered the summons.

"Could I see Mr. Lynd?" he inquired.

"What name shall I give him, sir?"

"Will Moffatt."

Within a few seconds she returned and showed him first into a waiting-room, and shortly afterwards into John Lynd's presence.

"Well," he began, abruptly, "what brings Will Moffatt to my house? Has he come to be driven from the door again?"

At the harsh, contemptuous tone, the hot anger of seven years ago stirred once again against this man of so inexplicable an enmity, who was also the father of the woman he loved. He took a quick step forward, but regained his self-control in an instant. That was seven years ago. He had learnt much since then. Learned assurance and self-command. Learned to think first, and act afterwards.

The older man watched him keenly, without moving.

Hatred may have caused each of them to somewhat underrate his opponent.

"Take a seat, Mr. Moffatt."

From his manner it was evident that he thought he held the trump cards. Will remained standing. He came to his point at once.

"Where is Red Ike, Mr. Lynd?"

"In jail."

"For what offence?"

"Poaching, and assaulting my keepers."

"*Your* keepers! Then I could make a good guess that what you say is a damned lie, and he is in jail on a trumped-up charge."

"Will Moffatt, be careful, or you'll find yourself where Red Ike is; my power as a magistrate…"

The threat and the claim combined to rouse Will Moffatt to say more than he had meant to do when he had entered the room. He did not raise his voice very greatly, but the words came clearly to those for whom they were not meant, and whom he had not known to be near.

"Your *what*? *You* a justice of the peace! You, the father of Jael the gypsy! You, the incendiary of Sandyflatts! You, who with Ben Faa attempted to murder Red Ike in the drift! You, who came but last week to my ruined house on a foul errand I could not even guess at until this moment! I warn you, Mr. Lynd, magistrate or not, if further harm befall Red Ike, you are striking at Jael Boswell, your own child. And, by a just heaven above, I'll denounce you publicly for what you are, if you take this further."

John Lynd's face whitened, whether from anger or fear, but he found no ready answer to this unexpected onslaught. Having no more to say, Will Moffatt turned to leave the house and beheld, standing in the doorway, his beloved Jean and her mother.

"Will," said Jean, "what is the meaning of this scene? And what of the strange words you have addressed to my father?"

"Madam," he answered, with a formality strange to his own ears (was this the Will who had come to her for comfort, and then stood tongue-tied at the gate, when he brought the news of his mother's death?). "Your father will understand. I came here for information concerning Red Ike, and I shall see him fairly dealt with, no matter what the consequence be to others."

Jean crossed the room to her father, and laying a hand upon his shoulder, questioned: "What is this charge against Red Ike?"

"He is in the hands of the law. His character in the past weighs heavily against him, Jean. I am but one of the ministers of the law, and am unbiased. His case can be dealt with upon evidence alone."

"If one gypsy," Will interposed, "be called to give evidence in the case, I shall take what course I think right to protect him."

"I have strong witness besides the gypsies. Joe Gream was present when the affair took place."

"Joe Gream! Is he the right-hand man whom John Lynd has ever depended upon to...."

"Hush!" said Mrs. Lynd.

Will turned to face her. As he did so, John Lynd rose, and leapt upon him. Had he been off his guard, he might have been borne down by the sudden fury of the attack. But he had realized the hatred and desperation of the man of whose past he had shown that he knew so much. As the man sprang, he stooped, grasped his ankles, and jerked him onto the flat of his back. His head struck a small black ebony table which stood at the side of the room, and which, at that moment, Will Moffatt recognized as being like the description of that one which Ike had seen in the gypsies' camp. Will felt Jean's grasp on his arm. "For the love of Heaven," she cried, "Will! Will! do not strike my father."

He made no answer to that, but lifted her hand, and saw there was no wedding ring upon it. Their eyes met for a moment, and then he turned and went out of the house, and on until he was once again in the solitude of the open moors.

Flinging himself down on a bed of bracken, he tried to think calmly and reasonably about John Lynd and his villainous conduct. But the vision of Jean in all her rare beauty, enhanced by the rich maturity of full womanhood, overpowered his more rational faculties. The wonder he had beheld in her eyes when he turned and saw her standing in the doorway with her mother, after listening to the storm of accusation that he had poured out upon her father, filled him with a fear of loss that was akin to despair.

What was she thinking now? He found no relief, guess as he would. Even if she believed the charges true, he was still her father.

Yet that she loved him he had no doubt, and even now there was an undercurrent of fierce joy in the thought. Jean Lynd was his, and had been through the seven years of self-inflicted exile. Though he might never possess her, she would still be his to the bitter end.

Yet, as his anger cooled, and his reason resumed control, he was unwilling, with the memory of the glance she had given him, to admit the possibility that he would lose her for ever. "If she love me," he thought, "should she not leave all and cleave to me? It was her father, not I, who was in the fault first, if not last. Had he not forbade me his house because he suspected my love for her? I was poor, God knows, but there is a remedy for poverty. To burn down a man's house is not the way to help him out of it."

But why had John Lynd burned down his house? Surely not because he had loved his daughter. Why had he not asked him this question, instead of charging him with the deed?

And now he remembered that John Lynd had not risen from the floor when he left The Bents; and he remembered too the curious black ebony table against which he had struck his head. Also, that he had not given a thought to Jean's mother. A cold shiver shook him like a leaf in a November wind. What had he done? Had he wrecked the peace of John Lynd's home? If he had done that, in the rash anger of his accusations, how could he ask Jean to forgive him?

But while he lay in the bracken, pondering the problems of strife and love, Destiny was working them out to their appointed end, and, for the moment, her actions were not unfavourable.

When John Lynd's head struck the small black ebony table, he lay stunned for some minutes, and, in the excitement that followed, he was the sole object of attention; and, on recovery, wishing to escape further questioning in the presence of Jean, he retired to his own room, followed by his wife.

There he made an absolute denial of all the accusations which she had heard, but his wife's fears were not allayed. He had always been more or less an enigma to her. Of his early manhood she knew nothing. She was a woman of great personal charm but of a sensuous dreamy temperament, trusting and trustworthy, and had been completely and unknowingly under the spell of his dominant personality. But now the wonder of a new light had dawned within her. Never more would his ascendancy over her be the same. The dormant or undeveloped side of her character had been touched to life. The darker and sterner aspect of his nature she had mistaken for wholesome strength, and had leaned upon it, not in glory and in joy, but feeling that it contained some essence that was right, and therefore she had not taken the trouble to understand it. But that day was gone. Henceforth, she became a changed woman, and John Lynd, as time passed, felt the rift between them, and chafed under the wound it inflicted upon his vanity and pride.

Meanwhile, with Jean there were strange happenings. She had never before that morning seen the small black ebony table. Ben Faa having brought it to The Bents within an hour of Will Moffatt being shown into the drawing-room.

The violence with which he had thrown her father against the table had dashed it against the wall, and sprung the catch, exposing the secret recess containing the black ebony box, in which were the letters, the gold chain, and the pendant.

Jean, mute with surprise, lifted the box and looked into it. Still more surprised, an exclamation of wonder escaped her lips when the exquisite beauty of the chain and the pendant met her gaze, and woman-like she clasped it round her throat, and stepped to the mirror to view herself. Then pressing the pendant spring, she exclaimed: "My father, and Jael Boswell."

Unclasping the chain, and placing it beside the letters in the black ebony box, she set the table upright, fixed the top, and then hurried with the box to her room and locked herself in.

Her first thought was to read the letters. Her second, would she be doing right if she did? No, she would return the box to its proper place. What right had she to pry into her father's secrets? She was about to obey the promptings of her better instincts when she heard her father and mother leaving their room together. Passing her door, they descended the stairs, entered the drawing-room, and closed the door.

"Thank God!" she murmured. Her next thought was the box. For the present it would be safe in her bed. She then fixed her bedroom window-latch, unlocked the door, and sat down to think. How long she sat she did not know; to her it seemed an age.

The sound of a strange woman's voice below roused her, and filled her with alarm. The woman was demanding the black ebony table.

"I tell you I bought it from Ben Faa," her father was saying.

"He had no right to sell it," yelled the old witch, flinging the money down. "Now hand me the table."

Her decisive manner of speech and action impressed Mrs. Lynd with a vague feeling that there was some veiled motive behind the peremptory demand, and taking the decision into her own hands, a thing she would never before have dreamed of doing, she said to Abegail: "There is the table, go and take it."

Jean saw the sibyl depart, and crept back to her room. What had she done? The box was in her possession. Had she stolen it? Was she a thief?

How to judge of her action she had no clear conception. Like all super-sensitive, emotional people, she magnified her impulsive act, and it tortured her because she could come to no ready decision as to what she ought to do.

Flinging herself face downwards on the bed, she buried her face in the pillows, and strove to steady her mind. It was all in vain, and leaping onto the floor again she paced silently its ten-foot length, torn with fear and anxiety.

Would the gypsy discover the loss of the box immediately, and return to demand it? Then, she thought, should she read the letters, and if they contained any defamatory matter regarding her father retain them? She resolved to read the letters, and, right or wrong, the thought gave her no further trouble.

A glance at the first letter confirmed her resolution. Hurriedly, fearing Abegail's return, by one of those strange coincidences of which life is full, she overlooked the very letter that Red Ike did not read when John Lynd attempted to shoot him in the drift years before.

The problem that now faced her was how to return the box without the gypsy knowing from whom it came.

Pondering on this for a few moments, and finding she could devise no way out of her difficulty for the present, she arranged her disordered hair, and then joined her father and mother in the drawing-room downstairs.

Here her first lesson in the hard school of real life began.

Hitherto, she had lived with the unconscious freedom of a bird, a veritable spirit of the wilderness. Never knowing a serious care, she had not understood how happy she was. All this was suddenly changed. She stood in the centre of a new world of which she had had no past experience to guide her, and no friends on whom she could rely.

CHAPTER XIII

WILL MOFFATT was still lying amongst the bracken in the opening of the dale of the fall of rock when the dusk of evening began to cast its weird shadows. A pair of night-jars poised and fluttered above him like wind-hovers. A brown owl floated past on silent wings. The air was alive with night-wandering moths, and the roar of a distant force, rising and ebbing on a light wind, was the only sound that broke the quiet of a desolation as profound as chaos itself.

With a dull heart, he gathered up a weary body and aimlessly crossed the moor towards Sandyflatts. When he had covered half the distance he became aware that someone was hovering in his wake. This roused his deadened brain, and he determined to take whoever it was by surprise. He wheeled, and commenced a rapid run, when a voice behind him shouted: "Will Moffatt."

He halted at the sound and called, "Red Ike."

"Yes." And the next moment they were standing once more together.

"Why, John Lynd told me you were in jail."

"So I was until a few hours ago. Then the charge against me of poaching and assault was withdrawn, and here I am."

"The scoundrel!"

"Who?"

"John Lynd." Then as they walked back, Will told him all that had passed at The Bents that morning.

The moon was at the first quarter, and lying low in the southwest sky. A thin mist overhung the ruined home, and they had approached it within a few yards when the slim figure of a woman stepped out of the branches of the bourtree that blocked the doorway.

"Jael," ejaculated Red Ike.

"No," she replied. "Jean Lynd. Will, I have come to speak to you."

"Oh, Jean, if I could take back what I said this morning...."

"That would not mend matters at the root of the evil, Will. I think you did right in some respects and wrong in others. I know it was in the cause of your friend. But I have come to ask you a favour, or for your advice."

By this time Red Ike had withdrawn onto the moor, guessing that they would be glad to be alone together.

"Jean, forgive me. I am not worthy to...."

"Nevertheless," she continued, "I have come to you. Now listen. When my father's head struck the table this morning, during the scuffle, he was stunned for a while, and shortly afterwards retired to his room. I found when alone that under the table-top was a secret recess containing a small box in which were letters sent by my father to Jael Boswell, and, in a pendant attached to a gold chain, were the miniatures of them both. Shall I return the box and the gold bauble to the gypsy woman? If so, how can I do it without them knowing from whom the box has come?"

"Jean, the miniature is of the woman who was Jael Boswell's mother."

A low cry escaped her lips: "Then what you told my father was right. The younger woman is my half-sister?"

He could not deny this. He only said: "Red Ike, and you may trust him, will undertake to have the box returned to where you wish before dawn."

"There it is, then," and handing it to him, she turned quickly and disappeared through the waning moonlight.

He did not dare to follow her. She had not even bidden him adieu. She was gone, and he had not had the grace to ask if he might see her home.

That was past mending now, and cursing his slowness, he stepped through the bourtree, and sat down in the darkness to await the return of Red Ike.

An hour passed before he came, and his first words were: "I shadowed Jean safely to The Bents."

After that they relapsed into silence, each occupied with his own thought. Till Will asked, "What has become of Prodigal?"

"Very likely he is chained up in the gypsies' camp. I'll be going there shortly, and may bring him with me when I return."

Then he hazarded another question: "Do you know anything of Peg Shore and Joe Gream?"

"Nothing," he replied, and rising from his seat, without speaking another word, he set off to the gypsies' camp.

It will be recalled that seven years earlier Peg Shore had been living at The Knoll, and Joe Gream at The Forge with his old mother. Tonight Will Moffatt determined to find out if they were still residents at the same places.

John Lynd's elevation in the world had puzzled him greatly. But his surprise was greater still when he found that The Forge had been razed to the ground, and upon its site stood a modern mansion similar to John Lynd's.

He was about to pass through the gate to observe the house more closely, when the sound of footsteps warned him not to proceed further. Withdrawing into the cover of a young, rising, dark pine plantation, he stood expectant.

He heard two folks coming towards him, and a few seconds brought them to where he was standing.

"I tell you," the man was saying, "Mr. Lynd had Red Ike released from jail today."

"Then," said the woman, whom he recognized as Peg Shore, "may the devils rise out of hell and tear them both to pieces."

"Tush!" said the man, of whose voice he was less sure. "There is Will Moffatt to deal with also."

Not wishing to play the eavesdropper any longer, he stepped out of the wood and barred their path, his sudden appearance causing the woman to cry "Joe! Joe!" and to cling to the man.

"There is Will Moffatt to be dealt with also, Joe Gream, and lo, here I am."

"Then you are here for an unlawful purpose, and trespassing on my premises, you poaching hound."

Will laughed at that. "John Lynd charged Red Ike with a similar offence, and withdrew the case today."

He did not understand then—nor ever fully—what there was in that to rouse the woman to fury, but Peg Shore sprang upon him like a wild cat. He threw her from him sprawling, into a runnel by the roadside.

"Will Moffatt," said Joe Gream, "I'll have the law at your heels tomorrow for assault and trespass."

"Will you? Have you yet to learn that a man cannot be charged with trespass between an hour after sunset and an hour before sunrise? Also, that you must produce the engines I was poaching with, or you'll not secure a conviction. As for assault on that woman, why, if the Brutchstone had a tongue it could have proved the charge against you, for her, seven years ago. Pshaw! Marry her and you'll make a fit pair. There's a ring to be found that Red Ike bought for Peg. He threw it into the boiling cauldron below the Stepping Stones. Is that right, Peg?"

But she was creeping away, like a guilty ghost, farther and farther into the darkness of the night.

Will walked away with some pity for Peg in his heart, and not over-pleased with himself for the part he had played at that interview.

He was not one who had a love for strong drink, nor any inclination to mix among the boisterous scenes that it engenders. It was a sudden impulse, born of his dissatisfaction with his own thoughts, that impelled him to lift the latch and step into the drinking-room, and remain with the rowdy company foregathered there.

At his appearance they all sat wide-eyed and open-mouthed, and no wonder, for not one of them was aware of his return.

The first to speak was old Simon Reed, the tailor. Clapping his hands on his knees, he bent forward, and, peering with his short-sighted, bleary eyes, he ejaculated: "It's Will Moffatt, or I'm a bishop."

"Yes," he answered, "it is, and you'll all have a drink with him, lads."

This request instantly put the company in the best of humour, and he was acclaimed welcome with more gusto than he had dreamed was in the whole countryside within a circle of twenty miles. Then, in a flash, he realized he was in the right place to learn all he wished concerning John Lynd and Joe Gream. He had but to spend freely, and lead the company with a few questions. He began cautiously. How to make them all three-parts drunk and remain sober himself was his first problem. He began with a simple ruse. Calling the landlord, he cried: "Fetch a gallon of ale onto the table, and we can help ourselves without troubling you so often." He fulfilled the order with alacrity. Then he nudged Simon Reed, and whispered, "Get someone to give us a song." A sly dog was Simon, and he nibbled his bait at once. Rising from his seat he shouted: "Gentlemen, would you like to hear my favourite ditty tonight?"

A young chap, already half gone in drink, and who had no roof in his mouth, set the house in a roar: "Sit yersel down, you old neudals, you've no more tune in your voice than a jinny-owlet. What do ye want noising and singing when you can get a cropful of ale for nothing?"

"Everyone doesn't like ale as well as you, Pyatt," answered Simon. "If I did, I'd drown myself, hang myself, and cut my wind-pipe."

"By the look of thy nose-end, Simon," rejoined Pyatt, "You've drunk yer own share, and several other folks."

"There you are, gentlemen," rapped Simon, turning to all present. "A man cannot be afflicted with the infirmity of indigestion without being subject to the taunts of a rapscallion, a rantipole, a scallywag, a dithermadow, a thing that will not speak plain English without trying to imitate the peculiar nasal drone of a gent from Oxford." And, pointing to Pyatt, he stood upon one leg, and with one arm crooked, and cried: "Behold him there, a specimen of either Kairo, the missing link, or a Yahoo from the land of the Houyhnhynms, a wonder, a marvel, a creature unbalanced with the exuberance of his own verbosity and egoism. And now, gentlemen, we'll have a song."

When the merriment caused by Simon's oration subsided, Will called for another gallon of ale, and said: "If those present do not wish to hear Simon Reed sing, will anyone else do so?" Instantly a burly farm-servant, intelligent, and whose voice rang with resolution and independence stood up: "I'll sing."

A clap went round the company.

SONG OF THE POACHER

On a night that is dry, when the wind's in the west,
And the moon will have set in an hour;
Oh, he says to his mates: "While the world is at rest
We'll away, and the countryside scour.
We've nets for the rabbit, the partridge, the hare,
The heathcock and pheasant as well,
Though keepers may watch them,
The poacher will catch them,
By river, vale, moorland, and fell."
Who knows half so well as the poacher
The habits of feather and fur?
His knowledge is deeper
Than e'er dreams the keeper;
And he laughs in his sleeve at a slur;
He laughs when the keeper may slur him
He laughs in his sleeve at a slur.

On a night that is wet when the skies wear a frown
Oh, he says to his mates, says he:
"There's naught but the rivers for us to fish down
On a night such as this you'll agree.
We've nets that will fish or the shallows or deeps,
And courage to use them as well.
Though bailiffs may watch us,
'Twill try them to catch us,
In the end, lads, we'll bear off the bell."
Oh, who knows so well as the poacher
The habits of fish in the stream?
The bailiffs though cunning,
Are not in the running,
When they would the poacher outscheme.
Oh, he laughs at their moves to outscheme him,
He laughs when they him would outscheme.

Ah, who knows as well as the poacher the wraths,
Where the rivers can safely be crossed?

RED IKE, BY J. M. DENWOOD & S. FOWLER WRIGHT * 71

Oh, who knows so well as the poacher the paths
Where a man in the dark can be lost?
Oh, who knows so well as the poacher the curse
What follows the life that he leads?
The curse that will follow
Him still till the hollow
Grave close o'er his strong heart that bleeds?
Oh, who knows so well as the poacher
The little-souled tyrants about?
Yet long as the river
Reeds flower and quiver
He'll laugh in his sleeve when folks flout;
Oh, he'll laugh in his sleeve when they scout;
He'll laugh in his sleeve when they flout.

As the singer sat down 'midst clapping and shouting, Simon Reed's shrill voice sounded above the din: "Durst you sing that song in front of Squire Lynd, Dick Stagg?"

"I dare sing it before the Queen of England, or the devil in hell," answered Dick boldly.

So Lynd was the Squire now!

"I'm not so sure," queried Simon.

"Well, you may be, I care for no man."

"But," persisted Simon, "Mr. Lynd is a squire and a magistrate."

"That's a fact, and he's a reptile as well. Why, Simon, the only thing to be made out of a rotten squire is a rotten magistrate."

"Mark my words, Dick, as sure as I'm a snip, your tongue will get you into mischief "

"Then I may happen get out of it again, as Red Ike did today."

At this sally there was a general laugh.

"Red Ike is a fine fellow, his heart is in the right place, for sure," muttered Simon. "When my old woman was lying sick, and work was slack, and we were nigh to starving, never a day passed but he brought her some dainty, fish or game or coney. But that was before he got into trouble at Carlisle Fair. He must have been mad drunk when he felled the blithering gypsy stiff. On the day of his trial we were flustered, more so nor had he been our own son, until we were told he wouldn't swing. I seldom pray, but when my old lass knelt down and was thanking the Lord that Ike was spared, I down on my knees beside her, a thing I've not done since, and added my thanksgiving to hers."

A strange silence prevailed until Simon finished his speech, then pint mugs were slowly and meditatively but deliberately emptied of their contents.

Will ordered another gallon of ale, and soon after that the din was as loud and merry as ever. Covertly he watched Simon Recd and Dick Stagg, and considering the amount of liquor both consumed, he did not wonder that one's nose was red, and that for the moment the other cared for no man. He now resolved to force the pace. Rising from his seat he held his pint aloft, and cried: "Here's to Red Ike, and to hell with squires, and game-laws, and magistrates!"

At once the whole company rose, and echoed his toast.

"Toss off your drinks," he exclaimed, "And, landlord, fetch another gallon; there's the money for it, and for a further gallon besides."

Simon Reed put on his spectacles, and looked him up and down, then blew his nose, and took a pinch of snuff, and finally folded his arms and ejaculated: "Well, I'll be damned."

Dick Stagg stepped up to him and held out his hand, and whilst he shook it, Will gazed into his frank face. Eyes greeny-grey, hair light brown, a clean well-shaped jaw, nose straight and slightly extended at the nostrils, and a mobile mouth of rare power and sweetness. He guessed his age at twenty-two.

"You sang the poacher song well, Dick. Who wrote it?"

"Red Ike," was his quick response.

"Then he is known as a poet, Dick?"

"Yes, and feared and hated by at least two men."

"And who are they?"

"Squire Lynd and Joe Gream."

"But what the devil has he done to them?"

"Nothing. It's what he might do that terrifies them." And Dick laughed in a low gurgling tone which had a world of meaning in it that he could not fathom.

"You're a shrewd fellow, Dick; what do you know of them?"

"If I were Red Ike, I'd move heaven and hell to marry Jael Boswell. They mean to drive him from the countryside or compass his death for fear he may wed her."

"How do you know this, Dick?"

"I was but a lad when a gypsy was killed by a fall of rock in the narrow dale across the moor yonder," jerking his thumb in the direction, "and I chanced to be in the gypsies' camp at Mirkholme when the dead body was taken thither. Abegail Faa was in a terribly excited way, but not about the man that was killed. They took no notice of me, being a boy, and I lounged against a van fascinated by a scene which yet I did not fully understand. John Lynd was there, and Ben Faa and Jael. Abegail was heaping all the curses of Bedlam upon Ben and Lynd, and demanding some letters from Lynd which I gathered from the jumble of her jargon had been in Red Ike's possession. There were also fearful bickerings concerning a carved stick which had been stolen from the gypsies' van.

"'I tell you, Red Ike had not the stick with him in the drift,' Lynd was shouting.

"'Then you should have forced him to say where it is, you nincompoops.'

"'Curse you for an old filth,' shouted Lynd, 'I wish that the moment that I first set eyes on you and yours, my sight had been blasted forever.'

"Abegail screamed out at that, and her face became livid with passion: 'But for you, John Lynd, I and mine should have been held in reverence and esteem the world over. But beware, or I'll be more than a match with you yet. Flesh and blood, even of a gypsy, have a limit of forbearance. Tempt me not too far, or I shall shatter the fabric of your schemes and dreams in ruins about your feet. You are not beyond my power. Beware! Beware! Beware!' and in a paroxysm of wildest frenzy she began to dance round an imaginary circle, and chant a strange incantation of which I could make nothing.

"A mocking laugh from John Lynd brought her to a sudden pause, and she glared at him with eyes blazing like the flames of hell.

"'You forget,' he sneered, 'that your mystic rite loses its efficacy unaided by the magic of the carved stick.'

"She turned fiercely upon him, and the evil of her malignant glance would have shrivelled him to a cinder could it have worked her desire. Her features contracted, and she couched like a wild cat preparing for a spring. When she spoke her voice sounded hollow and distant, and as if it had issued from the tomb: 'You reptile, you monster, well do I know you, you devil! But I hold the key to your future in my hand. I can unmake you at my wish.' And crossing her arms over her breast she hugged herself and chuckled with a fiendish satisfaction that was most uncanny to see and hear.

"Lynd stood unmoved, and said in cold deliberate tones: 'You must compel Ben and Jael to wed without delay. And stop your infernal threatening nonsense, or, by God, I'll stop it for you! I've had more than enough of you already. You've known others feel the weight of my vengeance. One false move on your part, if harm befall me through it, and I'll stamp you underfoot as I would a viper.'

"Turning on his heel, he was about to leave the camp when old Abegail shouted, 'Hold!'

"Lynd wheeled round and heed her again.

"'Well?'

"'Listen,' she hissed. 'I know you better than you know yourself. I am an old woman, but what of that? Would my death clear the way for you to fulfil your wishes with regard to Jael and Jean? You may think so, but it would not. Now, hand me the letters recovered from Red Ike and go. I could lay open the scroll of destiny before you, but the fool is blinded by his own conceit, and saith in his heart, "I am the master of my own fate." Again, I say, hand me the letters and go.'

"Lynd flung the letters to the ground at her feet.

"'There they are, and I fear you not.'

"'Come hither, Ben Faa, and you too, Jael. Give me hold of your left hands.'

"' What would you do, Abegail?' inquired Jael.

"'Pledge thee to Ben.'

"'Never! Never! Never! While breath's in my body.'

"'Come hither,' demanded the hag again, 'Thou art mine, and hast sworn to obey my behest. This is thy natal day. Tonight the moon will be under eclipse and the consummation of thy bridal must take place during the hours that earth shadows the queen of night.'

"'See,' replied Jael, and taking a bright steel dagger, unsheathed, from the folds of her dress, she drew the blade, and flashed it above her head: 'I shall not wed Ben Faa. I know too much of the life he leads, and the man who attempts to possess my body without my free consent shall feel this point of steel in his heart. Ben Faa my husband!' and she laughed aloud. 'The earth may eclipse the moon, but Ben Faa shall never eclipse me.'

"Then, turning on her heels, her loose hair flying in the wind, flourishing the dagger above her head, and daring anyone to follow her, she fled from the camp to the moorland, where she lay until night fell.

"Now," continued Dick, "After that, John Lynd with a brutal curse caught Ben Faa by the throat: 'Is what Jael says true, you whelp of a witch? Have you no more brains than allow your devilry to be seen by her? God! I am continually frustrated by the idiots who beset my path.' And lifting Ben bodily by the neck, Lynd threw him over his extended leg to the ground, and the wretch's head striking a stone, he lay still as death.

"The suddenness of Lynd's attack, indeed the whole scene, seemed to have petrified Abegail, but the sight of Ben lying motionless roused her to thought and action again.

"'Hast thou killed him?' she shrieked.

"'I wish to God I may have, it's the price of him.'

"Abegail leapt towards Lynd, and, fixing her talon like hands on his shoulders, glared into his face.

"'Thou wishest what, John Lynd? Thou brokest the heart of my adored and only daughter, and every day of life I mourn her loss. Now Ben Faa and Jael are the last ties I have on earth. My heart is set on their union. And thou,' her voice rising to a shrill pitch, 'thou wishest him dead. May palsy seize thy tongue, and damn thee to eternal silence! But listen and remember. For a short while thou shalt prosper in all thou doest. Yet the very height to which thou art climbing shall be thy undoing, because thou art building the foundations of thy prosperity with bricks burned in roaring fires of hate and hell. Thou scoffest at my prognosticating, but I tell thee, I have seen thy career from start to finish. At the acme of success thy end shall be bloody, and no man shall care for thee more than the carcase of a dog. Now go thy way.'

"Without another word, old Abegail lifted the still prostrate body of Ben, and bore him into the gypsies' van as lightly as if he were a child."

CHAPTER XIV

AT closing time Will Moffatt left the White Horse Inn with Dick Stagg for company.

He had much still to ask him, but chiefly the cause of John Lynd's and Joe Gream's rise in the world.

"That's easily explained," he replied. "The fall of rock in the narrow dale was the making of them both. A hundred years ago the quarrymen, who drove the drifts with which many of our fells are honeycombed, knew by the lie of the strata that the best green slate was to be found in the hearts of the mountains. You know that Lynd, being a landowner, had, in common with other sheep farmers in the district, a right of pasturage in the dales and on the fells surrounding the farms. His father having followed quarrying in early manhood, the son would no doubt have heard him speak of the excellent quality of slate metal spread widely over the district, and especially in the neighbourhood of the fall; and most likely Lynd, acting on this knowledge, resolved to inspect the fall of rock. However, on going thither he found Joe Gream had forestalled him, and there they had perforce to make a pact, and together they leased the mineral rights, and favoured by the huge fall which contained, ready to hand for working, thousands of tons of the best slate, their fortunes rose rapidly. Today John Lynd is one of the largest landowners in the county."

"And what kind of a landlord has he made, Dick?"

Again Dick laughed in that low gurgling tone that had such a world of meaning in it, and that Will found it hard to fathom.

"You ought to know by this time what kind of a man he is. If ever the devil incarnate walked the earth, he is John Lynd. But I forgot you have been out of the country for years. His wealth has given him influence, and like all men disposed to be tyrannical, a full measure of power has converted him into a savage. On the bench of the petty sessions he is nicknamed Nero. But like the Roman monster, he'll have his day and not a moment longer."

"And what of Joe Gream? Is he inclined to be a demi-god also?"

"He's John Lynd's right-hand man. But having had no education, and not having tried to remedy this defect by his own exertions, he is just showy and shallow. He comes to the front in church bazaars, flower shows, village sports, and suchlike festivities. And then at times he breaks out in wild drinking sprees, and buries himself for weeks in the lowest brothels in the neighbouring towns, seldom returning home until Peg Shore hunts him out with the aid of the police."

"He is not married then?"

"Married!" echoed Dick. "He has no need to wed. Peg is ever at his service. 'Tis common gossip that he has set his heart on Jean Lynd, but she..."—Then, recollecting himself, he exclaimed—"...Damn it, Will! I forgot that 'tis also said you are the stumbling-block in his path."

What else he might have said was interrupted by the shouts and curses of a number of men engaged in a free fight on the moor. They paused to gather, if possible, the import of it. Dick had grasped his arm, and he could feel his body quivering with excitement: "It's keepers and poachers," he cried. "Come on, Will, and we'll see the sport." And without realizing the gravity of their act, they dashed over the moorland in the direction of the fray.

They arrived on the scene when the fight was at its height. Favoured by the darkness, they both dropped flat on the ground to get a better view of the conflict. There were a dozen men all told, and the sound of smashing blows and hoarse curses, and the sight of dark and shadowy figures contending for mastery, made the night hideous. Now and again they could see between the earth and sky two antagonists fall with a thud and grappling each other as if the issue were a matter of life and death.

Suddenly with a loud voice someone shouted: "Hey, lads, the b—'s bludgeoning me."

"Then let his guts out with a knife," roared another.

"Nonsense," yelled a third, "Don't use any weapons; use your feet and fists. Lynd's here himself, and they'd swear the angels from heaven into hell at his bidding."

A loud groan told of a man in extremity. "Lynd's punching me to death."

"Curse him, where is he?"

"Here I am, who wants me?" jeered Lynd.

"I do," was the rejoinder, and in a moment the two men were fighting with the fury of snarling demons.

Round and round, and up and down they fought. Now standing upright, launching terrific blows at each other, or locked in a wild embrace, endeavouring to put the wrestler's skill into practice, of which each was a master. Anon rolling over and over on the moorland and trying to throttle each other.

"Ah!" the voice was Red Ike's, "Your tricks won't act with me, John Lynd." And then they saw Lynd's body double up and roll on the ground, and knew that he was winded from a blow in the pit of the stomach.

"Look out! Ben Faa's creeping behind you."

Red Ike leapt round, and before the gypsy could regain his feet he was in the hands of a madman.

"At last we have met again, and at the right time. Blast you for a dog! I'll leave my mark upon you tonight, so that if we do not meet again until we are old men I'll know you at a glance."

A howl of fear broke from Ben, and he began begging for mercy, when John Lynd sprang upon Red Ike's back, shouting for help to secure him. A black, silent, shadowy form bounded through the darkness like the spirit of evil. A snap of sharp teeth and the jaws of Prodigal were fixed in John Lynd's face.

He staggered backwards paralysed in the grip of this new foe, and fell within a yard of where Dick and Will were lying. "Call the dog off!" Will shouted.

At the sound of his voice it came and stood beside him, and he grasped and held it by the neck.

Lynd peered through the darkness and groaned, "So it's you, Will Moffatt."

He did not answer, but stood up and moved away, followed by Dick. Meanwhile, Ben Faa had fled from the fight with Red Ike in full pursuit.

Laying his hand on Dick's shoulder, he said: "What should we do now? I'll be in a devil of a mess tomorrow."

"Let's clear off. There's Lynd shouting again for help. He's evidently feeling in a bad way, and I hope…"—and again he laughed in his low gurgling tone—"…that the dog has nipped off his nose."

The callousness of this remark repelled Will Moffatt, and feeling the silence, he went on, "I'll tell you shortly why I hate John Lynd."

Now they were nearing Sandyflatts.

By the side of the cattle pool formed by the meeting of the three runnels, and in which Red Ike washed himself on the memorable night of the burning of Sandyflatts, they paused, and ere they shook hands and parted, Will said: "In the morning, Dick, there'll be a hue and cry over this night's work, and I want you to promise that you'll say nothing about it, unless I ask you to do so. 'Twas evident that John Lynd did not recognize you, so that you'll not be hunted."

"But I can prove that you were not mixed up in the affair," replied Dick.

"Perhaps you can, and perhaps you cannot," he answered. "If you try to clear me at present, we'll both be charged with being there, and how are we to prove we had nothing to do with the job? You had better lie low. Besides, from a remark you made to me you have at some time been at cross-purposes with Lynd."

"Yes," said Dick, "my only sister was servant at his house. He seduced her and she died in childbed, and had been dead and buried for months before I learned the full history of the case. Lynd had provided her with money to hide herself. No one in the district knows the facts of the case but my mother and myself, and she, being of a sensitive nature and deeply religious, begged me not to expose Lynd. However, I met him shooting on the fells during September, and my blood boiled and I could no longer restrain my tongue. High words on both sides were the result, and he pointed his gun at me, threatening to shoot. At this I laughed, and he looked puzzled. The moment he lowered his weapon, I leapt upon him, and felled him with the breach; and, to tell the truth, I had half a mind to put a charge of shot into his skull, and finish the devil within him forever. But better reason prevailed. I threw the gun from me, punched his carcase with both my feet, and left him lying to come round or perish as the outcome might be.

"Next morning instead of the police, I received a note from Lynd offering me hush-money on condition that my mother and I left the district. I did not answer, but cursed myself there and then that I had not blown the mean cur's soul from his body. I still have the note, so that I have no fear of John Lynd. And now if you wish, Will Moffatt, I shall dare him to touch you."

Will had listened amazed to Dick's story, and wondered that John Lynd, of all men, should have so little foresight as to place himself within the power of his enemies in the manner he was doing continually. He thought that the fact must be that, though his physical courage on the spur of a moment, and urged on with excitement, was undoubtedly great, when he came to reflect on the consequences of his evil acts, he had not the moral courage of a primitive savage. He was a bully and a tyrant by the power of the wealth behind him. Had he been born in the gutter, he would have remained there until the jail and the hangman's rope had sent him a short cut to a bed of quicklime, and to the doubtful realities of another state of existence.

"Well," said Dick, after they had paced several times back and forward by the cattle pool, "What would you have me do?"

Will answered: "I have many reasons for asking you not to take action in my defence, at least not for the present. Will you do what I ask?"

"Yes, but remember you are still holding the lurcher that attacked Lynd. Is it your dog?"

"No, it belongs to the gypsy, Ben Faa."

"The devil it does? Then let the brute go to its master. That fact is the best piece of news I have heard tonight." And he began to roar with such hilarious laughter that the night-shrouded moorland rang with his merriment. Has the man gone mad? Will wondered. When the fit left him he cried: "Don't you see that if the dog belongs to neither you nor the poachers, the gypsy will have to bear the onus of its attack on Lynd? It lies with him to whom the dog belongs to get out of the scrape. Lynd's nose is bitten off in more ways than one." And again Dick laughed louder than ever.

His point of view was too forcible not to be appreciated. Will released Prodigal, and instantly, as though appreciating the position in which he had placed his friends, he bounded away in the direction of Mirkholme.

Will's idea of Dick's sagacity was now considerably enlarged, and he debated within his mind whether or not it would be better to act on his suggestion, and allow him to force John Lynd to hold his hand, and keep his lips sealed.

But he returned to his first resolution, and determined, for good or evil, to let the event take its course, without attempting to influence it. He may have been wise or foolish in this, but his intention was not a selfish one, nor could he have guessed a tenth part of what it would afterwards mean to him. One thing it did for him was to prove the worth of Jean, and her wholehearted and abiding love.

He resolved not to stir on the morrow from Sandyflatts, lest he might give the appearance of avoiding any enquiry which might be made, but to wait patiently, though he was torn with anxiety.

At noon he beheld a party of horsemen crossing the moor at a gallop, and judging they were out for his arrest, he walked to meet them. They instantly surrounded him.

He neither spoke nor moved when the warrant was read, but was struck with the fact that he alone was named and charged. The wording was thus:

"That Will Moffatt, whilst night-poaching on a portion of John Lynd's estate called Badkins meadow, did unlawfully resist the said John Lynd's gamekeepers in the execution of their duty, and in company with other unknown men did unmercifully beat, with intent to do grievous bodily harm to the said gamekeepers, and did also endeavour to murder the said John Lynd with the aid of a ferocious dog belonging to the said Will Moffatt, and that the said dog at the instigation and the encouragement of the said Will Moffatt, did worry, maul, and disfigure the said John Lynd almost beyond recognition, and to such a degree, and in such a manner, that his life is despaired of."

And having read this, and finally cautioned him to be careful in answering the charge, the officer placed him under arrest.

He spent three days in the lock-up before he was formally brought before the Bench and remanded to stand his trial for the offence at the forthcoming Assizes to be held at Carlisle the following week. When asked if he had anything to say, he gave no answer. Before being removed to the cell, he glanced round the court, and beheld Dick Stagg gazing at him with a puzzled look upon his face. Also, he saw a woman deeply veiled, but whom he could not fail to know.

The reader will wonder why he suffered thus without a word of explanation. In the first place, he was not guilty. The second and more powerful reason was that he knew who were.

He knew, beyond that, that he had on many earlier occasions engaged in the same unlawful poaching which must, sooner or later, lead those who so adventure into violent conflict with the keepers who are appointed to protect the game.

But there was a further reason, quite apart from his quarrel with John Lynd, why his heart inclined him to stand by them, even at the heavy cost which must now be paid.

His own father had perished, broken in body, though not in spirit, by the rigours of the poacher's life. Actual want had first induced him, in his earliest years, to take toll of the wildlife of the moors and fells. Then the jail had inflicted a sense of loss of standing among his fellows, with consequent difficulty in securing work, and the irritation of malicious tongues, to which he had reacted in a spirit of open hostility to the social order around him.

He had preached the creed that no man could have a better right than another to the wildlife that wanders on the tameless moors; or rather, if such a right could be claimed by any, it was his who matched his human skill against their sleepless caution.

That any man should uphold the game-laws as they were applied to the protection of the wildlife that finds its own sustenance, had been sufficient to bring from him a stream of invective and ridicule, which spared no man, whether from prudence or fear. That such laws should be enforced by armed men at the risk—or rather the certainty—of murderous struggles resulting from the orders which they received, seemed to him an intolerable evil, such as could not be justified by any argument of expediency.

Yet, apart from the doubtful aspect of his poaching activities, he had been a man of honest and sober life who had been liked by many, and trusted implicitly by those who had really known him.

So Will Moffatt sat in the narrow cell pondering on the events that had brought him to that position, without doubting that he had acted rightly. It was not for him to turn informer to clear himself, and without doubt he must let events take their course and suffer the consequences of his misfortune. And then in the solitude his thoughts became centred on Jean Lynd, and, heedless of all else, he conjured her before his mental vision, and wrapped in the joy and meditation of a fancied happiness with her, he forgot his surroundings, as they walked once more as of old, arm-in-arm, 'mongst bracken and whin and broom, by crystal beck and craggy dale, where heart's-ease blows and bleaberries ripen on the glorious Lakeland fells.

It is an old saying that a clear conscience is music at midnight.

His thoughts occupied with love he took no heed when the cell door opened and closed again, until a soft voice behind him called, "Will."

He turned, bewildered. "Jean! Jean! What brings you here?"

"My love for Will Moffatt."

He took a step towards her, as if to take her in his arms.

"No! No! Do not touch me, but I must learn from your own lips if you are guilty of the murderous attack on my father. I cannot rest until I know for sure."

"I am not guilty, Jean."

"Then why did you not attempt to clear yourself?"

"There are times when a man must suffer to shield the guilty."

"Then you know?"

"I do, Jean."

"And you mean to suffer to save them?"

"Yes."

"Will you not tell me in confidence?"

"I am in jail, and in jail the walls have ears. I won't tell you now. Perhaps I shall suffer, but what of that? If I do, I shall go out of prison with my self-respect untarnished in my own sight, and with a knowledge that I have won the trust of at least half a dozen men, and one of whom I love as a brother."

"But my father, Will, has he no claim to the consideration of justice?"

"None from me, Jean. He has never given me nor those against whom he led his sorry keepers either consideration or justice. He has oppressed them, and hounded me from you, and from the country-side of my birth. Jean, I love you. I shall always love you. But do not ask me to do what I should regret till the last hour of life. Would you care for Will Moffatt, the informer?"

"Was it your dog that worried my father, Will?"

"Jean, I have no dog. The list of the licence holders at the police station will confirm this."

"Then whose dog was it, Will?"

"I can't say that."

"You know then, Will?"

"I do."

"Then you'll tell me nothing further?"

"Nothing, Jean, except that I love you, and am not guilty."

"I believe you, Will, but oh, my father! Will! Will! If you saw him! He's dreadful." And she shivered and covered her face with her hands as if to blot out a foul sight.

Until now he had not realized that what Dick Stagg so coarsely alluded to might be a fact, nor that he stood in terrible jeopardy.

"Oh, Will, that I had flown with you before this fearful affair happened! Why did you not ask me? I would have gone with you, even as an outcast, to the world's end, and now you are lost to me for ever!"

He cried "No!" to that. "No! We have found each other for ever." But she held out her hands as before.

"Do not touch me, Will." Withdrawing from him, she crouched moaning against the wall of the cell.

For a moment he stood over her in a misery of irresolution, and then with an effort of will and courage he urged upon her that the future is never so black but that men and women can win through, and grasp hope and then peace from even the depths of despair. "Jean," he said, "suppose I told you what I know, are you sure that justice would follow? I can tell you something. It was the dog that was the real culprit. No one urged it on. It only obeyed a natural instinct to rush into the fray as any dog will do to help its master or friend.

"Besides, Jean, I wasn't there when the fight began. I don't know who was most to blame. But do you think anyone would listen to that? You know as well as I that the poachers would have to bear all the blame, that the full force of the law would be employed for their punishment, irrespective of the actual measure of their guilt."

"Will, do you mean that my father was in the wrong?"

"Not legally wrong, but there is a moral law which is higher than those which are made by men. Because one man has money to buy land, is there no limit to how far he may restrict the liberties of his neighbour? I, too, may wish to fish and shoot, and wander at my will and pleasure by moor and fell and tarn and stream. The privileged enjoy the rights of their fellows, or it would not be privilege."

"But, oh, Will, if you had seen my father!"

"Is my present position giving him any anxiety? No, Jean, he would gladly have me driven to penal servitude. Yet, without malice in my thought towards him, I shall not aid him to punish the men who resisted his attempt to arrest them. They, and he, and I, are all the victims of a selfish system. Were there no game-preserves, there would be no poachers. I wonder that any self-respecting educated man should degrade himself with preserving game, well knowing the injury he will have to inflict upon his fellows to protect it."

"But are my father's assailants to go unpunished, Will?"

"Who would have punished your father, had one of his dogs worried me, Jean? You yourself know of many cases which have happened in this district of poachers being bludgeoned and maimed for life. Did you ever know the assailant of a poacher go to prison? You did not. He goes scot-free with murder in his heart, and the voice of an ill-informed public opinion lauding him for his deed, under an English sky. Jean, the heart that has pity for the downtrodden is touched with the richest attribute and the sweetest known to man. Without pity this world would be a hell indeed."

"Have you no pity for my father, Will?"

"Jean, you press me too hard. I pity your father, but if I told him so, he would fling it back in my teeth. Yet I do feel for him."

She stood up, white-faced and wretched, holding out an uncertain hand. He drew it to his lips, kissing it passionately, and the next moment she had left the cell.

CHAPTER XV

ON the morrow, after Jean's visit to him in prison, Will felt like a new man. He had now no doubt about the course he had taken. To do the right thing is the surest way in the end to win the esteem of one's fellows, and above all to plant more firmly the roots of love for one's self in the heart of a true woman. A young oak sapling is a tender thing to look upon, and the winter comes, and rains beat, and winds blow, yet these are but the means that cause the frail plant to clutch tighter with its buried fibres at the heart of its mother earth. So do the storms of adversity help men and women to the realization of themselves, causing them to grope, sometimes blindly in the dark, for the sustenance of the life of love abiding in their hearts, and to find therein all that is best in the world, and all that the world has to give that is worth finding.

Meanwhile, the fierce fire of a quickened and absorbing love became intensified in Jean's breast. She did not sleep during that night, but sat before her bedroom window until the dawn broke, revolving within her mind the problem of what she considered her duty towards her father and her love for Will.

And he, blind egotist that he was, had then barely glimpsed the great radiant nature of the woman whose love was his. No wonder he had loved her. Her serene soul, sweet and pure and true to the loftiest sentiments, combined with an indefinable charm of personality, compelled an instinctive deference from others. And what was he that she should love him, suffer for him, and bear patiently with all his infirmities of mind and conduct?

On the next morning we have seen that her love had brought him to a more confident manhood, but while he was elated thus, it is a strange thought that the same event had brought her to the greatest trial that her life had known. During her absence from home, her father had asked for her repeatedly, and his first question as she entered the sick-room was, where had she been the previous day? With perfect self-command. Jean explained everything and declared their love for each other. Her father listened to the end. and then, pointing to the door, said, "Go," and with characteristic devilry, and in spite of all protestation on the part of his wife, he rose from bed, his head swathed in bandages, and dressed himself and descended the stairs to the drawing-room, and calling the whole household together, he openly renounced his daughter, and drove her with curses from his presence.

So rapidly had Lynd acted that Jean's mother was not aware of the full meaning of the circumstances that had occasioned her husband's wrath, before her daughter was beyond the precincts of the house and grounds, an outcast upon the wide moorlands, penniless but not friendless, though she had shortly a further trial to endure that served a destined end.

To collect her thoughts, she retired within a dense growth of whins and bracken and sat upon a crag of outcrop granite, a favourite spot with her, where she had often, in past days, spent many delicious hours storing her mind with romance and poetry, or dreaming of him who after long years of silence had suddenly filled her life again with trouble—but what of that? He was innocent; she loved him, and her love was returned; and the knowledge of this gave a sweet sense of security and content that pervaded her whole being.

By this time John Lynd's wife was thoroughly alive to her daughter's position, and she attempted to reason with him.

His reply was to forbid henceforth any mention of Jean, with the added remark that the mother could follow the daughter, if she wished. He was master in his own house, and meant to remain so. And without another word he returned again to his bedroom, locked the door, undressed himself, and lay down again as though nothing had occurred.

Jean's mother was helpless. She had no means in her own right, Lynd had made no settlement upon her, and never until that moment had she felt so entirely at his mercy. Her spirit rose in revolt at the thought of her absolute dependence. She knew that if she voluntarily left the shelter of her husband's roof without adequate cause, the law would allow her no claim upon him. As Jean had none, the future to them both was black indeed.

She would stay with him for the present, and be of what service she could to Jean.

And now one of those strange coincidences that occur we know not how nor why, was taking place within a short distance of Jean. Red Ike was lying watching the comings and goings at her father's house. Since the fight, he had not returned to Sandyflatts, nor did he know that Will Moffatt had been arrested, nor that Prodigal had so badly worried John Lynd.

When Ben Faa fled from the fight with Red Ike in pursuit, the gypsy made straight for Mirkholme, and only escaped his pursuer's clutches by turning and catching him in the stomach with a stone, which made Ike helpless for hours. And it was with great difficulty that, before morning broke, he managed to reach the drift in the dale of the fall of rock where the carved stick was hidden.

Luckily, he had stored some food there in case of need, and did not leave his shelter until he was well and fit. And now he was anxious. Seeing Jean leave The Bents and withdraw herself from view, he thought she might have there an assignation with Will, and he lay low to wait and see, hoping later to learn the news there might be abroad concerning the fight. It will be remembered that Red Ike did not know that Will Moffatt had witnessed the struggle.

An hour passed and Jean sat almost motionless, until the sound of a footfall tramping through the whins and bracken made her start to her feet, and turning round she was confronted with Joe Gream.

With an effort, Red Ike, who had been lying in the whins near to Jean unknown to her, suppressed an exclamation of surprise. By the devil in hell! Was she waiting for a low-lived, bloated lump of animalism like the man before her? If Jean Lynd would degrade herself thus, could there be any honesty and purity among women? He would wait and see. And the memory of his early love for Peg Shore, and of the man's connections with her by the Brutchstone years ago, stung his soul into fierce hate; and he swore a deep oath within his heart that, if Will's trust was betrayed like his own by this man, he would kill him for the pest he was.

As a lion crouches and watches for a favourable moment to spring upon its victim, so Red Ike crouched, unseen, curious, and with eyes riveted on the man and woman confronting each other. And wonder began to creep into his brain. There was no friendly greeting between them. Yet on Gream's part a certain fiendish triumph, but half smothered in his eyes, betrayed the working of his soul. And Red Ike marvelled that Jean did not move from his presence. Alas! He did not know that she was homeless and penniless. Looking upon her face, he was struck by its serene expression and exquisite beauty, and he loathed himself for having doubted her for a moment.

Here was no harlot, but the virgin stainless and true; and he whose arms would enfold her would find the greatest treasure in life.

Still, Red Ike could make nothing of the position. What had brought them together?

Joe Gream was on his way to The Bents, and by the merest chance had left the highway, and called to look over a fox-earth he had constructed recently on the open moorland, and afterwards taking a near cut had thus stumbled upon Jean. With as much courtesy as he could command, he bade good morning to her, and then asked after her father.

Jean spoke truthfully, saying she had no knowledge of his exact condition, but that Gream could learn by going to the house.

"Will you not return with me?"

"No."

"Will your father get better?"

"I hope so, but that depends upon whether complications set in or not.

"Have you heard that Will Moffatt is the only poacher arrested in connection with the affair?"

"Yes, I have heard so. But, will you please go? I do not wish to speak further on this subject."

"Come, Jean," he said, "Is it not time the constraint you impose between us be put aside? Will you marry me?"

Now was her time to speak.

"Marry you!" Jean echoed. "Are you not already by every moral and physical obligation under heaven tied to Peg Shore? Why do you insult me again and again with your importunity?" And she turned from him, and sat down again upon the outcrop crag of granite, not realizing the danger about to befall her.

Livid with passion, and with pent-up lust for the woman who once again scorned his repeated offer, he cried: "Then I'll compel you to my will," and with a bound he clasped her in a mad embrace. The next moment his throat was in the grip of a vice, and he was lifted bodily, and dashed against the granite outcrop, where he lay still as death itself.

"That was a near thing for you, Miss Lynd."

Bewildered with terror, Jean looked upon her deliverer, and beheld the shaggy-haired and unrecognizable figure of Red Ike, and shrinking from mm she ejaculated: "Who, who are you?

"Your friend and the friend of Will Moffatt. And you, Miss Lynd, were once a friend of mine, but long since I fell upon evil days, and this world has no room and no use for the man fallen from the esteem of his fellows. But we'll let that pass. I heard you discussing matters concerning your father and Will Moffatt. What of them?"

Gathering courage from the mild manner and speech of the man before her, Jean answered him fully. When she finished he said: "I was in the fight. Will Moffatt was not there. There was but one dog on the scene. It belongs to Ben Faa the gypsy. That it worried your father I cannot say, but I shall find out."

"But," said Jean, "when I visited Will Moffatt in prison yesterday, he admitted being present at the fight, and that he knows the men on both sides, and to whom the dog belongs. But further than that he will not speak."

"Then I shall visit him in prison myself tomorrow, Miss."

A moan from Joe Gream reminded them of a fellow creature in physical need, who, opening his eyes, begged for water.

Red Ike, taking a flask of whiskey from his pocket, poured the spirit down the man's throat, and eased him into a sitting posture against a whin bush and then, turning to Jean, said: "If you wish to return home, I'll see Joe Gream safely to The Forge."

"You'll hell as like, there is no Forge. I'm a gentleman now," cried Gream, his vanity touched to the quick by the reminder of his poverty-stricken days.

A loud laugh came from Red Ike's throat.

"Yes," said he. "That's what you call yourself, is it? Don't you see that you're a hog with wealth as you were one without it? Pshaw, man, there's not a particle of you worth making manure of."

With an effort, Joe Gream staggered to his feet:

"I'll get even with you yet, Red Ike. You'll be glad to lick the mire from my shoes. Had you got your due, you should have been hanged ere now."

"If ever I'm hanged, Joe Gream, it will be for you, so you'll get little satisfaction out of the job. And now, since you're fit to walk, your road lies back to The Forge. Out of my way. I warn you that if you follow Miss Lynd to The Bents, I'll go there and denounce Peg Shore's handyman to John Lynd as the attempted ravisher of his daughter. Remember my words. Were it not that filth and slander stick to the innocent and guilty alike, you should have been lodged in jail today."

Jean sat on the granite outcrop a silent spectator of this altercation, wondering at Red Ike's easy expression of speech and the dignity of his manner. She had recognized him now, despite his wild unkempt appearance, and, struggle though she did with revulsion of feeling against the man whom she knew had slain his fellow, she divined something about him that compelled her admiration and trust.

"Well," he said, after Joe Gream's departure, "I'm glad I was of some small service to you, Miss Lynd. I shall now keep you in sight until you reach home safely, and then I shall go my way."

This was a supreme moment to Jean. Should she throw herself on the protection of this man? He had saved her from violence within an hour. Did she dare to solicit his help now? There was nothing of the well-groomed conventional hero about him. He was not even as respectable in appearance as one of the farm hands, whose drudgery, by fell and ploughed furrow, told so heavily against them in the show of things. He was on a par with the gypsies, except that his body was clean, and his conduct and speech with her exemplary.

Seeing her hesitate, and thinking she wished to be rid of him, he gathered from the ground his favourite cudgel, and turned to leave her.

"Stay!" she cried. "You shall not leave me thus."

He wheeled round again, and stood attentive; deferential, and with a sign of pleasure and surprise in his frank bold eyes.

"I cannot thank you sufficiently, and thanks are a poor return for service such as you have rendered. You spoke to me a moment ago about my going home. I have no home."

He looked on her amazed. Had she suddenly been transformed into marble he could not have doubted his senses more.

"What do you mean, Miss Lynd?"

"Today, because of my love for Will Moffatt, I was driven from my father's presence, and forbidden his home. I am penniless and shelterless."

"But what of your mother? Can she not aid you?"

"She cannot. Except for the roof that covers her, she is as destitute as I."

"Have you no friends to whom you can appeal?"

"None but Will Moffatt."

"Then I shall be your friend."

"Can you trust me?"

"Will you go with me now? But stay, let me explain. There are two places where I can find you a temporary abode; one is Sandy-flatts, the other a hidden drift in the dale of the fall of rock. The former is of doubtful security owing to the gypsies; the latter a veritable refuge unknown to anyone but Will Moffatt and me. Choose for yourself. I shall see that at either place you remain in safety until

Will Moffatt's trial. After that we will consider what is best to be done."

"I'll go with you to the drift."

"Then," said Red Ike, "we'll go there now."

The early close of a dark autumn day had filled the dale with shadow when Red Ike and Jean reached the entrance to the drift. Removing a large boulder which cunningly fitted the aperture, he asked Jean to pass into the refuge. She hesitated. He laid a hand upon her shoulder and remarked: "See, Miss Lynd, there is a rowan tree in full berry, ripe and red, overhanging the entrance. Self-set in a crevice of the rocks, it has flourished, year after year, in a meagre soil, trusting to the beneficent power that broods over all things to guard it while it fulfils its destiny. 'Tis a happy omen that no evil shall befall you in the drift. Do you remember the old rhyme:

"Rowan berries and red thread
Keep the devil fra his speed."

Her glance fell before the calm manly look of Red Ike.

She saw that he understood the delicacy of her position, and, full of trust, she passed through the entrance into the darkness of the tunnel.

Red Ike was beside her instantly, and after blocking the entrance again and lighting a candle, he explained to her the nature of the place.

From the main drift there were several shorter side drifts in which the olden quarrymen had followed the richer veins of slate metal, and had abandoned them on coming to a fault.

In one of these side drifts was a rudely constructed bedstead thickly littered with dried bracken. A coarse Hessian bag full of bracken served as a pillow.

A huge undressed block of stone supplied a table, another a seat. On a ledge were canned foodstuffs, meats, fruits, biscuits, and milk in sufficient quantities to feed a healthy man for a month. There were no signs of a fire. Red Ike had never lit one in the drift, nor had he felt the need. Buried in the very heart of the fell, he was secure from all weathers, and his vigorous vitality, but lately inured to the rigours of a penal prison, had long since lost all desire for the effeminate luxuries of modern civilization. Use is second nature. He was at home anywhere. His six years' confinement, and the discipline of jail life, had thrown him back upon himself so constantly that he had ceased to care for the fellowship of other men. His natural reserve had become a habit, and in the deepest solitude his was never a lonely soul.

Jean beheld evidence of Red Ike's manner of living with strange feelings. Being an educated woman, of fine sensibilities and varied reading and highly imaginative, she felt as though she were suddenly thrown back into a primitive stage of life, but was recalled to the present by the sight of several volumes of new poems, plays, and novels which she had lately seen discussed in the literary columns of the daily papers.

Red Ike allowed her time to take full stock of her surroundings, and then said: "Do you think life here for a time will be endurable, Miss Lynd? If you can dispense with much that is of doubtful necessity, and to which you have been used, I shall do my best to see that you want for nothing you need. The bed of bracken there is at your service. I shall sleep in the drift next to yours, in which I was preparing a bed for Will Moffatt in case he arrived. I have a full supply of candles and oil, so that you can keep a light burning constantly. I have a small oil-stove on which you can cook fresh food if you wish. There are books if you care to read, and, if you wish to write to your mother, I have materials, and shall see that any message you have to send is delivered safely.

"I have but one request to ask of you, and that is that you will not leave the drift by day or night alone without my knowledge. You will wonder at this, but I will explain my reason so that we will understand each other.

"I wish my abode here to be kept secret. Not that I desire to practise any illicit acts, but rather the reverse; and with which if I accomplish my aim, I shall be delighted to acquaint you. Further, were it known that I am living here, your father would have me driven hence immediately. The slate royalty in this dale is either his or under his rental, and this drift is within the bounds of his agreement."

Jean held out her hand to Red Ike, which he shook heartily as she said: "I agree with your proposition."

The next morning Red Ike left the drift before daybreak to visit Will Moffatt in jail. He had great difficulty, owing to his past police-court record, to gain admittance, and but for the intervention of the prison chaplain, the naturalist, he would not have succeeded. Will was idly dreaming of Jean as he stepped into the cell. And thinking a warder was overlooking him, he scarcely lifted his head, but started with surprise when Red Ike's well-known voice bade him good morning.

Then he grew anxious, and asked, "Have you been arrested, Ike?"

"No," he answered, in a tone as cheery as a thrush's in the first warm breath of a sunshiny April morn. Then in a whisper, he added: "I have news for you, Will. Jean is staying with me in the drift. Her father has disowned and driven her from The Bents. Can you trust her with me until you are free?"

"Ike, you outrage my feelings with asking such a question. If she is content; she could not be in safer hands. But why has she been dealt with thus hardly?"

"Because she declared her love for you, and visited you in jail."

"Oh, heavens!" Will groaned, "that I am fastened up here like a rat! 'Tis a pity the lurcher did not rive out his throat, the fiend. No! No! I do not mean that. God forgive me for the evil thought. What can I do for her, Ike?"

"I have come here to help you and Jean. My life is not worth a dead dog. I cannot sink lower than I am now in the estimation of my fellows. I have no earthly ties. Whether I am in prison or not matters nothing. Let me stand in your place. I can take the blame upon myself."

"But you are little more guilty than I am, Ike."

"I was in the fight, Will. You were not."

Will stepped up to Red Ike, and looked him squarely in the eyes: "Tell me, my oldest friend, do you think for one moment that I would be a party to the act you propose? You have known me from my boyhood, and yet have you seen no deeper into my nature than dream I should allow you to step into my shoes in this case? Heaven and hell! Is Red Ike my friend that he insults me thus? Have I, without knowing it, sunk lower in his sight than is a common informer? Let me hear a denial from his lips now, that I shall know this is not so. Art thou yet my friend, or wouldst thou cast me body and soul into the depths of self-degradation?"

Astounded at this outburst, Red Ike replied: "Forgive me, Will; I see that I proposed you should do what I would hate like hell to be guilty of."

And grasping each other's hands they had need of no further parley.

So do men grow in understanding, faith, and love, and in the knowledge that sweeter than life itself are honour and the divine bond that was between David and Jonathan.

CHAPTER XVI

WHILST the interview between Will and Red Ike was taking place in the prison cell, Jean sat reading in the drift by the aid of a small lamp, absorbed and oblivious to her loneliness and surroundings. Volume after volume she glanced at and then laid aside. They had failed to arouse any great interest in her mind, until she noticed a pile of manuscript, and lifting a sheet was surprised to see in a neat hand the copy of a song.

OH, WERT THOU, LOVE

Oh, wert thou, love, the fairest rose
That grows on yonder tree,
I'd pluck thee lest a stranger came
And saw and gathered thee.

Oh, wert thou, love, the daisy wild
That decks the open lea,
I'd near thee stay by night and day,
Lest trampled thou shouldst be.

Oh, wert thou, love, of maids the maid
That fate had formed for me
In right or wrong as life were long
I'd only live for thee.

This slight effort appealed to her. Her peculiar position helped, no doubt, to intensify the predilection she had for verse. Her romantic nature responded to the impulse, and, turning leaf after leaf, her wonder grew as she read lyrics, sonnets, and poems richly wrought, or charged with rare spontaneity, that carried her on wings of rapture into realms that belong to the soul alone.

Unknown to her, situated and engrossed as she was, under the spell of beautiful verse, the sun climbed over the highest peak of the fell in whose heart she sat, and reaching the zenith it sank again and stepped, a god incarnadined, into the distant Solway Sea.

Through the gathering dark of evening, Red Ike, after a hurried tramp from Carlisle, crossed the Hill of Devils, glad to be once more on the far-spreading moorland. As he passed the White Horse Inn, a sound of drunken revelry through a half-open window arrested his attention, and, pausing, his blood ran riotously as he listened to Dick Stagg singing in a voice, wonderfully modulated to the tune, that old poaching song called *Bill Brown*. A roar of delight followed the finish, and Dick, elated with the approbation of the company and the amount of liquor in him, declared himself ready to do battle with any three keepers that Lynd or Gream might set to watch him.

"Thou's only a dummel-head at either poaching or fighting, Dick. Red Ike can beat thee hollow. I've known him catch more game and fish in a week nor thou could poach in a month; and I'll back him to lick the devil out o' hell if the old lad didn't spit fire and brimstone at him." And then Simon Reed, the tailor, took a pinch of snuff while the laugh went round against Dick.

"I'll tell you what, Simon, if you knew more about some things and less about others it would be better for you. I heard you say that Red Ike was your best friend when you were hard up and your old woman was ill."

"That's true enough, Dick, but I've said nothing against Red Ike. What I did say was that he's a better poacher and fighter nor thee; and as true as the Lord's above us, I'd give him the shirt off my back if he needed it. Out of his poverty he gave me abundance, and to do this he risked his liberty. I shall never be able to repay him, but I can do the next best thing, and that is, give him the respect of an old man, and I know when a man's worthy of it. There are some who'd like to crush Red Ike under the sod, or drive him from the countryside. I know them, Dick Stagg. But they'll not succeed, mark my words."

And Simon, taking another pinch of snuff, relapsed into silence.

The hoot of an owl three times repeated, *Too-whoo-o-o, Too-whoo-o-o, Too-whoo-o-o*, caused the whole company to look towards the half-open window, but Dick Stagg alone knew the signal, and from whom it came, and after a few moments he slid quietly from the house.

In front of the White Horse Inn grows one of those mighty yew trees, so common in England, whose age no man can guess, but which in the old days were planted and fostered by our forefathers because of the superior quality of such wood for the making of bows. Many of these trees may have been standing rooted in the self-same spot since Harold, on the field of Senlac, fell before the superior numbers of William the Bastard.

Dick Stagg placed his back against the yew tree and then stepped twenty paces onto the moorland and stood still. Why? Because the poacher never makes a practice, for obvious reasons, of discussing any question beneath a tree, nor of placing his catch against a tree in the dark. He uses a tree as a mark, and for nothing else, well knowing that other folks use trees for hiding-places and for shelter.

A figure within a few yards of him rose from the bare ground, and called, "Hist!"

Dick repeated the sound, and Red Ike advanced towards him.

After a hearty handshake and a hushed friendly greeting, both men moved further into the darkness and solitude.

"Well, I was surprised to see you in the fight with John Lynd and Ben Faa," said Dick.

Red Ike did not answer for some moments. Then: "Will you do me a service, Dick? I want certain articles, not for my own use; and I shall be your debtor if you'll get them for me.

"I'll do anything that lies in my power for you, Ike."

"Then we'll go to Sandyflatts, and I'll make you out a list of the goods, and you may fetch them to the cattle pool on the moorland after nightfall tomorrow. I do not wish to be seen about here for some weeks, but I shall be at Carlisle during the trial of Will Moffatt, which takes place within a few days. And now, Dick, how did you know I was in the fight?"

"I was with Will Moffatt."

"Then your evidence would clear him?"

"He will not allow me to speak. He made me promise that I would do nothing without his consent."

"The devil he did. Then without losing his friendship we cannot help him."

Red Ike now began to wonder how far he could trust Dick.

However, for the present, he determined to say nothing about Jean being in the drift, but could not resist the desire of asking if he had heard anything of her at The Bents. With a negative answer he was satisfied, and they walked along in silence towards Sandyflatts.

As they passed the cattle pool on the moor, Red Ike's quick sight beheld in its depth a huddled shadow which he knew was not the reflection of any natural fixed object. That there would be a solitary sheep near the pool was doubtful. What might it be? They had passed thirty yards beyond the pool when a gun-shot rang out and instinctively both men dropped flat onto the ground and lay still.

Presently, a dark figure came creeping half-double towards them. Slowly, carefully, it picked its way eerily, and scanning the ground as it came. Never a sound did it utter, and Red Ike's bold heart quaked. At last it was within a few yards of them, and, lo, its head was swathed in white.

Luckily for them, there were some clumps of stunted whins near where they lay, and the figure mistaking these for Red Ike and Dick raised its gun and fired a charge of shot point blank into them. A moment afterwards, ere he could re-charge the weapon, it was wrenched from his grasp and Red Ike had the man by the throat.

"Strike a light, Dick, and we'll see who the would-be murderer is."

Dick obeyed, and a yell of horror broke from his lips.

Red Ike lost his grip of the man, and fell back.

Neither man recognized who the figure was as he snatched the gun from the ground, and fled away.

"Be quick, run for your life, Dick; he'll charge the gun and fire again."

And the words were scarcely uttered ere the proof of the warning sang past their heads as they raced out of gun-shot.

"This way, Dick, we'll circle as a hunted hare, and lie in waiting, and watch The Bents until morning if needs be. Do you think the figure was John Lynd?"

"I'm almost sure of it. And oh, God, may I never look upon his face again! I would not go near The Bents for the world. Besides, there's murder in that man's eyes."

Dick's nerves were now thoroughly unstrung, and Red Ike, seeing this, proposed returning home with him by the Stepping Stones. Before parting, they agreed to meet again the next night at the cattle pool at a stipulated time.

Red Ike now turned again in the direction of The Bents, determined to satisfy himself who the man was that had dared so recklessly to attempt murder. Coming to the crossroads, where years before he had lost the lurcher previous to his going to Carlisle Fair on that memorable day on which he killed the French gypsy, he paused and knelt down, and with his ear against the bare hard ground listened intently, and could distinguish in the distance the regular tramp of approaching men.

"There are two of them," he muttered to himself, and hastily rising he stepped from the road and lay down on the moorland. As he surmised, the men stopped opposite him and began to parley, and his heart thumped in his breast at the sound of their voices.

"Keep a watch on the White Horse Inn tomorrow night, and let me know immediately if Red Ike or Dick Stagg be there. Curse you for a cur! Had we both fired together one of us might have hit them. I've half a notion of putting a charge of shot into your head for not doing as I ordered. If such a thing occurs again, I'll blow you to hell as sure as I'm John Lynd.

"But...," replied Ben Faa.

"Blast you and your buts! You want Jael, and yet you have not the courage to get her by the surest means. Unless you take her by force, she'll hold you off while Red Ike lives."

"I dare not shoot until the carved stick is recovered."

A sinister laugh rang out on the still midnight air, and then Red Ike roared: "Shoot them down, Dick; the world were better rid of such a pair of vipers."

With a yell of terror, Ben Faa fled into the darkness, but John Lynd stood his ground, and cried: "Shoot, you damned dogs, I'll die game." And raising his gun to his shoulder, he fired in the direction of Red Ike's voice.

From another quarter of the moor came a mocking cry: "You've missed again, Mr. Lynd. Go to! I now understand that you wish Dick Stagg and me out of the road before Will Moffatt's trial. We'll be there to give evidence that the dog that maimed and disfigured you for life belongs to the coward who has but fled and left you alone. You can put down your gun. It is pointed yards out of range from where I am standing."

As Lynd did so, Red Ike continued: "And now I may tell you that I am unarmed, that Dick Stagg and I parted at the Stepping Stones an hour ago, and that neither of us will be at the White Horse Inn tomorrow night. Get hence and home, and remember that I am master of the secret of the letters hidden under the top of the black ebony table, and that by the Eye of the Pyramids and the Carved Stick, you cannot harm me. Farewell, John Lynd, and the Lord be with you." And laughing ironically, Red Ike's voice died over the moorland and all was still.

Red Ike's first thought now was to go and acquaint Dick Stagg with what had just passed. This done, he would return to the drift, and study his plans for the next few days.

Jean had not slept during the night. In fact the passage of time, sitting as she was alone and in the heart of the mountain, had no meaning for her. Like Elizabeth Barret in her darkened room, day and night were one and the same.

When Red Ike, an hour before dawn, entered the drift and spoke, she looked up to him with a smile, and said: "I have been reading the manuscript poems you left lying on the ledge, and I congratulate you on them."

She spoke with an evident sincerity, and yet with a note of restraint which he was quick to recognize.

He answered, "You speak kindly, but you do not really like them."

Jean hesitated in her reply. She had enough judgment to recognize that they were of an unusual quality, and to wonder at their range of thought and emotion, and at the standard of their technique. But how could she say to him, who had shown her such generosity, that she had been frequently repelled by a savage and open satirical bitterness—a bitterness not directed against laws and institutions only, but often against individuals? Yet she would not insult him by the dishonesty of a merely conventional answer.

"I like some of them very much," she said. "I thought *The Poacher's Christmas Eve in Jail* struck a true note, tender and deep. I thought—forgive me—that it is an unworthy use of a great gift to satirise those who are living around us as you sometimes do, and that there was less of the true spirit of poetry in those that deal with subjects which are most suitable for the statesmen, or, at least, the prose-writer."

"What you say," he answered, "may be true enough of what I have written; but I cannot agree that any subject of importance to the welfare of humanity is outside the scope or spirit of poetry. I read and thought much on such subjects while I was in prison. If poets are not honoured today, is it not that they are not great enough for the art they practise? Did not the dread of Aristophanes' ridicule hold in check the vices of ancient Greece? Did not Horace hold equal place with Maro by the side of Augustus in Rome? Did not Rouget de Lisle achieve more for the world with the *Marseillaise* than all that Tennyson ever wrote? To write so may not always be the way to fame, or to win the applause of men, but to serve and perish in a righteous cause, and sink at last into an unknown, forgotten grave, has it not been the lot of countless thousands before us? Even Jesus wept over Jerusalem, not that its glory should perish and its temples fall, but that it was corrupt, and full of evil and oppression."

Jean gazed at the man before her. In the wan light of a flickering lamp that dimly lit the subterranean drift, he seemed transfigured. His eyes shone with animation, and every nerve in his body was tense with suppressed emotion. His shaggy red hair and beard, his soiled, unkempt dress, combined with his gestures and forceful utterance, lent him a strange fascination. She felt as though she were in the presence of one of the prophets of old, and stood awe-struck and speechless before him.

As his mood passed he saw her gaze riveted upon him, and thinking her alarmed, in soft and musical tones he asked her not to mind his wayward speech, as he was addicted to such outbursts when overpowered by the torrent of pent-up thoughts.

"In the loneliness of a prison cell," he went onto explain, "I accustomed myself to the giving of imaginary discourses. The shadows of the iron bars from the windows thrown onto my prison walls were my only auditors. With them I became friends, and often enough I touched them as I would the fingers of a human hand, persuading myself they responded to my longing for fellowship and sympathy. And sometimes, when the moon was at full, and the clouds in the wide, free expanse of heaven, wind-driven, raced over its face, and the shadows on the wall appeared and disappeared as rapidly as the clouds fled, I revelled with the flitting shadows, and fancied myself on the wild moorlands, the companion of moon and stars, of winds and clouds, and all the wandering habitants of borran, cave, and rock. Forgetful of my position, I whooped with the owl, and raced after the scared fox until the first grey streaks of dawn brought me back to the realities of the hell I was in. Perhaps I was stark mad when these fits were upon me; yet had I not had such relapses, I should have gone permanently insane."

Jean stepped up to his side, and placing a hand upon his arm pleaded: "I am sorry I have caused you to remember the past. Please forgive me." And with glistening eyes and faltering voice she sank to a stone seat and leant her head upon her hands in silence.

"I have something to say concerning yourself, Miss Lynd," he then began in an altered voice, and proceeded to recount his visit to the prison, and his useless endeavour to move Will Moffatt from his resolution; and explained finally that the trial would take place on the next day. Jean looked up at him perplexed: "Then it is a day sooner than had been fixed?"

"Nay," rejoined Red Ike. "I was at Carlisle all day yesterday, and did not return until daybreak this morning, and it is now noon."

Jean was still more perplexed: "How long have I been by myself in the drift?"

"A full day and night. And now I wish to explain my plans for you in case anything unfortunate should happen to me. I have a small leather trunk in which I keep my papers. This you can pack with the apparel I have bought for you, and I shall have it taken to the Red Lion Hotel, Grasmere, where I have hired rooms for you for one month paid in advance. With you I shall leave my watch, so that you will not lose the reckoning of time, a thing I have found is easily done when one is alone in the drift. Tonight after dark I shall show you over the path that takes you direct to Grasmere, and in case you have to go there by yourself, do so on the second day from now, and leave the drift when you see the Great Bear resting on the edge of

Glaramara, for then, at this season of the year, the dawn is about to break.

"Here is a purse containing sufficient money to tide you over present needs or longer, also a draft payable to you at the Bank of Kendal. If you have occasion to leave this district, send your address sealed to be left until called for at the bank, and with orders for it to be delivered up to Will Moffatt or myself, if either calls. I have prepared everything against an emergency, unless you have some wish of your own to make known."

Jean rose to her feet, her eyes shining with a radiance that told of unbounded trust in the man before her: "Who am I," she exclaimed, "that I have found such a friend? Until the last few days I have heard your name bandied on the lips of men and women with anathema, and have often shuddered at the thought of your presence. I speak this to my shame. You will forgive my plainness of speech, I know, now that I have found you out to be a true gentleman. I have no other favour to ask. Whatever you direct, I shall do without question." And stepping towards him, she pressed his hand in hers, and from that moment life to Red Ike, the poacher, became again full of light and hope.

CHAPTER XVII

NIGHT fell once more over the lone dale of the fall of rock, and then Red Ike set out to meet Dick Stagg at the cattle pool. He strode with free carriage, and erect as one of the great upstanding stones of the Druids' Circle, which, as he passed, were marked in steady shadow on the short wiry grass in the bright moonlight.

Dick was at the appointed place, and received him with a warm hand-clasp in silence.

"I want you to execute this commission at once for me, Dick. Do you know any young woman who could buy for me this list of articles? The night is yet early, and with a little exertion on your part you can catch the train to Penrith, and I shall wait here for you after the last return train."

Dick agreed to the proposition with alacrity. He too had his love affairs, and was delighted with the prospect of meeting his lass, Nell Glen.

"Be careful that no one shadows you, Dick; this infernal moorland is alive with sinister devils."

"All right, Ike, I'll take every precaution."

Little did Dick think that this simple service to his friend would rouse jealous fire and distrust of him in the unsophisticated heart of the young woman whom he induced to help him in the undertaking. Yet so it was. Reaching Penrith, he went straight to the Royal George Hotel, and after the usual familiar greetings explained his mission to Nell, and within half an hour was ready to return to Red Ike. Passing out of the smoke-room and through the hall, he encountered Joe Gream and Peg Shore.

"I have always the devil's luck," he muttered, and rapidly crossing the street, took shelter in an alley opposite, to watch if either followed him. His movements being suspicious, a police officer dogged him, and demanded to know the contents of his parcel, and Dick, to save delay, returned with him to the hotel. Nothing more unfortunate could have happened. Nell Glen was called, a full explanation resulted, and Dick was thus placed in the hands of his two most inveterate enemies.

After consulting together, Peg and Joe determined to probe the matter further. Nell admitted buying the articles, but whom they were meant for she could not guess.

"You little fool," said Peg, "and you fancy he loves you! Why, he has no sister, and can his old mother wear those things?"

A shadow, dark and full of doubt, settled over Nell's face.

"Whom do you think they are for?" she questioned.

"Some favoured chit who has supplanted you."

And Peg laughed in such a tantalizing manner that Nell flushed scarlet to the roots of her hair.

"He's made a pretty use of you, getting you to buy finery for your rival."

And Peg chuckled to herself, as she watched the effect of her poison taking effect upon the girl before her.

On the morrow, Peg met the old gypsy sibyl, Abegail, on Penrith Street, and persuaded her to call at the Royal George and tell Nell her fortune. The way had been well prepared by Peg the day before for parting Nell and Dick. Peg now explained all to the gypsy. A baleful light glittered in the hag's eyes as she listened to Peg's recital.

"Who's the other gyp that Dick Stagg's after?" asked Abegail.

"I don't know, and what does it matter? We must strike at the whole gang. If you manage the girl rightly, we'll ultimately be able to use her against the others, as well as Dick."

Abegail nodded her head, and glanced at Peg and questioned: "What is there in the job for me?"

"A fortune for Ben Faa and Jael, if Red Ike were out of the way," answered Peg.

Abegail started. "How know you this?"

"I know, and that's enough for the present. Do what I tell you, and you'll find that Peg Shore's right. Tell her that Dick Stagg is unfaithful. That another girl, dark-haired and blue-eyed, called Madge, is in an interesting way. That he has been to Carlisle several times of late to see Madge, and that he is there for that purpose to-day, and will call tonight at the Royal George Hotel."

Still old Abegail questioned; "What is there in the job for me?"

"Damn you!" said Peg, "Here's a sovereign, and do as I tell you."

The hag clutched at the coin, and then went on her nefarious errand.

At the moment when Dick's lass was listening with greedy ears to Abegail's blasting of her love and hopes, Jean was on her knees in the drift, praying for Will Moffatt's acquittal, and he stood at the bar of justice arraigned on the charge of night-poaching and the inciting of his ferocious dog to the worrying and doing of grievous bodily harm to John Lynd. Red Ike and Dick Stagg were both in court, passive spectators of what appeared to be the last act of a drama in which he was about to suffer rather than break faith with his principles. The indictment was read out, and the question put, "Are you guilty or not guilty?"

Silence fell over the court, but he did not answer.

"Do you refuse to plead, Will Moffatt?"

Still he gave no answer, and the crowd in the packed Court of Assize became more hushed and intense.

The judge thereupon said: "Enter the plea of *Not Guilty* for the prisoner."

The counsel for the prosecution then called the several witnesses, until the last to give evidence was Ben Faa. He was about to be sworn, when Jael Boswell rose in the centre of the Court, and dared him to speak.

"If you do," she cried, "I shall see that you will soon stand charged with perjury where Will Moffatt is now."

An usher called silence, and the judge interposed sternly to order the removal of Jael. She protested, but was dragged through the court, and thrust outside the door.

Ben Faa breathed more freely when he saw her disappear, but Jael's threat had daunted him, and his answers to the lead of the prosecuting counsel were so unsatisfactory as to be almost worthless.

The counsel supplied by the Crown for the defence now rose to speak. Until Jael's outburst he had been without a brief from his client, but seizing the opportunity her intervention gave him, he asked the judge that she might be detained and called upon to give evidence on behalf of the defendant. This was allowed, and Jael was put into the witness-box and sworn.

"Do you know the defendant at the bar?"

"Yes."

"Do you know him to be a poacher?"

"Yes."

"Do you know that the dog the prisoner incited to the worrying of John Lynd belongs to the defendant?"

"The dog belongs to Ben Faa. It was born and bred in our camp. It would not attack any man at the bidding of Will Moffatt."

"Do you know where the dog is now?"

"Yes. It is chained up in the stable behind The Roaring Militia Man."

"Have you any other evidence to give?"

"None. I know nothing about the fight, nor who were there on the poachers' side."

Ben Faa now attempted to slink from the court, but the judge ordered him to be detained, while enquiry should be made concerning the dog, and it should, if possible, be brought into Court. Poor Prodigal was soon brought into the court muzzled, and true to its natural instinct, on beholding Ben Faa, it endeavoured to break loose from its keeper and approach him. It ignored Will Moffatt entirely.

The sensation in Court caused by Jael's revelation was great, and the judge was visibly moved in the prisoner's favour, but quickly assuming again his impassive demeanour, he ordered that Ben Faa should return to the witness box.

But he stood there in a sullen silence, refusing to speak until the judge threatened him with committal for contempt of Court, and said: "I ask you for the last time, is the dog yours or not?"

"Yes," was the reluctant answer.

When the time came for the judge to sum up, he commented with severity upon the unsatisfactory nature of some of the evidence for the prosecution, and particularly that of Ben Faa, and he directed the jury that they must acquit the prisoner on the more serious issue. The dog, not being his, and he having no control over it, he was exculpated from the charge of personally instigating its attack on John Lynd, but they might think it equally clear that the prisoner had been present at the affray, and find him guilty on the minor charge. They did this without leaving the box, and the judge passed sentence of fifteen months' imprisonment.

Will Moffatt stepped from the dock with a light heart, waving a recognition to Red Ike and Dick Stagg, and calling a word of thanks to Jael for the courageous manner in which she had stood forth in his defence.

That night in his cell his mind ran over the whole events which had happened to him since his return to Sandyflatts, and he thought that fortune had surely favoured him, despite the prison in which he lay. Had it not proved beyond all manner of doubt that Jean Lynd was his, no matter to what depth he might have fallen in the eyes of the world? In fifteen months' time he would be free to hold her to his heart, and to walk side by side with her across the wide moor and broad-bosomed heathery fells, by shining, sunlit becks and sparkling tarns, and thundering forces whose misty manes flung in the winds are a wonder to behold. He gazed into the future, seeing himself again at Sandyflatts with Jean as his wife, busy about her household duties, and her serene presence filling him with delight. The vision so overpowered him with its seeming reality, that he rose from the stool in his cell and stretched forth open arms to clasp her to his breast, in such an ecstasy that he was unconscious of his narrow surroundings, and time and imprisonment were not.

And then a "change came o'er the spirit of his vision," and Red Ike and Jael, and Dick Stagg and a fair girl whom he did not know, and a host of other friends, warm and true, were with Jean and him, and Sandyflatts was still the scene, and he marvelled at the peace and happiness he felt, though he had a darkling sense, that weird and spectre-like shadows of great past sorrows and tribulations hovered on the edges of the realm of his vision and disturbed his thoughts; but all the time he knew that, if they came within the light of the circle of his happiness, they would be dispelled like the shades of night within the diffusive glory of day.

Gradually the vision changed again, and he was wandering over the moorland around Sandyflatts, and whomever he met greeted him with familiarity and friendship and respect, and he returned each salute in kind; and at last he came to the cattle pool where the three runnels meet, and behold, standing on its brink was Red Ike, gazing into its depth on the reflection of whin flowers yellow as gold, and heather purple as blood, and the sword-like leaves of iris, and the rapiers of tapered reeds, and of flowers innumerable. The lines of deep thought were marked strongly on his face, the sure index of a fixed purpose, long and faithfully followed. He was leaning on a slender staff, and the sunlight, streaming through a rift in a cloud of the morning sky, shone upon him, and Will Moffatt wondered in the vision, wondered at the scintillation of his staff—for in his hand he held a carved and enamelled stick, the Gypsy's Luck.

And then the vision passed, but he realized that he had triumphed that day, and would reap his reward in many others to come.

Now whilst he was under the rapt delusion of his vision, Dick Stagg was in the Royal George Hotel at Penrith. Unable to resist the allurement of Nell Glen, he had hastened thither, and was astounded at the reception he received. His old love checked his advances with a disdain that chilled him like frosty wind from the top of Skiddaw. In vain he tried his utmost art to soften her asperity of manner, and wondering and doubtful, he was about to appeal to her for an explanation, when, through a mirror opposite him, he saw the gloating features of Peg Shore and Joe Gream. Wheeling suddenly round he confronted them, and divining that somehow they were the cause of Nell's estrangement from him, he taunted them openly with being free lovers and worse. This roused Peg to fury, and in retaliation she poured a torrent of abuse upon him so utterly false that he stood dumbfounded before her. Nell was watching with critical eyes, and thinking Dick unable to refute Peg's charges, she held out their engagement ring on the palm of her hand, and told him to take it back. Hastily snatching it, he threw it into the fire.

A low cry broke from Nell's lips, but with a laugh Dick crushed it into the centre of the grate with his boot, and then, turning fiercely upon his tormenters, he snarled: "Now, tell me the meaning of all this."

Peg shrank back before his threatening attitude, but Joe Gream with a self-confident air presumed too far on Dick's forbearance in his temper and situation at that moment, and exclaimed: "No decent-minded lass wants anything to do with a poacher, and an associate of gangrels and murderers. There's not anything nor anybody safe in the countryside with such fellows as you prowling about. The old transportation laws need putting into operation again to clear the country of such scum." And glancing at Nell he ended, "You did right to break with an idle good-for-nothing."

With a bound, Dick caught him by the throat, dashed his head against the wall, and then flung him insensible under the table. Peg screamed, and Nell fainted. The landlord rushed into the room, and seeing how things were, closed the door and sent for the police. Dick stood with his arms folded, and, when the officer arrived, said: "I shall go quietly to the lock-up providing you don't attempt to handcuff me, otherwise I shall fight every yard of the way thither."

"You talk like a dictator, young man," replied the officer, "but I'll trust your word—come along."

At a special sitting of the Court next day, Peg Shore with Nell, awed and terrified, swore against Dick, with the result that he also was sentenced to a term of imprisonment, and that night he was lodged in the cell next to that of Will Moffatt.

Meanwhile, Red Ike had returned to the drift, and acquainted Jean with the story of the trial. She listened patiently to the end, and then buried her face in her hands and wept—not tears of sorrow alone, but of joy also. In our weakest moments we see things clearest, and Jean saw that Will's self-abnegation was her glory as well as his, and that he had strength of character and self-reliance on which she could lean as on a firm pillar, in love and worship. When she again lifted her head, Red Ike marvelled at the wonderful beauty and resignation of her face; it was as though it had been touched into spirituality by the hand of God himself.

I am not worthy of Will Moffatt, she thought whilst he was thinking how unworthy he was of her. There is no surer guide that the souls of two human beings are in harmony with each other than that each exalts the other above the ordinary mass of humanity by which we all measure ourselves. The ideal man or woman of one's imagination represents the true moral stature of each of us.

Now, when Dick Stagg on the first morning of his imprisonment was on exercise in the prison yard, Will beheld him with amazement.

Two days before, at his trial, he had sat in the centre of the Assize Court with Red Ike. What had happened, he wondered? As luck would have it they were told off together to scrub down the corridors, and Dick was thus able, with the connivance of a good-tempered warder, to tell all that had happened. As he did not mention Jean, Will concluded rightly that he was not aware she was living in the drift.

Will Moffatt now needed all his natural and acquired philosophy to help him to discipline his soul into patience until the term of his sentence expired, and, but for his reliance on Red Ike to succour and protect Jean, he would indeed have been plunged into an agony of suspense and despair.

Meanwhile, and during the next few days, Red Ike became perplexed at the non-appearance of Dick Stagg about their favourite haunts. For several nights he hovered round the White Horse Inn in hope of getting in touch with him, and then after a full week had elapsed, he suddenly decided to solve the matter at once, and walking into the drinking-room sat down and called for a pint of ale. His appearance, wild, unkempt, and unexpected, and the fact that he was not known personally to several of the younger men assembled, caused a hush to fall over all present. The landlord, recognizing him at once, refused to serve his order, and demanded that he leave the house. Rising from his seat, Red Ike grasped his cudgel, and holding it over his shoulder, defiantly commanded the drink to be brought him: "I came here in peace, and am prepared to pay for my requirements, and if I am treated civilly I shall behave so, otherwise the blame of the consequences will fall upon those that molest me. Is there a man here whom I have wronged? There is not. And there is no just reason why I should be treated with contumely, and like an outcast. What I have done I have suffered for, and who amongst you has got his full deserts for all the evil he has done his fellows? I am not going to try to justify my conduct in the past, but I shall not suffer any man to upbraid me with it and cast contempt upon me with impunity. There is not a grown man amongst you but to whom I have shown respect and friendship, and though I am not asking the same in return, I insist on being behaved to as a man. Drive me with my back to the wall, and, by God, I'll fight, though I shall be hanged at last. Now fetch me the drink I ordered, or I'll smash every damned picture and ornament in the room, and knock the first man down that tries to hinder me."

A murmur of disapproval arose at this challenge, which might have broken out next moment into open violence had not Simon Reed, the old tailor, seizing his pint, strode up beside him and cried: "Here, my friend, I'll share my ale with thee. Drink, and may the devil in hell roast the man that denies refreshment in thy need."

At this unexpected act, Red Ike lowered his cudgel, and sat down again.

Simon turned to the landlord, and taking a pinch of snuff said: "I'll have another pint of ale, and be sharp over bringing it, or I'll never again darken the door of the White Horse Inn as long as I'm quick."

"I'll do nothing of the sort," quoth the landlord.

Red Ike rose again to his feet: "Fetch the drink, and be civil."

"Fetch the drink," roared the company.

"I'll do hell as like," was the answer.

At this moment the landlady, bearing two pints upon a salver, entered the room and placed them on the table. "There you are, my lads," she said in a cheery voice, and the storm that seemed about to break was dispelled through her tactful interposition.

Nevertheless Red Ike was ill at ease and, for the first time in his life, he looked the fact squarely in the face, and realized the almost hopelessness of his present position, if he continued to live amongst those who knew his past life. His soul rebelled against the thought of fleeing before his foes, and he swore a great oath deep down in his heart that he would stand his ground, and dare the worst, and wrest from his fellows esteem, and honour, and love. He remembered again, as he had so often done during the last few days, that Jean Lynd trusted him, and had held his hand in friendship, and that tonight Simon Reed stood forth and called him comrade, and that even the landlady had given him some consideration.

The new spirit born within him was strengthened with the thought of these things, and he rose to leave the room forgetful of his purpose in coming thither.

"Nay, sit thyself down again, we'll not part without having another drink together," said Simon, "and then for the sake o' t' company I'll sing one of thy old songs, and if thou'll make us a merry ballad on Dick Stagg."

"What's happened to him?" said Red Ike

"He was mad drunk in the Royal George Hotel at Penrith, and in a jealous fit over a bit o' sunshine half murdered Joe Gream."

"Well, and what then?"

"He is in jail for that," replied Simon, "and now I'll sing thy song."

SWEEP

When Autumn comes round and the stubble lies white,
And merry hares romp in the bonny moonlight,
When far over moorland, and mountain, and fell,
The hollow winds whistle, the eerie owls yell,
Away goes the poacher, light-hearted and free,
A lord of creation till daylight is he.
Above him the stars in their glory are spread,
Beneath him the grass gives no sound of his tread,
Hurrah! lads, whatever he catches he'll keep,
And who is his helper but gallant old Sweep?

A dog and a wonder is Sweep, I'll be bound;
His marrow is not on the earth to be found,
How he arches his back and erects his great tail
When the scent of a hare is borne down on the gale;
At a wave of the hand he will speed through the night,
And makes the bold poacher's heart throb with delight.
Hurrah! though the rich to the land may lay claim,

The world's a preserve ever filled with fat game;
And where is the dog that has slain such a heap
In double the lifetime of gallant old Sweep?

To sing of his feats is my pride and delight,
My joy to be with him a-poaching by night;
Where Howard rules over the Greystoke domain,
And away on the lands of proud Lowther and Vane,
I've seen him full often kill hare after hare,
Until we had more than a strong man could bear;
He flees in the chase o'er a gate like a bird,
And pauses the moment a stranger is heard;
My lord and my lady would scorn him to keep,
But gifted, for all that, is gallant old Sweep.

Come, lads, now I know you delight ill good ale,
And next to it love an old song or a tale;
So drink up your pewters, to fill them I'm fain,
Since Sweep will refund me the wherewith again.
Hurrah for old Sweep! If he knew his own worth,
He'd strut up and down like a proud sprig of birth.
I'm sorry one cannot too stand him a treat,
However, let every man rise to his feet,
And drink to the toast a pewter pint deep,
Hurrah! lads, hurrah! for gallant old Sweep.

Simon sang with gusto, though in a voice shrill and broken with age, and during the whole time of his singing he kept his eyes fast closed. When he finished and looked towards Red Ike's chair, it was vacant.

The poet-poacher was pacing the wild moorland seeking in solitude to calm the tumult of his soul, and grieving for the loss and the unjust suffering and imprisonment of his friends.

An hour before daybreak, he crept through the opening into the drift. Jean rose to greet him, and he returned her salute with such a frank spirit, mingled with warm feeling, that her eyes fell before the ardour expressed in his. Quickly noticing her slight embarrassment, he spoke freely: "I have news for you, Miss Lynd. I learned last night that Dick Stagg has been imprisoned this week for an assault on Joe Gream. The affair took place in the Royal George Hotel at Penrith. Dick is the man whom I got to buy the list of articles for you; he also hired the room at the Red Lion Hotel, Grasmere, in case you should need it. I did not make a confidant of him with regard to you, though; had you had to leave the drift, I should have confided in him, and enjoined him to secrecy. He is a trustworthy lad, fearless and hot-blooded. But I fear there has been some underhand work used against him. Now, I have a proposition to make. The decision I shall leave to your discretion. You'll understand that if by any chance we should be discovered living together in the drift here, that the world will pass a free judgment upon us; not that I value the opinion of others where and when I know I am in the right, but I feel I must put our position in its proper light before you, as I put it before Will Moffatt when last I saw him."

"What did Will say to you?"

"He paid me a compliment by saying that if you were content to stay here with me until his return, you could not be in more honourable hands."

"Yes," Jean answered, "and Will Moffatt is right."

"You love Will Moffatt, Jean? Pardon me, but he'll make you his wife if you are willing."

"I am willing."

"Then we understand each other perfectly. And now, do you prefer staying here until his release, or will you go to more congenial surroundings? The winter is before us, and we might be snowed up here for weeks together. My sole object in speaking thus is to serve you and Will to the best of my ability. I shall watch and protect you, no matter which place you choose to stay at."

"I shall stay here with you, Red Ike."

"Your health would break under the strain of the long confinement, Jean. I must find some place where you can live quietly for at least a year; after that we can again consider things over. I know the very place suitable. I have some; friends in the Isle of Anglesey. I'll write them tonight. Were you once there, you would be free from molestation until Will gains his liberty. If all goes well with me till then, you can return to the drift and wait for him."

"I agree to anything you propose to do," said Jean, "I know you will act for the best."

Red Ike laid a hand upon each of Jean's shoulders, as Will Moffatt had laid his upon him in his prison cell, and, looking her straight in the eyes, said: "Jean Lynd, you and your future husband have made a man of me again. He was the first to hold out the hand of friendship to me after my release from prison; your confidence is a memory which exalts me every day of my life. I bless you and love you as a sister for it."

Jean was abashed at this simple truthfulness of manner and speech, but Red Ike continued: "Now, I wish to be at Penrith by daybreak in the morning, and shall not return until after nightfall. While I am there, I will write to the friends of whom I have spoken."

And so it came to pass that Jean was lost for a year to her father, mother, and the gypsies.

BOOK THREE

CHAPTER XVIII

AFTER Jean left the drift, Red Ike lived alone for a year. Though within an easy walk of daily converse with his fellows, he was by choice a veritable Robinson Crusoe. His friend, Simon Reed, had little intellectually in common with him, and was too old to stand the fatigue of night-work. The poacher himself seldom stirred abroad by day for various reasons. His abstemious habits, and his disregard of dress, enabled him to save rapidly, despite the fact that he sent money monthly to Jean. And so the winter passed gradually away. An early Easter favoured Red Ike in a manner peculiar to such a man. This church festival gives a large portion of the people a week's leisure to wander at will by fell and dale. Then hotels and lodging-houses have a regular demand for fresh-water fish. Red Ike, knowing this, swept the mountain becks and tarns for the small brown trout abounding in them; and he cleared the large pools in the main rivers of shoals of salmon-smolts, most of which were sold to the principal hotels and placed by the proprietors into cold storage to be served at table, as the year advanced, as savoury potted char.

Autumn drew near again, and one morning Red Ike strode into Penrith with the dawn. To avoid the main road he had skirted Helvellyn by the old Roman road, and then cut across the country to Mell Fell. His sixteen miles' tramp over a rough way had not impaired his magnificent vitality. His sinews were as fresh as though he had just risen from his bed of bracken in the drift, and unheeding the glances and smiles of folks caused by his uncouth appearance, he lingered about until the shops opened, and then selecting a barber's shop which he thought likely to suit his purpose, he entered it and asked for a shave and haircut. The man laughed and declined to take the job on, but after some discussion as to price, at last agreed. Within an hour, shaven, hair clipped, and shampooed, he rose from his chair. The barber stepped back with amazement. Instead of a middle-aged roadster, there stood before him the strong figure of a robust man well under thirty, whose clear-cut mobile features discovered to an intelligent observer that a resolute spirit, high-minded and purposeful, was masked within the brain behind those frank calm eyes, that shone with the light of unfathomable power.

"Well," said he to the barber, "have you seen the devil that you stare at me like one demented?"

"I have seen such a change in a man as I never before saw in my life," was the reply, "and I'm glad of it. If ever there was a miracle performed, I've worked one this morning."

And then the barber and Red Ike laughed merrily together. Good humour begets familiarity, and harmless repartee is the soul of good-fellowship, and Red Ike said: "I would have asked you to go and have a drink with me, but for my appearance. Can you recommend a tailor from whom I can get a suit at a reasonable price?"

"We'll have a drink first," said the barber.

"No, I'll buy the suit first, and then return for you," and they both laughed heartily again.

Being the model of a man, Red Ike was soon fitted, and afterwards at the suggestion of the barber, they went to the Royal George Hotel. On entering the door, they encountered Joe Gream and Peg Shore. Peg started and stepped back. Red Ike ignored her, but her involuntary action did not escape the barber's notice.

"Have you met that man and woman before?" he asked.

"Yes," answered Red Ike.

"I should think so," snarled Peg. "I know you, scoundrel that you are, in spite of your fine clothes and suave tongue. If you do not clear out of Penrith at once, I'll have the police at your heels."

The barber began to sidle to the door, but was arrested by the commanding voice of his companion: "Landlord, call an officer of the law. I am threatened by this woman."

The landlord demurred, but as Red Ike repeated the request, he stepped to the door, and hailed an officer who was standing without.

"This woman," said Red Ike, pointing to Peg, "who is staying with that man, is not his wife, yet she calls me a scoundrel and threatens to lay the police at my heels unless I leave Penrith. Now I have reasons for thinking that she wishes me out of her way, and the man's with whom she is consorting. Landlord, sometime ago you had a young woman here as barmaid called Nell Glen; can you tell me where I shall find her?"

"After the affair with Dick Stagg, she hired as a servant with those two," said the landlord, motioning to Joe and Peg.

"The devil she did!" ejaculated Red Ike, "then I'm afraid she will have gone astray long before now."

How little Red Ike knew his surmise was correct.

"You poaching liar!" blazed Peg, "you have done time for killing a man, and are not fit to be at large."

"Peg Shore, part of what you say is correct, but I shall leave Penrith of my own free will, and shall return hither whenever I choose, for I can still go where I will; but you, the bondswoman of a licentious brute on whom I would not wipe my shoes, you shall be compelled to follow him until he tires of you, and you sicken of him, and then he'll cast you from him into the gutter, where all worthless women are thrown when men are satiated with them. I am sorry for you, but I am not to be daunted with anything you say or do." And with these words he turned away, and for once the wretched woman was sufficiently abashed to leave him the last word.

There was now nothing for Red Ike to do but to buy some necessary articles, and return to the drift.

With the barber and the landlord of the Royal George Hotel, he passed a pleasant hour and then departed.

But as he walked down the street, and in and out of the several shops, he noticed that a constable was shadowing him, and he strode boldly into the police station and complained of the irksomeness of being dogged about as he was. He was told that the officer was doing his duty, and the matter must rest there. Having no other remedy, and not wishing to leave the town until after dark for fear of being followed, he, with his bundle strapped on his shoulders, wandered into St. Andrew's Churchyard and examined the Giant's Grave, and then, without trying to elude the man who was following him, he walked up to the Beacon Hill and lay down under the cover of the wood that crowns that prominent spot. Within twenty yards of him lay the policeman; each watched the other as a cat watches a rat.

A whole afternoon passed, but Red Ike waited patiently until the shades of gathering night became dense enough for his purpose, and then leaping from the ground he plunged at top speed into the depth of the Beacon Wood, and was soon beyond the reach of surveillance and pursuit. Crossing the town on the outskirts, he passed the brickfields on his right, and was making for the main road towards Keswick when a fresh thought struck him. How if the authorities telegraphed or telephoned to the policemen of the neighbouring villages to be on the lookout for him? True, they could not arrest him. He had committed no offence, but he wished to keep his destination unknown, and he resolved to follow the railway line for the first ten miles of his journey, until he was opposite Mell Fell again

The night was yet early, and he strode along debating with himself whether he should go by the old Roman road along Helvellyn's breast, or boldly take the main turnpike way by the White Horse Inn. He decided on the latter, and when once he had resolved on a course of action, he held by it with assurance.

About a mile below the village of Troutbeck, and at the base of the Hill of Devils, a crossroad branches eastward and runs for several miles over one of the most desolate stretches of country in Cumberland.

A little distance from the end of this crossroad, on a patch of wild common, a gypsies' camp-fire, newly lighted, was shooting fitful flashes of flame into the darkness, and Red Ike could hear a woman's voice singing in such a sweet strain that he paused to listen, and his heart throbbed. Yes, he could not be mistaken, it was Jael, and her song was the same as she sang in the Roaring Militia Man at Carlisle on the fair-day night over seven years ago when he killed the gypsy. Vaulting over the drystone wall that hedged the road, he crossed towards the camp, and stood within twenty-five yards of it. On the steps of the van, Abegail was sitting smoking. Jael was squatted cross-legged on the ground, and as she finished one song, she struck up another and another, pouring her whole rich spirit, wild and untutored, into them, yet with that passionate feeling such as only a woman is capable of who has loved deeply and lost the man she loved.

And now Red Ike was astonished. A slim boy about six years of age stepped from the van, and throwing his arms around Jael's neck, fondled her as only a warm-hearted mother is fondled by her own child. Red Ike watched Jael lavish affection on the boy, and a tempest of strange passion swept through his being. He flung himself on the ground, not knowing what he did, and resting his chin on his hands, gazed long and intently on the woman and child, but was unable to comprehend the feeling that agitated him. He could bear the sight no longer, and turned his head aside.

"So," he thought, after trying in vain to compose his mind, "Jael has consorted with Ben Faa after all," and with clenched fists he leapt to his feet with a deep curse on his tongue, but the next moment the truth dawned upon him. He was in love with Jael, and had not known it, and now she was lost to him.

A devil rose in his heart. He would have her yet. He would go now, and ask her to flee with him. He knew she would do so.

He was obsessed by the idea. And then he thought of the child fondling its mother. He would take it with them. No! No! He could not bear the sight daily of Ben Faa's brat creeping about him. And turning, he fled through the darkness in a tumult of rage with himself, and the torment of a gnawing passion in his heart.

During the next hour he lay on the Hill of Devils until he reasoned himself into composure, and gradually his resolute will triumphed over his weakness, and he laughed at the folly he had thought of committing.

Jael, he knew, had an absolute right to dispose of herself as she chose. He had heard her lay claim to such a right years ago. Besides, he had given her no reason to hope anything from him; indeed, his past conduct towards her might have led her to believe the contrary. He would play the man now, and abide by the consequences. Without knowing it, he had cast his love into the arms of Ben Faa, his deadly foe. What the fates had willed, he would submit to. Resigned to the inevitable, he resumed his journey.

There was a goodly company at the White Horse Inn, and as he passed it, Simon Reed was shouting at the top of his shrill cracked voice, and amid uproarious laughter:

> "My father died a month ago
> And left me all his riches,
> A feather bed, a wooden leg,
> A pair of leather britches;
> A coffee kettle without a spout,
> A jug without a handle,
> A 'bacca box without a lid,
> And half a farthing candle."

Red Ike stood irresolute for a moment. Should he go into the public-house or not? He was a man who had never loved drink for its own sake; indeed, his earliest habits of life in the first flush of his young manhood had been studious. His lapses were due rather to the want of association with men of higher intellectual capacity than to any inherent depraved tendencies. Besides, his poverty was the chief hindrance to his advancement. He was a proud, self-contained man, hating dependence in appearance or reality; a man not to be patronized by the wealthiest aristocrat in the land. He was still debating with himself when the cold muzzle of a dog pushed itself into his hand. Stooping down, he felt all over the animal's body. Yes, he could not be mistaken, it was the lurcher Prodigal. He patted the poor faithful brute, and turned from the allurement of the boisterous company at the White Horse Inn.

As he passed the yew tree opposite the door, he fancied there was a movement in the branches above him. He could not be sure, but he would make sure. Stepping briskly forward for about fifty yards, until he knew the sound of his footsteps would not be audible to anyone in the tree, he completed a half-circle and then dropped upon his hands and knees, and crept forward and lay motionless within the length of the tree's shadow.

The dog was at his side.

Suddenly several branches of the tree broke with a crash, and the thud of a heavy body striking the ground told its own tale.

"Damn it! I might have known the whole thing was rotten. 'Twas lucky I did not fall on the dog, or I should have crushed out its guts."

"Hist," said another voice, "someone may hear you. Who the devil do you think was the man that passed under us a few minutes ago?"

"I can't guess. Some fool listening to old Simon Reed singing. I hope he was edified for once in his life. Hell-fire! where is the lurcher? I tied him up to the bole of the tree, and he's got loose, and yet 'tis strange he should leave us. By God, the man that passed must have been Red Ike! Had I known it was he, I'd have shot him dead."

"What are we going to do now?" The voice was Ben Faa's.

"We'll take a short cut to Sandyflatts, and fell him as he steps through the bour tree that blocks up the doorway."

"It's a desperate job to risk."

"Not at all; nothing venture, nothing win. Come along."

"But the dog?" questioned Ben. "I couldn't trust the brute, mine though it is, if it saw us do him an injury."

"Then why the devil have you not put it down before this? At any rate, we have no time to lose. Dog or no dog, we'll finish him once and for all tonight. Were his soul in hell this minute, no man here would enquire after his carcase."

Red Ike could hardly believe his ears, and drawing a revolver from his pocket he levelled it at the last speaker, and murmured: "So Joe Gream is planning murder again? It will be better to shoot first this time."

The trigger clicked, but the weapon missed-fire. To the two scoundrels the sound was an ominous and unmistakable warning to flee.

The revolver fell from Red Ike's grasp, and his body shook like an aspen leaf.

"My God! What was I about to do? I, who but yesterday swore to my own soul to do no more wrong to any man on earth, no matter what injury I might have received."

In a spirit of self-despair, he was half resolved to end his troubles at once by putting the muzzle to his own head, when he became aware that, hovering near him was another presence, and raising his head from the bracken in which he lay, he beheld the form of a woman, and the warmth of her body began to pervade his. A soft voice breathed his name, and he murmured, "Jael," and leaped to his feet, and would have clasped her to his heart, but that he remembered the child that fondled her earlier during the night. Steeling his heart, he dropped his hands to his sides.

"Come," she said, "'tis not safe for you to linger here," and together they passed deeper and deeper into the night.

"Whither would you go, Jael?"

"Whither wouldst thou go, Red Ike? Thy habitation is not unknown to me, nor the woman who will shortly again be living with thee there. Thou hast the carved stick, Red Ike, and but three folks in the world know where it is hidden. Thou, Will Moffatt, and I. Nay, this is no wonder that I know. I behold by vision every important incident in thy life the moment it is taking place. I saw John Lynd shoot at thee in the drift years ago, and though I have not been there, I know its every particular as well as I know the van I dwell in. To convince thee further, I saw thee lying within twenty paces of the policeman under the Beacon Wood at Penrith today. Tonight I felt thee near me whilst I sang before our camp-fire, and I closed my eyes and mentally saw thee rush from the sight of me and the child that fondled me. Why—why didst thou do that, Red Ike?"

"Because," said he, "the child is Ben Faa's."

Jael clutched at her bosom with both hands, and stifled the cry that rose to her lips.

"Ben Faa's!" and then the truth dawned upon her, and her heart throbbed within her breast, and she longed to throw her arms about the man before her and smother him with a deluge of passionate love and caresses. But instead of this, she withdrew further from him, afraid of the great happiness she had divined. Red Ike loved her. Red Ike, for whose love she had not dared to hope; the man for whom she would have passed midst the flames of hell itself, aye, for whose love she had given her body years ago, and for whom she had kept herself inviolate from their first night's wild embrace at Sandyflatts. And now she crept closer to him and touched his arm, and in a hushed voice said: "Will Red Ike kiss me once more for old time's sake, and then I shall leave him forever? Just once, no matter though Ben Faa stand between us. I was on a time sweet to Red Ike, and perhaps in the days to come when my lot is drab, and years and sorrows and hardships have stripped me of all womanly charm, I shall remember and be happy with the thought that the one man who is throned in my heart kissed me for the delight I felt in asking him to do so."

Standing with bowed head before him, she waited until his warm lips touched her brow, and then, flinging her arms about his neck she spent her soul upon his lips, and thus left him like a dark shadow, bewildered and alone.

Red Ike stood transfixed, not knowing where he was, nor what had come over him. Had he been with Jael? It all seemed a dream, vaguely indistinct, and then the revolver which was lying at his feet reminded him that life is all reality, no matter into what imaginary regions the mind may project itself during our moments of highly-strung nervous tension. He threw himself on the ground, and resting the back of his head upon his hands, gazed into the starlit sky above him. Past and around him the forms of denizens of the moorland flitted on wings of darkness between him and the stars, the winds in the whins and bracken made him strange music, and his soul became calm and suffused with the peace that nature has always in store, and is still ready to dispense to those who seek and love her. Yet he thought: by what means did his daily life become known to Jael? That she knew of its principal happenings was certain. But how? Was there such a thing as second sight? He did not know. Lastly, could he trust her not to divulge the secret she was possessed of? Yes, he could trust her, and wondering at the exaltation the thought gave him, he arose and strode onwards to the dale of the fall of rock and unwittingly to Jean Lynd.

When Red Ike crept into the drift and stood erect, he was surprised to see a dim light shining in front of him. Thinking he himself had left it burning, he walked briskly forward and sat down on the stone seat beside the ledge on which were his books. Stooping to unloose his heavy boots, he saw at his feet a volume of Shelley's poems lying open. Hastily gathering it up he found that someone had been reading *The Masque of Anarchy*, and instantly blowing out the lighted lamp, and throwing himself flat to the ground, he called out:

"Who is in the drift with me? Speak, or I shall fire a revolver-charge into the side drift."

"It is I, Jean Lynd. I did not recognize you until you spoke, Red Ike, not knowing you were such a handsome man."

"How is that?" said he, forgetting the changed appearance the barber and tailor had made of him. As he relit the lamp, he laughed merrily, and replied: "Peg Shore did not think like you today, or if she did, she called me a scoundrel, and threatened to set the police at my heels in the Royal George at Penrith.

Then he told her the whole story of his love for Peg, and the cause of his flinging the engagement ring into the cauldron of the waterfall below the Stepping Stones, and of several other outstanding incidents until his meeting with Peg that day.

"You love her yet?" inquired Jean.

"I know now that I never loved her, yet I did not learn this until tonight. I love Jael Boswell, but she has a child to Ben Faa."

Jean looked upon Red Ike with astonishment.

"You love my half-sister?"

"I do, and save for the barrier between us, I should marry her tomorrow."

Jean felt within the folds of her dress, and snapped a silken thread, and then on the palm of her outstretched hand before Red Ike's gaze, lay Peg Shore's ring, set with six small rubies and a diamond.

"I found it on the edge of the cauldron. Take it to the woman you love, and wait patiently for the consummation of your desire. It is bound to come."

CHAPTER XIX

FROM the day that John Lynd was mauled by the dog Prodigal, he was seen no more in public; and even at home he had his meals served in a private room. His wife was not allowed to sit at table with him. His servants were forbidden his presence except when he rang the bell. He gave all orders with his back to them. Under no consideration could he be induced to leave the house by day, but as soon as night fell, he haunted the moorlands, gun in hand, with a huge, half-bred mastiff and bloodhound by his side.

Luckily, the dale of the fall of rock was a desolate place at all times, and some three miles from The Bents. It had never harboured game in any quantity, so was seldom visited by sportsmen. Its farther end being blocked by steep towering crags, barren almost from base to crown, like those of Stickle Pike and Napes Needle, invited no one to explore it save an occasional party of rock-climbers, and these only in the holiday seasons, or on special set expeditions. During the autumn and winter months, a shepherd in search of stray sheep might at odd times pass the mouth of the drift, and his dog smell at the opening, or, curious, hold its head sideways as if in wonder at the odour of human beings in such a place. Therefore, Red Ike and Jean were almost immune from the danger of discovery, and though Red Ike had often by night heard the report of firearms in the distance, he had thought little about it until an event happened that alarmed him considerably.

Leaving the drift one evening, he climbed over the fells on a round of several tarns that in the autumn are nightly visited by flights of wild duck. His intention was to lay night-lines baited with savoury morsels of which duck are very fond. The poaching of these proving lucrative had also commended itself to him because of the quietness of the method, and because few poachers had enough grit in them to face the undertaking, At midnight he was by Teufit-tarn with his lines set, and he lay down beneath a whin-bush to wait the hour on which he must begin his return journey. The loneliness of the place gave him a sense of security, and he fell into a deep sleep, and a dream of Jael, and was awakened by a huge dog sniffing along the length of his body. His first thought was to leap to his feet, his second to lie still. A shrill whistle sounded from the opposite edge of the tarn, and the brute bounded away in answer to the call.

A man of less nerve than Red Ike would have made haste to quit the scene, but one danger passed, another might not be near. He would see. For a full half-hour all was still, and then the sound of rushing wings circling the tarn, and the *quack! quack!* of a leading drake, told of expected arrivals; and the next moment the report of a fowling-piece spitting its message of death broke the midnight peace.

"The devil," muttered Red Ike, "that's spoiled my game for to-night."

And creeping deeper under the whin-bush, he unclasped a knife that Jael had given to him, and crouched ready if attacked.

He could hear the dog swimming the tarn, questing the shot duck, and a man's voice hoarse, and as if his mouth was roofless, urging it on. And now the man skirted the edge of the tarn until he stood within a few yards of Red Ike, and his foot came in contact with one of Red Ike's duck-lines, and laying down his gun he drew the line from the tarn, and seeing its nature broke into a torrent of wild curses. Taking an electric flashlight from his pocket he held the line up to the light, to examine the hook and the bait. Red Ike shuddered as he recognized the hideous, noseless face of John Lynd. And then John Lynd, holding the flashlight to the ground, scanned the edge of the tarn in search of more lines, and Red Ike crept from the whin-bush and seized the gun, and when the huge half-bred dog swam from the tarn he raised the weapon to his shoulder and shot the brute stone-dead. And then, fleet as a fox, he ran down the fell-side, with horror and pity of the man tearing vulture-like at his heart.

To have stood his ground would have been to invite murder. To have allowed the dog to live would have meant a fate to him similar to John Lynd's. Of these evils he chose the safer and the lesser, the dog's death and his own flight.

At the sight of the slain dog, John Lynd went raging mad, and seizing the gun from the ground where Red Ike had thrown it, he raced wildly and aimlessly round the tarn swearing vengeance. His blaspheming fell only on whin bushes and waters shimmering under the stars, and on the crags whose shadows seemed standing in awe at the sound of his fearful imprecations. The solitude echoed his curses again, again, and again.

Realizing he was baulked, livid with passion, and with his still unhealed face smarting and twitching with pain, he was a fearful object to behold. Yet the darkness was merciful even to him. It hid his foulness under a cloak of shade; maybe, the shade of the hand of God himself. Meanwhile, Red Ike was flown to a safe distance, and not fearing pursuit, paused and cast his body down on the sweet restful earth that denies the right of repose to no man. A great star, red as blood, was rising up the eastern sky, and Red Ike, raising his hand to his brow, saluted the beautiful image. As he did so, his eye caught the sight of the Brutchstone by his side. He was lying on the spot where Peg Shore and Joe Gream lay together years ago, when his trust in Peg was betrayed.

And then and there Red Ike laughed to himself and thought: "'Twas better that I found Peg out before than after marriage, otherwise I should have killed her. Surely the hand of destiny is in all things." And his hand clutched his breast, and he felt there Peg's ring that Jean had suspended round his neck with a silken cord, as a talismanic memory that he loved Jael Boswell. The thought strengthened him again, and rising to his feet, and laying his hand on the Brutchstone, he swore, by the remarkable formation of this peculiar rock, that as Peg Shore was, and could be, nothing to him, he would forgive all her past offences towards him; he would be forbearing with the infirmities and shortcomings of others, no matter how spiteful their usage of himself might be.

After all, the Brutchstone typified the inherent instinct of man and woman to reproduce their kind, and who was he that he should set himself up to be a judge of whether Peg Shore did right or wrong in committing a purely natural act? That his pride was wounded and his feeling lacerated at the sight of the act was a matter of concern to him alone. He would put the thought of it behind him, and wait patiently until Will Moffatt's release, and then seek a new country and, under an assumed name, start life afresh.

Thus resolved, he moved rapidly away, and within a few hours visited several tarns, and collected his night's catch in which, besides many duck, were a wild goose and a cormorant. The next night, through the agency of Simon Reed, he disposed of his produce at a good price, to the great satisfaction of Simon and himself.

After this, he poached the tarns no more for weeks, but confined his activities to the land and rivers, and reaped a rich harvest.

Simon Reed's old wife now cooked and baked for Jean and him, and they fed on the finest game the countryside afforded; and with a persistent regularity that almost seemed irony, John Lynd's game-preserves were made the support of his off-cast daughter, under the protection and through the intrepid boldness of his poaching foe.

That there could be a more glaring example of the futility of the game laws than this is difficult to imagine. And yet Red Ike was under no delusion as to the thing he was doing. He planned his course of procedure deliberately. He cared no more about the breaking of such a law than about snapping a rotten stick.

One night, after sweeping with a pole-net the low-lying lands for partridge and pheasants, Red Ike found the nearer return journey to the drift lay past Sandyflatts. It was a moonless night. (It is useless trying to net birds by moonlight.) An east wind was soughing over the moor, and blowing upon his face from the direction of the ruined house. The memory of certain happenings there saddened his soul, and he felt inclined to give the place a wide berth, when he heard distinctly a dog give a short yelp. That anyone should be there within an hour of daybreak made him curious, and stepping cautiously, the wind being in his favour, he crept to the rear of the house, clambered over the garth wall and dropped into the old well-pit.

Disposing of his game and nets in the tunnel between the well and the milkhouse, he eased the flag-stone that covered the opening in the floor, and in a moment was listening to the conversation of three men standing behind the bour tree that blocked up the doorway of the roofless kitchen before him.

"I tell you..."—the voice was Joe Gream's—"...Ben and I have watched the place night after night, and devil a mortal has come near it. There are spiders' webs across the branches of the bour tree that have not been broken for weeks. I placed some soil on the milkhouse sconce, and it is still there. No one is living there."

"Then we must watch Simon Reed's house, and failing to find out anything there, see that you shadow all the grocers' and butchers' carts. Red Ike must have accomplices to help him dispose of his poached stuff."

"Very well. I'll instruct the keepers to watch the incomings and outgoings of the carts, and Simon Reed's house, and the White Horse Inn. If we fail to learn anything during the next week, Red Ike must come into the district from a distance."

Ben Faa had remained silent during this conversation, and John Lynd turned savagely upon him.

"Have you nothing to suggest, you hell-hound? Have I to keep you and the old hag, and the gyp whom you dare not touch, supplied with money and protection forever, without any help from you? I would not wonder but that you are in league with the Red Devil yourself," and he raised his doubled fist as if to strike the gypsy.

Ben did not move, but a baleful light gleamed in his eyes.

"I have not seen Red Ike to be sure of him for some time; and as for your money and protection, I have need of neither. What I would like is to keep clear of this business, and but for the fact that Abegail insists that I shall help you have Red Ike sent back to penal servitude, I should throw up the sponge at once."

"You half-hearted cur, then get to hell from here."

And kicks and blows were showered upon Ben with a ferocity that was as remarkable as the equanimity with which the assault was borne.

"Well, are you satisfied?" said Ben, after the attack ceased.

"I'll be satisfied when I've finished you," roared Lynd. And, snatching his gun from against the bour tree, he raised it to his shoulder, as though to shoot.

"Hold!" said Ben, "before you shoot, let me tell you something. The letters are missing again from the recess under the top of the black ebony table."

"You're a liar!" gasped Lynn.

"It's the truth, so help me God!"

This was as great news to Red Ike as to John Lynd, and dropping quietly back into the tunnel, and replacing the flagstone, he climbed out of the mouth of the well, vaulted over the garth wall and sped like a greyhound across the moorland to Simon Reed's cottage. The old fellow was lighting the fire when Red Ike stepped into the room. Hurriedly explaining himself, and pressing some money into Simon's hand, he said:

"Meet me in the Twa Dogs Inn at Brigham tonight at eight," and before Simon could reply he was gone again, and racing at top speed towards the dale of the fall of rock.

A faint light of dawn was tingeing the eastern sky as he crept through the opening of the drift, and he could hear Jean breathing regularly in a sound sleep. Stepping up to her couch, he gazed upon the calm beauty of her face, and wondered that the man whom she called father could be the sire of such a fair, sweet creature. Her lips were slightly parted, and the shadow of a smile lingered about her mouth and closed eyes. His coming had disturbed her dreams, and she murmured, "Will, Will, Will!"

Fearing she would waken, Red Ike withdrew himself again, and retired to snatch a few hours' rest. He was ever a light sleeper, and the moment he heard Jean moving, he arose.

After breakfast, resting his elbows on the rough ledge that served as a table, he said: "Miss Lynd, I saw your father last night, or rather this morning early, at Sandyflatts with Joe Gream and Ben Faa. They were lying in wait there to kill me. Jean, should they at some future time succeed, or if ever I do not return after three days from my leaving here, you'll remember that a room at the Red Lion Hotel, Grasmere, is still reserved for you. I have seen to that."

Jean nodded assent.

"I heard your father give orders that Simon Reed's house and other places must be watched, and my whereabouts located. I myself could live content here for months without stirring abroad, and tire them out at their vigils, but this is not my wish. In the course of their conversation, mention was made by Ben Faa of some letters of importance, which are missing from a recess cunningly contrived under a black ebony table-top. Those letters, with the exception of one, I have read."

"I have those letters," said Jean, and she explained how they came into her possession. "I have read most of them. Now we shall read them together," and she drew the packet from her bosom.

A few moments later a low cry escaped her lips, and Red Ike looking over her shoulder beheld in her hands the marriage certificate of John Lynd and Jael's mother. This then was the meaning of the power old Abegail held over him. And as its full import became plain to Jean, she turned her face to Red Ike and cried: "I am not Jean Lynd, but Jean Kennedy. This certificate is dated one month prior to my mother's. I remember Jael's mother dying at Mirkholme; she lies buried on the open moorland, and my father had the grave fenced round and a yew tree planted above it.

"I have often stood beside it with Jael when I was a young girl, and I have seen her leaning over the fence and singing strange chants beneath the full moon, and at all times of the year. Poor Jael! 'Tis she and not I that should have been educated, and pampered amidst luxury, and looked up to with respect at The Bents.

"And oh, my mother! What has my father made of her?" And Jean dropped her head upon her breast, overcome with shame and sorrow.

Red Ike placed his hand under her chin, and, raising her eyes to his, said: "We are commanded to forgive our enemies seven times seven, and can you not also forgive and love your father, no matter what he may have done or been?"

"I love my father," replied Jean, "but can never go back to The Bents and take the place of Jael unless she be there to bid me welcome. 'Tis her home by right of inheritance."

"Then," said Red Ike, "I shall visit Jael tonight, and if she be not already bound to Ben Faa, I shall wed her, and The Bents shall one day be your home whatever happens."

"She is not wedded to Ben Faa, and you, Red Ike, are the father of her child."

"How know you this, Jean?"

"She christened it in your name. I stood godmother to it."

"And the godfather, Jean?"

"Dick Stagg. Jael brought the babe to church, and insisted that the rite be gone through with. The priest at first demurred, saying she had to come again at an appointed hour, besides, where were the sponsors? And with a shrug of his shoulders, he was about to depart, when I laid a hand upon his arm, and said, 'Stay!' Then turning to Dick who was standing within the church porch, I said: 'Come, man you and I will stand for the child.'"

A mist swam before Red Ike's eyes, but with a mighty effort of will he stemmed the tide of rising tears, and turning aside moved with downcast head into a side-drift and threw himself onto his bed of bracken.

"How does it happen," he thought, "that I never surmised such a contingency? I am the father of Jael's child, yet she did not disabuse my mind when last I saw her. What a short-sighted nincompoop I am! I might have guessed as much by the wild delight with which she clung to me. I shall go to Jael, and right myself with her. What love she must have had, and what sorrow have borne for me, through the years of my imprisonment." And then a great shame took possession of him. "I have doubted Jael's constancy even to her face, and yet she forbore to upbraid me."

He was roused from these thoughts by the voice of Jean. Stepping into the main drift, he was pleased to find her cheerful and composed, and taking her hands in both of his, he praised her sweet graciousness, and suggested that he bring Jael to see her.

"When?" asked Jean.

"Tonight, if you wish."

And now Red Ike resolved to show Jean the carved stick. An exclamation of wonder and delight broke from her lips when the treasure met her gaze, and she begged him to explain the meaning of the figures marked upon it.

"The serpent twined round the stick," said Red Ike, "has from the earliest ages been a sign of wisdom, very often of worship. It plays a part in the writings of Zoroaster, the Persian Christ, who lived over a thousand years before the Christian era, and who is reputed to have been miraculously conceived and born of a virgin mother, like Jesus. This remarkable prophet and law-giver regulated the apparent progress of the sun through the twelve signs of the Zodiac, which you see are represented on the ivory ball the serpent holds between its jaws.

"That the stick is an old piece of work, I do not doubt. For, as you see, all the principal planets but two are marked and named upon it. And those two are of comparatively recent discovery. Uranus by Herschel, and Neptune by Adams and the Frenchman, Le Verrier.

"However, the sun is also represented on the ball, and is resting on the verge of Pisces, in which constellation it is in the month of March. Whoever carved the work counted the months numerically as the ancient Egyptians did, and the Freemasons and Quakers do now.

"The serpent holding the ball between its jaws may mean that it is in possession of all the knowledge and power of the universe. The Jews knew little about astronomy. Thales was the first eminent Greek to study it. The first five principal planets were certainly known to the Egyptians, from whom the Jews derived what little knowledge they possessed. Moses was educated in their enlightened schools. We do not read of the Jews being inventors or improvers of any of the arts or sciences. That they adopted and practised many of the grosser superstitions, and much of the magic that tainted Egyptian priest-craft, is proved beyond doubt. And as you are aware, their magicians and Moses before Pharaoh threw down their rods which turned into serpents, and that Moses' serpent ate up all the others. There was also a serpent in the Garden of Eden, and it was possessed of all the wisdom of the world. I am inclined to believe that the carvings on the stick and ivory ball are a conglomeration of myths and fables that have filtered through the minds of vanished civilizations from remote times, and on which all religions have been built, and which in fundamentals are separately indistinguishable to the inquiring mind.

"Sex-worship was perhaps the first religion, and after that came the more enlightened sun-worshipper, to be followed by the abstract notion of deity. The growth of the idea is easily traceable. The carvings of the animate and inanimate life on the stick show a wonderful skill, but, what is more pleasing, a soul rich in sympathy, and an eye that delighted to look upon the glory and beauty of all created things. There is another peculiarity here," said Red Ike, pointing to the serpent's head. "This head is so fixed that the eyes are looking in the direction of the east and the rising sun on the ball, a sure indication that whoever did the carving had a definite meaning in his task. From the days of the building of the Tower of Babel, certain sun-worshipping rites and ceremonies have been handed down through countless generations. We learn of the practising of such rites at the building of Solomon's temple, one thousand years before the Christian era. Euclid understood them seven hundred years later, whence they passed in garbled forms to the Jews, and from them to the then-obscure ostracized sect of whom Christ is the recognized head to-day.

"Many of the carvings on the stick are similar to those scratched on the sides of the catacombs underneath Rome. And is not Christ today represented as the Sun, the Light of the world, and the serpent next to Him as the power of darkness?"

Red Ike now pressed the serpent's jaws together; the ivory ball divided, and Jean beheld in blood-red lettering—*The Gypsy's Luck*.

Jean started, and he, laughing, remarked: "I stole the bauble from old Abegail's van over seven years ago. It has lain in the bore during the length of that time, and it and the letters are the only things I ever made myself a thief for."

"Then you will retain it no longer; I entreat you not to do so."

"I shall return it to Abegail on one condition—that I be left unmolested by your father and the gypsies. My life is, and has been for some time past, in constant danger. Why, I cannot say, except that they are in fear I shall wed Jael."

Jean bent her head in thought for a moment, and then: "You wish to see Jael? The moon's at full. She will be by her mother's grave at midnight."

"I shall be there, Jean." And then he replaced the carved stick in the bore.

Three hours later, Red Ike stepped into the Twa Dogs Inn at Brigham, Keswick. Simon Reed was already there, but pretended not to recognize the smartly-dressed, clean-shaven stranger that entered the room.

The landlord, with an eye to business, greeted him affably. Red Ike signed to Simon, and after a few minutes they left the inn separately. Crossing Calvert bridge together at a quick pace, they were soon at the road ends that branch to the right over Brundholme, and to the left down Little Crosthwaite. And now Red Ike handed Simon a letter, instructing him to receive from the game-dealer payment of money due. Then parting, they entered Keswick by separate ways. When they met again at the road ends within an hour, Simon had the money.

"I think we had better not return home together, Simon."

"Why?"

"Because," continued Red Ike, "I have met with trouble several times on the moorland, and anyone meeting you alone will not molest you. I shall go by the mountain road through Brundholme woods. Besides, I wish to call at Mirkholme."

And shaking hands they parted.

The moon was now halfway up the sky. By midnight it would be at the zenith. In the deep gorge below Latrigg Fell, the noisy Greta, tumbling white in the moonshine, would have charmed a less observant man than Red Ike. To him the poetical grandeur of the scene appealed with irresistible magic, and again and again he paused as if to draw its essence into his innermost soul. Around him stood the mighty bulks of England's mountain monarchs like huge stark shadows, at whose bases he knew lay crystal lakes amidst the fairest valleys that the plastic hand of nature has moulded into beauty.

When he came to the rude stone bridge that spans the brawling Lonscale beck, he sat upon the coping-stones, and looking at his watch, found it was still an hour from midnight. He debated whether he should go by the gypsies' camp, or direct to the grave of Jael's mother.

He decided on the former course, and then instantly ascended the steep narrow highway called Haglonning towards Mirkholme. And now a strange doubt began to take possession of him. How if Jael should refuse to wed him? He had not thought of that before. Might she not have scruples of her own about linking her fate with his?

True there was the child, and a longing to take it in his arms, and gaze into its eyes, and listen to its speech, surged through him.

Quickening his pace without thinking of doing so, in a short time he beheld the gypsies' camp fire in the distance. He proceeded more cautiously until he was within a few yards of the van. Then he sat upon his haunches. Abegail was standing by the fire. The child was lying huddled upon the ground with its head resting on Prodigal's belly. Jael was not to be seen. Ben came from the van, and demanded of Abegail whither Jael had gone.

"Thou must find out that for thyself," replied the sibyl. "Perhaps she is courting with Red Ike. How can I tell? Thou makest no furtherance with her, and if she takes a notion to stray, that's thy lookout, not mine." And the old witch chuckled sardonically.

"You she-devil," snarled Ben, "you profess to have rare knowledge on some occasions when it suits your purpose; if I thought you were trifling with me, I'd knife the three of you."

Abegail, rolling her eyes and pointing at him with a skinny hand, cried: "Attempt to do so, and I'll blast thy sight where thou stand'st."

Ben for the first time in his life mocked the threat, and broke into a hoarse laugh. The worm had turned at last, and with an oath he punched Prodigal in the back, and seizing the child began to belabour it unmercifully, roaring, "Bastard! Bastard! Bastard!"

In a moment he was gripped by the throat, and but for Abegail's interference the wretch would never have seen another morn. As it was, he felt himself forced to his knees, and finally lifted bodily and thrown headlong onto the fire. Abegail pulled him from the flames, whilst Red Ike roared: "Beware that anyone of you lay a hand on the child again. I shall ever be near when least expected. Should such a thing happen again, I'll finish you both." And turning away, he left the petrified pair gazing after his retreating figure with terror in their souls, and a vague misgiving that Red Ike had his strong hand on the helm of their lives, and could steer them to destruction if they opposed his will.

A mile from the gypsies' camp, with the head facing the north, is the grave of Jael's mother. On several occasions Red Ike had wondered why old Abegail had sworn by the North Pole and the eyes of the Pyramids. And now, standing by the grave, he realized that the oath was a relic of the belief in astrology which was held by the ancient Egyptians to be a greater science than astronomy, centuries before Copernicus gave the death-blow to it by declaring the earth to be one of the planets.

The proof that the Pyramids were not built for sun-worship is that the eye of each looks due north, whence the sun never shines, whereas all Christian churches and Freemasons' halls and such-like buildings, whose rites and ceremonies are rooted in sun-worship, are situated due east and west. "Where stands your master?" "In the East." "Where stand your wardens?" "In the West." And are not the Baal-fires lighted even to this day in Northern Ireland and in Scotland? Further, St. John's Day being midsummer, high festival was held on that day by the Druids, who were sun-worshippers. It has also yet a symbolic meaning to Freemasons.

Red Ike, leaning over the fence by the mound of a lonely pariah whose grave was dug and whose body was lowered into its shallow trench without priest or prayer, wondered if there would be a hereafter, and, if so, would her soul have stood in more jeopardy before the great "I AM," than the thousands of blasphemous dignitaries of established religion who, whilst here, lived like princes, and fawned on the tyrants that robbed and crushed the poor, aye, and even in the name of Christ slew each other by fire and sword because they could not agree on the interpretation of the mild, gracious, and beautiful doctrine inculcated in the simple phrasing of the Sermon on the Mount.

And would it matter, he thought, if death were the end of all conscious life? Better, it seemed to him, a million times that separate individuality should perish utterly than that one soul should suffer the pangs of eternal damnation. For his part, he had no faith in the notion of hell-fire. This, he thought, could have been avoided by a beneficent all-powerful and all-knowing God. Besides, he thought, the uselessness of roasting men forever over things that are past and cannot be undone is to mock love and pity and charity with a vindictive vengeance unworthy of a demon.

And Red Ike, musing thus, heeded not the full moon above, shining in the yew-tree that shadowed the lonely grave—the tree which John Lynd had planted over the only creature be ever loved on earth, but who, owing to a false pride, he had not had the moral courage to stand and justify before the world as his wife, and so save himself and others from future shame and misery.

Unconsciously, Red Ike uttered Jael's name aloud.

"Well?" she questioned, and the tone of her voice was as soft as a silver bell.

Not knowing she was by his side, he turned abruptly, and would have clasped her in his arms, but motioning him off, she stood with a hand raised above her head, and cried: "What would Red Ike have with me, that he comes to disturb the vigil I keep by my mother's grave when the moon's at full? Thou art the first soul that hast ventured hither at midnight for twenty years. Even John Lynd shuns this haunted spot."

"That's a lie. I, John Lynd, am here." And his dark figure strode forward, and stood between the twain.

Jael uttered a startled cry, and thrusting him aside leapt before Red Ike, as if to shield his body.

"Stand back, John Lynd, and let no harm befall anyone near this place."

"All spots are the same to me," he ejaculated. "I would as lief three were buried here as one, and the sooner the better. Dead folks tell no tales."

"Why then did you not kill me years ago?" she questioned.

"Because I was a fool. Stand aside until I first finish with the brute behind you." And he laughed in such a cold-blooded manner that Jael quaked with horror.

Red Ike removed her gently from before him, and holding his arms aloft said with the utmost composure: "Shoot, you unnatural devil."

The suddenness of the situation took Lynd off his guard, and that moment his chance was lost. The gun was wrenched from his grasp, and the position reversed. But he was never a man to be daunted. Brute courage was the greatest trait in his character, and he exclaimed: "You will not always get the upper hand of me, Red Ike. The next time we cross each other I shall shoot at sight, so would you save your skin, your chance is now,"

And folding his arms, and with his back to the fence of Jael's mother's grave, he stood defiant.

"Pshaw," cried Red Ike, "I wish you no harm, John Lynd, and have never done so. I shall see that your gun is returned to The Bents, and if I am left in peace, I shall keep the peace."

"You keep the peace, you murderer, blackguard, and poacher! You should have been hanged years ago."

"Yet, John Lynd, if you shoot me, you will be as I am. And have I not been with you poaching in my early youth, aye, many times? You are the man from whom I learned the craft. Who knows the game better than you?"

During this conversation Jael had crept behind Lynd and standing upon her mother's grave threw her arms about him, and cried: "Get out of the way, Red Ike. He dare not harm me. I shall hold him until you are from sight."

And so, to save further trouble, Red Ike ran breakneck into the darkness of the moor.

When Jael released Lynd, he turned and faced her, and the moonlight shone full upon his face, and horrified and terror stricken, she crouched to the earth and held out her hands to ward him from her.

"My God!" she shrieked, "I thought you were John Lynd."

"So I am, or the scarred carcase of what's left of him," he rejoined bitterly. "And yet, Jael, you hinder me from getting even with the man whom I hold partly responsible for my appearance; and still I am…"—He was about to add, "your father," but checked himself, and turned the thought—"…an unsightly monster condemned to walk the world by night." And with a howl of rage he dashed off in the direction Red Ike had taken.

All night he prowled the moorland, circling it again and again from Sandyflatts, across the Stepping Stones, and by Mirkholme and the dale of the fall of rock.

Thrice he lay in wait by the cattle pool, in the hope that Red Ike would pass that way, until at last, wearied out, he was about to return home, when the figure of a woman flitted by him in the waning moonlight. With an oath he sprang after it. The woman turned and faced him. She was Jael. Seizing her roughly by the shoulder, he demanded where she had been.

"Star-gazing," she replied.

"With whom, you infernal bitch?"

"With Red Ike, John Lynd." And holding her left hand before his face, so that he could see the rings upon it, "I have married him."

"Hell and damnation! Are you mad?" he yelled.

"I was never more sane in my life."

"Under English law, for a marriage to be binding, it must be legally sanctioned."

"I am a gypsy. My word is my bond. A fig for your laws. You yourself have broken them at your will with impunity. Cared you for the law when you married Jean's mother, and cast mine off? A kind, considerate father I've had! Red Ike cannot be less so as a husband. Besides, he is my child's sire."

The exultant ring in Jael's voice drove John Lynd to the verge of lunacy, and grasping her throat, he shouted: "I'll throttle you for that."

A gleam of bright steel flashed in the moonlight, as Jael struck her dagger through his wrist.

"Come near me again, and I'll drive it to your heart. You have never shown compunction for me. Why should I for you? You renounced all guardianship over me, and if I choose to live with Red Ike, married or unmarried, 'tis solely my own affair. Now go."

"Jael, Jael!" he cried, and staggered and fell forward, limp and insensible.

Red Ike rose from the shadow of the whins where he was lying a silent watcher of the scene, and lifting a hand of the fallen man, felt his pulse.

"My God! He is bleeding to death."

Jael, hastily unwrapping a silk scarf from her neck, bandaged the wound, and together they sat for some minutes waiting for a sign of returning consciousness.

"I'm afraid I'll have to bear him to The Bents, Jael. He'll not come round without help. You take the gun." And Red Ike, shouldering his mortal enemy, strode homewards with him.

The rim of the moon was just visible through Winlatter Pass when Red Ike knocked at the door of The Bents. Jael did not approach the house with him. Jean's mother answered the call, and started back at the appearance of a stranger bearing the body of her husband, but being accustomed of late to Lynd's wayward mode of life, she quickly recovered her self-possession, and throwing open the sitting-room door, motioned towards a couch, and seizing a spirit-decanter poured its reviving contents between his lips. A low moan escaped him, his breast heaved, and sitting bolt upright he gazed around exclaiming: "Jael, Jael, my Jael!" and then fainted away again.

"You had better call the servants, Mrs. Lynd, and send for a doctor."

"I dare not do that," was the reply. "I myself shall nurse him to life or to death. But who are you, sir, and what has occurred to bring my husband to this position?"

"I am not at liberty to say, madam."

"But, sir, surely I ought to be told?"

"If your husband recovers, ask him. If he dies, I shall explain to you. Further than this, at present I shall say nothing." And Red Ike, leaning his ear to John Lynd's heart, continued: "He will be all right within a short while. I shall now depart."

When Jael returned to the camp, the first gleam of dawn was shooting its faint ray through the window of the gypsy's van. The fire on which Red Ike had thrown Ben Faa during the night was smouldering under the beul-pan that hung over it. Abegail was on the look-out for Jael, but did not see her until she ascended the steps and was about to enter the van. Ben and Prodigal were lying asleep in a tent a few yards away.

"Hist," said the old witch, "there was the devil to pay here last night."

"I know all about it, and had I been here when Ben thrashed the child..."—and Jael made a significant movement with her dagger—"...I should have taught him a lesson."

Abegail snittered, and then a dark shadow, evil as hell, settled upon her face: "Red Ike has the carved stick, but who has the letters, Jael? Thy mother's marriage-certificate is amongst them. She was lawfully wedded, not according to the gypsies' rites, but in an English church. Where hast thou been wedded? I see the sign upon thy finger." And leaping from her couch, she clutched Jael by the shoulder, and glared into her eyes.

"That concerns me alone, Abegail," was the quick retort.

"I'll see whether it does or not. Ben! Ben! Come hither!"

The piercing pitch of the sibyl's voice charged with the venom of a baulked woman, roused Ben and Prodigal, and both rushed together to the van.

A mocking smile curled about Jael's mouth, and shaking Abegail from her, she snatched a bludgeon from a table and cried: "Why have you called this creature from bed? Who is he? In what relation does he stand to you? Answer me. I have been fooled long enough!"

"Jael, thou art not yet wedded. Ben Faa has to be thy husband. I'll see to that."

"Here I am then, Abegail, let him come and take me if he can. You forget that John Lynd is my father. Could you ever mould him to your will? In spite of the boundless love he had for my mother, his was still the master-hand. And I warn you I am like him in that respect, though a woman. Why, I'd rather lie with Prodigal the lurcher than with Ben Faa. Now let him come and take me!"

Abegail had shrunk back to her couch. Ben had not dared to step into the van. The old hag's toothless jaws were working as though she had the palsy, and saliva like foam was running to her chin. Her eyes set in their sockets were staring vacantly at Jael. Her years of cunning and plotting had come to naught. Like thousands of other foolish mortals, she had striven for the world's riches, and found she was grasping a handful of worthless dust.

CHAPTER XX

THE road to the city of destruction is as straight as the way to Paradise. The land on both sides is bright with poppies, fragrant and full of charm. In the glow of youth, when the blood runs hot and life is all in the future, who can blame an erring soul that unwittingly wanders down that pleasant road, and, finding it sweet, for the time being lingers upon it?

Nell Glen, when she hired her service to Joe Gream and Peg Shore, knew little about either of them. She had heard idle rumours concerning their connection, but had given no serious thought to such. Her unsophisticated mind was bent only on selling her honest labour for the high wages she was offered. She was to learn very shortly to her honour's cost the nature of the wretches for whom she was going to work. A few weeks after she entered on her duties at The Forge, Jael was sitting in the grey light of dawn on the steps of the van, when she saw a woman crossing the moor towards Mirkholme. Her free carriage and jaunty air bespoke her a person of consequence in her own esteem. She was fashionably dressed. Jael watched with curiosity the approaching figure, and shading her eyes with her hand, muttered: "Yonder comes Peg Shore." Casting a glance of contempt towards Ben Faa, who was lying wrapped in a coarse rug beneath the van, Jael arose and went to meet Peg. To the most casual observer as the women faced each other, it was evident they were antagonistic.

"Well," queried Jael, "what ill wind blows the devil's agent over the moorland at such an early hour of the day? Has she come to have her fortune told again? This will be thrice in a month. Does she need another sugared story to please her fancy?"

"What does it matter to Jael Boswell?" retorted Peg.

"Only this," was the reply, "that I have read your horoscope once for all. Your nativity was cast under the baleful planet Jupiter when it was about to cross the cusp of the eighth house of the Zodiac. Joe Gream will never wed you. He has already taken a rival to you in his arms. At this moment they are locked to each other's breast."

"Jael Boswell, you are an infamous liar," cried Peg.

"Then to prove what I say, return to The Forge, inspect Joe Gream's bedroom. It has not been slept in. Last night he lay with Nell Glen."

With a smothered superstitious cry, Peg turned upon her heels and retraced her steps over the moorland. Arriving at The Forge, and fearless of consequences, she rushed into the house and upstairs to the bedroom in question. It was empty, and the next minute she burst upon Nell and Joe Gream situated as Jael had foretold. A fearful scene ensued. Leaping from the bed in a half-drunken condition, the filthy sot endeavoured to push Peg through the door, but underestimated his opponent. With the viciousness of a tigress, and a cry like one, she flew upon his body, and hurled him against a wash-stand that smashed into splinters beneath the force of his weight. Then, seizing Nell by the hair, she dragged her onto the floor, and jumped upon her. Joe Gream, snatching a broken leg of the wash-stand, aimed a blow at Peg, but missed her and hit Nell, felling her as still as a stone. Swaying with the miscarriage of his blow, he stumbled over Nell's prostrate form. This gave Peg her chance, and raising a chair aloft she struck and laid her seducer insensible beside her rival.

Somewhat sobered by the effects of her violence, Peg turned the half-nude figures onto their backs, went for a pail of water, and threw it over them, and then sat down to await their return to con-sciousness.

Nell was the first to revive, but when her half-dazed eyes met the mocking glance of Peg's, she fainted away again.

At that moment Joe moaned, rolled over onto his side, and then sat up; and passing his hand over his forehead, gazed around: "What's to do, Peg?" She neither answered nor moved. "What the devil are you in the sulks for, Peg?"

"Look on the woman lying beside you, Joe."

"Lord! I had forgot," he replied, rising to his feet. "And a sweet morsel she was. No more old women like you, Peg, for me after this. I remember the fracas you kicked up a while ago. By God, you've a hell of a temper, but this sort of thing won't do. I'll be boss here, and have whom I choose about me henceforth."

"And where have I got to be, Joe?" she questioned tauntingly.

"Out of this," he blurted with brutal candour.

"What," she hissed, "does Joe Gream speak thus to me? Me, whom he debauched in the sight of my promised husband? I dare you to cast me off."

Her words were wasted on a callous scoundrel. With a loud guf-faw, heedless of Peg, he lifted Nell from the floor, saying: "Come, my sweet," and placed her upon the bed, chafed her hand and chor-tled words of endearment, such as she had heard him use to herself a thousand times.

This was almost more than Peg could bear, and she rose to leave the room, while Nell moaned with returning life: "Oh Dick, Dick, Dick!"

As if hell itself had opened at her feet, Peg started and realized the enormity of the deed of which she was guilty in using this frail unsuspecting girl as a foil against Red Ike and his associates. And she saw, too, that what she had done had recoiled upon herself with tenfold force. Nell had supplanted her in the volatile and lustful heart of Joe Gream. Cursing her lack of foresight, and with a tormented soul, she decided that she would leave The Forge. And yet, though she longed, she could not bring herself to do so, but stood with eyes riveted upon the maudlin dotard fondling the inanimate form of Nell. At last she could stand the sight no longer, and with a swift revulsion of feeling, she fell upon him, seized him by the hair, and dragged him backwards to the floor. His head struck a brass kerb before the fireplace, and again he was rendered unconscious.

Letting him lie, Peg now busied herself to restore Nell. Had she foreseen the immediate result of her endeavour, she would have fled from the house as from a plague. When Nell opened her eyes, the soul was fled from them.

A loud, hysterical, hollow laugh sent a shiver along Peg's spinal chord, and shrinking back from the bed, she tumbled over the body of Joe. A woman of less nerve than she would have been daunted, but Peg gathered herself together, and the thought of danger steadied her up. Cautiously approaching the bed again, she spoke gently, but all manner of speech was alike to Nell, who neither heard nor saw aught but the phantasms of her clouded brain, and these were the flickerings of love-scenes with Dick Stagg. Now she seemed in the wildest delight, and, Ophelia-like, sang sweet snatches of popular songs old and new that had taken her fancy, because in happy hours she had associated them with river and fell, and entwined and blended their truthfulness and poetry with cherished moments and incidents in her own life. Anon, pausing and inclining her ear as if listening to the sound of departing footsteps, she whispered, "He is going, but will come again tomorrow night." Then a smile, radiant with vague happiness, lighted her face, to pass away again into a meaningless stare. And then she stood upon the bed, and gazing at the blank wall, arranged her disordered hair as though she were looking into a mirror; and her face flushed, pink as a wild rose on a June morning, and she cried: "'Tis my wedding day." And turning an imaginary ring upon the third finger of her left hand, she kissed it again and again. Peg Shore, rooted to the floor, watched her. Suddenly Nell, flinging her arm above her head, shrieked: "No, no, Dick! Do not stamp my ring into the flames!" and leaping from the bed, she ran round and round the room frantically gesticulating until she was exhausted. Then, crouching into a corner in an attitude of hopeless despair, she gnawed her fingernails until the blood trickled from them.

"My God! What am I to do now?" thought Peg. And looking round, she saw Joe Gream sitting with his arms folded round his knees and gazing on Nell. This roused Peg to action, and, shaking him by the shoulders, she growled: "Fool, don't you see the girl's gone mad! There's no time to be lost, come let us dress her, and put the house shipshape, and send for the police. It's your only chance to save your skin. Delay will mean the jail for you."

"Or for you, Peg."

"Nay, the damning evidence will go against the man. I could not rape her."

"Who can prove that I did, Peg?"

"I can, and on one condition I'll hold my tongue."

"And that, Peg?"

"Is that you marry me."

"Never, Peg. I'll see you in perdition first."

"Very well. I'll go for the police now."

"Hold, the winning card's in your hand!"

"Give me a written promise of marriage."

"All right, get me pen, ink, and paper."

And these two friends, in the presence of an insane helpless woman, bartered her honour there and then in an evil compact, while the woman crouched in the corner munching at her fingernails. The sun rose high over the Hill of Devils, and a slant ray passed through the window and between the two plotters, and touched the mad woman's head with light, and, lo, an aureole like to that which circles the mother of God gathered round her head and invested it with glory.

Now, Nell Glen's condition was but temporary, and she submitted passively to all that was done with her. Luckily, there were no bruises upon her body, and when Peg led her into another room, she lay down and fell into a sound sleep, and was still slumbering at noon when the police arrived to take charge of her. Assembled in the sitting-room prior to going upstairs, each holding a glass of spirits, the police beheld Nell walk in amongst them, and without glancing at anyone else, she touched Joe upon the shoulder, saying: "I wish to speak with you in private. Turn all these other folks from the house. What are the officers here for, Mr. Gream?"

"To take charge of you, Miss Glen."

"Of me, and why?" she questioned.

Peg Shore stole from the room and fled to the moorland, and as she passed the cattle pool where the three runnels meet, a mocking eldritch laugh from behind the clump of whin-bushes, from amongst which John Lynd had shot at Red Ike and Dick Stagg on a memorable night, caused her to quicken her pace, and old Abegail watched her fleeing as though from the wrath to come.

Joe dismissed the police, and Nell and he stood facing each other alone.

The low cunning of the mean soul of the man showed him in his true light as he held out his open arms invitingly: "You are not vexed with me, Nell? I would do you no harm, but, situated as we were, you saw I could not avoid the scene that passed this morning. I shall make amends to you at once, and shall leave The Forge for the winter months. Will you accompany me? In due course I shall marry you, and all will be well."

The insinuating tone of this address, and the position in which she was placed, overruled Nell's judgment.

Dick Stagg's image rose before her, but the thought of him in prison was repugnant to her pride, and the glamour of the wealth of the sot to whose embrace she had submitted, combined with the sexual desire he had intensified within her, made the woman in her as potter's clay in his hands.

Peg Shore returned to The Forge on the following day, and the house was closed. She prowled around it like a forsaken dog, whose master has abandoned it to the merciless chance of finding a new protector. A fierce hate flamed up within her heart, and she cursed the name of Joe Gream, and his body, and his soul.

She swore to pursue him, no matter whither he had flown with Nell. The pride that sustains a good woman in purity and in glory was something unknown to Peg. She had been flung from her mole-hill of a false position, and could but wallow in the mire in which she found herself, and hope for future vengeance.

CHAPTER XXI

PRINCE'S STREET, Edinburgh, was ablaze with light when Gream and Nell ascended the gangway from the railway station. Nell had never before been beyond the towns that stand on the borders of her native moorland, and the brilliant sight of the modern Athens filled her with wonder and delight.

The flaring streets and gardens, the huge crowds of folks, the busy stream of vehicles, the thoroughfares through which they thronged, seemed endless. Long vistas of pleasure opened to Nell's imagination, with no clouds lowering and dark to warn her of the perilous path she had begun to tread. She was a woman of great possibilities, and under favourable circumstances would early have developed talents of an order capable of fitting her to adorn a higher station of life than that into which she had been born. An omnivorous reader, she had stored her mind with legend and romance of the Borderland, and Scott's novels being her favourites, particularly *The Heart of Midlothian*, her whole nature was stirred to its depths amidst the scenes of that story; and during the next few weeks she revelled in the glamour of the Northern Wizard. The wonder was that, being in love with Dick Stagg, she did not sicken of the sottish wretch who now possessed her body.

He had no interest in aught but the indulgence of his physical appetites, and of such pleasures as helped their excitement. The architectural beauty of Holyrood Chapel, the strong massive buildings of Cannongate, the graves of Burns' Clarinda and the unfortunate poet Ferguson in Cannongate churchyard, the rugged strength and commanding position of the castle frowning from its lofty height, the beautiful monuments in the open squares, the paintings and works of art in museums and churches, made no impression on the dull soul of Joe Gream. He refused to accompany her on visits of sight-seeing. He would only go to plays and dances and other places of amusement. By degrees she began to wander by herself, and Calton Hill and Arthur's Seat became her favourite walks. In one of these she came face to face with Peg, who, with a cold cynical smile of triumph and a mock greeting, held out her hand saying: "Who would have thought to meet you here, Miss Glen."

At that moment Nell became a full woman, alert, watchful and distrustful. Hitherto she had been largely a creature of impulse. Her first lapse with Joe Gream had not been of her seeking. He had taken advantage of a position in his own house which he ought to have honoured, and which Peg should have foreseen, had her desire to injure Red Ike not blinded her to its possibility.

"You don't seem very glad to see me, Nell. Are you afraid I have come to steal your new lover? He's a jolly dog, isn't he? Far jollier than Dick Stagg. I'm sorry the poor jail-bird never thought of accommodating you before the unfortunate event in the Royal George at Penrith. When Dick is free again, do you think he'll care to pick up one of Joe Gream's old cast-off shoes? He thought too well of Nell Glen to soil her himself; what he'll think now I cannot guess."

Nell answered her in a quieter voice, but with equal spirit.

"Peg Shore, you and I will very likely make a pair of Joe Gream's old cast-off shoes unless I chance to fit the right foot. You at present have belonged to the left one. Whether our positions will ever be reversed again remains to be tested. If you have come to Edinburgh to prove the case, well and good. If I choose to fight you, I can win; but whatever now happens I would not degrade Dick Stagg by allowing him to take me within his arms. There is one thing neither you nor Joe can destroy, and that is my love for Dick."

"Then why the devil have you taken up with Joe?"

"I did not take up with him, he took up with me, and you helped to bring me to the pass with which you taunt me now. Have you no sense of womanliness left within you? I did not understand the meaning of what I did until after I fell within the scope of your machinations. And now what am I? A creature like you, Peg Shore. A soiled woman than whom, even in her own eyes, there is nothing so utterly valueless. I have heard a story that Red Ike, the poacher, was once in love with you. Can you tell me why the match was broken off?"

"Because I chose to break it."

"You know, Peg, that's a lie. I believe it was the same with you that it is with me and Dick now. Joe Gream's ruined us both."

Peg had no answer to that, but as Nell's mind went back to the happy innocent days of a love that seemed lost to her for ever, it seemed to the watching woman that the light of insanity began to flicker in her eyes again, and she turned and fled in terror from the woman she had deceived and ruined.

When Nell returned to their rooms at the Cockburn Hotel, Joe was sitting dressed and waiting for her company to the theatre. Seeing she was perturbed, he was about to question her when Nell forestalled him.

"I met Peg on Arthur's Seat an hour ago."

"The hell you did! Then we'll leave here tonight."

"Whither shall we go?" Nell queried.

"Anywhere. London if you choose, so long as we get clear of the bitch."

"Why?" questioned Nell. "Is there need that we should fly from before the face of anyone? What is Peg to us? I do not fear her. Why do you, Joe?"

A look of blank astonishment came upon the coward's paltry face, and he stood gaping at Nell like an idiot.

"What should we do then? I—I can't think."

"We can marry tomorrow," was the instant reply.

"No, no. At least not here. Anywhere but here."

"Are you already secretly married to Peg, Joe?"

"Heavens, what the devil has put that into your head? I could not manage her in single harness. Damn the double!"

"Is that what you'll tell me at last? If so, I need not go to London to be abandoned. Go yourself, and leave me here."

And the light of insanity again flared up in her eyes.

Joe saw the danger of driving the woman before him to an extremity, and in terror he ejaculated: "I'll do anything you wish, Nell."

"Then we'll leave here at once."

Hastily packing their trunks, and settling accounts, they took the Flying Scotsman for London. But in the same express Peg Shore journeyed thither. Night and day she followed their track like a bloodhound, but they shook her off at last in the London crowds, and to support herself, having no other means of doing so, she stooped to the unholy traffic of frequenting public places of amusement and selling herself to the highest bidder. Her youth and good looks, combined with a light vivacity born of reckless abandonment, procured her admirers.

Meanwhile, Nell was yet unmarried. Whenever she mentioned the subject, Gream avoided controversy by giving vague promises, and then buying her costly presents. She was not blind to his prevarication, and tried to content herself by thinking that at least he was kind, but she saw that he had no real love for her, and blamed herself that she could not create it in him.

She did not see the uselessness and hopelessness of trying to make a man out of a toad.

Peg Shore, hanging on to the skirts of chance with the wild hope of meeting Joe, came across him at last in the drinking bar of the Leicester Lounge. He was in a half-maudlin condition, when, edging up to him, Peg whispered over his shoulder, "Joe." He started, and turning, beheld Peg smiling triumphant by his side. His first inclination was to leave the room, but as she had often won him before by exerting persuasive art, so she cajoled him now, and together they passed forth into the London streets, and hailing a cab drove to Peg's mean lodgings. For three days he revelled in drink and mire. On the fourth he returned to Nell, and thenceforward, during another month, he kept up a continual intercourse with the two women. At length the consequences of his evil living became apparent to him and Nell, and recriminations on either side began that ended in a state of rupture between them.

And now the utter worthlessness of the man showed itself in the worst possible light. Assuming an indifference to the trouble, he endeavoured to persuade Nell that all would be right with them in the course of a week, and that he would marry her. Half believing him, she became more pacified, and then they set out together for the opera. On the way thither he paid her great attention, and after conducting her to a box, excused himself for a moment, but did not again return. Hurrying back to their hotel, he hastily packed his trunk, paid their account, and gathering all Nell's jewellery together, departed, leaving her to the charity of the wide world without a penny.

He was about to take a taxi for St. Pancras Station, when Peg accosted him on the step, but roughly shaking her off with an oath, telling her she would find her other sister of the night at Covent Garden, he ordered the driver to proceed to his destination.

With a satisfied heart, he left the express at York, and the cold-blooded scoundrel hugged himself at the thought of being free of all encumbrance once more.

Nell sat out the first act of the opera, and then, becoming alarmed at Joe's continued absence, retired at the interval, and, hiring a cab, hurried to the hotel.

As she stepped into the brilliantly-lighted thoroughfare at the end of her journey, Peg Shore faced her.

"You need not stare at me so high and mighty, Nell Glen. Joe has fled and left us both."

Without yet fully realizing her position, and ignoring Peg, Nell hastened onwards, fear tearing at her heart, and a maniacal light in her eyes. On entering their room and examining it, the hideous meanness of the man to whom she had given her body appalled her. Not only her trinkets, but every article of dress, necessary and unnecessary, were gone, and with a wild cry, she rushed from the hotel, and sped demented through the crowded London streets towards the Thames Embankment.

Peg Shore, sure of the position, had waited outside hoping things would thus turn out, and chuckling with devilish glee, she followed in Nell's wake.

What object Peg had in following Nell she herself could not have explained. That she might turn upon and rend her never entered Peg's mind, as she did not realize Nell was stark mad.

However, as Nell ran, and as if the whirling frenzy of her brain was acting on a rational impulse, she began to divest herself of the gewgaws and finery that Joe Gream's money had bought, and one after the other flung them from her, until at last she was half nude. And still she fled, and men and women paused to stare as she passed, wondering at the strange sight; strange even in London where 'tis said there is nothing new to be seen. And now freak took possession of her. Leaping to the plinth of Needle and assuming a pose, like to the prima donna in

RED IKE, BY J. M. DENWOOD & S. FOWLER WRIGHT *

she had lately seen, she began to sing that wild Border ballad called *Carlisle Yatts*. The weird music of the air blended with the mad spirit of the singer, and as it floated through the night, and over the shimmering waters of the rolling Thames, the gathering crowd that had followed the wild, fleeing woman stood bewitched, and listened until the last word and the last note of the beautiful but woeful song fell from her lips. And then Peg, moved at last to pity for the girl she had so fearfully wronged, laid a hand upon her arm, and said: "Won't you come with me, Nell?"

And passive as a child, she allowed herself to be led to the Bedlam, which is preferable to the slavery of London's flaring streets, while Peg, swearing that she would put her past life forever behind her, returned to her lodgings at Soho, gathered her small stock of things into a bundle, and by midnight was bound for the North at express speed.

She arrived at York, where she knew that Joe must change his train, and would be likely to stay, as the grey dawn was breaking over the eastern wolds, and stepped from the train to the station platform almost penniless, hungry, weary, and diseased.

Passing by the Tudor Hotel, by chance she glanced at one of the upper stories and beheld the evil but amazed face of the man she was seeking. He had thrown up the lower window-sash, and leaning over it, was holding a half-smoked cigarette. The sight of Peg rooted him to the spot. With a wave of her hand, she crossed to the opposite side of the street, and then stood with her gaze fixed upon him.

It now seemed to the moral coward as if by a weird instinct she could divine his movements and track him no matter whither he went; a vague numb dread of her half paralysed his senses, and his body trembled like a single reed, standing frozen and lorn by a moorland tarn.

Peg waved again to him, and he, gliding unsteadily from his room, down the stairs, and from the hotel, dithered to where she stood.

"You brute!" she exclaimed. "May the power of hell mete out to you the full measure of punishment you deserve."

"Why have you followed me hither, Peg?" he chattered.

"Why did you flee from London, and leave Nell? She went stark mad, and is now in Bedlam."

A new light came into the monster's eyes, and he said: "Is that true, Peg?"

For some moments she did not answer, but gazed curiously upon him.

"Is the creature standing before me human?" Peg thought. Yet stifling her feeling she replied: "'Tis a thousand chances to one you ever meet her again. She's as good as dead to the world."

"By heavens! That's great news, Peg. Come and we'll have a tot together."

Loathing him though she did, she crept up to his side; the old craving for stimulants so suddenly appealed to her in her weakened condition, that for the moment she was irresponsible for the action, and, he linking his arm in hers, they sallied along the street in search of a drinking-bar.

"Whither were you bound when you caught sight of me, Peg?"

"Nowhere," she replied. "I was going to hang about until the forenoon, and then ask at the hotel for you."

This deliberate lie again startled the sot, and she felt him shiver, and there and then she resolved to use for her advantage her new lease of power over him.

Meanwhile, as on a former occasion, Nell's lapse into insanity was banished by a sound sleep, and had she been in good bodily health, all would have been well with her in a few days. The doctors seeing this, and attributing her madness to her physical condition, had her removed to hospital, where under medical treatment she made rapid recovery. Her vigorous vitality soon became evident, and on the morning pending her discharge as fit, she was offered a position as a maid-servant in the official quarters of the institution, and accepted it.

Now, had Nell been an ordinary woman, she might have ended her days as a servant within asylum walls, but what the fates will must come to pass. By a strange coincidence, a few weeks later, some friends of the doctors called and were asked to stay to dinner, and the conversation turning upon the new opera which was now running, one of the guests remarked that he heard a young woman stark mad sing from the plinth of Cleopatra's Needle, and that if she were sane she would make one of the finest artists of the day. Nell at the moment was serving at the table, and several pairs of eyes were at once turned upon her with evident curiosity. Rising to the occasion with splendid nerve and tact, she said: "Gentlemen, I'm sorry to be the occasion of any comment amongst you. My infirmity I could not help, and I'm sure the gentleman who made the remark did not again recognize me."

"Bravely spoken, young woman; I did not again know you, and I tender my apology. Furthermore, if you would care to adopt the profession of a singer, I have a vacancy at the present moment, a small part, but still an opening for which I can train you. Will you accept it?"

Seeing Nell hesitate, he continued: "To prove that I am right in my surmise, will you sing *Carlisle Yatts* for the company present, and allow them to decide for you?"

Nell complied with the request.

'Twas a strange place for an artist to begin her career in, but this time the ears of many of the wild inmates of that living hell were strained to catch, not the frenzied outpourings of one of their crazy fellows, but Nell's gentle compassionate voice of wonderful compass and sweetness. It was that of a forlorn spirit but lately emerged from the most terrible ordeal that a mortal soul can pass through. And Bedlam became hushed with the marvel, until the finish of the weird ballad that is infused with such tragic power.

A generous burst of applause followed her effort, and she was pressed by the small critical audience to allow herself to be trained as a singer. With this proposal she agreed.

During the year that followed, her progress was a surprise to her teachers. Previously to this she had had some lessons in music, and now with untiring application, coupled with an excellent memory, and no ordinary natural powers of an actress and elocutionist, she soon mastered the scores and songs of several operas in the company's repertoire. Then came an unlooked-for opening. One of the principal singers falling ill, she was hurriedly called upon to fill a vacant position, and it was with this ballad that she sang herself into the responsive heart of London.

THE LASS OF BLENCO

What can soothe this great pain in my bosom still dwelling?
Shall I e'er find a balm for a soul ill at ease?
Since time that forms kingdoms brings me not my Ellen;
Is there naught under heaven my pangs can appease?
I oft roam alone by the moorland so dreary
And sigh when I come to the old trysting tree;
The loss of my Ellen has made life so weary
That nothing is left in the wide world for me.
The distant hills shine in the sunset of even,
The heather and bracken look rich in its glow,
But gone is the pleasure to me it has given.
I lost my young Ellen, the Lass of Blenco.

Now sadly I wander,

On Ellen to ponder,
In grief's bitter anguish alone I must go;
The joy of life left me,
When cold death bereft me,
Of beautiful Ellen, the Lass of Blenco.

Her face was as fair as the first flush of morning,
Her innocent smile was the light of my heart;
Oh, why should she pass like a star without warning,
And leave me in gloom that can never depart?
I've seen her trip over the moorland so cheery,
And wait for me there by the old trysting tree;
Alas, never more shall I clasp thee, my dearie
Thy memory is all that is now left to me.
The distant hills shine in the sunset of even,
The heather and bracken look rich in its glow;
But gone is the pleasure to me it has given,
I lost my young Ellen, the Lass of Blenco.

Now sadly I wander,
O'er Ellen to ponder,
In grief's bitter anguish I lonely must go;
The joy of life left me,
When cold death bereft me,
Of beautiful Ellen, the Lass of Blenco.

This sudden rise in Nell's fortune had such a beneficial effect upon her whole nature that the soul of the woman expanded and blossomed, and shed a radiance and sweetness round the orbit of her life. The world of supreme emotional art in which she now moved was reflected by her, and she became a favourite with her associates. And as she advanced rung after rung up the ladder of fame, she became known for an almost reckless generosity towards her necessitous fellow-artists, whom she never failed to relieve. And the dark shadow that lay across her past life caused her to be forbearing with others, and kind and gentle. And deep down in her heart still burned the smouldering fire of her love for Dick, with whom she had broken faith, and did not dare to hope for reconciliation.

Often in the lone watches of the night, perched in her snug apartment on the heights of Blackheath, and gazing from her bedroom window on the broad Thames in the glittering moonlight, she thought of the silvery gems of her native Lakeland, and the happy days she had spent with Dick, boating and fishing, or climbing to gather cranberries and bleaberries on the brant slopes of Helvellyn and Blencathra, and she longed to be there once more.

A cold shiver, icy as death, ran through her body at the thought that never again could she face her former friends. And she swayed backwards from the window, gasping: "My God, what a weak fool I have been!"

Then, losing all sense of time and space, she beheld the phantasy of her late past life glide in sequence before her mind's eye like a horrible nightmare.

But once, suddenly, the scene changed and she was with Dick midst their old haunts on the moorlands, and the clear Glenderamakkin was running goldenly in the distance, and the heather was a sheet of red flame, and white clouds crowned the fells, and the roaring waterfalls mingled their music with the single recurring note of the church bell in the valley below, and peace descended upon her, leaving her calm, radiant, and happy. Retiring to bed, she slept dreamless and untroubled the whole night through, for the first time during months.

On the morrow she pondered on the visions of the previous night, and, being of a sanguine temperament, it pleased her to think that they augured well for her in the future, and she resolved henceforth to take her destiny as it came. Until now she had not dared to go near the Thames Embankment, nor to the hotel where she and Joe Gream stayed, but after breakfast she drove to Cleopatra's Needle and gazed unmoved upon the plinth on which she had stood and sung in her madness. She then journeyed to the hotel, and afterwards to the asylum. The doing of this gave her such a deep satisfaction that she saw the plan she had taken, of facing the worst aspect of any circumstance, was at once a moral victory, and had a stimulating power incalculable in effect upon her mind.

And thus, step by step, she climbed the rough highway back to self-respect. And after all, no matter how we have sinned in the past, the rebuilding of our moral character is perhaps a greater achievement than the keeping of it untarnished within the sheltered environment of smug respectability. There is an old wives' saying: "'Tis an easy castle to hold that is never stormed." And did not Christ say to the woman taken in adultery, "Neither do I condemn thee. Go, and sin no more."

Meanwhile how were things faring with Peg and Joe Gream at York? Not at all badly for the woman. Her old desire to become possessed of him grew stronger day by day, and casting every other consideration to the wind, she insisted that he take her to the hotel with him, and give her money to buy dress and other requirements.

This accomplished, she endeavoured to push him to further extremes, and marry her. But the low cunning of the man never failed him, and growling that all women thought of was making unnecessary trouble, and wishing them all at the devil, he strode about the room fuming with rage.

Peg, fearing she had gone too far, pacified him for the moment, and saw at last that the only way to deal with him was to play his game and beat him at it.

She now began to humour his every whim, and mollified him to such an extent that he was led into extravagances beyond his means, and Peg, taking advantage of him to the utmost, and without scruple, and carefully hoarding her ill-gotten gains, gloated to see him gradually becoming entangled in money difficulties, until at last he was forced to retrench and return home.

By this time, a year of Will Moffatt's term of imprisonment had passed, and within three months, and on Christmas Eve, both he and Dick would be free once more.

Red Ike and Jean were again living in the drift. He took toll of the moorland, and lake, and river, in almost undisturbed liberty. Occasionally he saw by the glimpse of the moon, or under clear starlight, the shadowy forms of men following the same course as himself, but of these he took no heed; even when they chanced to cross each other's path they glided swiftly apart, glad to escape recognition, and to be left in peace to pursue their way.

And Red Ike's toll of the countryside was exceedingly profitable. With wise forethought he stored within the drift sufficient food and articles of necessity to serve Jean and himself until the spring, in case they were snowed up in the drift. And this, in fact, happened. He was glimpsed by night on the moorland no more for many weeks, and by then John Lynd's body was ready to be buried over the grave of Jael's mother.

CHAPTER XXII

NOW Nell Glen's star was rising rapidly to its zenith, and the manager of the opera in which she was appearing, resolved, before the close of the London season, to take the tide of success at the flood, and tour the provinces with a first-class company of artistes.

At this time the power of her matchless voice thrilled, and at times electrified, her audience into unbounded enthusiasm. Her art had the spontaneity that the too highly-trained artist often lacks. She played upon the emotions and the hearts of others by the sheer exquisite force, and richness, and expression of her own highly-strung, intensive, and imaginative personality. Perhaps the taint of insanity with which we have seen her afflicted was a trait of her power; and perhaps a course of very severe voice-training would have destroyed her charm. As it was, when singing she forgot even the impersonal heroine she represented; in fact, the part was herself.

In the course of a week or two of their tour the company was at York. Thence they journeyed to Durham city, and onwards by the east coast to Newcastle-on-Tyne; and the next stage was Edinburgh.

As the express steamed into Prince's Street Station, Nell grew faint and sick with the thought of the manner in which she last left it. During their stay in the city, she could not be induced to leave the hotel, except to perform her duty at the theatre, and much speculation was rife amongst the company at this unexpected attitude.

"Of all the places in the world, this is the one you should be the most delighted to see," they declared. But she remained firm in her resolution, and was glad when the company's stay there was ended. In Aberdeen she again became her old self, and under the stimulus of the reaction of her despondency at Edinburgh, and the passion of a burning love resurging through her, she sang with increased power and charm. Not fully understanding the magical influence she wielded, she yet felt that the indefinable longing that would not let her soul be at peace had some natural affinity with her native moorland and Dick Stagg. And hour by hour, and day by day, her love for both strengthened, and she began to look forward with impatience to the time when the company would journey to Glasgow and thence to Carlisle.

In this city they were appointed to perform during the week preceding Christmas. As Nell came within sight of the Cumbrian fells once more, a strange feeling took possession of her.

Hitherto, her ardent desire had been to behold them; and now she shrank from coming in close contact with the scenes that reminded her of so much former happiness and the beginning of her lapse into sorrow, and evil, and shame. When she stepped through the entrance from the Border city railway station and beheld the jail walls looming before her, in whose grim confines she knew Dick Stagg was yet lodged, she felt as though the ground were trembling beneath her, and an involuntary cry burst from her lips. Gazing upon her as if thunder-stricken a few yards away stood Peg and Joe, whilst within a stone-throw, and in his prison cell, sitting on a low stool, was her lover, teasing oakum, and rejoicing in the thought that the weekend would see him free, and humming to himself, under his breath, one of Red Ike's sweetest love-songs.

SONG

Again I hear the throstle sing
By Bonny Greta's side;
Again the first wild flowers of spring
Bloom sweet in vernal pride;
And high among the beetling rocks,
The shepherds tend their fleecy flocks,
Lest there the prowling mountain fox
The lambkins should destroy.
In greening woods the cushats pair,
The sunlight floods the valleys fair,
A 'witching spell pervades the air,
And fills the heart with joy.

Oh, sweet it is at this glad time
To wander lone and free,
And weave a tender happy rhyme,
My dearest one, to thee.
'Tis love inspires the lark to sing,
As up he goes on quivering wing,
The master-minstrel of the spring,
Whose song we prize the best.
'Tis love, fond love, so pure and bright,
That pub our carking cares to flight,
And fills the whole world with delight,
And makes us truly blest.

Now who can explain the ways of destiny? The old witch Abegail professed to do so, and deluded Nell to break faith with the man to whom she had plighted her troth. Jael forecast Peg's fortune, and with mockery drove her to acts of brutality. But neither sibyl foresaw the dramatic events that were now shortly to take place. The morning before Christmas, Will Moffatt and Dick Stagg were released from jail, and when they stepped forth to freedom, the first thing they beheld on the hoardings was the advertisement of the opera in which Nell Glen was appearing; and in attractive letterpress were abstracts from newspaper notices in eulogy of the new star. Whereupon they both went and booked seats for the evening performance.

'Twas a brilliant starlit Christmas Eve, and Red Ike and Jean were snowed-up in the drift; and from the entrance to it, the sight of the towering fells, clad in their mantle, was a delightful one. To the west, the mighty peak of Scawfell pierced the sky like a lance. To the north lay the huge bulk of Skiddaw. To the northeast towered Blencathra. And to the south stretched the long, broken line of the Helvellyn range. The two prisoners in the drift, fearful if they moved into the outer world that their footprints would betray their retreat to some wandering shepherd, had sat for hours together during the long nights for weeks past, watching the starry constellations march in majestic order over the arch of space. Red Ike had taught Jean how to distinguish the various groups as they rose from the east into view; and how the fixed stars can always be found by drawing an imaginary line from the Pole Star to them. Thus, he first drew her attention to the Great Bear and the Little Bear, and to the splendour of Arcturus; to Taurus and Aldebaran; to Cassiopeia, and Perseus; to the great square of Pegasus, and the beauty of the Pleiades. And when, in a clear midnight sky, during the loneliness of that Christmas Eve, he called Jean to the entrance of the drift and pointed out to her the planets then visible, and the glorious gorgeous form of Orion bound with his sparkling belt, and begemmed with the wonders of Rigel, and Betelgeuse, and Sirius, her delight knew no bounds, and her interest became so great in the study that she determined under Red Ike's direction to master the whole of the starry heavens of winter.

At that instant a meteorite rushed out of space and broke into a thousand flashes of light over Sandyflatts, and Red Ike said: "Will Moffatt and Dick Stagg would be released from jail today. I wonder if Will will venture through the snow to the drift tonight?"

Jean was about to speak when her arms fell powerless to her side, her lips trembled, her eyes seemed starting from their sockets, and she gasped for breath and moaned: "My father."

Red Ike, leaping to his feet, cried: "Where?"

"I saw him walk past the entrance to the drift," she whispered.

"Hist, and retire to your couch, and extinguish the lights. I'll stand on guard until daylight. No one can enter here, nor harm me, not if there be twenty men outside."

"But he's there, Ike. I saw him, I saw him, I saw him!"

"Never mind, Jean; do as I ask you. I'll stand before the entrance. If he shoots, he can but hit me in the legs. Now run and put out the lights."

"Never," cried Jean, with courage born of despair. "This time I shall share the danger with you. Stand aside. I'll go out, and face him."

Red Ike would fain have withheld her, but calmly she stepped past him into the night. Before her lay the dale, peaceful and white. The waterfalls and fell becks were muffled under the thick snow, or frozen into silence. Not the call of bird, nor bark of fox, nor bleat of sheep, gave to the grim desolation a touch of life; all was still as the grave.

"You have been mistaken, Jean," said Red Ike, standing by her side, "there is not, nor has been anyone near the drift tonight."

"Then," said Jean, "I saw my father's wraith, and for the first time in my life I have glimpsed the form of a spirit. My father is dead."

"Nonsense, Jean, 'twas merely a figment of your brain. Your long confinement in the drift is telling upon your nerves, and I am glad that the time is near when I hope to hand you into the safe keeping of...." He did not finish the sentence. Jean staggered against his side.

"My God! He is there." And pointing with her hand, she continued: "He is but a shadow. I can see the stars shining behind and through his body. 'Tis a spirit, and yet my father. And oh, Red Ike, his face is as it was before the lurcher worried him. See, he is leaving us and climbing upwards amongst the snowy crags, whither the foot of mortal man has never trod. And ever and anon he is glancing back upon us, and, lo, he is dissolving into air, or sinking into the heart of the fell."

"Jean," said Red Ike, "I have seen nothing in the direction you are pointing. 'Tis your imagination that pictures the figure before your mind's eye. Come, we will return into the drift."

During this scene midst the solitude of the fells, there were two other scenes enacted of equal import to those concerned in this story. At Carlisle Nell Glen, under the glow of the limelight, was captivating with her matchless natural artistry the heart and soul of her Border audience. And spellbound amongst the charmed host were Joe Gream, Peg Shore, and Dick Stagg. None of the three could credit their sight. Will Moffatt did not know Nell, and when Dick whispered that it was she, he smiled incredulously, thinking his friend infatuated with some likeness the singer bore to the girl with whom he was in love. But Joe sat with his eyes riveted upon Nell, and the magic of her power worked him into such a frenzy of lustful passion that he began to loathe the thought of Peg Shore sitting beside him. Peg, glancing at him from time to time, and knowing his nature too well, wondered if Nell were now beyond his reach.

It was hardly likely that she would descend again into the arms of the man who abandoned her to the cruel inhospitality and inhuman traffic of London's streets.

Still, she thought, judging Nell's standard by her own moral code, "A woman always hankers after a man with whom she has once cohabited." And she resolved to watch him like a thief. But Peg had not yet probed to the lowest depth of Joe Gream's rank grossness and sexual cupidity, and the fair body of Nell, surging with a great love that infused every note she sung, was alive with kindling fire. Men in the vast crowd before her responded to the appeal that she unconsciously roused within them. Joe Gream, having known the woman in the past, when she was sweet and pure, desired her again. At the close of the opera, with a brutal curse, he turned his back upon Peg and fled from her down a side street of the old Border city, and was soon lost to view in the darkness of the night.

Now from the start of the performance, Nell had beheld Dick Stagg amongst the audience before her. And often as the curtain was rung down between the acts, she peered from behind it with an aching heart upon the moorland poacher, who held the peace of her soul in his hands. What to her were the plaudits of humanity in the mass? For each of us the heart that beats in unison with our own alone is, so to speak, the pivot round which our life moves, and a woman is happy only within the radius of her love. Nell was under the personal spell of Dick Stagg once more. Her soul was reaching unseen hands out towards him, and yearning and beseeching him through the medium of her art to enfold her again within the compass and essence of his being. And the glory and charm of the magnificent power she evinced, combined with her mature physical beauty, and grace, and manner of bearing, daunted the daring of Dick, which had hitherto advanced on equal terms towards her. With grief and pain she shrank before the thought that, in spite of her splendid talents and success, she had fallen even below his notice. And her soul cowered within her in shame and humbled her to the dust. Had she but known her true position in his regard, how different would she have felt!

Dick knew nothing of her fall and degradation with Joe, and in the fullness of his unselfish soul, and real love for her, he could have watched her climb to the highest pinnacle of fame and wealth and social standing, aye, seen her married to another, and yet have rejoiced in the knowledge that she had once loved him. The jail and his sudden overthrow into the shadows of adversity had developed and brought to the fore the noblest and finest traits in his character. He had not known, and did not yet know, anything of the envy and hate engendered in the struggle of life for what most men deem the essentials of existence. 'Tis true he had poached for money, but then he had also worked hard for a bare pittance, and spent his slight gains from both sources with a free hand and ungrudgingly, and, his wants being few, and his pleasures inexpensive, he had not felt the poverty and hardship of his lot.

Nell Glen, during the last year, had often contrasted his free generosity towards her, prompted, she now saw, by pure love, with the fawning attentions of many of the ephemeral would-be lovers that daily fluttered about her. And when Dick Stagg, on that memorable Christmas Eve, left Carlisle to walk home over twenty-five miles of snow-clad moorland, he took with him the renewed and eternal love of one of the greatest singers of the day.

Christmas Day fell on a Saturday, and in the grey dawn of the morning, Will Moffatt and Dick pushed aside the frozen branches of the bour tree that blocked the doorway of Sandyflatts, and passed onwards into the old milkhouse.

Striking a light, Will examined the room, but there were no signs that anyone had been there for weeks, or perhaps months. He remembered the pile of stacked wood in a corner which he himself had placed there. Not a stick of it had been burned. Under the sconce was a small oaken chest. This he opened and within it were cans of preserved fruit, biscuits, and canisters full of tea and sugar. Evidently, Red Ike had not been here for some time. Everything was as he had left it fifteen months ago.

Dick Stagg watched him with a curious glance of which he took no heed, but hastily making a fire, he busied himself with preparing breakfast, and as the blue smoke curled from the milkhouse into the crisp morning air, Red Ike calling Jean to the entrance of the drift, pointed out the welcome sign to her, saying: "There is a tenant at Sandyflatts; Will Moffatt is free from jail."

"And see," cried Jean, "yonder's a dog crossing the moorland, a huge animal; 'tis coming towards the dale here, and is alone."

And Red Ike, through a pair of field-glasses, watched the approach of the animal. Onwards it came, its bounding great body scorning the obstructing snow, and laying a hand upon Jean's arm, he said: "It is Prodigal, the lurcher, the dog that worried your father, and it is coming to the drift."

Jean shuddered and ejaculated: "Oh, block up the entrance."

"Nay, Jean, the poor brute was never in the fault. Had it been your father's dog, it would have worried me instead of him. I shall shelter it at present, even if I destroy it afterwards. Why it has left the gypsies at Mirkholme I would like to know. They have driven it away for some reason. However, we can now leave the drift if you wish."

"Whither can we go?" asked Jean.

"To the Red Lion at Grasmere. I'll conduct you thither. My task is finished," and stooping down, he patted the head of Prodigal that was now crouching at his side.

When Jean and Red Ike arrived at Grasmere, the hotel was thronged to the door with a happy and animated crowd. The lake being frozen over had attracted folks from far and near, and laughter and shouting, and the clink of skates, gave a lively tone to the valley. Jean was glad that she could take up her quarters almost unobserved, which otherwise would not have been the case at that usually quiet season of the year. Red Ike arranged all, and then, bidding Jean be of good cheer and all would be well, he set out to cross the fells by the shortest route to Sandyflatts.

And Will Moffatt was sitting there waiting for him alone. Dick Stagg, after trying in vain to convince him that the prima donna was Nell Glen, had on his advice gone to Penrith to make sure that she was not at the Royal George Hotel; so persistent had Will been in laughing at the idea of such a notion, that he himself had begun to doubt the reality of it. As he walked by the old castle and down the hill before turning into Little Dockeray at Penrith, he stood for a moment irresolute, when a woman's voice by his side bade him a Merry Christmas, and glancing at her, he beheld Peg Shore.

Dick did not return the greeting, and was about to move away; but Peg was not to be thus cast off.

"Has Dick Stagg come to have a look at the old spot where his pretty dove forsook him?" chortled Peg. "And does he know that she is the new star that has risen so suddenly in the operatic world?"

"I've come to have a look at the old place, Peg, and what does it matter to you or me whether she be a star or not?"

This emboldened Peg, and she continued: "Are you interested to learn that whilst you were in jail she fled to Edinburgh and London with Joe Gream, and that he abandoned her on the streets?"

"You're a liar, Peg Shore."

"Hear me to the end," she replied. "I followed them to both cities."

"For what purpose, Peg?"

"Listen to the end. In London Nell went mad. I saw her taken to Bedlam. Tonight she is again consorting with Joe."

"How know you this, woman?" cried Dick menacingly, and taking a step towards her.

Peg did not move.

"I was at the opera last night at Carlisle, and I left them there together. Follow them, Dick Stagg, and learn the truth for yourself. Whither they go, I shall go. The woman I care nothing about, but I shall track him, if need be, to death. He is mine by right. When I fell to him I was his first woman, as he was my first man. Yet Nell Glen knew we were consorting when she took him from me. I have sworn he shall be mine at last, in spite of her, and heaven and hell." And with a wave of her hand, she turned and entered the Royal George Hotel.

Meanwhile Red Ike and Will were consulting together at Sandyflatts; and out on the moorland the wind was rising and great banks of black clouds, charged with thunder and rain and lightning, were sweeping from the distant Solway Sea. John Lynd, unknown to them, had been lying since the previous midnight murdered in cold blood at The Bents. The surrounding villages and farms were alive with rumours; Dick Stagg's and Will's footmarks, and it was surmised, Red Ike's, were measured in the snow, and the length of the stride of a dog's walk was also measured, and one of them dreamed of the calamity that was about to befall them.

Suddenly a loud roll of thunder shook the old house, and Red Ike remarked: "The storm has begun; before morning there will hardly be a pickle of snow on the fells, except in the gullies or sheltered spots, where it lies very thick, and the wind and the rain cannot sift it.

"All trace of Jean and me leaving the drift and crossing the fells through the snow will be destroyed. I had thought of not prolonging my stay in the drift, but of going immediately to London, and studying there until the spring, when I hope to bring out a work under more favourable circumstances than can be done in a provincial town. But now I shall stay in the drift until the spring, and husband my money resources."

"Hush," said Will, and blowing out the light they both stood up and listened. A blow with a heavy stick or a policeman's baton sounded on the door, and then a voice commanded: "In the name of the Queen, open the door.

"Come," whispered Red Ike, and together they lifted the flagstone that covered the tunnel to the old well and were soon crossing the moorland and making for the drift in the teeth of a raging storm.

"Well," said Red Ike, when they were both again safely harboured, "I wonder what fresh mischief the devil has been hatching for us? However, we are safe here until tomorrow night. I shall then visit Simon Reed, and learn the news. I think you and I, Will, had better clear off from the countryside altogether, or we'll be sent to penal servitude or hanged for something we know nothing about." And they both laughed merrily at the idea as a joke. How little they thought that such a doom was hanging threateningly over their heads! 'Tis a curious coincidence, and the subject is worthy of deeper study than has been given to it, that the human mind can at times divine future events or events that have happened, and can guess them truly without having the faintest reasonable knowledge that such things are.

Next morning, after a sound sleep, they arose in good spirits, and Red Ike, going to the entrance of the drift, and looking over the moorland, exclaimed: "The gypsies have left Mirkholme, and, by the Lord above, Prodigal was here when we returned last night, and he has departed too."

Together they examined the drift thoroughly, and Red Ike declared that everything was as he had left it.

"Is the carved stick still in the boring?" Will asked.

"Yes, it is still there," he replied.

There was now nothing to be done but to wait until nightfall again, and for Red Ike to visit Simon Reed, while Will would go at the same time to see Jean at the Red Lion Hotel at Grasmere

As soon as the dusk was so dense that a man could not be distinguished on all fours from a sheep within fifty yards, Will crept from the drift on his hands and knees, and in this manner ascended to the harrage of the fell, and when once he was beyond the skyline he leapt to his feet and made straight for Grasmere. As he passed the newsvendor's shop that stands opposite the road end that leads into Easedale, he saw on a hoarding in large letterpress:

DREADFUL MURDER IN LAKELAND

And, curious and interested, he hurried to the hotel with the daily paper. The waitress behind the bar was full of gossip, and said to him: "Are you a native of the district?"

"Yes," he replied.

"Did you know John Lynd, the murdered man?"

He again assented, and she continued: "There are three men suspected with being concerned in the tragedy. Two were but released from jail on Christmas Eve. The other is a disreputable, desperate character, who has been in penal servitude for murder before. I hope the three culprits are soon caught and hanged."

He let the paper fall to the ground in wonder. This, then, he thought, is the reason why Red Ike and he were visited by the police at Sandyflatts the previous night. Dick, Red Ike, and he were to be charged with the crime.

"Have any of the men been arrested?" he questioned.

"Not yet," she answered, "but one of them, called Red Ike, was here last night. He came from nobody knows where with Miss Lynd, the murdered man's daughter, and left her here."

"Is she here yet?"

The suddenness of his question caused the woman to startle, and she gazed curiously at him and answered: "No. Immediately the news arrived this morning, she ordered a conveyance and drove over The Raise."

Thus satisfied, he rose to depart. The waitress with arms akimbo leaned over the bar counter, and said: "I really believe you are one of the men wanted."

"What if I am?" he replied, and dashed from the room.

Night always favours a fugitive. Yet whither could he flee? 'Twas known that the three of them were in the district, and the main roads would all be watched. However, he must see Red Ike and Dick as soon as possible. He stood a moment thinking at the Easedale road end, and could hear a commotion at the door of the Red Lion Hotel. He would be pursued and caught if he remained longer. Running up the road and past the farthest cottage, he vaulted over a low stone-wall and struck over the flat that stretches towards the base of Halmcrag, intending to cross The Raise. On a second thought he saw this would be a desperate chance to take, and turned and faced into Easedale again, but kept his course along the breast of the fell, and time after time he thanked his lucky stars that the previous night's storm had cleared away the snow.

He was going at a breakneck speed, as though the whole force of the county police were at his heels, when suddenly remembering there was no need for doing so, and slackening his pace, he began to think calmly, and after a few minutes' reflection, saw clearly that the best way to do was to return to the drift, and wait there for Red Ike. He would see Simon Reed and learn all particulars. And then he thought, how if Dick be arrested at Penrith? What attitude would he assume, if challenged and charged with the murder?

Would he laugh the idea to scorn, and submit quietly, knowing himself innocent, or would he take alarm, fearing foul play, and striking out for personal freedom, do harm to someone in his hot blood? And strange to say, he thought, the last of all, of his Jean's sad plight. Would she be welcomed home by her mother, or refused admittance to her presence? He could not guess, but he knew for certain that he could not give her protection in any case, and that the issue of events was in the hands of destiny.

CHAPTER XXIII

WHEN Red Ike approached Simon Reed's cottage, all was in darkness. Even his good old wife, who usually kept indoors, had been moved by the spirit of gossip in the air, and was in a neighbour's house where the news of the day was always discussed.

Simon was at the White Horse Inn, and had been there all day. Many were the rumours concerning the murder, but all agreed that John Lynd had been done to death by either Red Ike or Dick Stagg or Will Moffatt. The company were discussing, in a babel of voices, the bearings of the case. The doctor had certified that the crime had been committed at midnight.

"I tell you all that Red Ike was never near The Bents that night that John Lynd was killed," cried old Simon Reed at the top pitch of his voice.

"How do you know that?" roared several voices at once.

"I know well enough, and I'll tell you how I know. I examined all the footmarks in the snow. Now when Red Ike walks on snow or soft ground, the toes of his shoes always leave a scraped impression, as if every step he takes his foot slips back a little. I can point out this peculiarity in his walk, and shall stake my life that none can gainsay my assertion. Not all the police in the world can get him convicted on the evidence of the footprints."

An all-round laugh followed this speech. And outside in the darkness, Red Ike was holding onto the window sill to steady himself in his bewilderment.

"John Lynd murdered, and I am blamed for it? Good heavens! When will wonders cease?"

And for several minutes he stood as if paralysed. But by degrees his resolute will gave him mastery of the situation, and with squared shoulders, and head erect, and the look of a lion in his eyes, he strode forward, lifted the door-latch and stepped into the centre of the room, and cried: "Who says that I murdered John Lynd? I am here and throw the lie back into the teeth of all present that dare to suggest such a thing. Until the last few seconds I was as ignorant as a man in his grave that any harm had befallen him. When was the deed done?"

A long pause ensued.

"Landlord," said Red Ike, turning to him, "will you answer my question? Surely to God there is no reason why you should not. Man, I'm as innocent of the murder as a babe."

"You'll have to prove that, Red Ike. Where are thy mates, Will Moffatt and Dick Stagg? You all fled from Sandyflatts to avoid arrest last night, though how the devil you got away nobody knows. But you'll all be caught and hanged."

"I have not seen Dick Stagg for over fifteen months, landlord; and Will Moffatt and I had no idea why we were visited by the police at Sandyflatts, and it is just as likely that you are the murderer as I am."

A wild burst of disapproval followed this, but the look of the lion came again into Red Ike's eyes, and raising a pointed finger above his head and in a voice of withering scorn he cried: "Yes, yes, I hear you all, and defy the lot of you, you brainless idiots. The last time I was here I remember the reception you gave me. You seem to have no fellow-feeling or sense of justice for a man placed in my position. When I charge one of you with murder you howl as if hell was let loose, and yet expect me to bear the same charge with meekness and patience. Go to, you sots. I would not wonder but that every man here except myself has had a hand in the murder."

"Nay, nay," said a thin voice from a corner. "Red Ike knows well enough that I am as innocent as he is," and old Simon Reed rose to his feet.

"Hold up your hands, Red Ike," said the landlord, levelling a fowling gun.

"Put down your weapon, and I'll submit to arrest; there are three policemen in the passage behind you, landlord."

Surprised at these words, he turned to look, and the next moment was hurled forward to the ground. The gun exploded, and Red Ike, daring anyone to follow him, rushed out into the night.

"Hurrah!" cried Simon Reed, "that was the cleverest trick that I've ever seen done in my life. Good luck to the lad that played it. He has too cute a brain to be caught by fellows like us." And the old chap laughed, and clapped his knees with delight.

"Get to blazes out of here," cried the infuriated landlord, rising to his feet. "I believe you are in league with the murdering crew, Simon Reed, you infernal old snuff-box."

"Just thee jump up, landlord. I'll go out of here when I please, and at my leisure, and I'll not visit the devil when I do go. And I'll tell thee something, old pimpled boniface, had I come here less often in the past, I might ere now have been parish clerk and should have had the pleasure of saying 'Amen' over thee one of these coming days, and seeing thy Mary Ann a blooming widow, as pleased as a dog with two tails."

At this moment the landlady bustled past her husband, and grasping Simon's arm led him to a chair, and patting the old fellow's bald pate, bade him hold his tongue, or otherwise sing a song.

And then this merry crew soon forgot all about the murder of John Lynd, and the misery of the three men blamed for the crime. Such is the variableness of human nature. And Simon, with a twinkle in his eye, sang Red Ike's ballad:

THE VALE OF ST. JOHN

One morn as I wandered to breathe the fresh air,
Where the broom by the Bure blooms sweetly and fair,
I met my young Mary as fresh as the dew
She brushed from the daisies unnumbered to view.
As clear as the dawn was her bright open face
No sign but of purity there could I trace;
A vision of sweetness and gentleness she,
And light as a sunbeam she passed o'er the lee.
Like a fairy she came, and when she was gone
No beauty I saw in the Vale of St. John.

That morn on Helvellyn the heather was red;
On the lofty Blencathra the bracken were spread
The ferns on the grey crags of Wanthwaite were green,
And every wild creature was glad and serene.
While I who had never till then known a care,
Was filled in a moment with love and despair.
Lest some favoured suitor sweet Mary could claim,
And leave me without either hope or an aim.
Though lowly my lot, I'd forsake e'en a throne
To dwell with my love in the Vale of St. John.

In the Vale of St. John there is set a green bower
I'll prize above all to my life's latest hour;
For there as each evening creeps down through the dell,
As shepherds return from their flocks on the fell,
I linger with Mary far into the night,
And fondle my darling with wildest delight.

164 * *RED IKE*, BY J. M. DENWOOD & S. FOWLER WRIGHT

Oh, blithe could I spend all the rest of my days,
A stranger to fame and the world's busy ways,
Had I my heart's wish, and a cot of mine own,
Beside the sweet Bure in the Vale of St. John.

When Red Ike rushed from the White Horse Inn towards the black yew tree that stands opposite the door, a shadowy figure glided from under the tree, and stood before his path.

"Hello, Red Ike, hold!"

Recognizing the voice, he paused, and exclaimed: "Jael."

"Yes," she answered, "'tis I." And linking her arm through his, she led him into the darkness and depth of the night-shrouded moorland.

"Whither are you going?" he inquired.

"I would it were into another world with thee, Red Ike. This one is full of tribulation for us both. I am sick of it unto death, and, but for the child that is thine and mine, I should free myself of it quickly. Often unknown to thee have I sat night-long by the tarn that lies in the hollow of the fell above the drift where thou hidest. And I have looked into the depth of the tarn when the stars and the moon were shadowed in it, and I have wondered if that I leapt from the shore of the tarn, I should find peace lying in the mirror of the stars and the moon."

Red Ike stood still, and folded Jael in his arms, and she nestled her head upon his breast, and broke into tears, and while he stroked her hair, and murmured words of love to her, the soul of this wild-spirited woman felt that it had at last found shelter from the buffeting of an evil fate that had ever been its lot.

They had paused by the wide of the cattle pool where the three runnels meet on the moorland, and Jael releasing herself from his arms cried: "Oh, my God! I forgot. I came to warn you to keep away from Sandyflatts, and I can see it standing as stark as a shadow in the distance yonder."

"Why should I keep away, Jael?"

"If you are taken, you will be hanged for the murder."

"I shall not be hanged, Jael. I did not commit the crime."

"But Ben Faa swears he saw you kill John Lynd."

"And do you believe him, Jael? You once told me that you foresaw, or saw when they were happening, all the chief events in my life. Did you see me do the deed?"

Jael crept up to him, and looked into his eyes, that were burning like live coals. Long and earnestly she gazed, and then, with a strange cry, exclaimed: "By the eye of the Pyramids, the North Pole, and the Carved Stick, you are innocent, Red Ike." And she leapt upon his neck, and clung round him in a transport of passion and delight.

"My child is not the son of a murderer. We are saved! We are saved! We are saved!" And she pulled his head down towards her lips, and covered his with a kiss.

"Hist! There's danger astir," she cried, drawing him away from the cattle pool. They crouched together in the darkness, like two stones close to the ground.

"'Tis the police, and Ben Faa," she whispered. "They are bound for Sandyflatts. Will Dick Stagg or Will Moffatt be there?"

"I do not think so, Jael."

"Then you return to the drift. Tomorrow midnight, if I have any news, I shall be at the South outstanding stone of the Druids' Circle." Before Red Ike could answer, she glided away.

When Red Ike returned to the drift, Will was already there, and when he walked along the tunnel and stood before him, his face was radiant, and he looked more like a bridegroom on his wedding night than a man who was being hunted for murder.

"Well, what news?" he questioned.

Will related to him his adventure at Grasmere, and during the recital he watched his face closely, but it gave no clue to his thoughts. When he had finished he asked: "And what are you going to do now, Will?"

The question nonplussed him, and he replied: "I do not know." And still gazing upon Red Ike's face, he realized for the first time in his life that he was in the presence of a man of superior will power and resource to himself. He watched a strange smile curl about his mouth, and his eyes brighten with animation, and he knew instinctively that he saw clearly where he could but grope through the mystery that enveloped the murder of John Lynd.

"Did you see Simon Reed tonight?" he inquired.

"Yes, and Jael too. And I stood by the window of the White Horse Inn and heard the crime discussed, and afterwards I entered the house, and gave the lie to the charge against us. Jael told me on the moorland that Ben Faa swears he saw me commit the murder. Tomorrow night I shall lie in wait for him, and shall see what he has to say about the case. I have yet to learn the exact time the deed was done, and all the known particulars."

"Have you thought of Dick Stagg?" Will said.

"I am going to Penrith now, Will, and shall be there by daybreak. If Dick be arrested, the daily papers will contain the news. If he be free, I shall hunt him up. In any case, I shall return to the drift within an hour after nightfall tomorrow."

Red Ike would not allow Will to accompany him, and requested him not to stir abroad until his return.

When he arrived at Penrith, the first thing that caught his eye in the glare of a street lamp was a reward of £500 for his own arrest. But, nothing daunted, he lingered on the streets openly until almost noon, when to his surprise he saw Peg Shore and Dick Stagg on their way to the railway station. By good luck, neither of them noticed him behind them, until he touched Peg on the shoulder, as they were stepping past the strip of the castle ruin that faces the station.

"Whither are you bound, Peg? Come with me a short distance along the highway towards Keswick. Not a word now, for the present, and if either of you gives an alarm, I'll blow both of you to hell. This way, Peg, and Dick will carry your handbag."

Had Peg Shore been hypnotized, she could not have obeyed Red Ike's command more helplessly.

Onwards he compelled them to go, until they were well clear of the town's suburbs, and then striking along a byroad, and coming to a patch of waste ground covered with coppice, he ordered and followed them into the screen of the trees and then, facing both, demanded to know how they came to be together.

"I shall shoot the first that I find lying to me. Already the price of blood is on my head, so it will not matter whether I am hanged for one murder or three.

"But first of all I want to know where Joe Gream is."

"Peg says that he is with Nell Glen."

"Go on; where are they, Dick?"

"At Preston. I was going there to satisfy myself that what Peg says is true."

"If it be true, Dick, believe me, the woman that freely consents to an incontinent act with a man like him, is not worth the trouble of seeking. Peg was unfaithful to me, and Joe Gream is the man with whom she fell."

"Is that true, Red Ike?"

"I never lie, Dick. Beware of the woman beside thee."

"Still, I shall go and see Nell, and satisfy my own heart."

"Dost thou know, Dick, that John Lynd is murdered, and that thou, Will Moffatt, and I are blamed for the deed?"

Red Ike watched Dick's face closely. A look of blank wonder passed over it. One sees the same look in the eyes of a dog that stands studying the attitude of its master when in doubt, its body rigid and tense.

Red Ike continued: "Neither you nor Peg had noticed the reward posted on the hoardings at Penrith this morning. My name alone is published, but do not doubt, Dick, that you and Will Moffatt will be arrested at sight. I shall not be taken until I have investigated the crime for myself. That I can run the culprit to earth I have no doubt." And holding out a revolver on the palm of his hand, he added: "If I am betrayed before I have solved the problem of the murder, my informer shall go with me to the grave. Swear both of you, that you will keep your own counsel about fleeting me."

"We swear," they both ejaculated. Bending his eyes upon Peg, he said: "I have also my friends that will avenge my arrest, if anyone at present breathes a word about me to the police. You are now both free to go your own ways."

Leaping into the depth of the coppice, he was heard crashing through the obstructing undergrowth.

Peg Shore journeyed with the afternoon express to Preston alone. Dick lay hidden in the wood until nightfall, and then crossed Shap-fells on foot, and arrived on the outskirts of Preston by daybreak next morning. Remembering that Peg had given him the address of an inn, he glanced at the direction, and resolved to take the risk, and put up there for the night. Before entering the town, he washed himself in a horse trough by the road side and then walked briskly and steadily forward. Passing several policemen, he cheerily bade them the time of day, and, satisfied that he was not suspected, he called in a public bar and ordered a drink. By the merest chance it was adjoining the opera house and several artists were lounging at the counter discussing the topics of the hour, and then conversation turned upon Nell and Joe Gream: "I tell you," said one of them, "the fellow persists in following her, and endeavoured to force himself into the ante-room behind the stage last night."

"Then why the devil was he not given into the hands of the police?"

"Miss Glen would not consent to such a thing."

"Was he drunk?"

"By the look of him I should think he is never sober."

A merry laugh rippled amongst the artists, and Dick Stagg wondered if the man referred to was Joe Gream. He was quickly relieved of all doubt. Dressed in what he doubtless supposed to be the height of fashion, the man himself stepped into the bar, and with a swaggering manner called for a drink, at the same time saying: "All the gentlemen present can have one with me if they choose."

Dick rose to his feet and slipped unnoticed through the door, but turning into a small side-room, he sat where he could hear all that passed amongst the company in the bar, and when he rose to depart he knew that Joe, whatever he had once been to Nell Glen, was nothing to her now.

As Dick stepped out of the public house, Peg, standing on the opposite side of the street, motioned to him, but waving his hand to her, he returned to the small side-room he had just left, and shortly after she joined him there.

"Well, Peg," he began, "the man you are seeking is in the bar drinking with the opera artists."

"I know that," quoth she.

"What are you going to do now, Peg?"

"I can do nothing, Dick. An hour ago I was refused admittance at his lodgings to see him. If I accost him on the streets, he will have me arrested for soliciting. I can but bide my time, and take my chance to overreach him when it comes."

Dick mused awhile.

"Why not go into the bar, and have a drink amongst the company there? He is a cur and a coward to his heart, and every time you push yourself where he is, you'll add to the fear he has of you, and you'll weaken further his nerves." Peg glanced at Dick and an unnatural light came into her eyes.

"Will you help me, Dick?"

"What to do, Peg?"

"To get him."

"I will, Peg. If it depends on me, you shall have him."

"Dick, I shall be frank with you. I meant to betray you to the police, but since you have shown a generous spirit towards me, I shall not move in the matter. Now what are you going to do with yourself immediately?"

Dick leaned his chin upon his hands on the table, and looked her straight in the eyes: "I am going to visit Nell Glen, and explain my position to her, and then, after wishing her a successful career, I shall give myself up to the police, and let things take their course. I am not guilty of the murder of John Lynd, and am not going to be a fugitive in the world for a crime I did not commit. I'd rather be hanged innocently than be hounded daily from pillar to post."

This was a new way of facing the question to Peg, and gazing on the man before her, she marvelled at his serenity.

"Do you mean what you say, Dick?"

"Yes. I would have given myself up at once had I not wished to speak to Nell. I do not value life unless I have personal liberty to go my own way within reasonable bounds, and without infringing on the rights and laws that govern my fellows also, so long as I consider both are just. Besides, I have but lately come out of jail, and I do not fear to return thither."

"Well! Well!" exclaimed Peg. She did not understand the temper of the type of man with whom she was speaking. He had walked through hell several times in his life, and could go through it again if needs be. He felt no shame of having been in jail, nor of being a poacher. He did not fear poverty. Only those placed above want fear it. The man who is nurtured and daily lives in poverty laughs its real and its vague terrors to scorn.

Peg continued: "Will you wait here until I return, Dick? I am going into the bar."

When Peg walked in amongst the artists, every man in the room but Joe raised his hat to her. He, wonder-struck, gaped in amazement, but quickly recovering himself, with an effort pretended to ignore her, but his surprise had been too evident not to be remarked by those present. One jolly dog of an artist, who had indulged too freely, tipped him on the shoulder, and signing with his head to Peg, asked: "Is this your lady love, my friend?"

"Yes," replied Peg, "he and I were at the opera at Carlisle on Christmas Eve, and he became infatuated with the prima donna. Is that right, Joe?"

"You bitch of hell! I'll choke you."

"What I say is true, gentlemen, and after we left the opera house he bolted, and left me on the street, and I have not seen him again until this minute, despite the fact that he has promised to wed me."

The utter shamelessness and *sang-froid* with which Peg spoke astounded her listeners, and smiling she continued: "Let him deny what I say if he dare. I hold him in the hollow of my hand." And with a mock bow, and a sweep of her body, she turned and left the bar.

"That's a poser for you, my friend," said the half-drunk artist. "I wouldn't have had such a letdown for all the ale in the kingdom, well as I like it."

"To hell with the lot of you, you gimcrack sponging Punch and Judy showmen," roared Gream.

"Hold, my friend," cried the jolly artist. "We, myself included, may be all you call us, yet men who use filthy terms of speech sometimes get punched on the head for doing so. You need not apologize, only keep quiet."

After this, Joe was ignored by the whole company, and finally he left the bar in high dudgeon, but like all men of his stamp, being self-satisfied and self-centred, his natural vanity soon gained the ascendance once more, and with a light laugh he dismissed the incident from his mind.

Not so Peg. She returned to the small side-room where Dick waited.

"You heard what passed in the bar?" she queried.

"Every word, Peg. You'll have done yourself with him forever."

"Devil the fear. I've played second fiddle to him long enough. Henceforth I'll be his master. He cannot shake me off, and if he now goes near Nell at the opera house, he'll get sneck-posset as sure as he's alive. Hist! He's leaving the bar. If you wish to see Nell, her address is on this card. I shall meet you here again tomorrow." And hastily leaving the room she began to shadow Joe.

Dick gazed on the card Peg handed him, and he mechanically turned it over in his fingers. He had walked from Penrith to Preston to see and speak with Nell, and now his courage oozed as it were into space.

"What," he thought, "has come over me?" He did not know. Like most people who are not given to self-analysis, the defects of his better qualities had not hitherto given him cause for thought. His fine moral nature, trustful and trustworthy, had been, despite his jail experience, in a state of deep repose until the revelation Peg had made to him concerning Nell and Joe shocked his feeling into tumult, and his thoughts into an activity that was new and strange to him. 'Tis true he had often wondered at Nell's attitude towards him in the Royal George at Penrith when he assaulted Joe, but he did not then know, nor yet knew, that Peg and old Abegail, the gypsy, had poisoned her mind against him. And now fresh doubts began to assail him. If she discarded him when a barmaid, would she be likely to look upon him with favour now that she was a great singer? He had not thought of the fortune she would be earning with her art, and fame was a thing he had never dreamed about; in fact, it had little meaning to him. His was not a small soul, but it was playing a part in another sphere of life, different altogether from that in which Nell was now moving. In a dim way he realized this, but did not grasp its full import, yet felt the distinction much in the same sense that a poor man feels towards a very distant-mannered rich one; that is, if the poor man be humble, and the rich one haughty.

So Dick wavered in his resolution to go at once to see Nell. He would hear her sing again tonight, and visit her in the morning. Not being guilty of the crime of murder, he did not think that he might be arrested any moment, until, hearing a commotion outside, he glanced through the window and saw that a policeman was posting on a hoarding the bill announcing a £500 reward for Red Ike's arrest. He shrank back into a corner of the room, sick at heart. Then he remembered the injunction Red Ike laid upon him and Peg in the coppice near Penrith; and his respect for the sagacity and fearless bearing of Red Ike emboldened him. Had not Red Ike said to him and Peg that if given time, he could run the culprit to earth? And Dick had never known him lie, nor turn aside in aught he set out to do. He must know the murderer. He never boasted. And now Dick heard folks crowding into the bar, and discussing the murder, of which details were in the daily papers. He wished to buy a paper, but dreaded to face the street which he imagined was filled with hostile crowds. Clenching his fists, he leapt to his feet with an oath: "Damn it. I'm losing my nerve. I'll go and see Nell at once. No, I'll have another drink first."

Leaving the little side-room, he walked into the bar again. Calling for a whiskey and soda, he lounged against the window, and felt that the sight of the folks outside and his mingling with those in the bar were having a beneficial effect upon him, and he was half inclined to drink himself into a cheery careless mood, when he saw Nell Glen pause before the hoarding opposite the window, and read the reward bill describing Red Ike, and the next moment Joe Gream stepped towards her. She started at beholding him, and one of the opera artists also catching sight of them, the little group of artists in the bar were soon gathered at the window watching intently.

Suddenly Nell turned and faced Joe, and it was evident, from her manner and his, that she was rebuking him, but he stood his ground as though determined to win his point at any cost. Dick was debating with himself whether or not he should interfere between them, when the half-drunk jolly artist left the bar and crossed the street, and, as if by accident, stumbled, and pitched his head into Joe's stomach, and doubled him up like a ball in the gutter.

"The devil! Who would have thought of doing a trick like that?" exclaimed one of the artists, who were laughing uproariously. Then they went to assist their comrade to his feet, and safely out of the way of the police.

Nell understood the ruse at once, and Dick, upbraiding himself for his slowness of wit and action, watched her move away without casting a glance towards the groaning and vomiting sot on the ground. Than this, Dick needed no further proof that Joe was nothing to her.

Then he saw Peg kneeling beside Joe, and, turning from the scene, he left the bar, and returned to the little side-room, and leaned his head upon his hands in silent thought.

BOOK FOUR

CHAPTER XXIV

AT midnight, previous to the happenings at Preston, Red Ike stood waiting for Jael by the south outstanding stone of the Druids' Circle. The moon was at full, and at the zenith. The atmosphere was hazy. Not a breath of air stirred the mountain solitude, and save for the wild hooting of the owls amongst the distant woods and crags, or the bleat of a solitary sheep that had wandered from its fellows, the heights of Castlerigg were as still as ere the birth of time or the creation of man on the earth. The planets and star groups shone dimly through the vault of night. Afar and near the huge bulks of the fells stood like stark shadows. In the distance, the moonlit surface of Broadwater glittered with sheen. To an imaginative man like Red Ike, whose mind and soul had fed themselves unconsciously on the beauty and mystery of night's witching glory, the scene around him was a boundless joy. The years he had spent in prison had created within his heart a stoical indifference to human companionship for its own sake, and his studious, retiring habits made him feel no loss of such. He was happy, alone with his own thoughts, and the friendly night, that was filled with shadows and horrors for other men of less daring mould, helped him. And, strange to say, in the darkest hour of night, he knew by instinct when he passed a stationary object whether it was living or not. Waiting for Jael, he beheld her coming towards him. He knew it was she by the rapid and fearless gait with which she advanced. He held out his open arms to enfold her, and with a glad cry she sprang towards him, but ere he could clasp her, she fell sharply back from him in awe and wonder.

"Why, what is the matter, Jael? It is I, Red Ike."

"I know it, I know it," she exclaimed, "and there is a halo round your head like the halo of the saints. I saw it once before a dim shadow, but tonight it is perfect and whole. And yet men say you are a murderer. And you say they lie, and now the Christian God has invested you with a sign to prove that you speak the truth, and I, the godless gypsy, am the one woman in the world chosen to be the first to look upon the marvel."

Red Ike listened to Jael with astonishment. What did she see about him that caused her to use such speech?

But ere he could question her she cried: "The glory is fading away; yet I have seen that which is bliss to me, life to me and to my child." And cowering to the ground, with her hair falling loosely over her form, she burst into a wild song of abandon and delight. The music, and the burden of her song, swelling strangely and sweetly amongst the great upstanding stones of the Druids' Circle, seemed like the weird echo of some spirit rejoicing to be midst the moonlit scenes of happy times, when life was full and free. A pastoral of love and mirth in a young and artless world. All the poet in Red Ike responded to, and revelled with Jael's ecstasy, and the moon and the stars shone upon them, and none but the moon and the stars and the great upstanding stones of the Druids' Circle were aware of their presence.

Suddenly, Jael ceased singing, and rising to her feet, and seizing Red Ike's arm, said: "Come." Together they passed from the heights of Castlerigg towards the dale beyond, and onwards to the waste moorland.

Neither spoke until they came to Naddle beck, to cross which Jael begged his assistance. Lifting her bodily in his arms, he leapt from bank to bank.

Avoiding the main roads and footpaths as much as possible, they breasted the fell to Teufit Tarn, and crossing the Bure beck, were soon upon the old Roman road that skirts the side of Helvellyn. Red Ike now knew they were bound for the grave of Jael's mother.

The gradual swell of the moorland to this particular spot, as Red Ike and Jael climbed towards it, slightly hindered them getting a full view of the grave, which was in the shadow of the yew tree John Lynd had planted above it, and within the shadow stood the figure of a woman in her night attire, waiting for the coming of Jael. As she and Red Ike were approaching the grave, the apparition stepped from the shadow.

With a low cry, Jael started, and clung to Red Ike's arm, but the woman, without speaking, glided forward with extended arm, and proffered a small packet to Jael.

Red Ike offered to take it, but the figure brushed his hand aside, and gave the packet to her.

The wan light of the moon was upon the woman's face which was of a deathly pallor. The eyes were fixed in the head. The lips tightly compressed. In fact, the whole features were rigid as those of a marble statue. Jael was speechless and tremulous, but Red Ike whispered assurance in her ear: "It is Jean Lynd, and she is sound asleep."

Jean at this moment turned and walked back to the grave and standing within the shadow of the yew tree leaned over the fence with bowed head. A pair of night-owls hooting their weird calls flew round the spot, but Jean was deaf to their clamour. Red Ike led her to the graveside, and gazing upon it beheld a new-made mound raised across the breast of Jael's mother. This was John Lynd's sepulchre. And both graves formed the sign of the cross. A wild whim of the murdered man's own conception and ordering, but whether in mockery or in trust is known to the gods alone.

Red Ike touched Jean upon the shoulder. A slight tremor ran through her body, and straightening herself up, she glided through the moonlight on her homeward journey to The Bents.

Now, had Jael been asked why she had half compelled Red Ike to visit her mother's grave that night, she could not have answered. Perhaps it was because the moon was at the full, a time when she was never in a normal state of mind, or perhaps it was the compulsion of destiny, one of those events that happen because they have to.

Jael had forgotten that she still held Jean's packet in her hand, and holding it up in the moonlight she wondered what were its contents. At the sight of its form, Red Ike said: "The packet contains letters from your father to your mother, also their marriage certificate. You are John Lynd's first and only legitimate child. Failing a will and a male heir, you are the legal owner of all your father's real estate."

"I know," cried Jael, "and Abegail knows—and Ben Faa, does he know, I wonder?" Jael's voice sank to a whisper, but with a terrible meaning in its tone. "I now see the drift of much that has been dark to me." And a low guttural laugh broke from the depth of Jael's whole being. "This," she said, "is why John Lynd allowed the gypsies unlimited freedom to camp at Mirkholme. This was the source of Abegail's power over him, and the reason why he had supplied her with money at will. Fool that I was. Why did I not probe to the root of the matter before? It has often perplexed me. Had I not inherited a goodly portion of my father's indomitable will and obstinate temper, I would long ago have succumbed to the wish and the power of the old sibyl, and would have now been a debauched vagabond like most of my tribe. My resistance to moral degradation, even to the panderer, Ben Faa, made my body all the more desirable to him.

But now I see there is another reason and just as powerful in addition—the lust for the wealth he knew was mine, providing my father had not willed his estate from me. And I now regret that I am not married to you, Red Ike, according to English law." Lifting her eyes, shining and dark, to his, she said: "Will you wed me in an English church tomorrow, Red Ike?"

"I should be arrested on the instant, Jael."

"I had not thought of that. What shall we do?" And clasping her hands behind her head, she sank down into a sitting posture; as when she sang by the south outstanding stone of the Druids' Circle earlier during the night, she gazed into the bright starlit sky for some seconds, and then leaping to her feet, and throwing the packet to Red Ike, she fled in the wake of Jean.

Glancing at the constellation of Orion inclined to the western horizon, Red Ike guessed the time to be about three hours before daybreak, and hurrying after Jael, he was soon within the shelter of the half-grown fir-wood that encircled The Bents, and he resolved to wait there until Jael returned. Why she had gone thither he did not know. Doubtless she had some object.

When Jael reached the mansion, the front door was standing open, but the hall was in darkness. From the foot of the stairway she could see a glimmer of light on the wall of the landing above her, and hastily ascending towards it, saw that it came from a side bedroom.

Pushing the door further ajar, the sight of Jean froze her to the ground. She was standing utterly naked. Her finely-moulded body was as white as the new-blown snowdrift. Her hair coiled behind her head, her arms resting one behind her head and the other on the left hip, not a muscle showed any motion; she looked like the figure of an upright corpse, beautiful in symmetry, but awesome and fearfully fascinating to look upon.

But Jael, the gypsy, was never for more than a moment daunted by the strange sight of anything she knew to be mortal, or the remains of mortality. She crossed the room to Jean, and ran her fingers from the nape of the neck down the spine. Jean's body suddenly relaxed, her arms fell limp to her side, and she would have sunk to the floor, but that Jael caught her and led her to the bedside.

Seeing a cordial on the dressing-table, Jael administered draught to Jean. The generous juice gave a warm glow to her body, and with the signs of returning animation she gazed vacantly at Jael, and then recognizing her, enfolded her with a burst of wild joy, crying: "My sister, Jael, my sister."

Wide-eyed within the doorway, and dumb with astonishment, stood Jean's mother surveying the scene. Her daughter's strange plight, and the presence of Jael, the gypsy, there at that hour of the night, were inexplicable to her mind, and she demanded to be told the reason.

"'Tis all easily explained, madam," replied Jael, with ready address. "Whilst out on the moorland tonight I met Miss Lynd walking in her sleep, and fearing harm might befall her, I followed her hither. Now that she is quite safe, I shall depart."

"No, no, Jael, you must stay now that you have come home to us."

A look of bewilderment again came into Mrs. Lynd's eyes.

"What is the meaning of your speech, Jean?"

"Mother, Jael is my sister, and we must keep her with us."

"Jael the gypsy, your sister? You are demented, Jean."

"Madam, may I come hither tomorrow to ask you certain questions concerning your husband's murder?" asked Jael.

"No, I forbid you the house."

Jael crept up to the woman, as once before she had crept up to Red Ike, and gazing through her eyes to the depth of her soul, demanded: "Who killed John Lynd? You know, and I know you know; woman, why are you hiding the truth? Nay, you need not wince. Where is the axe he was slain with? Red Ike did not do the bloody deed. Ah, I have no need to question you. You'll screen the murderer to the end."

And at that Jael rushed from the house, and down the drive towards where Red Ike stood waiting under the sheltering darkness of the fir-wood. As she was about to pass, he leapt into her path.

"Jael, what is the matter?"

"Come," she cried, "the spell of the devil lies over The Bents."

"Nonsense, Jael, tell me quick what has happened."

"I shall tell you, but come, or for the love of heaven let me pass."

Red Ike grasped her arm: "We will return to The Bents together."

This brought Jael to reason. "'Tis no use going thither. Come, I have much to tell you."

As they moved away, a dark figure rose from the depth of the fir-wood and followed in their wake. Like a panther it crept along, now standing erect to keep them in view, now running on all fours, but always keeping at a safe distance, lest some unlucky chance might discover its presence to them.

"Hist! Jael, the devil is behind us. I heard his movement on the slight puff of wind that passed us this moment. We'll hurry forward to the cattle pool where the three runnels meet on the moorland. You must wait there until I return."

The second they reached it, Red Ike wheeled round. The lust of the man-hunt was in his blood. Within five and twenty yards of him, a dark figure rose from the ground, and fled like a shadow. It might as well have tried to flee from the light of the moon. Every bound brought the pursuer nearer to the fugitive, until, at last, seeing no chance of escape, he stopped and stood on his defence, with an up-lifted axe, whose sharp edge gleamed like silver.

"Another step, Red Ike, and I'll smash in your skull."

"There's my answer then, Ben Faa," and a stone hurtling through the air caught the unfortunate wretch in the stomach, and he fell in a huddled mass. Red Ike picked up the axe, unknowing at the time that with it John Lynd was done to death.

Standing over the prostrate man as he came gradually round, Red Ike felt a great pity within him. Why were he and this man foes, he wondered? Seven years ago, at their first meeting, the spirit of antagonism was between them. And yet there was no real cause why they should not have been good acquaintances, if not friends. True, he had come between Ben and Jael, but the circumstances had not been of his seeking, in fact he had endeavoured to avoid an entan-glement with her. Yet the woman and fate had overborne every ob-stacle in the way he had wished to go. And, besides, had not other men before them loved one woman, and yet been good friends? Thousands of times this must have happened. There was no way of explaining the case, but that they were born enemies; had perhaps been so in a pre-existence, and would be through all time to come. Is it a law of Nature that opposites can never exist near each other in harmony? And that the proportions of good and evil are indissoluble in the soul and in the body? Were this not so, would life become spiritually and bodily inane, and pass, and leave the universe void?

Red Ike lifted Ben Faa from the ground, and slung him over his shoulder, and bore him to the cattle pool. Motioning Jael to stand within the clump of whin bushes that sentinel the pool, he placed his burden in a sitting posture, and waited Ben's recovery.

"Why not kill me at once, Red Ike?" Ben gasped at last.

"I'll leave the hangman to do that, Ben Faa. Who killed John Lynd? I or you?"

The gypsy writhed under the question, but his tongue refused to speak. A horrible conviction dawned upon him.

"Oh, for the axe and Red Ike within my grasp," he prayed.

"Ben Faa, you have noised it abroad that I am the murderer. You have even sworn that you saw me do the deed. You liar! I have yet to learn the exact manner of his death. Is this the axe he was slain with? If not, why was it in your possession to night? Answer me, or, by the living God, I'll brain you with it."

Jael cowered within the whin-bushes, her heart wrung with fear lest in his passion Red Ike should forget himself. He held the axe above his head ready to strike.

A snarl like that of a cornered fox sounded behind him, and ere he could turn, old Abegail, as though she had risen from the earth, leapt upon his back, and grasped the axe-handle, at the same time calling upon Ben Faa to defend himself. Red Ike wrenched the witch's hands away, and hurled the axe into the cattle-pool, and then, gripping the hag by the neck, drew her over his shoulder. A heavy blow aimed at him by Ben descended upon her head. A curse broke from the gypsy, as he rushed into the pool to recover the axe, but Red Ike was upon him instantly, and holding him by the neck forced his head under the water.

"For God's sake," moaned Jael, "don't drown him; let the brute go."

Recovering the axe, Red Ike flung Ben from him, but seeing he lay motionless, drew him onto the moorland, and laid him by the old sibyl's side.

A loud whistle rang across the moor. "Jael, 'tis the police. Whither will you go?"

"To Sandyflatts," she replied. "I'll hide in the old well. Even if I'm found in the milkhouse, I'm free of arrest, but whither wilt thou flee, Red Ike?" And, hanging upon his neck, she clung to his lips a few brief seconds.

"Good-night, Jael. At the grave tomorrow night. Thou understand'st. Good-night! Good-night!"

When Red Ike fled from the cattle pool, Ben Faa leapt to his feet and pursued Jael. He had heard her mention Sandyflatts, and the old well, yet where the latter was he could not guess. The disc of the moon had set beyond the distant fells, but its light was still visible on the western skyline. And as Jael stepped through the bourtree that blocks up the doorway of the old house she could hear the sound of running feet behind her.

"Stop," cried a voice.

"'Tis Ben Faa. The devil has been shamming," and groping for something with which to defend herself, she grasped one of Red Ike's cudgels.

"Another foot forward, Ben Faa, and I'll brain you," she cried. Not for a moment did he pause, and as his body emerged from the branches of the tree, Jael felled him to the ground.

A loud whistle again sounded over the moor, and Jael counted, one, two, three, four. "They are converging on the house," she thought, and hurrying forward, she lifted the flagstone that covered the passage to the old well, and descended to the refuge of the tunnel.

The hue and cry after Red Ike was again fruitless, and when the police closed in on Sandyflatts and found Ben Faa lying insensible, and not another sign of life among the ruins of the old house, each looked at the other with surmise.

How had Ben Faa come to be there alone, and who had felled him? If Red Ike, how had he evaded them?

To solve the question quickly was of the utmost moment, and they straightway set about restoring Ben to consciousness. But the wily knave feigned a relapse time after time, until one of the police punched him in the ribs, and told him to get up without any more damned nonsense. Ben, not to be outwitted, took no heed, and they departed, and left him lying there.

They came to the cattle pool, and found Abegail. The old hag had at the moment regained her senses, and mistaking the police for Red Ike and Ben, yelled: "Knife him, Ben, knife him."

"Has Red Ike been here?" asked one of the officers.

"Hell and the devil! Has he escaped? I laid you on his trail, and he has slipped through the meshes of your net again. Where is Ben? He'll explain all to you."

"Ben Faa is at Sandyflatts. You'll find him there. I believe you are aiding and abetting Red Ike. Be careful or I'll have you arrested on suspicion of being concerned in the murder of John Lynd. We have yet to find the axe with which the deed was done."

Low among the whin-bushes, within a score of yards of Abegail and the officers, lay Red Ike with the axe in his hand, and standing up he swung the weapon round his head, and flung it into the cattle pool, and then, with wild cries like the hooting of an owl, fled across the moorland to the safety of the drift in the dale of the fall of rock.

Abegail crouched by the side of the pool in dread and consternation. She dared not speak. If the officers recovered the axe, Ben's doom was sealed. The handle alone would prove it his. It was marked with his name, and the size of the incisions in John Lynd's skull would prove the blade his also.

Now the splash in the cattle pool caused the police to scatter. There is no telling where a stone will land at night time, if thrown by an unseen foe.

"Red Ike is there," they cried with one breath, and raced in pursuit of the fleeing shadowy form.

Abegail waded into the pool for the axe, chuckling with frenzied joy.

But destiny is ever at variance with human wishes.

By the grey light of the breaking morn, the old witch, thinking to rid Ben of the axe forever, dropped it into the well-pit at Sandyflatts.

Meanwhile, and long ere this, Jael had crept from the well, and returned to the gypsies' camp. Red Ike, whose exact knowledge of the moorlands by night easily enabled him to outrun his pursuers, was soon in the drift telling the news to Will Moffatt.

Once more the dawn broke over the Hill of Devils, and far as the eye could reach from the entrance of the drift, the moorland seemed as peaceful as on a Sabbath morn.

Leisurely the sheep wandered and browsed, picking the greenest patches, which lay in soft, damp places.

An outlander, looking on the scene, and with no knowledge of the grim tragedy but lately enacted there, would have scoffed at the idea that hate and terror, misgiving and uncertainty, and all the turmoil that these engender in the human mind, disturbed a single soul on that wild stretch of common.

"Where are the gypsies encamped?" Will enquired of Red Ike. He turned with a puzzled look upon his face.

"'Tis strange, Will, but since they left Mirkholme I have never once thought where they are. I shall ask Jael tonight." Then, grasping his arm, and pointing with his finger, he said: "See, Will, there is a search party coming towards the dale. They are meaning to find us if possible. And, by the Lord, they have the lurcher Prodigal with them! If they keep the dog on the leash, it may come hither, and we are lost. I shall give them a hunt over the fells. I shall leave you here. Block up the entrance to the drift, and remain here until I return. I'll cross the dog's path, and once it strikes my trail it will follow me, no matter whither I flee. I'll not be caught, and if they slip the dog after me, they'll lay hands on neither of us today."

He then crawled into the open, and Will watched him take to the cover of the fallen scattered rocks that lay in confusion where they fell years before. He could not resist looking through the entrance to the drift as long as he thought it prudent and safe to let it remain open. Lithe as a fox, Red Ike passed unseen from point to point, until he was on the farther side of the dale. He then began to ascend the fell under cover of the whin-bushes. When near the top, he suddenly leapt into view on the top of a jutting crag and in wild defiance halloed to the police two thousand feet below him. Will wondered what the search party would next do, and he had no doubt that Red Ike was wondering the same. His heart throbbed at the intrepid daring of the man, poised in the wilds above his pursuers, but fearless as a lion in its native jungle.

The police now began to deploy, and from different angles to climb the fell on which Red Ike stood. Seeing this, he moved from his perch, and then, as if urged by a second thought, returned to it again, and placing his arched hands to his mouth shouted through them: "Prodigal! Prodigal! Prodigal!"

Instantly, the great dog tugged on its leash, and Ben Faa struck it savagely, but the dog turned upon him and seizing the offending hand crunched it sorely. And then Will saw the great animal breasting the fell, and could hear Red Ike encouraging it on its way. He had now no need to take any further risk, and blocking up the entrance to the drift, he returned to his bed of bracken and lay down and slept peacefully until nightfall.

Red Ike told him later that fleeing from fell to fell, and always making from top to top where he could guard himself from being surrounded, he held his own against the police until dusk. Then, in the dark, and favoured by the thick mist, he descended to the edge of Wastwater, and knowing that though 'twas midwinter, this deep and dark lake never freezes over, he leaped into its depth, and with Prodigal by his side swam from shore to shore.

"The wonder was," he said, "that the chilled water seemed to revive my exhausted body. I felt a wild, mad-cap, devil-may-care delight in cleaving my buoyant way through the liquid mass and the white mist on its surface.

"Once or twice, I started a flight of wild duck that fled my presence with shrill cries and clangour of wings, but I know that no man, nor boatful of men, dared follow me in my perilous swim through the dark. I could have overturned a dozen boats in safety, and escaped afterwards. That the wild duck should betray my whereabouts I had no fear on any score. And when I reached the off bank I felt reluctant to leave the water. Prodigal shook his great body, and licked my hand. I believe, if I had paused in the water, he would have paused too and licked my face. Never before had I felt such a strong fellowship for a dumb brute as I felt for him then. He had still the leash fastened to the collar round his neck with which Ben Faa had held him during the morning, and holding it in my hand we turned and together faced the fells once more. And straight as a bee flies, I allowed him to lead me through the dense mist from fell to fell and from dale to dale, and with never a hitch we again reached the drift."

CHAPTER XXV

UNDER the influence of a sudden impulse, Dick Stagg leapt to his feet in the small side-room of the public house in which we left him at Preston, and with a settled look of determination on his face, looked squarely at the desperate position he was in. And he saw plainly that he must either give himself into the hands of the law, or dodge from cover to cover, his life a very hell, until he was run to earth. And he resolved to go on the instant and visit Nell Glen.

He had little knowledge of the world beyond the work-folks amongst whom he was born and bred, and with a natural impetuosity, he went direct to the hotel where Nell was staying and asked to see her, and was told that orders had been given that she would not see visitors that day.

"But I must see her, and at once," insisted Dick.

There were several guests and artists lounging about the hotel hall at the time, and curious questioning smiles flickered upon their faces. Dick noticed their expression, and it steadied his nerve.

Would they ask her to come and speak to him then?

Immediately the words passed his lips, he saw his mistake.

The small crowd tittered. The rusticity of his manner, and the strong accent of dialect in his speech, made the proprietor of the hotel more stiff-necked than ever, and with a gesture of his hand, he cried: "Be off!"

Drawing himself erect, and with his head thrown back and clenched fists, Dick retorted: "Be civil or...." He did not finish the sentence when the jolly dog of an artist, who had butted his head into Joe Gream's stomach but a short time back, stepped forward and said: "Perhaps the gentleman has a valid reason for his request? Will he allow his card to be sent to the lady?"

"My card! What do you mean?"

"Well, your card with your name on, or failing that, shall one of the maids give the lady your name?"

This dumbfounded Dick. How could he give his name to anyone? Even now it might be posted on the hoardings, or shortly would be, as that of a fugitive murderer. No, he would leave the hotel. And he turned to go

"Hold," cried the landlord, "if you stir without giving an account of yourself, young man, I'll put the police on your...."

Dick wheeled round and faced him. The necessity of immediate counteraction on his part brought the quick brain of the poacher, so keenly alive to the sudden danger, into play. And with a torrent of biting sarcasm hardly to be expected from him by his appearance, he replied: "Would you add injury to insult? I came here peaceably to see this lady, and I mean to see her before I leave. What's wrong? Is my appearance at fault? Is this your usual fashion of treating strangers? What right have you to treat me as you are doing? Don't think you can intimidate me. Send for your police, send for the whole force if you like. In any case, I shall not leave without seeing the lady."

"And you shall see her; wait here a moment until I return," said the jolly artist, and a few minutes later Dick was ushered into Nell's private room.

Holding out her hand to him with a frank smile, she said: "I am pleased to see you, Dick, but what brought you hither?"

"To see and speak with you for the last time, Nell."

"I saw you on Christmas Eve at the opera at Carlisle, Dick."

"Oh, I had just been released from jail, and Will Moffatt and I thought we'd like to see the new star before we walked home, and during that night John Lynd was murdered, and Red Ike, Will Moffatt, and I are blamed for the deed."

Nell turned pale, and grasped a chair for support, and a wild light came into her eyes. Dick looked upon her in wonder and astonishment, but did not move.

Gently she sank to the floor and crouched in a heap with both hands pressed against her temples while the wild light in her eyes faded to a dull stare. Then she rose to her feet again, and gliding up to Dick, whispered: "Tell me you are innocent, my love. Oh, Dick, you had no hand in the shedding of blood?"

She grasped his hands, and gazed upon them fondly.

"They are white and pure, and are my Dick's, my Dick's."

Dropping her voice to a still lower whisper, she stole from him again: "But I am not worthy to touch you. I, the soiled outcast defiled with the filth of Joe Gream. Would to God that I were dead."

"*Nell!*"

And the name fell from Dick's lips with such passionate intensity that the woman's body thrilled to its tone, and the wild light faded from her eyes, and the man and the woman faced each other with open arms, and, for the moment, the evil of the world, and the portions of evil that had been theirs, were as though such were not.

During her previous fits of temporary insanity, Nell had had to sleep off their effects, but now she burst into a storm of tears and found relief, and Dick soothed her into peace, and in the act forgot his own desperate position.

Was it Shelley who said that he was older at thirty than was his grandfather at eighty, meaning that life is to be measured by experience? Perhaps a full, free, intensive existence, in which the noblest passions of the human soul are quickened to fruition, is man's true goal.

The trials of life are as necessary to our development as are its joys. Yet who but the rarest spirits recognize this? Had Dick Stagg and Nell Glen divined it, they would have rejoiced in the midst of affliction.

Out of darkness comes the dawn, and resurrection follows death, and when love is triumphant all else is but vanity of vanities.

Dick was shown into Nell's private room at noon, and at dusk of evening he was still there. A frank and full explanation from both sides left them without doubt that they had both been the victims of a dark scheme, and that their lack of exercising careful thought had cost them many months of despondency and misery. What now was to be done?

Nell suggested that Dick return to Red Ike, and learn all the particulars of the murder; the exact hour of its happening, and where and with what weapon the deed was done.

"Would it do to hire a private detective? You had better ask Red Ike and Will Moffatt, and let me know as soon as possible what they think. Someone who could move about with absolute freedom to investigate the case is necessary to combat the police in their efforts to fix the crime on innocent men.

"Dick, I know you are not guilty, but the three of you are doomed unless you can prove it. All hinges on this, and no time is to be lost."

"Then," said Dick, "I shall return to the moorlands immediately."

"And I shall expect you back within three days," counselled Nell, "and meanwhile I shall hire a detective to consult with you when you return. And now, God speed you!"

Ere he turned to go, he gazed upon the lair creature before him, and overwhelmed with his great love he would fain have clasped her again to his heart, but with an extended arm she motioned him off.

"No, no, do not touch me again, Dick. Things can never be as they once were between us. But oh, forgive me, Dick, forgive me!"

"Nonsense, Nell. We have thrown the past behind us forever. And with your help, I shall again be a free man to walk the world and look upon my fellows eye to eye; and then, whether you will it or not, whither you go I shall go, and live in the light of your presence always. If not as a husband, or lover, or friend, as a stranger I shall hover near you, hoarding the joy in my heart that I was something more to you than a remembered name. Do not forget this, Nell; for whatever betides I shall love you as I have always loved you. Let me kiss you once again for old times' sake."

She suffered his lips to touch her, and the next minute he was striding along Preston's main thoroughfare, happier than he had been for months, and bound for the moorlands miles away.

Preoccupied and being a rapid walker, he ran against a man coming carelessly from a side-street, and seized him to keep him from falling.

"Hello! my friend," the man cried, "we've met again." And Dick beheld the jolly artist who had helped him to see Nell. "Who the devil would have thought to tumble over you?

"Whither are you bound for so fast? Come and have a drink, lad. You're a lucky man to be in the good grace of the new star. I'd give my last shirt to stand in your shoes. And well, I'll be damned, when one gets a fair look at you she has not such bad taste after all's said and done. Come and have a drink. Come and have a drink. I'm on my way to the theatre, and have just time for one." And with a slap on the shoulder, as if they had been friends for a lifetime, he did not give Dick the chance to refuse the kindly meant potion.

Seated in a quiet snug of The Red Rose of Lancaster, the artist sized Dick up in the twinkle of an eye. He saw that his want of polish and manners was not due to lack of intelligence, but solely to his peasant upbringing. Given an opportunity, he would soon remedy these defects, and he knew, by the ease with which he had expressed himself to the landlord of the hotel where Nell was staying, that he had a gift of speech, and he wondered if Dick were the new Star's brother or lover. Still, this did not matter to him, he liked Dick, and being a true Bohemian and man of the world, wished to be friends with him. It was lucky for Dick that the artist's time was short.

"Can I be of further service to you, my young friend?" he asked.

"Not tonight. I am leaving the town immediately, but shall be back shortly."

"Then I shall be delighted to meet you here when you return. I shall call at this hour each evening as long as we remain at Preston. Now, shall we have another drink? I must be off."

"Yes," said Dick, and ringing for the waiter, he threw a florin on the table.

"Damn it! I did not mean you to pay for it."

"But," replied Dick, "you paid for the first drinks."

The artist held out his hand. And then, leaving the snug, each went his way.

That night, Nell was a greater marvel than ever before to her audience. Hitherto, the magic of her voice, charged as it was with suppressed and hopeless love, and tinged with the fire of insanity, had swept men out of themselves with its direct appeal to the sadness inherent in the great hungry heart of humanity that is ever waiting the vibrant touch of the supreme master to awaken and captivate it into one mighty whole. But now there was a change within her, and the note in her voice was transformed and clarified to one of triumphant exaltation. Victory was hers. Not the winning of applause, fame, or money. She was standing on the apex of the heights of life, and pouring forth to a listening world, through her song, a liquid message, a mating symphony, a call that was being answered in the spirit of the annunciation. She had emerged from the darkness of defeat and woe into the morning sunlight of boundless love, and the joy and richness of her happiness she scattered bounteously amongst her fellows, as a thanksgiving offering is poured forth by the giver of all good. Her spell was irresistible, and the audience, carried to the extreme of enthusiasm, acclaimed her wonderful power. She knew that her love for Dick was the source of it. The jolly artist who earlier in the evening had been with Dick shrewdly guessed the truth of their relations, and chuckled with self-satisfied glee. His was a generous soul that scorned the jealousy that hinders some men from exulting with pleasure at another's success.

Meanwhile Dick, with his face to the North Star, was taking advantage of every cross-country shortcut to reach Kendal by midnight or shortly after. The hue and cry was out after him, but the fact that he was journeying north in the direction of the scene of the murder of John Lynd told in his favour, and he allowed no man to pass him without a cheery good-night. However, as he was about to enter Kendal, a policeman challenged him: "Whither are you bound so late, young chap?"

"Home," Dick replied maunderingly, and as if affected with drink.

The officer attempted to grasp him by the collar, but Dick squared himself erectly, determined not to be arrested.

"Stand aside and let me pass. What the devil do you want with me?"

The vision of Nell rose to his mind. To be taken now would be to surrender the chance of proving himself innocent, and seeing the policeman about to draw his truncheon, Dick landed him a blow between the eyes and bowled him over into the gutter. Then doubling back the road he had come, and vaulting over a hedge, he passed Kendal Castle ruins on his right, and struck out towards the outline of the distant fells, and afterwards faced again for Windermere. On reaching here, he determined to journey along the main road, and passed safely over the bridge at Troutbeck, but when nearing Lowood Hotel, the sound of galloping horses made him take to the fields again, and lying low in the shadow of the hazel coppice that skirts the main highway, he awaited the approach of the horsemen. At the corner of the road that leads over Kirkstone Pass they paused. "I don't think we need go farther," said one to the others, "we are on a wild-goose chase." And they laughed together.

"Nay," said another, "we were ordered to ride to the foot of The Raise, where most likely we'll meet with the officers from Keswick; and if they have not met with the supposed fugitive, it has been some drunken fool that knocked the wind out of Capstick, the blatherskite."

"He sees double at times," said a third man jokingly, "especially when on night duty. Ginger pop's cheap then."

"Come, come, I could sup a pint now," said the first speaker as off they set at a trot towards Grasmere.

Dick now realized that to reach the moorland safely by daybreak he would have to cross Kirkstone Pass and go by Ullswater and Dockray to Cobble Ho. Evidently the police were scouring the main roads for him, and he would therefore be in no danger crossing the highways over the wild fells in midwinter. Bracing himself for the ordeal, he pushed mightily forward, and was soon over the top and descending the farther side of the pass. Brotherswater, as he was passing its still mirror, reflected a thousand stars, and he paused to gaze upon its glory, and thought of the cattle pool where the three runnels meet on his native moorland, and by whose side he had often sat with Nell Glen when the stars shone in the depth of the pool, and the glow-worms on its edge.

"But I have no time to waste," he ejaculated, and hurried to the dale below. Going at a free pace through Patterdale, he passed under Stybarrow Crag and thence to Dockray and Matterdale and onwards to his destination, the wide wild moorland above the Vale of Threlkeld. Leaving the stark mass of Mell Fell behind, he turned westward along the Roman road over the common till he reached the site of the old settlement above Birkett Bank. Here he threw his body down amongst the brown bracken and black heather, and rested himself, and not until now had he thought of the position in which he was placed. Thus far had he come, but he had no friends on whom he could rely for shelter in his desperate need. After a long debate with himself, he resolved to go to Sandyflatts and trust to luck, a decision he was fated not to fulfil.

As he raised himself from the ground, a dark figure rose with him, and he would have turned and fled, had not the voice of Red Ike commanded him to stay: "I have waited here since nightfall for you, Dick. Jael foretold to me your coming. She even knew the route you would travel. I laughed at her, but she prevailed on me to come hither."

And Dick replied: "I am here by the express desire of Nell Glen to confer with you."

"And where is she?" asked Red Ike.

"At Preston. She is the new opera star whom Will Moffatt and I heard sing at Carlisle on Christmas Eve when we were released from jail."

Red Ike mused and whistled softly to himself.

"Did she see you and Will Moffatt at the opera?"

"Yes, but she did not know Will nor he her."

"Did you both sit out the opera, Dick?"

"Yes, and we walked together to Sandyflatts afterwards."

"Will told me that. But are you sure that the new star is Nell Glen? It seems almost incredible to me, Dick."

"She has sent me hither, I tell you. Damn it! The position you and Will and I are in hardly warrants me to play the fool. She offers to hire a private detective to investigate fully the murder of John Lynd. Will you aid him in the case?"

"Come with me then," said Red Ike, and together they journeyed to the drift in the dale of the fall of rock.

As they passed Sandyflatts, Dick wondered whither they were bound, and when they came to the cattle pool and struck across the moorland to the southwest, he ventured to ask Red Ike if he had mistaken the way. On being answered in the negative, he was content to follow the lead taken, knowing that his companion knew the district better by night than he did by day. They were about to pass Jael's parents' grave when they were commanded to stand.

Without a word they both turned, and fled pursued by three mounted police.

"This way," cried Red Ike, and they plunged in amongst the thick, upstanding whin-bushes, through which no rider could follow them, and no man could distinguish them in the dark from many of the bushes that stood the height of a tall man.

"There is a good sheep-track within fifty yards of us, Dick, and once we strike it we can defy pursuit. It leads to the fell tops; the whin-bushes flourish halfway up to the tops."

Together they raced for life, pursued only by the shouts of the baffled police.

"That was touch and go, Dick, but halfway up the fell the bleaberry bushes not growing so high will afford us easier travelling, and if we meet with no one else, we will yet accomplish our journey before daybreak."

As the day broke, Will Moffatt welcomed Red Ike and Dick within the drift. Prodigal was lying on a bed of dried bracken, but he swung his great tail like a whiplash over his back with delight. Dick beheld with astonishment the ample meal spread out on the rocky ledge. Here was undoubtedly a refuge where a man could defend himself until starved out, if his hiding-den were discovered, an unlikely happening.

Though Dick was not a book-lover, he noticed the piles of volumes arranged on projections from the quarried rock-face. As Will shook his hand and said: "Well, lad, is the prima donna your lady-love?" he was still marvelling at the things about him, so Red Ike answered: "She is, Will, and the very fact that she is has saved you and Dick from the gallows."

This caused both Dick and Will to start, but Red Ike affected not to notice their amazement, and struck off into another line of thought.

"Jael was right, Will, as she foretold. Dick crossed Kirkstone Pass last night, and came by Ullswater to the moorland. I met him where she told me to wait, and she gauged the time of his arrival. She also told me last night that Dick and I would go to Preston, and directed the course we should take. Until Dick turned up last night, I had no faith in her predictions, but now I feel bound to follow her advice. Nell Glen is at Preston. She offers us, through Dick, the service of a private detective to investigate the murder of John Lynd, but I must see him before he comes hither. And Will, Joe Gream and Peg are both at Preston."

"How do you know they are?" exclaimed Dick.

"Jael told me so," said Red Ike, looking keenly at him.

"And how does she know?"

Red Ike, still watching Dick, said: "How did she know you would cross Kirkstone Pass last night? You'll remember, Dick, that you and Peg were going together to Preston from Penrith. She knew this also, though I have not mentioned it to mortal being, not even to Will here. She also told me that had there been a full eclipse of the moon a week ago instead of a partial one, she could have foretold the whole outcome of John Lynd's murder. She was born under the full eclipse of the moon, and can divine things better then than at other times. However, she is able to say that no harm will befall you and me on our journey to and from Preston, therefore we shall set off at dusk; so you had better get a good meal, and sleep till then."

A few hours later, Red Ike and Dick were standing by the cairn on the top of Stake Pass. Langstrath lay in the gloom behind them, filled with the thunder of roaring becks that fell fifteen hundred feet, and seemed to make the darkness tremble. On their right lay Angle Tarn, glittering like glass beneath the stars. Esk Hawes frowned against the skyline. Rossett Ghyll, black and forbidding, warned them of danger. The Pike o' Stickle on their left held itself aloft like a lance. The huge bulks of Crinkle Crags faced them and grew more and more awesome to look on as the poachers descended to Mickle-den at the head of the Great Langdale Valley. Passing high Dungeon Ghyll Hotel on the left, they climbed the steep sandy road to Blea Tarn, the retreat of Wordsworth's Solitary, but which is not, as is generally thought by most writers, the point of vantage from which Wordsworth beheld the wonderful cloud scene described in *The Excursion*. Now they strode briskly along towards Little Langdale. The Pike o' Blisco stood between them and the Heavenly Twins. Wetherlam rose through the dark in front of them. On their right lay the rugged Wrynose Pass at whose base stands Fellfoot Farm, the meeting place of old-time smugglers, at a date when most of the mountain pony-tracks were known only to a few bold spirits like Lanty Slee and William Litt, whose names and exploits deserve more than a local notice. As Red Ike and Dick passed Little Langdale Tarn, a troop of wild swans swept trumpeting through the night, and plunged into the water. At Hall Garth, Red Ike paused a moment, then he turned to the right over Mossrigg, and said to Dick: "We will keep to the loneliest mountain paths until we are clear of the Lake Country."

Leaving Tilberthwaite's thundering force on their right, they crossed the Stepping Stones, and shortly afterwards passed the famous Yewdale yew-tree, and entered the ravine which Tennyson, while staying on his honeymoon at Tent Lodge, Coniston, named

Glen-Mary. A few minutes later, they skirted Tarn Hows laying bare to the stars. The main road to Hawkshead was now before them. Passing unchallenged through this old-world town, whose lake lay like a gleaming gem on their right, they walked rapidly to Newby Bridge. The country was now more open, and they decided to make first for Lancaster, and thence to Preston.

The evening was dark and heavy with clouds as Dick stepped into the snug of The Red Rose of Lancaster.

"Hello!" cried the jolly artist, rising to his feet. "Welcome, my friend. It never rains blessings singly. Meeting with you is one, and that I have a note for you is another, and the third is that I can drink your luck in a pint of prime Kendal stout."

"Good luck!" replied Dick, and they drank the toast together.

Later, when Red Ike, with the air of a well-to-do citizen, entered the snug and rang the bell, the artist glanced at Dick and lifted his eyebrows significantly but good-humouredly, and was surprised in the action by Red Ike, who, with a smile, said: "Will you two gentlemen have a drink with me?"

"I'd drink with the Queen," said the artist, "that is, if she asked me, which is unlikely."

"There are all kinds of kings," replied Red Ike, "and those are not the least sociable who are uncrowned. Here's a health to you both."

"Your health," said the artist, "and I beg your pardon for the ungracious act you surprised me in."

"There's no offence where none is meant, my friend, and the man that cannot enjoy a joke even at his own expense has but a poor spirit."

And Red Ike saw and was satisfied that the man, though a jolly dog, was trustworthy in his own way.

CHAPTER XXVI

WHEN Red Ike and Dick left the drift on the journey to Preston, Will Moffatt, to drive away his oppressive loneliness, began to read Chapman's translation of Homer's wonderful poetical romance.

Unlike Red Ike, he had been, during the last seven years of his life, a wanderer on the face of the earth. Restless and without a definite aim, he had drifted from province to province in the New World, and during that time he had read but little. His unappeased love for Jean Lynd had gnawed unceasingly at his heart, and now the story of Helen's abduction, and the love the Homeric hero had for her, wrought strangely upon his mood, and his blood mounted, and surged through his body, until the ravishment of his feeling became almost unbearable, and he laid the book aside in a transport of wild longing to be with Jean once more. The lurcher, Prodigal, lay curled on its bracken bed, and he was about to stoop and clap it, when it rose slowly to its feet, and stood rigid as a block of granite with bristling back, and ears cocked forward and wide-eyed, looking to the entrance of the drift.

"What is there, Prodigal?"

The dog did not move. Hitherto it had been as bold as a lion in the face of danger.

"Good lad!" he said, and yet the dog did not move. And now he could hear the rustle of garments somewhere down the dark tunnel, and he held the candle above his head and gazed through the gloom.

"My God!" he ejaculated. Gliding towards him came the form of a woman, clad in a lawn nightdress that reached to her bare ankles. On her feet were a pair of thin slippers; and her hair fell loosely to her waist. Her eyes were fixed and staring and sightless. She was fast asleep.

"'Tis Jean," he cried, and moved to clasp her in his arms. But she fell back as though conscious of his nearness, and yet not a muscle of her face showed the least sign of life. She was indeed a walking corpse. Her soul was working the limbs of her body, but was not of it. 'Twas in some far-away mystic region unknown to psychological research. A disembodied entity that no doubt impelled the slumbering mortal part of Jean Lynd to obey an instinct that in her waking senses she would not have understood, and which she would have shrunk from in fear and awe, had she been awake and able to think about it. And Will Moffatt held the lighted candle, and watched her.

Mechanically she moved about the drift, and pausing she lifted Longfellow's *Evangeline* from its shelf of projecting rock, and murmured: "Gabriel, my Beloved." But her voice had a faraway sound in its tone, as though she spoke from some innermost recess of her being, and without the use of any of her faculties other than that of her tongue. 'Twas evident to him that Jean was acting under some powerful attractive force. And it dawned upon him then that but a short time back the Homeric story of Helen of Troy, and the loves of the rivals for her, had roused his own emotions to such a pitch that he could read no more, and that the wild longing for Jean in his heart had become unbearable, and in a flash of insight he saw that this was the cause of her coming to the drift. His thought, love-charged, had flown to her on the wings of ether, and even in coma she had answered his call.

What would she do next, he wondered? And with amazement he saw her remove the carved stick from the boring in the rock face, and hold it in an upright position before her and press the jaws of the serpent so deftly outlined upon the stick, and when the ivory ball between the serpent's jaws opened in halves, she held the stick at arm's length and spelt letter by letter, "The Gypsy's Luck." Then she replaced the stick in the boring, and turned to the bedside, and knelt and prayed audibly for her dead father, and for comfort for her mother, and for her own reunion with himself. And still he held the lighted candle, and Jean prepared for herself the bed of bracken, and then glided forward and extinguished the light in his hand and lay down to rest. After a few moments, he relit the candle, and a low sweet voice behind him breathed his name and Jael stood before him.

"I have come to inquire after Jean. I met her by the moorland grave, but ere I could arrest her attention she fled my presence. In vain I pursued her. Fleeter than the shadows of night that sometimes baffle my comprehension whither they come and go, she passed from my view. I have since been to her home and to Sandyflatts and have not found her; yet I thought I glimpsed her by the cattle pool where the three runnels meet on the moorland. Is she here?"

Will handed Jael the candle, and motioned her to the bed of bracken, and they both gazed upon Jean sleeping peacefully as a child.

"What is to be done now?" inquired Jael.

"We can do nothing until she wakens," he replied. "She has come hither in her night attire, and cannot again leave the drift until she is clothed."

"Her mother," said Jael, "is leaving The Bents tomorrow, and Jean should accompany her."

"Whither are they going, Jael?"

"I do not know. However, in any case, Jean needs some clothing, and I shall risk the getting of it for her."

And ere he could question her further, she fled down the tunnel of the drift, and passed into the night.

He took the lighted candle and waved it over Jean's closed eyelids, but she did not move. Yet he knew she was now in a natural sleep, by the regular heaving of her bosom, and the serene composure of her features; and he dared to stoop and kiss her on the brow.

A smile flitted over her face, but quickly passed again into the blissful dreamland whence it came.

"Jean," he whispered in her ear. He could not resist the temptation to recall the sleeping wonder of his treasure.

"Will," she exclaimed, half rising from the bed, and leaning her head upon her hand. "You here? Oh, for the love of God, begone, or you will be taken by the police."

"Nay, we are in the drift," he answered.

"In the drift. How? Why? What has happened?"

"You came hither alone an hour ago, my love," and he laid his hand upon her head and continued. "Out of the night you came, in answer to my passionate call. Deep calleth unto deep. And 'tis well that at last we have come together by means that are beyond our control. I cried out to you in my great love, and you in the love you bear for me could not but answer my appeal. How else can your presence here be explained? I know that in a normal state you would have been afraid to pass through the weird loneliness of the wintry moorlands by night, but you came as you are, unprotected from the cold, and with love and prayer upon your lips."

Not for a moment was Jean at a loss, and without hesitancy replied: "I remember distinctly hearing you call upon me, Will, but where I was at the time I have no knowledge. I must have been asleep at home. Or how comes it that I came hither as I am now?" Rising from the bed of bracken, she stood before him in all her exquisite loveliness. And she took his head between her hands, and he felt the warmth of her body enveloping him, as though with a garment. Yet he dared not embrace her, so great was his longing to possess her.

Midnight was long passed ere Jael returned to the drift, and Will saw by her face that something untoward had happened. He welcomed her, but passed no comment on her altered look.

After handing him a bundle of Jean's clothes, she squatted on the ground with arms wound round her drawn up knees, and fell into deep thought. Hitherto he had possessed very little personal knowledge of Jael, and he silently contemplated the rare type of beauty before him. Her olive complexion, enhanced with the glow of pure physical health, her dark eyes, and black hair, a wealth of profusion but strong in fibre, bespoke her the born gypsy. 'Twas the cast of her features, the lofty brow, the straight nose, delicately formed, but slightly extended at the nostrils, the oval face and the mouth and chin that betrayed the blend of Celtic blood in her veins. In repose, one would have been puzzled to define her nationality, but later when he began to converse with her, and beheld her alert and seething under the stress and fire of emotion, he knew that her super-sensitiveness was an inheritance from the wayward and passionate soul of John Lynd.

A slight movement on the bed of bracken in the side-drift farthest from them caused Jael to look up at him, and then, as if suddenly remembering where she was, questioned; "Is Red Ike here?"

He answered: "No, he has gone to Preston."

"Yes, yes," she replied, "I had forgotten for the moment. He will be back tomorrow night. Meanwhile, Jean must stay here." And rising from the ground, with clenched fists and drawn face, and a wild look in her eyes, she faced him, her whole body tense with suppressed passion.

"I saw Ben Faa at The Bents tonight."

The abruptness of her speech, and the import of it, startled him, and he ejaculated, "Well?"

"He was with Mrs. Lynd, and they were striking a bargain, and I was the chattel of their trading. By fair means or foul, my body has to become the property of Ben Faa. The price of his success, a thousand pounds, is already paid over. But I shall have a say in the matter. Hist, is Jean asleep?"

He nodded.

"Before morning I shall bring the money to you. Will you keep it safe until I require it again?"

"I should be aiding and abetting you in a theft, Jael."

"No, Will Moffatt, you will be helping me to keep myself inviolate. I shall never return to the arms of Red Ike, unless my body has belonged to him alone. Until now he is the one man that has possessed me, and by the child that I bore him he shall be my one and only man henceforth. The money, when my aim is achieved, I shall return to Mrs. Lynd. I do not covet it, nor shall Ben Faa reap the reward of an attempt upon my chastity. Again, Will Moffatt, will you help me?"

"On the conditions you propose, I will, Jael."

"Good," she replied, and prepared to depart for the gypsies' camp. He escorted her to the entrance of the drift, and exhorted her to use every precaution in what she was about to attempt, but elicited no response. Without another word she slid into the night.

He returned to his stone by the ledge of rock, and tried to interest himself once more in the story of Troy City, but all in vain, and he laid the book aside, and took the lighted candle, and went and looked upon his Jean once again.

She was sleeping soundly, and had been during Jael's presence in the drift. He was glad of this. She had trouble enough to bear.

Why add to it until circumstances compelled the necessity of doing so? And he bethought him of the clothing that Jael had brought. He would undo the bundle and place them by her side.

He began to think of the tangle of events in which he had become involved, and could see no immediate definite clue by which the mystery of John Lynd's murder could be solved. But the workings of destiny are not of man's ordering, though men are the puppets through whose agency destiny achieves its purposes.

Had he dared to have left Jean alone in the drift, he would have followed Jael to the gypsies' camp. He was afraid that Ben Faa might do Jael bodily harm if he caught her taking the money; and he was no less afraid that Jean, in one of her fits of somnambulism, might, during his absence, return to The Bents. He was relieved in his anxiety by Jean herself.

"Will," she called, and in an instant he was by her bedside. "I have had such a strange dream," she continued. "I thought Jael was in the drift with us and my mother and Ben Faa; and there were also two dark shadows hovering about us, but these were formless, and I could not gather from what objects they were cast. And I thought that, though I was present, I was not of the company, nor could I be seen by any of you, nor hear a word that passed amongst you. And I wondered at this, and endeavoured to make myself known to you all, but in vain. And I laid my hand upon your arm, Will, but found that you were not conscious of my touch, and that I could pass through your body, and the bodies of all present, without resistance or feeling on the part of any of you, and yet I was not afraid. In fact I myself had no feeling, I was simply spirit, yet in likeness and shape to the physical body I now am. And my power of perception was so great that I knew what thought was passing in the minds of you all. The expressed thought was not a hundredth part of your thinking. And the desire to conceal thought was great in all of you. And I saw, Will, that your love for me made you waver again and again in your relations with others. You wished to help Jael against Ben Faa, and you thought of me. But Ben could not harm Jael. One of the dark shadows that were hovering in the drift placed itself between them, and, Will, it formed itself into the shape and likeness of my father. And Ben's soul shrank within himself, not because he could see my father's wraith, but because my father's soul's thought dominated Ben, being greater than he. All this may seem strange to you. However, the other dark shadow that hovered in the drift glided towards my mother and sombrely spread itself around her, and I knew its influence was evil. I thought her thought with her. And her wish to protect me urged her to evil thinking and doing. And she plotted with Ben Faa to destroy Jael. And my father's wraith seemed power-less to interfere between them, and I glided towards my mother, and the dark shadow in which she stood fell backwards from about her, and I followed it, and it sank through the solid rock-sides of the drift, and I knew then that the Power of Darkness cannot prevail with my mother if I remain steadfast to protect her, and, by the help of God, I shall do so."

Will could not but marvel at Jean's story. She believed it a dream, yet nevertheless he saw it was no mere dream, and that the course of events past and future would ultimately prove it to be true. And the knowledge of this gave him courage and hope.

Until now, Jean had not spoken of Red Ike. Nor had he come into the vision of her dream.

Will was sitting on a huge block and facing the entrance to the drift. Jean was lying on her bracken bed. Her hand lay in his. The flickering gleams of the candlelight gave to the sides of the main drift a weird appearance where the jutting portions of crag cast strange shadows, human and animal-like, on the smoother portions of rock. In happier hours he might have taken a pleasure in amusing himself and Jean, by tracing out figures as he had often done, mak-ing them with his fingers in years long past on the walls of Sandy-flatts. But now a fresh shadow startled him, and Jean's hand was clutched in his with fear. On the wall of the main drift a shadow, the height of a man, advanced towards the entrance of the side-drift. They watched it moving, but could not hear the sound of a footfall, yet they knew that the body from which the shadow cast was in mo-tion. And, lo, the shadow turned its head, and they both exclaimed: "Prodigal?"

The great dog was walking on its hind legs towards them. He called it, but it stood waving its forelegs, and then, dropping to the ground, glided away to the entrance of the main drift. Will then re-membered that after Jael left him to return to the gypsies' camp, he had securely blocked up the opening. Without a second thought, he hastened, and gave her admittance. As she advanced up the drift, Jean, who was unaware of Jael's coming, welcomed her with a glad cry and arms open to embrace her. Yet Jael gave no sign of friendly feeling or otherwise, and a shade of disappointment came upon Jean's face. He watched them intently, and knew by intuition that Jael was about to make some disclosure that might cause an es-trangement between them, and gypsy-like she came to the point at once:

"I was at The Bents tonight, Jean, and I saw your mother and Ben Faa together there. I heard them discuss certain questions concerning me with great freedom. Do you know that Ben has visited your mother frequently since your father was murdered?"

"I have not see him there since that event, Jael."

"I believe you, Jean."

"Jael, you know that I know that you are the legal heir to all our father possessed, and that I am his natural daughter, with no legal claim upon his estate."

"Yes, yes, Jean, but do you know that for your sake, your mother is plotting with Ben Faa to defraud me of my rights?"

"I do not, Jael; nor shall I ever keep one groat's worth of what belongs to you. I once possessed the proofs that your mother was our father's first wife. These I should have given you, but I lost them. How I cannot say. Yet I know that neither my mother, nor Abegail, nor Ben Faa has them."

"How do you know that, Jean?"

"I refuse to say, Jael."

"Then you know who killed John Lynd." And Jael leapt to her feet in a frenzy of passion, and would have flown at Jean had Will not restrained her. And Jean, self-possessed and calm, gazed upon Jael in wonder and answered: "If I knew that, my sister, I should have the murderer hanged without regret. I loved our father. With all his shortcomings, he was a kind father to me. Bear with me, Jael, if you think I am hiding something from you. What came of the proofs mentioned I do not know. More than this I shall not say."

"May God forgive me, Jean. I forgot! I forgot! You gave the proofs to me by the grave cut crosswise over my mother's grave, the night before our father was buried. You were walking in your sleep, and were therefore quite unconscious of what you were doing. Indeed, I followed you to The Bents. You remember my words with your mother there, when you woke from your sleep, and were astonished to find me with you. I gave the proofs to Red Ike."

Jean stepped forward, and laid a hand upon Jael's head.

"If I did as you say, my sister, I know it not. Surely, you can now trust me to the uttermost knowing this. That I gave the proofs to you, to whom they rightly belong, whilst I was in a subconscious state goes far to prove that I meant them for you in my rational moments.

"Now tell me what you know of my mother and Ben Faa."

Jael unloosed the fold of her dress, and holding a bundle, of banknotes towards Jean, said: "There is the price paid by your mother to Ben Faa, on condition that he compel me, by fair means or foul, to become his wife; and the compact on your mother's part was that she hold her tongue with regard to the murderer of your father."

And turning to the boring, in which was hidden the carved stick, Jael drew it forth; and planting it upright in the drift, glided three times round it, muttering: "By the Eye of the Pyramids, the North Star, and the Carved Stick, things sacred to the whole gypsy tribe, I swear in the presence of Jean Lynd and Will Moffatt that what I have said concerning myself and the murder of John Lynd is the truth, the whole truth, and nothing but the truth."

The weirdness of her motions, the strange intonations of her voice, and the contortions of her features as she muttered the oath filled Jean and Will with awe; and as if to complete the rite the great lurcher rose on its hind legs and circled three times round the carved stick, whining plaintively, and all the while waving its fore paws.

This done, Jael cried, "There," and tossed Will the banknotes. He laid them on the ledge of the rock, beside the Homer he had been reading, and then replaced the stick in the boring.

Jean glanced at him and he felt compelled to explain his position with regard to the money. A pained expression crossed her face as if she were thinking he had not trusted her fully in the past. Only for a moment did its shadow darken her look, and he inwardly rejoiced to see it pass. He could not bear to think she doubted him for a moment. In his own mind he had resolved to risk going to Kendal the next day and banking the money in Jael's name, and should have done so had she herself not suggested an alternative.

By the edge of the old Roman road that lies along the breast of Helvellyn, there are occasionally unearthed old stone coffins in which, at a very early period no doubt, had been buried the remains of some chieftains, or men of mark in their day. However, Jael, in her lonely wanderings, had discovered one of these sepulchres near the surface, and had had the temerity to prize open the coffin-lid, and look on the dust that had lain there for at least two thousand years. The marvel was that the grave was unknown to the countryside. Perhaps it had been discovered and rediscovered, and forgotten again and again by shepherds who had no interest in such things; and perhaps Jael was the first to learn of its being there, after the death of the last man in whose memory lingered the name or fame of the occupant of the grave.

However, Jael would have the money hidden in the grave. Will was pleased rather than otherwise at this suggestion, and that night Jael and he deposited it there.

Afterwards, he could not persuade her to return with him to the drift. She would go to the gypsies' camp. But he suggested: "How if Ben Faa has missed the money?"

"So much the better if he has," she answered, with a low guttural laugh. "He dare not harm me whilst it is in my possession."

He bade her good-night.

"Nay, I shall see you again before morning," she replied, and glided away.

After parting with Jael, the desire possessed him to visit Sandy-flatts, and he turned his steps thither. There was no reason for doing so, but he could not resist the impulse, nor did he think of the danger of arrest he might be running, nor did he use any caution when he got there. He simply strode through the bour tree that blocked up the doorway, crossed the floor of the roofless kitchen, entered the old milkhouse, and striking a light examined the place.

The bed of bracken Red Ike had made, the pile of wood he had chopped and heaped into a corner, in fact everything in the room, had been placed in a heap on the centre of the floor and burned to ashes.

"Ben Faa has been here, by God!" he exclaimed.

"He is here now," said a voice behind him. Will turned and beheld him standing before him.

"Where is Jael?" he demanded.

"I am here, Ben Faa."

He leaped round at the sound of her voice, and Will sprang upon him, and with his knee in his back, and his throat between his hands, he held him powerless. He gripped him until he sank to the ground in a heap.

"There is a rope hanging from the beam in the milkhouse. Bring it to me, Jael."

He tied his arms behind his back, and then ordered him to stand up. He feigned unconsciousness, but Will swore he'd hang him to the cross-beam of the kitchen, if he did not arise.

"To the cattle pool where the three runnels meet on the moor-land," Will commanded. He obeyed implicitly. And there he tied his legs together and left him. At dawn a butcher, stopping by the pool to water his horse, found Ben and released him.

Will returned alone to the drift in the dale of the fall of rock. It was tenantless; even Prodigal was gone.

Morn would break within an hour. The world by daylight to him was forbidden, and weary in body, and perplexed and anxious at the disappearance of Jean, he retired to bed. At nightfall again he would go to The Bents, and until then he slept through a dreamless day.

CHAPTER XXVII

WHEN Dick Stagg read the note Nell Glen sent by the artist, he gazed upon him with blank amazement. Red Ike noticed the change upon Dick's face and wondered. The note was brief and to the point.

> Hotel Plantagenet,
> Preston,
> Tuesday.
>
> DEAR DICK,
>
> You can show this note to the bearer, Mr. Thomas Mayne, and trust him with your case, and arrange with him to see me at any time during the day.
>
> Ever yours,
>
> NELL.

Dick handed the note to Red Ike, and the artist thrust his hands into his trousers pockets, and glanced inquiry at them both. He saw that the two men were friends, and that their meeting at The Red Rose of Lancaster was not a chance one.

After a few moments' reflection, Red Ike passed the note to the artist. The jolly dog became all seriousness. To look upon, he was another man, quick and vigilant, and tapping the note with his fingers said: "Well, how can I serve you, gentlemen?"

"Have you a private room where you are staying?" said Dick.

"I can soon procure one. Come with me."

"We dare not be seen together on the street."

"Is your case so bad as that? However, I'll pledge you my word that with me you are safe. Still, if you would rather, come separately to the Hotel Plantagenet, and I shall give orders to have you admitted to me there."

On their arrival, the artist and Nell were awaiting them. Nell explained briefly how she had decided to enlist his service on behalf of her friends. She knew that he had been engaged for many years as a detective before he took to the stage; she had felt that she could place implicit confidence in him.

The bold bearing of Red Ike and the straightforward manner and address of both men assured the artist that, whatever their past had been, he was in the presence of men not guilty of John Lynd's murder. A full explanation of the case, and of their movements during the time of the crime according to the doctor's evidence, pointed beyond doubt to their innocence.

"The deed was done with an axe," said Red Ike.

"Is the axe in the possession of the police?"

"No," he replied, and then, suddenly remembering that he had thrown one into the cattle pool on the moorland, he jumped to the conclusion that it would still be there, and that it was the one required to prove the case.

"Well," said the artist, studying Red Ike, "do you know something about the axe?"

"I think I can find it."

"To whom did it belong?"

"To the gypsy, Ben Faa. He was going to brain me with it, and I winded him with a stone and cast the weapon into a moorland pool. Curse, what a fool I was to let it slip through my hands."

"If it was the axe with which the murder was done, it will not be there now. The gypsy will have seen to that. However, you were in the drift during the whole of Christmas Eve and Christmas Day. Have you proof of this?"

Red Ike paused. To answer the question meant the disclosure of Jean's being with him there, and he hesitated to reply. The detective saw this and said: "I must have your whole confidence, otherwise I shall not trouble to investigate the case. Besides, what you say to me is strictly private."

"Then," said Red Ike, "John Lynd's daughter was staying with me in the drift at the time of the murder."

Nell Glen rose from her chair in astonishment; neither she nor Dick could believe their ears.

"I understand," said the artist.

"No, you do not understand," rejoined Red Ike. "Her father drove her from home because of her refusal to marry."

"Hold," cried Dick, "the man she refused to marry is the one who follows Nell from city to city. The man who was butted into the gutter when he accosted her the day before yesterday."

"The devil, is that so?" ejaculated Mayne.

Red Ike continued: "Her father drove her from home, and I sheltered her until her lover was released from prison with my friend here." And he laid his hand on Dick's shoulder. "Neither he nor Jean Lynd's lover, Will Moffatt, is guilty of the crime. It was committed at eleven o'clock on Christmas Eve. At that time they were both to-gether at the opera at Carlisle. I think Miss Glen can prove this."

Nell Glen grasped the back of her chair for support, her whole body shaking with uncontrollable feeling. Dick Stagg stepped to-wards her, and, full of emotion, she flung her arms about his neck, crying: "I can save you, Dick. I can save you! Thank heaven, I can save you!"

Then remembering in whose presence, besides Dick's, she stood, she shrank abashed with shame, and sank into her chair.

"Is that the way the wind is blowing?" cried the artist, with a glad light in his eyes. "I was once young myself, and by the Lord, I wish I were young again. But, by the way, who was the woman who supported the fellow's head within her lap, and escorted him to his hotel?"

Dick looked at Red Ike, and Nell watched him curiously. But neither his face nor voice betrayed any feeling.

"Answer him, Dick."

"Had she or he anything to do with the murder?"

"No," answered Red Ike.

"Then we'll pass them over for the present."

Had he known that at that moment Joe Gream was with his fel-low-artists, drinking in the bar close to the opera house, and disclos-ing Nell's past life and his whole relations with her with a gusto and colouring and a minuteness of detail that made the most outspoken amongst them squirm with revulsion, he would have found means to make the fellow quit the city at once. For though he shrewdly guessed much of the truth concerning her, he was one of those who find pleasure in sunning themselves in the light of others' success. And Nell Glen was to him one of those rare spirits that occasionally cross the world's stage to charm and elevate with the wonderful gift of song their less-favoured fellows. He had no jealousy in his soul, and therefore what he could not rival nor surpass, he could enjoy exquisitely, and his appreciation and advice, on several occasions, freely given without stint or patronage, had helped Nell during many a sore trial; and she was grateful, and he knew it, and this made them warm friends.

That night, whilst the artist was hurrying northward to the scene of John Lynd's murder in the role of private detective, Nell Glen was receiving her first real rebuff from her fellow-artists. The scurri-lous news circulated by Joe Gream spread quickly, and she found herself the butt of envious raillery, pointed with dark meaning, that she was quick to focus in her mind with true perception.

And at the close of the performance, in a wild and dangerous outburst of passion, too near the verge of insanity to do herself justice at the time, she pulled up the offenders, and poured out her wrath upon them: "What," she cried, "if I have on occasion fallen into error, who in this company can point an accusing finger at me? I know you all. Man and woman. And whatever I have been, or am, I shall stand no disrespectful treatment, without retaliating, from any of you. Have I given any one of you cause that I should be treated other than a fellow-artist amongst you? The men I have held at a distance, the women I have been kindly and considerate with, and my advice to you all is to leave me to go my way without molestation, and mate amongst yourselves, or do as you choose. I admit I have passed through hell on earth, and I shall say further that I have been too fearfully scorched in the fires of my own-made hell ever again to possess the clean spirit that is the joy and sustenance of a good woman's pride. But surely I deserve the measure of sympathy and helpfulness I have extended to all present, or to be left in peace."

"By God!" cried the manager of the company, "that's the way to defend one's self, straightforwardly, bluntly, and honestly. Now if anyone has aught to say in reply, out with it."

A dead silence followed, and one after another they slunk from Nell's presence.

When the last one left, the manager continued: "I am sorry things are happening as they are, but if you bear up, and face the wave of slander as you have faced those," and he jerked his thumb over his shoulder, "the issue need cause you no further trouble."

Now, had the efforts of Nell's enemies been confined to the circle of artists in which she moved, all might have been well henceforth with her. But Joe Gream, baulked in his desire to bring her again to his feet, and finding that her fellow-artists, though envious of her success, and therefore inclined to humiliate her, had no power to destroy her position, he began to beset her on the streets, and followed in her wake wherever she went; until the annoyance became so great, she had perforce to stay indoors for days to avoid him. This infuriated him more than ever. Yet, left to himself, his lust might at length have dissipated itself, had he not met with a drunken newspaper hack who soon divined the sensational copy that Nell's history would make, and finding in Joe Gream a pliant tool to work with, he suggested the matter be written up for the daily press, and next morning to Nell's utter bewilderment she beheld, under striking headlines:

NELL GLEN: HER LIFE STORY

This was a phase of attack of which she had never dreamed, nor did she know how to combat it. It seemed as if the fair prospect that had opened out to her was again darkened with irretrievable disaster. She shrank from the newspaper as from a viper, and her soul revolted in an agony of despair against the injustice of such a foul measure of revenge, knowing, as she did, from the first-hand knowledge possessed by the author of the infamous sketch, that Joe Gream was the instigator of the work, no matter who might be the writer. How could she again face an audience? What would Dick think when he read the press? And she gave way in utter abandonment to solitary hopelessness, and longed for death. The thought of death gave her a strange thrill, but leaping to her feet she cried: "Why should I die? I too shall take revenge. Ere I lay a finger on myself I shall send Joe Gream where he belongs."

She began to prepare herself to put her resolve into execution. Her unsophisticated mind, primitive in its instincts, decided her. She would kill not for the lust of killing, she would remove him from her path, as her progenitors, in the far distant past, removed the wild beasts that menaced them in the wilderness.

But, lo, the miracle happened. Nell beheld herself through a mirror, and her glance fell before her own reflection. She saw not the supreme glory of her loveliness, but a hideous shadow of her evil self stamped on every feature with hate that engenders murder; and sinking to the floor, she covered her face with her hands, and wept herself to peace.

The evening came and brought with it one of the severest trials it had ever been Nell's lot to face. She dreaded some hostile demonstration by her audience, and with great difficulty was prevailed upon to step into the limelight. She felt the tension she had to impose upon herself almost past bearing, but the moment she appeared a free burst of generous sympathy thundered through the house for several minutes, and overwhelmed her with its genuine spontaneity. She trembled with the reaction of her nerves, but the respite the long ovation gave her enabled her to collect herself, and when she began to sing 'twas a paean of gratitude that she poured forth over the vast crowd that sat entranced under the golden power and melody of her voice. Thus was the love of fair play shown by the mighty heart of an English audience, and thus it is ever repaid by its great artists with reverence and service and love that are its due.

Joe Gream and the hireling newspaper hack, under the impression that they had blasted Nell's career for ever, were astounded at her reception. And Nell, seeing the former in the pit, was sorely tempted to denounce him to the audience during an interval of the opera, and might have done so had the manager not pointed out to her the futility of such an act. Her enemies were defeated, and the acclamation given her by the populace had endorsed her triumph. "Better let well alone," said he. "'To stamp the dust raises a stoor.' Besides, Joe Gream can be dealt with another way, less public, yet just as effective. Wait till tomorrow. After then, he'll cause you no further trouble."

At the door of the theatre, Peg Shore stood waiting for Joe. She too had seen the exposure of Nell's past life in the press, and been witness of the night's event, and doubted not but that she herself could profit by the turn things had taken.

"Come," said Peg, accosting him as he emerged. "I have something important to say to you."

He shook her off roughly, and she chuckled ferociously.

"A word from me, Joe, concerning your attack on Nell Glen, and the crowd about us will maul you to death. Be careful, or I'll let hell loose upon you."

The mean coward was cowed at once, and Peg stepped to his side, and escorted him to a cab in waiting.

"I have saved your skin again," she continued, "and yet you have never a civil word for me; you are not the least grateful for a good turn done. However, unless you clear out of Preston at once, you'll be in jail before morning."

"What the devil for?" he snarled.

"You will soon learn," she answered. "Nell Glen's manager has already put the law in motion against you. You have slandered her, and must bear the consequences of your folly."

"What I said is true, Peg."

"Yes, I know that. But the greater the truth, the greater the libel, if you have injured her career as an artist."

As the serious consequences of his action dawned upon his dull, soddened brain, he collapsed into a corner of the cab, his teeth chattering and his whole carcase breaking into a cold sweat.

"I warned you many times," said Peg, gloating over his discomfiture.

"You did hell as like, you she-devil."

"All right, Joe. Whither shall I tell the driver to convey you? I'm sick of skulking at the skirt-tails of Nell Glen. Shall I tell him to stop while I alight? I am not going with you to the Hotel Plantagenet."

"What are you going to do then, Peg?"

"I intend leaving Preston, and the fear of a jail, behind me, by taking one of the midnight trains from here."

"To the hotel then," he said, "for our trappings. I'll stay in the cab until you bring them."

"You drive at once to the station, I'll meet you there," replied Peg.

Two days later saw the pair at Dover, on board ship bound for Paris. But even far removed from their native moorland, and in fancied security, they were to learn soon that destiny had laid its axe at the very root suckers that fed Joe Gream's fortune, and severing the arteries through which his wealth flowed, compelled their return to England and The Forge, at the base of the Hill of Devils.

Now, by a strange coincidence, at the very moment Joe and Peg embarked for Calais, fleeing from imaginary arrest, Red Ike and Dick stepped on board the small steam-packet, *The Lady Eveline*, bound from Fleetwood to Barrow, to face the real danger of being hunted from wild to wild like a fox to its borran.

From Barrow they took the tramcar to Furness Abbey that is situated so charmingly in the Vale of Nightshade. Thence, on foot, they journeyed to Dalton, and over the bleak stretch of countryside to the Duddon estuary.

Avoiding the sleepy little market town of Broughton-in-Furness, they silently hastened along the Duddon Valley, and over Wrynose Pass and Lingmoor to Chapel Stile, and climbed out of Great Langdale by Dungeon Ghyll, crossed Easedale, and onwards to the crest of Armboth fells to the refuge of the drift in the dale of the fall of rock.

Immediately Red Ike crept through the opening of the drift, he was aware that it was tenantless, and spreading his arms wide so that they touched both sides of the tunnel, he whispered to Dick to do likewise, and follow him.

By this means were anyone standing in the passage in the dark, he would find escape impossible.

Cautiously the advance was made until the first side-drift was reached, then Red Ike struck a light.

"There is no one here, Dick, not even Prodigal. I wonder what has happened." And thrusting his hands deeply into the bracken beds he added, "Nor has anyone slept on the beds for a couple of nights; both are quite cold to the centre."

On the ground was a tin platter, from which Prodigal was fed. The food it contained had remained untouched since he had placed it there himself. He counted the candles; but one had been burned. He knew this, because he had opened a fresh pound-packet the night he left for Preston.

He examined the canned food; it was also as he had left it. Turning to Dick, he was about to speak, when he caught sight of several articles of ladies' underwear thrown carelessly over the bed on which Jean Lynd had slept during her sojourn in the drift. Lifting the garments, he spoke his thoughts: "They have been here again, Dick."

"Who?" echoed Dick.

"Jean and Jael. See, this wrap belongs to Jael, I have seen her wearing it. 'Tis strange that these things are left here. How long will it be ere day breaks, Dick?"

"It was about to break when we entered the drift."

"Then we must content ourselves until nightfall again."

After a hearty meal, each man threw himself onto his bed and slept through the short winter day. With the weird call of the first night owl, they were abroad once more. Each had his work to do, and the finding of Will Moffatt was the chief part of it. "Perhaps," said Red Ike, "Will has been belated, and taken shelter in the old well tunnel at Sandyflatts."

Red Ike determined to go thither. Dick would waylay old Simon Reed on his nightly visit to the White Horse Inn, and learn if he knew aught, and they would meet at midnight by the grave of Jael's father and mother. This arranged, they parted.

At a swinging pace, fearless but cautious, Red Ike crossed the moorland at an angle, and arrived at Sandyflatts without mishap. He stepped through the bour tree that blocked up the doorway, entered the milkhouse carelessly, nay almost defiantly, and struck a light and examined the room. Seeing the heap of ashes, the remains of the burned bracken-bed and sawn wood-blocks, a deep curse escaped his lips, and grasping an oak cudgel that had been overlooked in a corner, he lifted the flagstone, descended into the passage to the old well-pit in the garth behind the ruined house, and crawled to the farther end.

Will Moffatt has not been here, he thought, and a chill of apprehension passed through his body. Had Will been taken by the police, or what had happened?

He was about to rise to his feet and ascend the well-pit when his hand came in contact with a cold steel and a bundle of clothing. He struck a match, and examined the articles. His wonder knew no bounds. There were Ben Faa's axe, and doubtless the clothing he had worn at the murder of John Lynd. However, he would make sure that the clothing belonged to the gypsy, and climbing from the well-pit, he hastily returned to the drift.

Untying the bundle, he shook the garments separately and held them up to the light, and a grim smile crossed his face. By one article alone Ben Faa could be condemned, and this was an old-fashioned sealskin cap, blood-soaked. A thousand people could be found to swear it was his. He was wearing it when Red Ike felled the French gypsy in The Roaring Militia Man at Carlisle seven years ago. The bundle also contained a brown corduroy shooting-coat and a pair of buckskin trousers, and both these articles had once belonged to John Lynd's gamekeeper. Red Ike searched the pockets of the garments. In one was a jockteleg. In another an envelope containing a draft for a thousand pounds made payable on the Bank of England to Ben Faa. The draft had been stopped by John Lynd's order.

This, then, was the reason why he had been murdered. Now, in all men of great soul and boundless love for humanity, there is an unfathomable wealth of pity. The culprit, not less than the victim, is grieved over long after the hangman's well-soaped noose has completed a useless vengeance.

And Red Ike, who had walked through hell himself, sat in the silence of the drift in the heart of the mountains, and pondered deeply over Ben Faa.

Now that he alone was in possession of the evidence that would hang Ben, he felt a reluctance to move in the matter, and was inclined to flee the country rather than stand in the witness-box facing Ben whilst the judge pronounced the death sentence. Not that Red Ike was tainted with moral cowardice, but his heart bled for Ben, on whom a dire doom would be inflicted by the soulless hangman who, without any provocation, commits a score of murders, under cover of the law, for a few paltry pounds. To be sure, Ben was a murderer. He had a personal grievance against John Lynd, whose treatment of him had been mean and brutal and gross in many ways. But it seemed to him that Ben Faa, bad as he was, was not as bad as a hangman who dares, in the presence of his Maker, to stand with the halter in his hand, whilst a priest, priding himself on being a servant of God, reads the burial service over a drug-doped culprit before he is hanged and dead.

Whirled in the tempest of his emotions, Red Ike paced the tunnel of the drift, unable to decide the course he ought to take. In the drinking-room of the White Horse Inn, dressed as a travelling tinker, sat the detective, Thomas Mayne, listening to Simon Reed singing Red Ike's songs at the top pitch of his cracked voice, whilst outside, in the shelter of the black yew-tree, stood Dick, waiting until the clock struck the hour when the boisterous company would be turned out of the inn onto the moorland road.

A wild burst of laughter caught Dick's ear, and he crept to the window of the drinking-room.

"You're all liars, every one of you," shouted Simon Reed.

"You still think Red Ike innocent then?" asked the landlord.

"Think? Think? There's no thinking about it. I'm sure."

"Bah! We'll see what Will Moffatt has to say tomorrow when he is brought before the magistrates."

"I'll be there," cried Simon, "and devil a word will they get out of him until he is ready to speak, and that won't be tomorrow."

"When and where was he caught?" inquired the tinker.

"At The Bents the night before last, as he was trying to force one of the windows. After a chase the gamekeeper felled him."

"Who was with the keeper?" questioned the tinker again.

"Ben Faa," answered several at once.

"Humph!" exclaimed the tinker. "Was Will Moffatt trying to force the window from the inside or the outside? And is it true that he is sweet on Jean Lynd? She's a bonny lass, they say."

"Who says?" quoth the landlord.

"I say, and a good one as well," snapped Simon Reed.

"And I say so too," chimed in the tinker. "I saw her today. She's a reg'lar Venus. Charming from top to toe."

A dead silence followed this sally. And Dick drew back from the window into the shelter of the black yew-tree. He recognized the tinker's voice, and his part of the night's work was finished. He need not wait to speak with Simon Reed, and so decided to return to the drift.

There he would be safe until midnight, when he must meet Red Ike by the grave of Jael's parents.

And Red Ike, absorbed in deep thought, and oblivious to all but the question that occupied his mind, sat on a block of rough-hewn stone with Ben's axe in his hand and the blood-stained clothes at his feet. When Dick entered the drift and accosted him, for the first time in his life Red Ike was taken unawares.

"I have been to the White Horse Inn, and the artist-detective is there, and Will Moffatt's taken."

Red Ike leapt to his feet as if electrified.

"Who said so, Dick?"

"The landlord of the inn. I stood by the window outside the house and heard him bantering Simon about it."

"And you heard the detective there as well?"

"He is drinking with the company. He's dressed up as a tinker."

"Then we'll go and bring him hither."

"Is there no danger in doing so?"

"I'll bring him hither myself, Dick."

The blood mounted hotly to Dick's temples, seeing which Red Ike said: "Nay, lad, I do not doubt thy courage. I spoke in haste. Come, we have no time to lose. The clock's on the stroke of ten."

Together they sped to waylay the tinker-detective on the road to Keswick. At the foot of Burns Brow, where the Bure and the Glenderamakkin meet and form the river Greta, the tinker was about to cross the bridge that spans the confluence of the becks, when two dark figures stepped from the thick growth of broom that grows rankly there, and walked by his side.

"Well met! Do you know either of us, my friend?" said Red Ike.

"I can make a good guess at you both, and am glad to meet you. Whither are you bound?"

"I have news of importance. Will you accompany us?"

"I'll go anywhere with you."

"Then we must not speak again until we are under cover." Never, I think, in the history of crime, had a man a stranger experience than this man in Red Ike and Dick Stagg's charge. This man, who in his earlier days had tracked many a culprit to earth in the crowded centres of our larger cities, was led by tarn and fell and knee-deep through roaring becks and spongy peat mosses, where the flushed bittern boomed on hasty wings, and wild-duck beat furiously the water in the trenched soughs, in desperate attempts to shun the bold intruders of their night-shrouded haunts.

Had he been forewarned of his experience, he would have laughed at it as a wild romance. Nevertheless, he showed no sign of reluctance as they strode by beetling crag or darkling wood, or when the startled fox barked within a yard of him, or the terrified rabbits and hares leapt about his feet, or the wild owl flew hooting round his head.

But his wonder was increased greatly when they halted at the entrance to the drift, and Red Ike dropped on his hands and knees and crept into the tunnel.

However, he followed suit, determined to face boldly the adventure to the end.

And now, in the candle-lighted drift, he stood gazing about him unable to credit his senses. In his wildest dreams he had never imagined anything so strange. In these rude surroundings in the heart of the mountain, was a choice library of the best English literature, the latest poetry, belles-lettres, and many excellent translations of ancient and modern foreign works.

Being a man of some culture and natural talent, he saw that, whatever the outcome of John Lynd's murder proved to be, the men in whose presence he stood were not of a type to be dealt lightly with. Of this he became doubly sure on a further acquaintance with Red Ike, when he discovered the great soul that burned within him, ardent, unquenchable, and fearless.

CHAPTER XXVIII

WE must now turn to Will Moffatt and the events that led to his capture.

When he returned to the drift and found that Jean had fled, he waited till the fall of night, and then again hastened to The Bents, anxious to see for himself if all were well there. The house was new and strange to him, it having been built after he left England, and, as he approached, it was in darkness save for the solitary gleam of a lamp hanging in the hall that shone through the fanlight above the front door.

He had an idea that the place might be watched, and that he would need to be circumspect to avoid arrest.

Unfortunately, his long absence had made him a stranger to the dogs, those keen sentinels that ask but little in return for the service they give.

Avoiding the carriage-drive, he was creeping cautiously forward when his foot struck a wire and immediately the report of a gun rang out, and he felt a stinging pain in his ankle.

"The brutes!" he ejaculated, "I have sprung a trap-gun," and stooping, he groped along the wire, and found the weapon. But now he could hear the barking of dogs and the shouting of men, and see lanterns swinging in the dark at a rapid pace towards him through the half-grown larch plantation in which he stood.

The dogs, he knew, would soon be upon him, and snatching the gun from the ground, and snapping the wire attached to it, he fled for the open moorland. As he cleared the plantation fence he heard a dog immediately behind him, and turning upon it he felled it to the ground with the gun stock. A minute later, he had to do the same with a second, and then a third.

"Damn it!" he thought, "is there a full pack of dogs after me?"

However, he could now have easily outrun his pursuers, but he felt that the foot in his right boot was sopping in blood from the gunshot wound, and that he was growing weak and dizzy

With a curse, he flung the gun into a clump of whin-bushes, and awaited the coming of those whom he knew would soon close in upon him. As they approached, he shouted: "Hold! I am bleeding to death from a wound in the foot caused by your trap-gun."

He might as well have whistled to the wind to stop. With a rush like a pack of wolves on a stricken deer they leapt around him. He counted eight, and heard Ben Faa shout: "It is Will Moffatt," and for the moment he regretted that he had cast away the gun, though it was as well he had done so, or he might have dashed out the man's brains as he approached.

When later he came to his senses, for he had almost been beaten to death by the gamekeepers and the police, his foot was bandaged, but the pain in it was excruciating, and a soul-tormenting thirst pervaded his whole body. He would have given his life for a drink of cold water. He lay in the dark, hour after hour, a prey to the most clamouring desire that a sentient being can be inflicted with.

"For the love of Christ!" he moaned, again and again, "A drink! A drink!"

And all the answer he got was the echo of his own voice, a mocking echo that drove him to despair, until at last he swooned into forgetfulness, for how long he knew not.

When again he awoke, a doctor was bending over him and then he was removed to the jail hospital, and guarded day and night.

Knowing the uselessness of asking any questions, he lay silent, and allowed the officials to do with him as they chose. On the third day of his incarceration, Jael came to visit him.

"Where is Jean?" he at once inquired.

Jael studied him a moment, and answered: "She, with her mother, left The Bents the morning before you were taken by the police. Do you know where they are, Will Moffatt? I wish to find them."

"Will you believe me, Jael, when I say that I have not seen Jean since we left her in the drift?"

"My God! Have you forgotten in whose presence you are speaking, Will?"

He had forgotten, indeed, and by an incautious remark had betrayed to the police at his bedside where, with Ben Faa's aid, Red Ike and Dick could be found. Would Ben remember the drift? He did not know, and dared not trust himself to speak again to Jael; and in agony of mind and body and utter helplessness, merciful nature gave way under the strain, and he sank again into a stupor that lasted for several hours.

Meanwhile Mrs. Lynd, thinking that she had bribed Ben Faa to secrecy concerning the relationship between her husband and Jael's mother, and that Ben would find means to compel Jael to marry him, and, above all, thinking that she had Ben in her power, knowing that she knew he had killed John Lynd, was imagining that nothing could transpire to jeopardize her worldly position with regard to the inheritance of the wealth of which she had quietly taken possession. She did not realize the full contents of the letters, nor the marriage certificate that was hidden in the drift, nor that Jean had been there when she returned home from her sleepwalk. Lulled into a fancied security, she had hurriedly prepared to leave The Bents for good and bury herself and Jean abroad, preferably in the South of France or in Italy. Under an assumed name, she hoped to pass the remainder of her days in safe obscurity.

Hence, whilst Will Moffatt was being mauled well nigh to death by her keepers and the police, she and Jean were following hard in the wake of Joe and Peg, bound from Dover for Calais; and following the usual route of such passengers, they arrived in Paris and engaged rooms at the Hotel Vivat Republica.

Until now, Jean had made no resistance to her mother's wishes. The noon following their arrival, with surprise and consternation, Mrs. Lynd saw Joe and Peg take their places opposite Jean and herself. They had flown into the very presence of those whom she, of all people, wished most to avoid, and if she did not desire a scene, good breeding demanded that she treat them with courtesy. Had she registered at the hotel under her own name, her position would not have been so complicated. She would now have to explain to Joe and Peg, and consider about other matters afterwards. But events seldom adjust themselves according to our plans.

She invited them to her private room, and now, for the first time in her life, Jean opposed her. Under no condition would she again associate with Joe Gream. In vain Mrs. Lynd cajoled, and finally threatened to deprive Jean of money, and leave her stranded in the French capital.

Thus both women were roused to opposition. The long servitude of Mrs. Lynd to her husband's stormy nature and imperious will had developed within her a cold, calculating spirit. And now that she was free of his dominant personality, she went suddenly to the opposite extreme, and became herself a petty tyrant.

But John Lynd had begotten Jean. He had transmitted his strong will to her, and the mother was now to learn this.

Red Ike, by J. M. Denwood & S. Fowler Wright * 215

With a light laugh Jean said: "I shall apply to the British Consul for help to return to England at once, and never again shall I touch a coin of yours until Jael is given her rights.

"I had no idea we were coming hither when we left home. I understood our destination was London, and that the settlement of your affairs was our object there."

"You shall do as I bid you, Jean."

"I shall do as I wish and think right, no matter what the consequences. And never again shall I stand willingly in the presence of the man who made an attempt upon my chastity."

"But what if his intentions are fair, and he'll wed you, Jean? Joe Gream has wealth, and...."

"Then wed him yourself, Mother. I shall not."

Mrs. Lynd leapt upon Jean and dutched her by the shoulders, her face flaming with wrath.

"You dare to insult me?" she cried, and so violent was her passion that she shook Jean as a dry reed is shaken in the wind.

Jean unloosed her mother's hands and flung them from her, but the infuriated woman, with her back to the door and in a menacing attitude, exclaimed: "You dare to speak about chastity! You, who lived for months with Red Ike hidden in a hole in the fells, like a bitch fox. You shall wed Joe Gream, or I shall choke you."

"I shall not allow you to choke me. Stand aside and let me pass, or I shall rouse the house."

"I shall disown you unless you do."

"You have already done so, and are my mother. Again I say stand aside and let me go, or I shall use force."

A loud knock sounded on the door, and immediately both women assumed a composed air.

"Open the door, Jean," said Mrs. Lynd, stepping away from it. Jean threw it wide to the wall, intending to depart, but Joe stood smiling evilly upon her.

"You here?" she exclaimed. "Eavesdropping again."

"No," he retorted. "I am here by appointment."

"By whose wish?"

"Your mother's."

"She is at your service then. Allow me to pass."

He attempted to bar her exit, but Peg had crept up behind him, and she grasped him by the nape of the neck, and swung him from the doorway.

As Jean passed from the room, Joe Gream, livid with rage, turned upon Peg, but she held up a warning finger, saying: "If we get into the hands of the authorities here, we shall be expelled the country. Have you all lost your wits?"

"You go to the devil," he snarled.

"I'm going to him fast enough with your help, and when I meet his majesty, I'll present you to him," Peg replied mockingly. "Meanwhile we must come to an understanding. See here." And producing an English newspaper she showed them the announcement of Will's arrest.

> "Will Moffatt, one of the alleged Lakeland murderers, was captured after an exciting chase subsequent to his attempted burglary of The Bents. He killed three dogs before he was run to earth. The arrest of the other two suspected men who are yet at large is expected at any moment."

White as a ghost, Jean glided towards Peg, and snatched the paper from her hands. Pointing to the paragraph, she said: "Unless I am supplied with money to return home immediately, I shall denounce you all as having something to do with this affair."

"You dare not!" exclaimed Mrs. Lynd.

"I dare do anything, and shall stand no refusal. And you, you wretch!" she cried, flaming upon Joe Gream, "do not cross my path again, lest I kill you with as little compunction as Ben Faa slew my father."

"Hush! For the love of God, Jean."

"I have spoken, Mother, and you know it is the truth."

Helpless and speechless, Mrs. Lynd gazed upon Jean.

And Peg, gloating over Joe's rebuff, and triumphant with the knowledge concerning the murder thus placed within her hands, grasped greedily at the power it gave her. But she did not know the full truth, and though it gave her a temporary ascendancy over Joe Gream, it availed her nothing in the end.

At midnight Jean recrossed the English Channel, leaving her mother, Joe Gream, and Peg at the Hotel Vivat Republica.

And meanwhile, how had things fared with Red Ike and Dick?

They were sitting in the drift, discussing particulars of John Lynd's murder with the artist, when Prodigal bounded along the tunnel, and stood upon his hind legs waving his front paws, and at the same time turned to face the entrance.

Red Ike extinguished the candle, and said: "Come, we may yet have time to escape; our hiding-place is discovered."

All three, preceded by the dog, rushed for the entrance, and a mile away, lanterns were seen flashing through the night, advancing to the dale of the fall of rock.

"We had better climb out to one of the fell-tops and watch how things go with the search party. Wait a moment. I shall return for the axe, and the bundle of clothing belonging to Ben Faa."

"You are too late. The police are almost upon us," said the artist.

"Nay," replied Red Ike, "the distance between us is greater than you think. 'Tis the darkness that deceives your judgment. They are yet a long way from us."

Half an hour later, from a vantage point above, they perceived the police enter the opening of the drift in full force, counting ten lanterns as they disappeared one by one, two remaining outside on guard.

After a few moments Red Ike, with a low chuckling laugh, remarked: "I wonder what the police are now thinking? Most of them will be too thick-headed to understand the treasure trove, entirely intellectual, they will have found. Tomorrow they will need to bring a donkey-cart to remove their find. Could I have been there to pack and save my books and manuscript note-books from harm, I should now be happy."

The artist mused and marvelled at the even tenor of the speech he heard, and this fact was borne upon him that, outside the sphere of art, wherein it is understood and practised by the great leaders of thought and action in the artistic schools midst which he had moved in the world, there are men wandering along obscure byways full of the fire of genius, who are doomed never to emerge into the full glare of notoriety, but who are nevertheless true lovers of the beautiful, and devout workers for the spreading of the knowledge of the fine arts; and that the desire to know and enjoy things intellectual is not the prerogative of the cultured and leisured classes alone. He realized also that Red Ike was a rare soul, calm, self-reliant, and high-minded, a credit to himself and the class from which he sprang.

Long and patiently the three watchers waited until the police emerged from the drift, and Red Ike counted the lighted lanterns as they flashed in turn through the dark. When the tenth reappeared he said: "They are again all outside the drift."

"What are we going to do now?" inquired the artist, as the search party were well on their return journey.

"I shall go to Keswick with you at once, and later during the week, when my plans are matured, I shall acquaint you with my intentions. In the meantime, Dick and I will take no harm sleeping out on the fells for a few nights."

They were about to skirt the spur of the fell on which they stood when across the dale came the cry of the midnight owl. "Too-whoo! Too-whoo! Too-whoo!"

"Hark," said Red Ike, and the wild note sounded again. "'Tis Jael Boswell calling me," and he immediately answered the summons in such perfect mimicry that the artist could scarcely credit his hearing.

And then, a few seconds later, the shrill whistle of the curlew rang out, and this was followed by the long-drawn-wail so familiar to all who study the bird. And Red Ike mimicked the wail, which Jael interpreted thus: "I'll be there. I'll be there. I'll be there."

"What do you mean by that?" questioned the artist.

"I'll meet her by a moorland grave before daybreak," was the answer, "And now come, we'll to Keswick."

After seeing Mayne safely to his destination, Red Ike and Dick parted at the Druids' Circle on the wilds of Castlerigg, having previously agreed to spend the whole of next day together amongst the bracken that grows so densely above the remains of the old British fort, whose ramparts are still visible on the shoulder of Shoulthwaite fell.

"I must now be off, Dick, to meet Jael. Keep clear of the highway. Cross the road by the lonning foot that leads to the Vale of St. John, and climb out to the Brutchstone, then keep to the breast of the fell until you come to the force that, when winds are high, falls, waving like a white flag, to the Naddle beck below. There you will be safe, and I shall join you before daybreak."

Jael, within the shadow of the yew-tree by her parents' grave on the wild moorland, was waiting for him.

Absorbed in deep thought, she did not notice his approach until he spoke her name, and then, with a half-smothered cry and in sheer abandon, she flung her arms around his neck in a transport of love as unmistakable as it was boundless and sincere. She gave herself to him in just such another wave of passion, long years before at Sandyflatts, when their child was begotten. And Red Ike folded her to his heart, satisfied that whatever her shortcomings were due to her gypsy upbringing, she was the one woman in the world for him. And smoothing back the wind-blown hair from her forehead, he returned her raptured caress.

"Oh, take me away from this unfortunate countryside," she exclaimed. "I am weary unto death of the constant turmoil in which we live."

"Whither can we go, Jael, until the murder of John Lynd is cleared up? To flee openly would be to court arrest. If I stand my ground until I am taken, and then clear myself, I shall have to denounce Ben Faa, and on my evidence he would be hanged. And, by Christ above, Jael, I loathe the thought of being the means of bringing a man to the gallows. Were it not for thy sake and our child, and because I cannot now bear to part with you, I should weeks ago have flown the country."

"What is to be done then?" she asked in bewilderment.

"I do not know the best course to take at present. Perhaps the fates themselves will decide without my intervention. What has to be, will be."

"You are a fatalist?"

"Yes, Jael, I am. I believe that a man's destiny is entirely outside his control. He is a creature of circumstance. If he will a thing and accomplish it, 'twas his destiny to do so. If he will a thing and fail, the same rule applies. His only salvation is his ignorance of what destiny has in store for him. A blind hope keeps him alive, and often deceives him at last, as it deceived your parents lying buried at our feet."

"Were they both deceived by destiny?"

"Your father broke your mother's heart, Jael, and brought her to an early grave, despite his great love for her. 'Twas his destiny to hide his marriage with a gypsy to save his social position. His second marriage, whilst your mother was alive, involved him in endless scheming to hide his fault, and placed him within the power of Abegail and Ben Faa. Even when he held the proofs of his guilt in his own hands, strong-willed as he was, he dared not destroy them. Did not Jean hand them to you over your parents' dead bodies on this very spot? If such happenings are not the workings of destiny, I know not how to account for them."

"Where are the proofs?"

"They are hidden in the drift in the dale of the fall of rock."

"Now listen," said Jael. "Mrs. Lynd gave Ben Faa a thousand pounds on condition that he used force to compel me to wed him. I stole the money from him, and Will and I hid it in an old forgotten tomb by the side of the Roman road that skirts Helvellyn. Let us take the money and flee the country. I could join you anywhere abroad."

Red Ike took her face between his hands and looked into her eyes. They were burning like two stars through the dark.

"Would my brave-hearted Jael counsel me to do wrong? No, I know she would not. Shall I flee the country and leave Will and Dick to face their trial without me?"

The light faded from Jael's eyes.

"I do not understand," she said. "Do what you think is best. I only wish to be with you."

"Was Ben Faa with the police in the drift tonight, Jael?"

"Yes," she replied, with sudden energy, "and he and Abegail are returning thither even now to search for the carved stick, and the letters given to me by Jean."

"And for the thousand pounds, Jael. Their quest will be in vain. Come, I shall go with you to the camp."

"No, no, they might return, and find you there."

"Well," said Red Ike, clasping her closer to his breast, "suppose they do? What will it matter? Besides, I wish to see our boy."

"He is here," replied Jael, disengaging herself, and lifting a well-wrapped form from the shadow of the yew-tree at their feet, "many a night we have slept by the grave together. 'Tis a peaceful spot shunned by the superstitious, but beloved by the wildlife of the moorland. Several times of late a flock of fieldfares have lodged here with us, and their company has been a solace to me. 'Tis a happy omen that the birds should trust us so."

It now dawned upon Red Ike that Jael was persecuted, and bore it patiently through her love for him. And upon him fell a great awe. He took the child from her arms and held it up to the bright glow of the frosty starlight, and gazed earnestly upon its face. It was the very miniature of himself, and the paternal yearning was roused to such a pitch in his being that he hugged the awakened and wondering boy to his breast. Jael leaned against the yew-tree, and knew not what to make of the emotional man before her.

During the enacting of this scene, Ben Faa and Abegail were toiling up the dale of the fall of rock towards the drift. It was a rough journey through the dark for the old sibyl.

They dared not take a lighted lantern with them for fear of being detected, hence it took them double time to get there. Arriving at last, after much cursing and grumbling, they crept through the entrance and then blocked it up.

"Now we are all right," said Ben.

"How if the Red Devil returns and finds us here?" asked Abegail.

"Then I'll shoot him like a dog." The words were scarcely uttered when Abegail started, and grasped his arm exclaiming, "There is someone here."

Ben held the light above his head, and peered through the tunnel.

"Humph! 'Tis the lurcher."

"Shoot the brute," cried the witch.

"Not until we have searched the place. The report of the revolver might bring somebody upon us. "

They now advanced forward, examining carefully every yard of the sides of the drift, until they came to the first side-tunnel in which Red Ike had always slept.

To a man with any sense of culture and decency, the neatness and cleanliness of the place would have made a strong appeal, even had he had no special leaning to book-learning, but Ben Faa the gypsy knew nothing and cared nothing for the amenities of life. He was gross and sensual in all his appetites; in fact, he was almost an animal in everything but shape, yet crueller and more cunning because of slightly higher development of reasoning power than the beast possesses.

"Be quick with the work," croaked the old sibyl. "Search the bed first."

Ben scattered the bracken over the floor of the drift: "There's nothing here, Abegail."

"See if there's a recess behind the books on any of the rock-ledges. We have no time to waste."

Ben swept row after row of them with his hand to the floor, and examined the wall.

"By the holy Gods, we have found it!" And he drew the carved stick from the boring.

Abegail clutched it and danced with excitement, a weird figure in the candle-lighted drift. Her transport knew no bounds until Ben reminded her of their situation, and then she cried: "We'll find the money and the letters yet. Be quick, be quick, be quick! They'll be hidden in some hole like the stick."

Ben ran the lighted candle close along the walls, and by chance ignited a fuse that had been laid to a charge of dynamite in an unfired boring, overlooked by quarrymen when first the drift was made full twenty years before. Neither he nor Abegail understood the danger they were in, but stood watching the burning fuse and expecting it to fizzle out. Prodigal, the lurcher, crept away to the tunnel-mouth and whined when it found the exit blocked up. And Red Ike and Jael, a mile away on the night-shrouded moorland, heard a thunder boom in the dale of the fall of rock, and the echo of it rolled from fell to fell until it died gradually in the distance like a faint moan.

"My God, what has happened, Jael? A mountain has fallen asunder, or the drift has been blown up," cried Red Ike.

"'Tis destiny working its own ends," she answered. "Come with me to the gypsies' camp. You will be safe there at present, and after tomorrow for all time in any place."

Morn was breaking, and Dick, buried under a heap of bracken and shielded by the ramparts of the old British fort in the depth of Shoulthwaite Ghyll, lay waiting the coming of Red Ike. He too had heard the thunder roll, but could not guess at the cause.

However, a quick movement among the dry rustling bracken, and a well-known signal three times repeated, made him leap to his feet, and through the grey light of dawn the bold figure of Red Ike came in view. He hailed Dick in a voice that startled him with its clarity, and then said: "I have been to the drift, and found there the corpse of old Abegail; and Ben Faa alive, but maimed and almost beyond recognition. He did not recognize me when I examined his wounds and bandaged them. He had fired an old dynamite charge in a boring in the drift. Did you hear the roar of an explosion during the night, Dick? Jael and I heard it a mile away. I was puzzled to guess its cause, but Jael, by some strange power that I cannot fathom, divined both it and the result, and to satisfy myself whether she was right or wrong I returned to the drift and found things as she said.

"I then sent word to her by Prodigal, instructing her to acquaint the authorities, and also Mr. Mayne, with the case. Tonight I shall visit him myself. And now, as we can do nothing further at present, what say you to a good sleep, Dick? I wonder how Will Moffatt is getting along?"

With him things were going hard. His wounded ankle had received scant attention. He was looked upon as a murderer now, and as an erstwhile incorrigible poacher who had bid open defiance to law and order. And, since his arrest, he had refused to answer all questions put to him. What made things worse still, he had no friends to whom he could apply for help. Thus racked at once with physical pain and mental worry, there was little to wonder at that his condition was deplorable. Yet he was not without hope. He knew that Red Ike was still free, and that while he was so, no stone would be left unturned until he unravelled the mystery surrounding John Lynd's death.

Many a time in the darkness of his prison hospital, he pictured in his mind's eye that bold commanding form striding over the moorland in the full glory of manhood. And he wondered what manner of a man he would grow into in the days to come, when he would be free to follow his bent, with Jael by his side to urge him to the fulfilment of his destiny. He thought that he should yet live to see him hated and feared and honoured, as are all men who are the salt of the earth.

CHAPTER XXIX

IT was on the third morning after the police raid on the drift that Will Moffatt was ordered to be removed from hospital to his cell.

The warder in attendance on him said he must walk to his quarters. He refused this, saying that without assistance he could not do so.

After some exchange of threats and expostulation, the jail governor was called, and being somewhat more humane than his subordinate, or having some further purpose in mind, sent for a couple of prisoners to assist him, and to his astonishment they were Red Ike and Dick. Whether they had been brought together by design or chance, he could not guess, but, ignoring all rule and discipline, he bade them a cheery "Good morning."

Red Ike answered, and the warder made no attempt to check the conversation.

"We gave ourselves up to the police last night, Will. Ben Faa fired by accident an old dynamite charge in the drift. Abegail is killed, and Ben Faa wounded near to death. Jean has returned to The Bents; we shall all three be released from jail within a few days."

Will Moffatt made no answer, though but for his wounded foot, he could have leapt for joy. Red Ike took him bodily up, and strode off with him to his cell. Until then he had always doubted the story of the prowess of Red Rowan, the starkest man in Teviotdale, bearing away Kinmont Will, irons and all, from Carlisle Castle with the bold Buccleugh, but now to him the feat became quite credible. Red Ike could have borne him for miles, though he was then a man weighing thirteen stone.

Will had now nothing to do but settle himself down and wait patiently the culmination of events that would release him from prison. However, there was yet another surprise for him in store that day. He was sitting on the edge of his bed, daydreaming of the future and building castles in the air, when the door of his cell was thrown open, and Jean stood before him.

Meanwhile, in Paris Mrs. Lynd became the prey of a thousand doubts, and feeling the need of companionship, she foolishly allowed Peg Shore free access to her presence, and reposing confidence in her, unwittingly let slip many thoughts, showing the fearful anxiety under which she laboured. This aroused Peg's curiosity and suspicion, and by artful means she led her to discuss the details of the crime, as far as Mrs. Lynd was aware of them.

Peg divined that Ben Faa was the last man seen with Lynd, and that he threatened the exposure of Jael's mother's marriage, unless paid to hold his tongue.

Really, Mrs. Lynd cared little about the scandal the story would create, but she dreaded poverty, and never gave a thought to the question whether she was doing right or wrong in withholding the light she could throw upon the case. Yet her very fears were groundless. Had she had the moral courage to face the worst at once, all would have been well. In Jael she would have found a generous, compassionate soul far above her own conception, and infinitely beyond her deserts. 'Tis the misfortune of lower minds that they judge others by their own standard, thereby missing the good they grasp at but cannot reach.

At last, her anxiety became unbearable, and she resolved at all costs to return home, and without a word to Peg, she packed her luggage and recrossed the English Channel ere she was missed.

From Dover, she hurried to London, and thence by the Northern Express, reaching Penrith at midnight. There she hired a hackney carriage, and arrived at The Bents in the early hours of a dark winter's morn, leaving her luggage.

Driving along the avenue, she beheld with wonder the house lighted up in every room and the front door standing wide open. Trembling with apprehension, she ordered the driver to stop, and alighted, saying she would walk the rest of the way. The driver turned his horses, grumbling at his curt dismissal, and was soon out of sight and hearing.

At The Bents, Ben Faa lay nigh to death. Jean had had him taken thither from the gypsies' van.

By his bedside with her stood Jael, watching the flickering flame of life, now waxing in sudden spurts, and as quickly waning again to so low an ebb as to be almost gone.

"Do you think the doctor will be long, Jael?"

"He may be here any moment, Jean. Has Ben made any confession?"

Jean shook her head. A slight rustle of silk in the doorway behind; a few quick steps, and Mrs. Lynd stood beside them.

RED IKE, BY J. M. DENWOOD & S. FOWLER WRIGHT * 225

"Whom have you here?" she exclaimed.

"'Tis Ben Faa; he has been injured in an accident."

"Would to God that he were dead."

At the sound of her voice, Ben opened his eyes.

"You wish me dead, Mrs. Lynd. Yet I am not the only one you would like off the earth." And moving his eyes to Jael, he held out his hands imploringly, and said, "Kiss me, Jael."

She obeyed the wish, and a look like that on the face of a pleased dog crossed his face. All his life he had loved her in his own way, and this was the first time her lips had touched him. The contact seemed to invigorate his whole body, and rising to a sitting posture, he cried: "The doctor is coming."

"Yes, I am here."

"Then listen, Doctor. I killed John Lynd because of his treachery to me, and I do not regret the deed. And Jael, the woman standing there..."—and he pointed to Mrs. Lynd with the word— "...would have had me trample upon you. Had I lived to make you my wife, I should have skinned her of the wealth she possesses, as the gypsies skin a hedgehog of its hide.

"She thought I was bought off with the thousand pounds I compelled her to give me. This was the price John Lynd agreed to pay me on condition that I wedded you, Jael.

"He stopped the cheque at the bank and mocked at my impotence to win you, and I felled him like an ox. I could no longer bear his insolence. I shall slip through the hangman's hands tonight." Then with a horrible oath, in a voice full of fiendish exultation, he cried: "Yes, I slew the devil. I slew him."

And with hands raised above his head, as though he were wielding an axe and striking a frenzied blow, and with a loud chuckling laugh, he leaped from the bed, and plunged head foremost onto the floor, a quivering corpse. The doctor gazed on the three women before him, and said: "You all heard Ben Faa's confession that he killed John Lynd?"

"He was a liar, Doctor."

"He told the truth," said Jael.

"You also are a liar."

Jael pointed a finger towards Ben's body, and with eyes fixed on Mrs. Lynd: "I hold notes to the value of a thousand pounds given to him by you. That you owned them can be proved by the numbers at the bank."

"He was a thief, and stole them from me."

"You lie; over Ben Faa's dead body you lie, Mrs. Lynd. I hold the receipt given to you for them. I found it on the moorland, and I shall return the notes to you."

Until now, Jean had watched the scene silently. The one word, "Mother," escaped her lips, and turning she fled from the room. Jael followed, and together they walked to the gypsies' camp. At the door of the van, Prodigal was lying on guard.

"Well, Mrs. Lynd," said the doctor, eyeing Ben's corpse. "What has to be done with the dead body there?"

"I'll have it carted away, and tipped onto the moorland, Doctor."

"Nay, I'll give it decent burial myself, madam. Allow it to lie here until I return. I'll be back as soon as possible."

"Not a moment longer than is necessary shall the carcase remain, Doctor." And Mrs. Lynd rang the bell for attendance, and ordered its removal.

Morn was breaking o'er the Hill of Devils as Jael and Jean were looking on old Abegail's mutilated body in the tent that was Ben's, when the cart bearing his remains drew up at the camp. A grumble from Prodigal announced the strangers, and a glance at the party was sufficient to read its import.

"Bring him hither," said Jael, motioning them to Abegail's corpse, "lay him by her side. They shall lie in death together." Then, turning to the doctor, she said: "Will you give me the certificates of death? I shall have them buried on the moorland at sundown today."

There, in the tomb of the Roman commander that lies by the roadside skirting the breast of Helvellyn were laid side by side the bodies of Abegail and Ben Faa. And Jael caused a cairn of stones to be raised above them which remains to this day.

Events now began to shape themselves rapidly. The death of John Lynd brought disaster and complications on all who had had dealings with him. His was the mastermind, dark-dealing and shrewd, that to trust was to court financial ruin.

First and foremost to bear the full weight of his villainy was Joe Gream. In John Lynd's hands he had ever been as potter's clay. From his dream of security he was awakened as with a thunderbolt, to find himself almost beggared and stranded in Paris. He had been lulled and tricked into the belief that he was co-partner in the wealth derived from the fall of rock, and in other quarrying ventures. But now he found, by an agreement signed under his own hand, that he had had but a share of the profits during John Lynd's lifetime, and had not any claim on the real estate from which his income came. And further still, the very house he had built on the plans, and under the instructions, of Lynd, belonged to the man whom Ben Faa had slain.

In despair, he rushed into the presence of Peg, to find her apathetic to his clamour.

What was there to care about in a broken man whom she herself had plundered? Had they not used each other in the service of lust and self alone? Now that there was nothing further to be gained from him, she was glad to be free of the encumbrance of marriage, and took the chance of breaking with him there and then. While he, exasperated at her brutal indifference to his unforeseen and hopeless difficulty, broke into wild violence of manner and speech and threatened her life; she waved him aside with a scoffing laugh, daring him to do his worst, and seeing that the end had come between them, he allowed her to depart and pass out of his life.

Henceforth the way of them both was that of the evil-doer. Drink and degradation, imbecility and the jail for him; for her, London's streets and prostitution; and at last for each the homecoming to a pauper's grave within the shadow of the Hill of Devils.

After the carting away of Ben's body from The Bents, Mrs. Lynd dismissed her attendants, ordering them to secure the house, and not disturb her no matter who called, until she herself summoned them to her. She now saw plainly that to save herself from poverty and humiliation she must act promptly, and wished to be alone to plan the best course to pursue. Had she known of the existence of Jael's mother's marriage certificate, she would have been constrained to more violent measures than she ultimately resolved on.

Fortunately for herself and all concerned, she judged the case to be an irregular connection of no legal weight, or one that could be disposed of with money. Finally, she resolved to double the thousand pounds already in Jael's possession, and thus settle the question for good. That her harsh conduct during Ben's death scene and afterwards would have prejudiced her in the minds of those present never entered her thoughts; therefore, with a satisfied conscience not keen at the highest, she retired to bed and soon was sound asleep.

Meanwhile, the police were overhauling the contents and the debris of blasted rock in the drift; and to safeguard the welfare of Red Ike and his fellow-prisoners, the artist detective was there taking notes of books, manuscripts, and every article likely to be of value to his clients. When the Carved Stick was found intact, his exclamation of delight at the wonderful workmanship attracted the police around him. He pressed the serpent's jaws together, the ivory ball opened, and the glare of the candle-light scintillating on the polished disc of the split ball, the marvelling group of men cried as with one voice: "The Gypsy's Luck."

And, now, immediately on the renewal of the search, the packet containing the letters of Jael's mother and the marriage certificate was found.

"I require," said Mayne, "that those proofs of John Lynd's connection with the gypsies be placed in my charge."

"And who are you?" demanded the police inspector.

"My credentials are here," was the reply, and the officer, after some hesitation, allowed the claim.

The doctor, leaving Ben's corpse with Jael, went directly to the police-superintendent, and acquainted him with all that had taken place at The Bents.

His well-known integrity and local standing placed his deposition beyond question, with the result that the police-station became a scene of activity unparalleled in its history, and somnolent Keswick saw the red-letter day of its existence.

Public feeling had run high for weeks on the murder, and as the innocence of the prisoners, coupled with Ben's confession, were bruited about, the streets became thronged with groups of folks discussing the latest phases of events as they came to hand. And when the cart containing the contents of the drift rumbled through the town, guarded by the police and followed by a huge crowd of various partisans of those concerned in the murder, the cheering and booing became such a babel that it was an impossibility for a fair-minded observer of the scene to place any reliance on the judgment of the howling mob he beheld. It is ever thus when emotion, and not reason, is the arbiter on the actions of men.

There now remained little to be done but to place all available evidence in the hands of the authorities, before the three prisoners became free men.

Without delay, Thomas Mayne hurried to Carlisle and acquainted Red Ike and Dick Stagg and Will Moffatt with the turn of events.

From Red Ike he received instructions where the axe and Ben Faa's blood-stained clothing were to be found, and after getting and delivering them to the police, this part of his work was finished.

His next thought was of Nell Glen. Ringing her up on the telephone, he poured into her glad ears the great news that rejoiced her heart.

He then, to fill up the good work of a perfect day, determined to visit the gypsies' camp, but arrived there too late to accompany the funeral of Abegail and Ben Faa to the burial in the Roman grave on the old highway along Helvellyn.

But his investigations did not end here: His was one of those curious casts of mind that must see every actor in a case, and an hour later he drove to The Bents.

At first he was refused admittance, but sending a peremptory demand to Mrs. Lynd, he was finally ushered into her presence.

In a few words he explained the object of his visit, showing her the futility of resistance to the rights of Jael, and counselling caution; and when Mrs. Lynd treated this advice with contempt, vowing to disinherit Jean so far as lay in her power, and laughing to scorn the claims of Jael, he said: "Read this," and spread the certificate of John Lynd's marriage with Jael's mother on the table.

"You are entirely at the mercy of the guardians of Jael's son. By the right of inheritance, all the real estate belongs to him, and the personal estate is divisible between him and his mother. Need I explain things further to you?"

With a cry like a tigress bereft of its cubs, Mrs. Lynd sprang and endeavoured to grasp the certificate, and failing this threw herself upon him in such a frenzy that he had the utmost difficulty in restraining himself from doing her an injury. Her mad raging aroused the domestics, and a further scene of intensified confusion began when they rushed into the room.

"He has stolen some of my property," cried the infuriated woman. "I charge you all to recover it from him, letters and a certificate."

The detective backed to the wall, and drawing a revolver said: "Mrs. Lynd is a liar. The property she speaks of belongs to Jael Boswell. I, incautiously and with the best intentions, showed the articles to Mrs. Lynd. The first man or woman that interferes with me again I shall shoot. Stand clear of the doorway and let me depart hence. Out of the road, I say, all of you. To the fireplace at once. Anyone that molests me does so at his peril."

Still facing the cowed domestics, he backed from the room and into the hall.

As he stepped from the house, Mrs. Lynd fell forward to the floor, her face ghastly livid, and blood issuing from her mouth.

Her tale was told.

Too deeply injured to be judged harshly, may she rest in peace.

That night the White Horse Inn was packed to the door. Simon Reed was in his glory. The day's news had brought together from far and near the whole male population of the moorland; men who seldom or never were seen in a public house were there eager to hear the latest details.

The burial of Abegail and Ben Faa in the Roman grave had been no less a wonder to them than had been the burial crosswise of John Lynd over the gypsy woman's yew-tree-shaded sepulchre. And now the question was asked: "Where would Mrs. Lynd be buried?"

"That we'll see when the day comes round to hap her up," said Simon Reed.

"Do you pretend to know, Simon?" chimed in the landlord.

"I know a varst of things thy thick sconce never dreamed on. Did I not tell you all that Red Ike was not guilty of John Lynd's murder?"

"You did, Simon," chorused a dozen voices at once.

Encouraged thus, the old fellow waxed eloquent.

"In all my life I never met a lot of pilgarlicks like as we have on the moorland; they can't see past their nose-ends. For all I told them a dozen times that the footmarks in the snow were not Red Ike's, they would not have it I was right. But, I knew, I knew, I knew." And Simon, with delight, chuckled and hugged himself, with arms folded over his breast.

"Simon is one of the seven wonders of the world. He should be put in a glass-case and exhibited on fair-days as a marvel," said the landlord.

And Simon, holding a pinch of snuff between his finger and thumb, glanced round the company and chortled.

"Gentlemen, if I'd a dog as daft as some folks, I ken I'd drown it."

This thrust of ironic satire, pointed indirectly at the landlord, made him wince, but swallowing his choler, that was rising to the point of exploding, he banged his fist on the table and cried: "I'd banish from the countryside such scoundrels as Red Ike. Mark that, Simon Reed."

"No doubt, landlord, no doubt. But when Red Ike steps on the moorland again, he'll be the Squire."

A loud guffaw followed this assertion.

"The Squire?"

"Yes," answered Simon, "the Squire at The Bents."

And even as he said, so it came to pass. Red Ike became Squire at The Bents, and The Forge passed by purchase into the hands of Dick Stagg and Nell.

Will Moffatt's ambition was a modest one. He rebuilt Sandy-flatts on its old plan, refusing all overtures from Red Ike that he be allowed to raise, at his own expense, a more modern dwelling on its site. But in spite of him, Red Ike and Jael had five hundred acres of moorland fenced in, and turned over to Jean as a wedding present. And in the peace and quiet of rural seclusion, with the wind and the clouds, and the wildlife of the moorland for companionship and pleasure, they together, for long years since, have watched, with unbounded satisfaction, the star of Red Ike's career rise in the literary sky.

In the centre of the mantelpiece in the drawing-room at The Bents, standing upright, is the Carved Stick, an object of curiosity to all who delight in exquisite workmanship of a rare kind. And though Jael was never crowned the Gypsy Queen at Carnac, she reigns supreme in the heart of a great soul. A kingdom of more vast importance than any shadowy empire on which the sun never sets.

This is ephemeral; that is indestructible. And who can say that destiny, that at times seems to us so untoward in our relations of life, is not our best friend and helper? Perhaps it is the very mainspring of life itself, urging us to achievement or defeat, and by both means purifying and ennobling us beyond our realization in this, a finite state.

If there be no end to the universe, nor to time, then we, who are part of the universe, and without whom time would be meaningless, must be meant ultimately for something great, as are our most splendid imaginings

But the tale is told. And the worst that can happen to a mortal here, if this life be the end of all, is death. Death and a quiet grave, like John Lynd's and the gypsies, on the wild moorland within the shadow of the Hill of Devils.

ABOUT THE AUTHORS

SYDNEY FOWLER WRIGHT (1874-1965) penned over seventy volumes of science fiction, fantasy, classic mysteries, historical novels, poetry, and non-fiction, many of them being published by the Borgo Press Imprint of Wildside Press. Please visit his website at:

www.sfw.org

JONATHAN MAWSON DENWOOD (1869-1933) wrote the first draft of *Red Ike* in 1922, but was unable to sell it until 1930, when he was dying of heart disease. When the book became a minor bestseller in 1931, he lamented his late success, saying that the money thus earned might have saved his life if only it had appeared several years sooner. He also penned a half-dozen other books, but none gained the public's eye like this thinly-disguised adventure based around his father's life.

www.ingramcontent.com/pod-product-compliance
Lightning Source LLC
Chambersburg PA
CBHW021243260626
47155CB00004BA/1283